WILD CHILDREN

RICHARD ROBERTS

A Division of **Whampa, LLC**
P.O. Box 2540
Dulles, VA 20101
Tel/Fax: 800-998-2509
http://curiosityquills.com

© 2011 Richard Roberts
http://frankensteinbeck.blogspot.com

ISBN: 978-1-62007-120-5 (ebook)
ISBN: 978-1-62007-121-2 (paperback)
ISBN: 978-1-62007-122-9 (hardcover)

TABLE OF CONTENTS

ACT I, SCENE I 4

ACT I, SCENE II 38

ACT II 77

ACT III 119

ACT IV 160

ACT V 236

DENOUEMENT 285

About the Author. 287

ACT I, SCENE I

FOR THEIR SINS

I think I was nine the first time I saw a Wild Child. A lot of Wild Children have been tamed, but this one was wild in every way.

Wild Children weren't allowed in our village. It's not a rule, but I didn't understand things like that anyway. I was nine! I just knew I'd never seen one before, and that my parents kept me in on Walpurgis, and that sometimes my mother would be talking to someone else's mother and they'd mention them. All I understood was they were saying something really, really mean about somebody.

So, I was nine. I was in church, and Father Birch was giving his sermon, or maybe he was reciting the... actually, you can already tell, can't you? I was bored. I was leaning back in my pew, wondering when there'd be more singing and things would get at least a little interesting again. I knew I was asking for trouble, but I was so bored even getting yelled at seemed like a good idea. My head rolled to the side so that I could stare out the window at the sunny day I was missing – and there was a Wild Boy!

He was a wolf. His ears were all big and pointy and fuzzy, and so was his mouth. He had this nose and mouth like a wolf, and all the hair and fur I could see was grey. I guess it should have been creepy, but it was really cute. And I knew he was a wolf. When you see a wolf and a dog you know which is which, right? But the best part was his expression. I could so tell

4

that he thought Father Birch was full of it, that the whole thing was dumb, like he understood exactly what I was going through.

So here I was, bored out of my mind, and all of a sudden there's a Wild Boy looking in the window! One second my whole body was heavy and everything dragged, and the next I felt so alive I itched. And I thought, when was I going to see a Wild Boy again? I whispered to mom that I had to go, you know, excuse myself. Man, was she mad. It took a couple of minutes to convince her and I knew I'd hear more about it when we got home, but – a Wild Boy, right?

You get a lot of stares when you slip out the front door during church. There's no good way to do it. But it's kind of funny because while they're giving you a look, other people are giving *them* a look for not paying attention to Father Birch. Anyway, I slipped along the walls, which is probably the dumbest way to do it, and I got outside and ran around the corner, and there he was, sitting under the window eating something. Jerked beef, I think.

He grinned at me and his teeth were sharp, but not ugly and hooked like real dog teeth, and he was cute like a puppy and at the same time the wildest thing I'd ever seen. I sound like a nine year old, don't I? He hadn't said a word, and I was so excited!

Of course, I froze. What to say? I didn't want to say something stupid. He was so different and he had that grin, and it was like he wasn't a kid like me, like he'd seen it all. That's what I was thinking. I felt like an idiot and I didn't want to make it worse.

Not that I had to worry. He was all confident. He got up and walked right over and leaned against the wall and said, "Ducking out on Father Boring?" I just about busted a gut trying not to laugh!

I don't know how long we spent talking. I don't know what we said. I spent most of it feeling like every word out of my mouth was the dumbest thing ever said by anybody, but he never seemed to mind. He didn't tell me much. He told me Father Birch was trying to keep him out of the village so he couldn't talk to the other kids. We kind of spent most of the time making fun of Birch for one thing or another, which is why I just about fell on my butt in terror when I heard the Father yelling behind me!

"BLASPHEME!"

I swear, he really talks like that! And the Wild Boy took off like an animal. I've never seen a person run that fast, and sometimes he was on all fours. I wish I could have run. Instead I had to turn around and see Father Birch standing over me so mad he was shaking.

"Wicked little hussy," he snapped, and that may sound hilarious to you but I was shaking like a leaf. "What are you doing talking to that filthy animal? Do you know what he is, girl?"

"Isn't he a Wild Boy, Father?" It was all I could say!

"And you don't know what that is, do you?" he yelled back, and I just felt worse because he was right. "You don't know because you don't pay attention, you don't have respect, and you don't obey. Wild Children are monsters. They're mistakes. Children who fall from innocence don't get a second chance. You become like THAT," and he pointed after the wolf boy, "forever."

"Is that really so bad, Father?" I had to ask, "He doesn't seem bad, or unhappy."

I thought he was going to hit me. I guess he didn't because of what he saw behind me. Instead he leaned down and looked me in the eyes, and I had to look into his because I knew he really would hit me if I didn't. But he was so angry even the memory of his voice makes me sick. "He's happy," he told me, and he just seemed more furious because now he was quiet about it. "He's happy because he's the worst kind of monster. He looks like a wolf because that's his sin. He preys on the weak and stupid and selfish. On children like you. That is, until he's caught and caged. A slothful child like you probably thinks that sounds like a good life, but you're not going to end up like him. You're going to end up like THAT."

Father Birch's hand grabbed my shoulder, and it hurt, and he twisted me around to point at the street. At first I didn't understand because he seemed to be pointing at a fancy carriage and the young man and woman in it and, well, I'd never seen anyone dressed that well. They were obviously rich. I wondered if they were nobles, even. They weren't from anywhere near our village, I knew that, and didn't seem to be stopping. And then I realized what he was really pointing at.

A girl sat on the back of the carriage. She was, I don't know, ten? Twelve? Only she wasn't a girl, she was a Wild Girl. She had big, hairy brown ears and a tail, and below the hem of her skirt the legs dangling over the edge of the cart ended in hooves. And her face wasn't a girl's face. Like the wolf boy she had this snout, but hers was a donkey's, kind of bulbous at the end. She wasn't pretty, but she was certainly cute.

I didn't want to be her, though. Not at all. Because her hands and feet were in shackles and chains, thick and iron, and she had a collar locked around her neck. She looked so sad, and she just stared at the ground as the carriage rode out of sight.

Not that I got to see it, because Father Birch yanked me around to yell at me some more. "That is what waits for you, tramp," he told me. I didn't want to hear that. After seeing that girl, I didn't want someone to tell me this. "That boy became a wolf because he is evil. You're just stupid and lazy and disobedient. Take one step too far down that road and you'll become like her. Children who become wolves are hunted because they're monsters. Children who become donkeys are sold. We don't want them corrupting our village with their sin."

I could tell that he was just getting started. Father Birch can go on for hours. But he'd spent so long shouting at me that the church people were starting to peek out the doors and windows at him. So he gave me back to my mom, and we went home, and she yelled at me too, but honestly I don't much remember that part. After what happened at church it didn't seem important.

And then when I was going to sleep the wolf boy peeked in my bedroom window at me. I thought I must have imagined it, but I didn't.

The next time I saw the Wolf Boy was at school. Mister Thornback is our teacher. We only have one school and one teacher in our village, but my mom and Father Birch say that living as far out as we do we're lucky to have a school at all.

You might think because I don't pay attention in church I don't pay attention in school, or that because Father Birch is such a jerk I have that problem with all adults. Actually, I like school and I like Mister Thornback. Don't get me wrong, he can be as hard as anybody. I've felt his ruler a few times. He broke it on Joseph Wheaton the first year I was in school, but Joseph had caught a squirrel and had his foot on it and was squeezing it slow to hear the noises it made. Thornback just about lost it. That's how he is. He doesn't bend much, but he's not mean. If he gives your knuckles a whack for talking in class, you were talking in class and you earned what you got.

I'm a little soft about him because really, I like school. It's not my favorite part of the day, but Mister Thornback is smart and he's got a pile of books he got from all over and he wants you to learn. If you can multiply in your head he'll mess with your hair and tell you you're ahead of the class, and then give you a bigger list of harder problems to see how you handle those. If you're having trouble adding up big numbers he'll sit down with you and show you how to do it, step by step, even if he has to stay behind after all the other kids go home.

In case you can't tell, I'm the 'multiply in her head' girl.

Now, the school is sort of a barn. Not a literal barn, but that kind of feel, you know? One big wooden room, all by itself. I think maybe there's an attic and Mister Thornback lives there. There's a couple of windows, but they're big and high up on the walls. I couldn't reach them. I couldn't reach them standing on a barrel. I never found out how the wolf boy ended up peeking in through them, or why none of the other kids saw him, but he kept doing it all day. I'd finish spelling the word 'sassafras,' which was tough because I have no idea what that is, and I'd look up and there'd be these eyes and gray hair and pointy ears looking over the window ledge behind Mister Thornback.

You know what I did? I didn't do anything. I wasn't even sure what I wanted to do. School wasn't like church. I didn't want to get in trouble here. And I was scared too, but I was mad at Father Birch for the way he treated me. Mostly I didn't want to make the teacher mad.

And then Mayor Pomter stopped by and had a chat with Mister Thornback, and he told us that he was needed in the village. He handed out a bunch of worksheets and said he'd be back. Eventually.

Only a couple of people started to goof off. It's not that Thornback expects us to finish the worksheets. Some of that stuff was crazy hard. But if you don't know when he'll get back, even the lazier students get kind of diligent.

I don't think of myself as one of the lazier students. Okay, I get bored really easily, but digging through the teacher's book pile to find out what the difference between a Vandal and a Visigoth is sounds like time well spent. How often do you get to see the word 'pillage' used in a sentence? But a wolf boy at the window raised a whole new level of curiosity. I helped a couple of kids dig out a book and then, you know, I kind of sidled out the front door for a breath of fresh air.

There he was. Insouciant (it was on the worksheet) grin and everything. This time I felt less like an idiot. Instead my head was just racing around! It had to be an act, right? But you know, with what Father Birch said, that meant he got turned into a wolf because he was really like that already?

"You don't have a lot of fun, huh?" he asked me, "What's your name?"

"Jenny." I tried not to pull on my hair or mess with my skirt. Was I still that nervous? Sheesh. Also, I couldn't believe we hadn't asked each other our names the first time we met. "And you...?"

"Wolfgang." He grinned wider.

"Nuh-UH." I couldn't help myself. I sounded like an idiot, but did he expect me to believe that?

He laughed, and I knew I'd caught him even before he spoke. "Okay, but see, when you become a Wild Boy, you get a new name. You're never allowed to keep your old one. I guess nothing's stopping me from going back to being Pepper, except maybe it's a stupid girl's name. But I don't."

I had to giggle too. "It is, isn't it? Wolfgang or Pepper, huh? I can let you get away with Wolfgang, then."

Then he grinned some more, and now you couldn't doubt it was real. He looked so proud, like nobody I'd ever met. "Nobody has to let me get away with anything anymore. I get away with stuff all by myself."

"No wonder Father Birch thinks you're evil. If he heard you say that he'd have you in the stocks or something." That didn't seem to faze Wolfgang in the slightest, so I pressed on. "So, is it true? You really get turned into an animal for your sins?"

"I don't know. What's a sin?"

"You know exactly what a sin is," I told him. I wasn't going to let him talk down to me! Even if he was charming while he did it. Were all Wild Children like this?

"Yeah, I know," he told me, and then he leaned close and I got that 'stupid' feeling again. His eyes were grey, everything about him was grey, and they and his teeth were all I could see for a minute. "Listen, Jenny. I'm older'n most of the adults you know. Wild Children don't live forever, but you know, we never have to grow up. I don't need adults anymore. I can live in the woods and eat mice if I gotta. I bet you go 'yuck', but I get the thrill of the hunt that you or an adult will never have."

And then he stopped for a second, and… and I thought he was going to kiss me. And, again, I was barely nine. I'd have said that wasn't just sinful it was gross, until he was so close I didn't know how I felt. Instead he whispered to me, "Well, maybe you will. It's not too late for you. Because Father Birch has one thing right. Maybe the only thing. I became a Wild Boy for my 'sins', alright. But did God curse me, or was it a blessing? And it's not easy. He told you you just have to put a foot out of line, right? If that were true, do you know any kids who wouldn't be Wild Children?"

I could certainly think of plenty of kids in the village who ought to have changed, yes. Like Rose (I hate that name) Creeper, who right then walked right out the door and saw us. I bet she just gave up on the work and was going home. That is, until she saw a Wolf Boy and yelled, "Oh god, oh god… get out here, Ivy! Everybody get out here! There's a Wild Boy!"

And that was it. I mean, for me talking to him. He didn't run away. I think he liked giving that grin to other kids, 'cause he just stood there and grinned at them as everybody in school rushed out and stared and stared. And the funny thing was, they all stood right behind me until they figured out he wasn't going to run away or bite them or something. Then Ivy pushed herself in front of me and goes, "You're a Wild Boy?"

And he goes, "Uh-huh."

And she asks, "How'd you get into the village?"

And I didn't even hear the answer because suddenly everybody was talking at once, and I guess he answered some questions, but I couldn't make anything out. I wasn't really trying. I was pretty mad. I was also wondering when Mister Thornback was going to come back.

He didn't. Eventually we all went home. The next day he apologized, kind of stiffly, but that's Mister Thornback. Said the Mayor really needed him. He was pretty upset – I could tell.

After that Wolfgang was… around. I'd see him, sometimes at school, sometimes at church, sometimes at home. I didn't get to talk to him much. Most of the time I didn't have the chance. When I did have the chance I'd drop off a bucket of rutabagas or something in the kitchen, slip out the back, get as far as "Hey, Wild Boy," and five other girls would be standing around us and they'd start yammering at him. And where you've got five other girls, you've soon got five other boys. And in about ten minutes some grownup would see a bunch of kids gathered around and start yelling something about what's going on, and everybody would scatter. Wolfgang could move so fast I wouldn't even see where he went.

And then Ivy mouthed off to Father Birch.

Maybe it was because she'd gotten to talk to Wolfgang way more than I did. I wouldn't sneak out of school, right? But she would. And she'd always shove herself to the front to be the one to talk to him. Ivy's a couple years older than me, and she's acted like that ever since I met her. She didn't like church, I knew that, but she didn't like school either, or… well, anything that inconvenienced her.

I'm sorry. I shouldn't talk bad about her. I just never got along with Ivy. That morning she didn't even pretend to pay attention in church. Her head lay back on the pew and I could hear her snoring from across the aisle. Ivy gets away with a lot of stuff because her uncle is Mayor Pomter, and I don't know, maybe she thought she could get away with this. I was stewing and jealous that she was skipping out on the Parables, but I forgot all about that when Father Birch stopped the service and started walking down the aisle to her row.

I stopped feeling mad at her and started feeling sorry for her.

She wasn't even awake until he started yelling. Her folks didn't try to wake her, didn't try to cover, nothing. I could see it in their face that they were as afraid of old Birch as I was, but she was their daughter! My mom woulda- I hope she would. I always thought she was trying to protect me.

"Sinning harlot!" bellowed the old man, and when I say 'old man', listen, Father Birch was a big guy. His hair may have been grey and white, but he could have broken me or Ivy in his bare hands. When he yells, you're afraid. And as she jumped he grabbed her blouse and dragged her out of the pew and threw her down in the aisle, I know it hurt. "Little Ivy Pomter believes that sleep is more important than God. Is that it, Miss Pomter?"

I could see her fear in her face – and I could see that she wasn't afraid enough. And then she actually opened her mouth and told him in front of everyone, "Yeah, I guess I do."

He... he hit her a few times. He yelled a lot. Her parents just sat there like stone. I guess I can't blame them for that. I started crying before she did. I put my hands over my face and tried not to listen.

It wasn't over then. It was just beginning. Thankfully, a lot of it's kind of a blur. A lot of it I don't want to remember. Father Birch dragged Ivy out of the church, out to the middle of the village square. All the while he was shouting. A lot of it was at her, but a lot of it was at us. About our duty to God, and virtue. About punishing the weak and immoral and sinful. Everyone wanted to be quiet, but there were 'amens' and 'hallelujahs' to be said, and by the time the Mayor came out everyone was shouting. A lot of them at Ivy.

I can't tell you about the look on her face. I'm sorry.

The Mayor said that Ivy had committed a crime and she would spend until tomorrow morning in the stocks. He and Birch dragged her over to them and locked her in themselves. A lot of people laughed, and a couple of them slapped her. I didn't do anything. Or say anything. I hadn't said anything since Ivy was caught snoring, and I wasn't going to start.

Then Father Birch chased everyone away from the stocks. Standing between Ivy and the townspeople, he raised his hands and delivered another speech.

"But this, my flock, is not just about one girl who has turned her face away from God. Her soul was weak and rotten, but the weak twig doesn't snap by itself. This girl was corrupted. She was lied to and tempted and misled. Yes, there are more sinners among us-" and I swear looked straight at me, and I thought my heart would stop. Then he went on, "but this is something worse. I have been speaking to the Mayor about this, but it is time for you all to know. I have seen a Wild Boy in the village. A wolf. He has been lurking among our houses, spying on our children."

Father Birch grabbed a fistful of Ivy's hair and lifted up her head so that everyone could see her face and explained, "He has gotten his teeth into this lamb. Maybe a night of shame will teach her that God punishes sin and rewards only virtue."

And there was Wolfgang. And like always he was the center of attention just by being there, so everybody was looking at him already as he retorted, "Maybe it will teach her that you care more about pride and wrath than you do about virtue, Father."

Father Birch doesn't debate. He grabbed a stick. In fact, he pulled a fence post out of the ground and lunged, then as Wolfgang ran he chased him out of the square, and so did the Mayor, and so did all the adults and about half the kids, especially the older ones. The only adult left was Mister Thornback, and only briefly. When the rest of the adults left he just shook his head and walked off in the other direction.

Which left me, a bunch of kids, and Ivy, who was locked into the stocks bent over and crying. Me and the others looked at each other, and we didn't know what to do. I'd never liked Ivy, but I wasn't going to leave her. After a while I went over and put my hand on her back. She didn't say anything, and I didn't say anything.

And then Wolfgang was back again. He jumped down off a roof, and for a moment I was mad at him because he was showing off at a time like this, and then I was mad at me for caring when Wolfgang showing up might have saved Ivy's life. You're allowed to do anything to someone in the stocks. Anything you think the people watching will let you get away with.

Wolfgang didn't act like he was saving her, though. It was me he paid attention to as he walked up. "You look mad."

I was mad. I was so mad at Father Birch, at the Mayor, at the other adults, I barely had room to be mad at Wolfgang. But I didn't say anything.

"What do you want to do?" he asked me.

I looked down at Ivy. I knew the answer to that. "I want to let her out."

12

"Then we'll let her out." As if it was as simple as that.

But it wasn't as simple as that. "We can't do that, Wolfgang. You know we can't!"

"Why?" He was making fun of me, at a time like that! "Because Father Birch says so?"

For a second I was worried he might be right, but- "No! Because when the adults come back, if Ivy's not in the stocks… it'll be worse. Even worse! They might burn her at the stake! Maybe you can run off and live in the woods, but Ivy can't. All we can do – all I can do, Wolfgang –is stay here with her and make sure that anyone who tries to make it worse for her knows someone's watching them." Yeah, I was starting to cry again.

But Wolfgang still grinned. It was like he had life all figured out. "They're not coming back, Jenny. Not before morning. By then she's allowed to be out anyway, and nobody will be thinking about it. Adults always do the same thing together. As soon as they were far away and I knew Father Birch was going in the wrong direction I knew the rest of them would follow." Leaning closer, he repeated, "So let me ask you, Jenny. What do you want to do?"

I couldn't stop crying. Maybe it was because I was crying, but I didn't think about it at all. I just believed him. And I started grabbing the lock and pulling on it, which was stupid. I couldn't budge it at all and the Mayor had the key. So I started crying harder, but I didn't give up. I looked around and tried to figure out what I could do.

"I'd suggest an axe," Wolfgang said.

It was like a fever. I was still crying, but it didn't matter. I went and kicked the door of the nearest house. And I beat on the door of the next one. All the adults were gone, it didn't matter. Then I found a shed that I could knock open, and I grabbed a wood chopping axe, and I ran back to the stocks, and I hit the lock again and again and again until it fell off.

Some other kid opened up the stocks. It was Wolfgang that helped Ivy out and who she held onto as she cried. I couldn't let go of the axe. Wolfgang stood in front of the stocks and spoke to all of us.

"Ivy can go home now. Her parents won't say anything, I bet, because they're afraid they'll get in trouble too. That's what adults are like. After what you just saw, is anybody going to argue with me?"

Nobody did.

"Father Birch goes on and on about virtue and sin, but he's just an angry old man. He didn't lock Ivy up because she disrespected God. He locked her up because she disrespected him. Mayor Potato locked up his own niece. He didn't have to. He didn't try to argue. Adults don't love you, they just want you to follow their rules until you grow up just like they did and make your own children follow the rules."

Then he took the axe out of my hands and it was me he looked in the eyes as he told everyone, "You've heard about Walpurgis Night. That's the night the wolves come to town. The adults are afraid of us. They think they can't face us on Walpurgis. One night a year, the children are in charge. Do you want to grow up like them? You don't, or you wouldn't have stayed here with Ivy and Jenny. Walpurgis is coming soon. Come with us, so that when you go back to your homes the next morning, part of you will remember that you're not just another sheep with the rest of the sheep, and maybe when you grow up this village won't be full of people who let someone like Father Birch make the rules." And he grinned a little wider and added, "Maybe if you're really not a sheep you won't have to grow up at all."

I don't think he said anything else. The other kids made a lot of noises. They were angry and they agreed with him, and they wanted to stay with Ivy as Wolfgang took her home to her parents, who I guess really didn't tell anyone. Myself, I just sat there on the broken stocks and cried.

There were still... I think three weeks until Walpurgis. Life got back on track, sort of. Ivy didn't attend church and no one, not even Father Birch, said anything about it. She did go to school, but I'm not sure why she bothered. She was quieter than she had been before, and when she did speak it was usually to say something nasty. She hardly did any schoolwork and became an instant expert in slipping out the front door when Mister Thornback's back was turned. I could tell the whole thing bothered him, but Mister Thornback doesn't bend. She felt his ruler more than a few times, and it didn't seem to mean anything to her either way.

One reason she was ducking out was Wolfgang. He played a game of tag with the adults of the village those three weeks and he was always watching us. I thought at the time he was keeping them from thinking about Ivy, about whether she'd really paid for her 'crime.' I thought that all the more because she was the only person he spent any time with. Mostly he couldn't show up anywhere for thirty seconds before an adult spotted him and there was a fuss. A big fuss at first, and then less of a fuss after he got away a dozen times. Maybe that was the idea. By the time Walpurgis came around, adults were starting not to care.

But the schoolhouse isn't quite in the village. He could show up there, and only Mister Thornback might see him. Wolfgang could hide from one adult. So half the time Ivy slipped out, it was to talk to Wolfgang. She wouldn't get much time before Thornback wondered where she was and Wolfgang had to slip away, and all Ivy would say about those meetings is that she was looking forward to Walpurgis Night. She told me just once, when nobody else could hear, that she would do anything rather than grow up.

And what made me feel weirder about it all was that when Wolfgang would peek through a window or his shadow would hang over the doorway, I always saw him first. I got the feeling he was there to see me, not her, but I let her go instead.

And then it was Walpurgis Night.

The funny thing is, I didn't know then and I don't know now what the holiday is about. All anyone would ever tell me was that it was the night when the wolves ran wild. Adults generally didn't want to tell me that. I knew my parents kept me in on that night and there were sometimes funny noises, but I hadn't thought about it much. This year it was all I could think about. I was determined to get out and join the wolves.

The plan was simple. I'd go out in the late afternoon to bring in a tray of butter and I just wouldn't come back. I could hang out anywhere I wanted until night fell, and then it wouldn't matter. So I did just that. When the sun was low but there was still a couple of hours until sundown I told my mom I was going to bring in some butter – and she locked the door right in front of me.

She knew. And my father was home, too. They both knew.

"Walpurgis night," my mother told me. "No one leaves the house until morning." It was all she would say.

So I puttered around for an hour. For two hours. For three hours. I helped my mom make supper. I read the book I'd borrowed from school. I swept, although I wasn't able to sweep it out the door because the doors were locked. It was already dark, and I heard something like a howl in the distance, and I realized I was desperate, and I had an idea.

I scooped up the dust in the pan and told my mom, "I'm gonna dump this out the window." I only needed a few seconds where they didn't think about what I was doing. Our house isn't exactly big, but I went into my bedroom to open the window there. If I wasn't immediately in sight, that would be another few seconds. And the sound of me wrestling the window open wouldn't alarm them, because I was throwing out the dust, right?

I like to think kids aren't stupid. Well, neither are adults. It must have been a good plan, because I was halfway out the window before my mother grabbed my ankles. I didn't give in, and it didn't matter. She and my dad pulled me back in with ease. Then I heard a wolf, a real wolf, howling through the window. And after that someone shouting. Not words, just a sound, made by a girl's voice. By Ivy's voice.

I kind of lost it. I kicked and yelled and cried, and my parents actually tied me to my bed. I don't think I slept at all that night. I remember when the banging started on the door, and my father yelled that if they broke in and passed the cross on the door and the light of the fireplace they'd lose the protection of Walpurgis Night.

I remember my mom yelling, "I won't let my baby become a monster."

It must have worked. The banging stopped.

Eventually I remember the sun rising, and everything becoming very quiet.

I've mostly lost track of the next year. A year of nothing worth remembering. I'll tell you what I can.

In the morning everyone acted like they do every year, as if nothing had happened. For the children who hadn't gone out it was like that. The wolves came and left, but it was a dream. The kids who had gone out wouldn't say anything, and believe me for the first month I asked. I knew who had gone, because they'd been with me when we saved Ivy. They just wouldn't answer me no matter what I said. Rhubarb, who used to be the friendliest girl in school so that no one would make fun of her name, told me, "You wouldn't understand." The rest of them seemed to be mad at me. All of a sudden I didn't have many friends anymore.

I couldn't ask Ivy. Ivy was gone.

She wasn't alone. Clover, Rye, Hinny, and Morning Glory didn't show up to church on Sunday. Or school on Monday. They were gone, and no one, adult or child, wanted to talk about it. The kids who hadn't gone out on Walpurgis didn't even think it was that special.

That I understand. You're probably from a big city, but when you live in a little village way out in the country, families stay in one place, but kids move around a lot. We were used to someone just up and vanishing. They'd be sent off to apprenticeship, or the girl would be betrothed, or the family would decide he'd had enough schooling and was needed out on the farm, or they'd be fostered to some relatives in the next village because it was still family and it was more practical that way. Kids come and go all the time. Which is the only reason I can give that I hadn't realized, until that moment, that every year after Walpurgis Night a few children were always gone.

Nobody wanted to say why. And if they knew, would they tell me the truth? I wanted to think they'd become Wild Children like Wolfgang. That they were living in the woods and would never grow up, and all their troubles were over. I didn't want to think that they'd been caught and disposed of quietly. Or that something worse, something I hadn't thought of, had happened to them on Walpurgis Night.

I stopped asking. Hinny and Rye had been two of my best friends. Rye was just the most laid back boy you could-

Even today dwelling on them isn't a good idea. At the time I couldn't stop, and then I couldn't think about it anymore, and that was how I drifted into month after meaningless gray month. I didn't make any trouble in church, although I cared less than ever. I was polite and obeyed my parents, but I couldn't forgive them. School was the only thing that still made me happy at all. I didn't really have any friends there anymore, but I was still good at it, and Mister Thornback cared. He was worried about me, I knew. He didn't say anything. You can't expect an oak tree to bend. But while I was at school at least I was somewhere I knew I was appreciated, where I had some kind of purpose. I started staying late. I learned a lot of stuff that I'll never, ever use. And I didn't notice how the time was passing, or that summer, fall, winter were gone. That I was a year older. That I'd been nine when Walpurgis Night came around last time. That I was ten now, and it was coming again.

Until, of course, Wolfgang came back.

I'd been too wrapped up in my schoolwork. Mister Thornback was actually running out of work for me to do, or at least work that I could do without getting so far away from where the rest of the class was that he couldn't even teach me with the fourteen year olds. I didn't want to go home, and sending home someone who wants to learn is just something he can't do anyway. So he started sending me out on learning errands. He let me learn how to use a sextant, and order brushes for him because I knew what every kind of brush was good for, and gather different kinds of arachnids in glass jars.

And one day in spring he told me to go out and pick mushrooms so he could show the class which ones were safe and which were poisonous. Or rather, show everyone how hard it was to tell the difference. I didn't think he needed to. Our moms had drummed this lesson in hard as soon as we were old enough to walk out the door alone. But it was something to do, something to scratch away a few hours that wouldn't feel wasted.

So I stepped out the door, and it had been raining, so I was putting on those big old rubber boots Mister Thornback keeps beneath the overhang, and Wolfgang was just... there. I'd been having such a bad day, I thought I'd lost my grip at last and I couldn't tell dreams from being awake anymore.

I tried to hit him anyway. It was like trying to kick a snake. Not only did he duck under it, he stepped right up and hugged me. The jerk. I was so mad at him, so mad at everyone suddenly, and at the same time I felt like it had all been a dream and now I was waking up again.

"Your parents wouldn't let you go." It was a stupid thing to say, but I knew I didn't have to explain, because it meant he knew everything else, too. So I didn't say anything.

He had to let me go, but he was grinning. Wolfgang always grinned. He had it all worked out. It was all a big joke to him. God, was that ever true. "We tried to break you out."

"I guess we both failed, huh?" Yes, he'd made me feel less mad at him. But worse, I was starting to get that 'everything I say is dumb' feeling again. After a year apart I wasn't used to him anymore. But some things were more important.

"Ivy!" I whispered. "Wolfgang, what happened to Ivy? And the others? Nobody will say anything!"

"That's 'cause they don't know," he answered. "You know what a Mystery is, right? Some things you don't get to know until you've been through them. Becoming one of the Wild Children is one of them."

"You mean she really...?" I couldn't finish the sentence. Partly it was because if I did, maybe I'd be wrong. But mainly I felt so relieved I could barely keep my legs under me.

"Oh, yeah. In fact – hey, Whistle! I think we've found our contact."

And she walked out from behind the corner of the school. No, she... trotted out. Wolfgang is only a little bit wolf. At first I didn't think there was anything human left of Ivy. Her eyes, though. Wolves didn't have green eyes, did they? And she didn't walk like a wolf. The way she held her head and looked at me I knew this was Ivy, even before she spoke and her voice removed the last bit of doubt.

That and her kind of snide tone. Sigh. "Wolfy, we've been back ten minutes and you're hanging all over Jenny already." Chalk it up to the 'stupid' feeling, but I actually took a step away from him when she said that.

No matter what she acted like, I wanted to run up and hug her. "Ivy, you're alive! And you're a Wild Girl and everything!"

"You're still so human, Jenny." She sniffed at me, but her tail wagged.

Wolfgang, of course, wasn't going to let us fight. "She's mad 'cause you're still calling her Ivy, Jenny."

Wolves are expressive. Whistle pouted. "Wild Children don't keep their human names. You know that. You and Wolfy are the only people who know who Whistle used to be, and it's going to stay that way."

"Not for long." Even I was grinning now. "Every kid in school who hears your voice is going to know. I'll have trouble stopping them from having a party."

Wolfgang actually looked hesitant for a moment. But only for a moment. "None of them are going to hear her voice. Whistle's not coming back, not yet. You can't have too many Wild Children hanging around a village at once. I chose years ago to bring the children here over, so it'll be me — and anyway, she's too new at this. I really only brought her this far so that you and her could meet."

Wolves aren't known for rolling their eyes either, and Whistle looked a lot more like Ivy when she did it. "That's it? That's really it, isn't it? Wolfgang, you brought me all the way back here just so that Jenny and I could say hello, so that she'd know it could really happen to her. No wonder! I didn't want to come back to this awful place. I hate it here."

"Which is another reason you're not sticking around. Finding the kids who might be Wild Children, getting them to join us on Walpurgis Night — that's a job for a calm head." He shrugged and asked her, "So, you seen everything you want to see?"

She nodded. That looks kinda weird on a wolf too. "Yeah, Wolfy. No regrets here. They're all a bunch of humans. I'm with you all the way."

"Then I'll see you after Walpurgis. If we're lucky, I'll have a new friend or two. Maybe Jenny."

And Whistle gave me an odd look. This wasn't Whistle the Wild Child, or the Ivy we saved from the stocks. This was the old Ivy, the one I didn't like. "You don't know her as well as you think you do, Wolfy." And she ran off. She didn't have Wolfgang's ability to just disappear yet, but she was fast and she was quiet and if I'd blinked wrong I'd have missed her.

It was just me and Wolfgang.

I grabbed him by the cast-off shirt he wore (which was never as grubby as it ought to have been) and demanded, "Where have you been? I can't – I don't even know how long it's been!"

"About ten months." He answered like it was no big deal. "It's less than two months to Walpurgis. Whistle really isn't ready to live on her own yet, but I can't let a Walpurgis Night go by in our village without doing something. And I had to disappear for a while. For a long while, until the adults started to forget. They knew which kids could think for themselves and they knew I was talking to you. This time I can't be so obvious. If you don't come this year, making the run isn't worth it."

"The kids left from last year would go, I'm sure, Wolfgang. And I think my folks think I've forgotten. I think everyone thinks that. There's some new kids, but I don't know them really well. How are you going to talk to them without the adults finding out?"

"Easy," he told me, and he sure sounded like he thought it would be easy. "I find you and tell you where I'll be. You tell some of the kids from last year. A group gets together, and I talk to them. We may not have a passionate pack like last year, but we'll save a few from growing up like Father Birch."

"Don't say that name," I hissed at him. It was crazy, but now that I wasn't sleeping through my life again all the bad feelings I had for Birch were spilling out like they were fresh. "I'll do it. I don't know that I want my friends running off into the woods and becoming Wild Children, but if it's a choice between you and Father Birch-"

"Jenny McThresh!" And that was probably the worst time possible to have Mister Thornback walk up behind me. Wolfgang vanished, but it was too late.

Oh, it was so way too late. "That was a Wild Boy!" yelled Mister Thornback. He doesn't yell really loud. In a way, that's worse. He hasn't lost his temper. He really is that mad. "Worse, it was a wolf. Worse, it was Pepper Birch. Jenny, I didn't want to believe what they told me last year. What are you doing talking to a creature like that?"

My back was actually pressed against the wall of the schoolhouse. We were talking loud enough, everybody inside could hear us. And he knew it, and I knew it. We wanted them to. "He's not a creature. Whatever he looks like, he's as human as you or I. Maybe more! How do you even know his name?"

"Because I'm more than forty years old, which is how long it's been since that little beast was human. I'm not sure 'human' described him then, either. I don't understand why I even have to explain this to you. You can see him with your own eyes. He's been marked as a beast, like all Wild Children. He can't ever hide what he is again. How can you associate with something like that?"

"So that's it? You think Father Birch is right? Wolfgang is evil because he's a wolf? Because he doesn't want us to obey? To grow up and do whatever a stupid, mean old man tells us, because he claims to speak for God?" My eyes stung. I was almost crying. I didn't like arguing with Mr. Thornback, but I wasn't going to back down.

"I think – I know – that Wild Children are marked for their sins. I know that we're going to pretend you didn't say what you just said. I don't agree that being beaten in public or a night in the stocks turns a child from foolishness."

And then, and this felt like the weirdest thing to happen so far, he got down on his knees and put his hands on my shoulders. He was so angry he was shaking, but he didn't yell anymore. He looked me in the eyes and said, "That creature is evil. Stay away from him. I don't know how he could get his teeth into a girl like you. Maybe he offered you immortality. Maybe he lied to you about freedom, tried to tell you that just because a rule is wrong you can break it. But listen to me. Trust your eyes. He's a wolf now because that was his heart when he was human. Wild Children are cursed by God for their wickedness, and no matter what he may show you, it is a curse. Their humanity is gone. He will do everything in his power to make sure you walk that path until you're destroyed."

I was shaking too, and the odd thing was, it wasn't because I was afraid. I was angry. Even Mister Thornback accepted this kind of stupidity. He was the nicest adult I knew, but he just couldn't let go of the rules. "Are you going to tell my parents? Or Father Birch? Or the Mayor?"

The look of distaste on his face was as weird as the rest of this day. I was realizing I didn't know Mister Thornback at all. I wasn't sure I wanted to anymore.

And then he goes, "I'm not going to tell anyone. We make our own moral choices, Jenny. You have been told lies, and you have been told the truth, and you have to figure out who you trust. The fate of your body and soul depend on it." And he got up and he went back into the school, where the other kids were pretending not to listen.

Who did I trust? I trusted Wolfgang. I used to trust Mister Thornback. I was worried now that I didn't really know either of them. But Mister Thornback was with Father Birch on this, and I trusted that, whatever the question, Father Birch was wrong about it.

I knew Mister Thornback didn't tell anybody because this year it all seemed to work. Up until night fell on Walpurgis the plan, such as it was, went like clockwork. After that I had no plan, no predictions.

I think my parents suspected something because I was suddenly spending a lot less time at home. I just wandered around. I found an excuse to be everywhere. And sometimes, when no adults were around, I'd make sure that Wolfgang and some of the village kids showed up at about the same time.

I don't really know what he said to them. I didn't hang around. Looking back, I think it's clear enough to me. I was going through the motions, but it wasn't that I had signed on to Wolfgang's crusade, if that's what it was. It was more like after I'd missed Walpurgis the first time I'd fallen asleep, and I was waking up again just before the next one. This time I was going to do it right.

Not much even happened. If it had, we'd have been in trouble. The whole point was that this year the adults didn't suspect. They couldn't plan. They probably knew it would – you know, I don't know what they knew, and I don't care. Poor Mister Thornback knew. Kids ditched his classes in droves. I know he never told anybody. He just taught everyone who was left. He didn't even punish the children he caught. I skipped out a couple of times, but only a couple. I couldn't understand how someone could be so right and so wrong at the same time. I couldn't make it worse for him.

But none of this matters, right? You heard about it last year. Different words, same tune. I'll skip ahead to Walpurgis, because in my memory that's how it happened. That one whole year, from beginning to end, is just a blur. A gray blur at first, and then a shiny, broken blur at the end.

Because suddenly it was the morning before the night. My folks were on edge. All the adults were. My mom told me to be home well before sundown, though, and that's it. They didn't suspect us, they were just afraid of the night. My father even sent me down to the apothecary around noon to get some tobacco. I'm sure he wanted it to ease his nerves during the night. This time it was me barely ahead of them. I didn't come back. Probably a lot of other kids did the same.

Most of the area around the village is farms. Eventually there's the woods, but mostly it's farms. But that just makes it even easier to hide. Sit down under a cart, behind a rock too big to plow up, in a drainage tunnel, at the bottom of an empty irrigation ditch. Look at the flowers, listen to the wind and the birds as the sun stumbles and skips its way down from the top of the sky. That's what I did, until I woke up, surprised I'd been able to sleep, and the sun was setting and I heard in the distance the first howl of a wolf. The year ripped from my life was over. Walpurgis Night had begun.

I bolted out from my cover and followed the howl. The wolves would be coming from the woods. That's where I would go.

As I got closer, I saw more kids. Nobody stopped us or said a word. Every door was locked, a lot of the windows were covered, and no one was looking out for fear of what they'd see. What they'd see was their own children, defying them and everything they believed in. Seeking a new truth, I guess.

No, even then I couldn't buy that. Maybe the other kids did. I was looking for an adventure. I was awake again, and I could feel my whole body. I might find out who Wolfgang really was, and if I was like him, and what my destiny would be, but mostly I just wanted to do this for its own sake, even if I didn't know what it was.

I guess part of me was doing it to spite Father Birch.

Eventually we got to the woods, and just as we weren't quite sure where to go there was another howl. This one wasn't distant, or faint. It was strong and it was long and it wasn't human. One of us tried to echo it. I'm pretty sure it wasn't me, because I was running forward through the trees, following the sound until I found the wolves.

Four wolves. Wolfgang sat on a log in front, grinning as always. That grin was different with three other wolves pacing behind him. One only had a wolf face and paws and wolf eyes, but he moved like an impatient animal. When we'd stepped into the clearing we'd left human rules behind.

Wolfgang stood up and he held out his hand and he called. "Jenny, c'mere." That surprised me. But I walked over to him anyway, leaving the rest of the kids behind. He took my hand in his, and his was so coarse and furry, but it still felt human. I looked back at the others; I was stunned. There must have been two dozen children there. Half the houses in town must have been filled with terrified parents wondering where their children were. No… angry parents, mad that they were being defied, but too afraid to do anything about it. The tables had turned on them.

Wolfgang squeezed my hand tighter and leaned over and told me, "This is your year, Jenny." Louder, he asked the other children, "Do you want a speech?"

When no one answered, he laughed. "No, you don't. We all know what we're here for. But last year they took Walpurgis Night from Jenny. Tonight we're going to make it right. Let's go have some fun." Behind him the three other wolves howled, and then Wolfgang howled, and some of the kids started howling, and I… I didn't howl, exactly. I just screamed up at the dark sky and the bright moon. I hadn't realized how angry I was, how trapped I'd felt, and now the chain had snapped.

We ran! That was what the wolves were there for. They ran on all fours, even the one who looked almost human. They laughed, and they let out little howls and they weaved in and out of the group. We got to the village and we spilled into the main square. All the doors were shut, and the kids laughed and shouted, but for a moment they didn't know what to do.

I knew what to do. I ran up to the stocks and I started to kick them as hard as I could with the sole of my foot. And then Wolfgang was beside me kicking it too, and then the other kids, and I learned that a bunch of people, even if they're children, are strong. In a minute it was nothing but chunks of broken wood.

We ran a little wild for a while. A few kids threw rocks. Some of us chased chickens, until one of the wolves picked up the chase and ran it down and shook it. Killed it, I guess, but we just laughed at the feathers flying everywhere. I threw a rock at the Mayor's house. Another kid threw a rock. Pretty soon there was a whole group of us, throwing rocks and screaming who knows what. We were the kids who'd stayed with Ivy a year before. She wasn't there to see it, but we remembered. Oh, did we remember. I was thinking of moving on to the church, but Wolfgang probably knew where I was going and dragged me away.

Instead we played burglars for a little while. Houses were left alone, but even a village as small as ours had a few shops. There wasn't anything much fun in the apothecary, but we managed to break the lock off and get in and paw at things for a while until we got bored. The general store, where everything the village bought from the outside world was sold, was more interesting. I ran down the length of the shop, dragging my hands over the merchandise and laughing. When some of it fell out and broke, we all laughed harder. When we all spilled out onto the street again the store was a mess, but we hadn't taken much. We didn't care.

I did take a pouch of tobacco for my father. I don't know why. Trust me, that's the last you'll ever hear about it.

Aside from the Mayor's house, it was a game. All the rules were gone and there was nothing to stop us. We were being children, really, which is why it was Wolfgang whose whistle brought us all to the inn.

I'd never even been inside. It was a place where adults went to talk and strangers spent the night on their way to places more interesting. The front door wouldn't give, even when the wolves had a go at it, but the back door wasn't even locked. We spilled inside. The wolves stood on tables and counters. A couple of kids started banging pots and pans and throwing them around in the kitchen. We were all hungry, and I was amazed at how good some of the food in their pantry was. Of course, that wasn't why we were there. We were there so Wolfgang could start bringing up bottles and little casks out of the wine cellar.

If we hadn't been running around the village breaking into stores we'd never have dared, but soon we were all drinking something. There was a lot of laughter when some of the kids tried the beer and thought it tasted nasty, but I kind of liked it. I mean, it tasted weird, with this sort of sharpness that wasn't like the other drinks. You could taste the alcohol in those. Beer was just weird. Nobody wondered why we didn't just collapse, drinking this stuff. I guess Walpurgis Night had its magic after all.

But things did get a little mixed up after that. A lot of kids took to standing outside their own doors, yelling at their parents. A couple cursed them, but mostly they just howled. Wolfgang must have been pretty mad at my folks, because he stood outside their front door and told them that this year he had their daughter and they couldn't stop what she'd become, while his wolves clawed at the windows without actually trying to get in.

Eventually I realized we'd been holding hands almost the whole time since we left the inn. But that was about the time things changed. We trailed back into the square, and Wolfgang climbed up on top of the little stand by the ruined stocks where the Mayor usually made pronouncements and he told us, "It's well past midnight! We've had our fun, and I think we've made our point. For another year the adults will remember that they can't control all of us." There was laughter, and cheering, and howling. They didn't even let him finish. I'm not sure they all heard him.

"But we're not quite done! One more stop, the most important."

And we knew where we were going.

I would have thought Father Birch would have locked and barred the church on Walpurgis Night. He didn't. I thought it might have been because we'd have found some other way to break in. Wolfgang, of course, had been here before and knew it wouldn't be. We flooded inside. We pushed over pews. There actually wasn't much to do, but Wolfgang had thought of that. He'd brought a can of paint, and after a little while the walls were covered in hand prints and angry words that couldn't be read. After I wiped the paint off my hands we sat on the altar and howled. And then Wolfgang surprised us.

He shoved us all off of the altar, and he and his wolves set their shoulders against it and pushed it aside. Underneath were doors. Big doors. We all knew what this was. The village's storehouse, where the taxes and the emergency food and the building materials and anything thought of as a treasure was kept under the church. Local legend said it went down several stories in a series of basements. We were about to find out, but until now none of us had even known where the entrance was.

Standing on the doors, Wolfgang held out his hands, and we actually all got kind of quiet. "For some of you, the night is done. If you want to feel like a wolf for a few more hours follow my brothers. They're going back to the woods to run and hunt and play. If you're tired, go home. Curl up on your doorstep. When morning comes your parents won't say anything. They never do." The kids from last year nodded.

"What's down below is a Mystery. Are you here for fun, or are you here to see this all the way? All the way, no matter what it takes, no matter what happens? If you stay I can't say what will happen to you, but your life in this village is over. The rest of you can go home. Go home with my blessings. When you grow up you'll remember Walpurgis Night, and maybe you'll let your kids run wild, or maybe they won't have any reason to want to."

Up until then everything had been funny. I think it was the sudden seriousness that scared most of the kids. The wolves were standing by the door, and most of the children followed them. And then Wolfgang pointed at Bud, who was only nine, and Dahlia, who was seven, and he told them, "You two. I'm proud of you more than anyone. You can't join us, yet. But join the wolves next year, and the year after that, and you'll be ready. It's for kids like you that I keep the Mystery." And they slunk off, looking jealous. At the door tiny Dahlia threw her head back and howled, and I wondered if she was turning into a Wild Girl right there.

That left seven of us and Wolfgang. We helped him open up the heavy doors and we went down into the cellars under the church to learn the Mystery of the Wild Children.

At first, as a mystery, it was kind of disappointing. Well, I thought so. The others were whispering and laughing again already. It really was a storehouse. Huge barrels and salted meats and bales of hay and spare metalworks hung from the ceiling. One other thing rumor was right about – it wasn't the only cellar. There were more doors. I was impressed by that, because I thought this first room was bigger than the church.

Then Wolfgang slid his arm around me and he swung me around, and he laughed. "We did it, Jenny! We got this far! Here everything is decided. Tomorrow you'll be a wolf like me, I know it." I giggled a little. I was a little scared and confused. And then his furry mouth touched mine, and I was even more scared and confused.

Not only wasn't he scared, he didn't seem to think the kiss was a big deal. The others were already poking around. Opening taps, prying open crates. "You all must be hungry again, right? Feel free to have a bite. But first, we howl – all of us."

And he howled, and he howled like a wolf, like someone who really wasn't all human anymore. But we howled too, and I was surprised by how much like him it sounded. Were wolves and humans that different?

I guess I was about to find out. Wolfgang was dragging a box, some kind of small but heavy locker out from behind a crate. From it he took some old wooden mugs. They didn't seem that fancy, but he passed one to each of us like it was a ceremony. We were all quiet then as he went over to one of the casks lined up against the wall. It was a dusty one, smaller than most. He took a spigot from the locker as well, which he pounded into the hole in the cask.

"This is what I brought you here for. This village guards a secret. Father Birch knows, and the Mayor knows. They think they'd give their life to keep it from us, but on Walpurgis Night there's nothing they can do."

He took the mug from me and held it under the spigot and let it pour, filling it with a frothy golden brown. "You've heard of the Fountain of Youth, right?" he asked. "And you all know by now that Wild Children never grow up. This is why. You're all well on your way to becoming one of us. This will push you over." He held the mug up to me, and I took it and sniffed it and took a taste. More beer.

"The mistake adults always made was assuming the Fountain of Youth would be water."

We each took our mugs, and he took one for himself. We were all nervous now, but he drank, and we drank. I drank. It was beer, but this was a lot better than the other stuff. It was kind of sweet, and we drank and we drank until the mug fell out of my hands because I suddenly couldn't hold it.

Back at the inn? You know how I said nothing we drank really bothered us? All of a sudden I could barely stand up. I think I was the one who started the giggling, but it came out all squeaky and high-pitched, and then raspy. Even Wolfgang wobbled. He sort of staggered over to me and put his arms on my shoulders, and he couldn't quite do his usual grin.

"This is it, Jenny. You've come all the way. In a few minutes – oh, no way."

"What?" I asked him. He was staring at my ears, and they felt a little weird, but everything felt a little weird. I reached up to touch them, and they were… long. Long and hairy. Too long to be wolf ears. This was wrong. And I could barely feel them, but I knew what they were. They were donkey ears. I thought of the girl on the cart and brought my hands to my face, but my face hadn't changed. My hands had. They were hooves. I had hooves instead of hands. Rough hooves rubbing against my face.

The others. One of the boys had ripped his clothes off. Even his body was round and brown and hairy now. A girl sat in the corner crying, pulling on her tail. Her tail? Oh, yeah. I wagged mine. I had a tail, too. Then I nearly fell over as I went from having feet to having more hooves.

And Wolfgang just looked kind of disappointed, but not enough to stop grinning. "Sorry, Jenny. Well, I guess you're not Jenny now. I thought for sure you'd be a wolf."

I was about to punch him in the face and tell him what I thought of his 'sorry', but there were hands on my shoulders. Big, adult hands.

"Seven donkeys. No wolves. Nothing funny," a voice announced. My hands were yanked behind me. I was being tied – no, these were cold and hard. Metal shackles. With my hooves I'd never have a hope of getting out of them. And a collar around my neck. It hurt, and I was twisted around by a big man in black with a black mask hiding his face. Another man was putting shackles on some of the other children. We'd all stopped changing. Two of us seemed to be completely donkeys. The rest were a mix. I was the only one of those without hands. The one girl just had ears and a tail, and she tried to run but she was too drunk. The second man caught her before she reached the stairs. He shoved her down onto the floor, and shackled her and collared her, and then he pulled another, different pair of shackles down from the ceiling and hobbled her ankles. The rest of us wouldn't have been able to run. Learning to stand on hooves isn't easy.

He'd pulled the shackles down from the ceiling. I looked up. The hanging metalwork – collars, yokes, manacles, chains. There were a lot of them. This wasn't the first time this had happened.

"You can get back to the forest, you little demon. No puppies for you this year," snapped the big man to Wolfgang. Who was just standing there.

"I don't have to do what you tell me to, old man," Wolfgang retorted. "It's been forty years, and I've enjoyed every second of not having to listen to you." He looked me in the eyes, and all there was in his face was… disappointment. I couldn't see much else for tears after that, but his voice was clear and there was no pity in it. "You're right about one thing. There's nothing for me here. Ah, well. Ivy's waiting, I guess." All I could see was a blur, but it was a blur he wasn't a part of.

"Wolfgang! How dare you? How could you do this to anyone?" I yelled after him, "They said you were a monster, but I believed you!" Our captors seemed to think this was hilarious. They laughed a lot. Wolfgang didn't even bother to answer me.

After that they dragged us through a couple more rooms. There really was a whole network of cellars down here, but that didn't seem interesting anymore. We were chained together by our necks and dumped in a big, rough stone jail cell, one wall of which was just bars. There was one boy left who was pretty much a donkey from the waist down, the two who looked like real donkeys and I guess were boys to start with, and me and three girls. The one who looked almost human, and two others who looked more donkey than I did. But they still had hands. That was basically all we did for a while, look at each other and try to remember what the others had looked like before and figure out who had changed how.

Then the men in their black masks came back, and another man with them without a mask.

"Mister Thornback!" I yelled, and the men in the masks started laughing again. Mister Thornback just looked grim. He certainly didn't look like he wanted to laugh. He looked haunted. But he was here anyway, helping them.

The other Wild Children couldn't believe it either. "Really?" asked the remaining boy, and one of the donkeys lifted his head too, and stared. "Nuh-uh," he added.

The girl who'd barely changed had started trembling, and shaking her head and going, "Not him."

Mister Thornback never changes, though. Whatever he was doing, whether he was happy about it or not, he did it properly. "Open up the cell please and unlink them, gentlemen, if you want my professional examination."

The bigger man grunted, and the smaller man took out some keys. He opened up the cell and went down the line, unfastening the chains that held us together by the necks.

"Full transformations first, please."

They tugged one of the donkeys out of the cell. The 'wrist' shackles on him were too much. With four legs he could barely walk in them. Mister Thornback started looking him over, like an animal at any fair. Ears, muscle tone, eyes. He was checking the hind hooves when the Wild Boy said, "Please, Mister Thornback-"

He didn't really get to say anything else. Mister Thornback just sighed and told the men in the masks, "He can speak and understand, but other than that the transformation is complete. Even the teeth and eyes."

"Talking donkey, huh? Always a buyer for those," observed the smaller man approvingly. I wanted to hit him. For a second I thought our teacher did, too.

The Wild Boy was led back into the cell. Next out was the other donkey. He got the same look-over, until Mister Thornback got to his face he told the boy, "Say 'ah'." He didn't. The men went quiet, and Thornback lifted the donkey's chin and repeated, "Say 'ah'."

"Huh?" was the only reply he got. Except that, while that *is* what I heard, I heard something else, too. Not words, just an animal noise. And I tried not to think about what I was beginning to suspect.

Gently, Thornback took the keys from the smaller masked man and undid the shackles and the collar and gave the transformed boy a slap on the butt. There was another one of those sounds I heard as "Huh?" but also as a disgruntled sawing noise, and the boy trotted off into the next room.

"Complete transformation, gentlemen. Whoever he was to start with, all you have is a donkey now. He's not even a Wild Child."

"All of them are donkeys," the bigger masked man told the teacher gruffly.

"We'll never sell it. Might as well use it around the village," suggested the smaller.

"No. We get rid of all of them. No Wild Children here," retorted the big one. "That's the only reason I put up with that devil boy. This way we know when they change and can get rid of the new ones."

"Leather, then," said the smaller man. We all got real, real quiet. I even thought Mister Thornback was going to cry, but he just sat there.

"That one first," said the big man, pointing at the girl who'd hardly changed.

"Yes, of course," said Mister Thornback and sighed. "Come here, girl." He called her to, beckoning with his hand.

"You know who I am, Mister Thornback," she told him sulkily as she hobbled over.

"No, Wild Girl," he told her, gently but very seriously. "I know who you were. You don't get to keep a human's name, or pretend you're still who you used to be. I suggest you forget Violet Fromme. I'm trying to. Hold still, please, and don't say any more."

And he gave her a sort of brief medical examination, I guess, like he'd given the donkeys. It was a little embarrassing, but we had a lot worse on our minds. Eventually he looked up at the masked men and pointed at the extra shackles on her ankles. "Are those really necessary?"

"Yes," answered the big man coldly. "None of the others will be able to run for a couple of days. This one might try to escape."

"Well, then there's nothing I can tell you that you don't already know. The ears and tail are the only visible transformation. Her mind is obviously still almost at human sharpness. There's no question of what she is, however. She'll look like that for the next ninety years, probably."

Both of the masked men smiled. "She'll bring a lot of money into the village," observed the smaller one.

"We'll never be able to get full price. You'll have to sell her to a dealer in the capital. But whether we get a penny or a wagon of gold, we sell her first. Wild Girls like her are the worst. They all corrupt every man who sees them, but the ones like this breed sympathy."

"We'll work something out. She won't see daylight until I've found a buyer, don't worry."

Violet — could I call her Violet? — didn't know what to do. Mister Thornback helped her shuffle over to the doorway and sit down. He didn't say anything else. The only thing he said to the next two girls was, "Say 'ah'," and he seemed satisfied when they did. I didn't listen to what he said about them. I guess he must have done the boy with the donkey legs. I don't remember that at all. Because, of course, I knew that he'd done all the others, and now I had to face him.

"Alright, Wild Girl," he told me with the same soft, tired voice,."Come let me look at you."

I shuffled out into the light on my brand new hooves. I wasn't looking forward to this, and his expression when he saw me was more guilty and stricken than I would have believed. "Jenny," he whispered to me, and his hands clasped my cheeks. "How could this happen to you?"

"Why are you helping them, Mister Thornback?!" I yelled back furiously. The men in the masks started laughing again, and there were tears in Mister Thornback's eyes, although I'm sure I'm the only one who saw them. He would never let them show.

"He can't understand you," mumbled Violet by the door. I didn't need her to tell me, unfortunately. I'd heard my own voice. I knew what I'd said, but I also knew that what had come out was the mindless 'ee-aw!' of a donkey.

"No Jenny here," the big man announced to everyone. "We'll call this one Bray." And he and the other masked man had another good laugh.

I got less of an examination than anyone. My old teacher made a half-hearted show of it until he lifted my wrists and noticed my hooves. After that he just stood up. "I don't have to tell you anything about this one's condition, gentlemen. There's nothing you can't see for yourselves."

"That's right," husked the big man, and he and the smaller jailer pushed past us into the last cellar, a sort of crude dining area by the main storeroom. They sat down at one end in rough chairs at a rough table and poured themselves drinks from an old bottle.

I was being led to follow them. Mister Thornback's arm was still around me. It was such a strange thing for him to do, it made it really weird that he sounded so composed as he told the others, "Gentlemen, I examine your acquisitions every year. I make sure they're healthy and help you with the… difficult cases. You know I don't approve, but I do it for the village. I've never asked for anything. Now I'm asking. Let me have Bray, here."

"No," the big man told him gruffly, pulling off his mask so that he could take his drink. It was Father Birch, of course. I'd been too drunk and scared to recognize his voice, but his hatred was too familiar. "You think of her as human, Thornback. She's corrupting you already. That one is so full of sin it's a wonder she didn't turn into a wolf."

"You can't do very much else with her, Father," Mister Thornback answered him gravely. "No hands. She understands, but she can't speak.

She'd be useless as a servant. She can't do much of anything. But she can remind me of my failures, because I promise you, Father, I don't even have to look at her. Every time she tries to talk I'll know that she's just a Wild Child now."

The other man was taking off his mask too. He was the Mayor. I didn't know him well enough to have recognized him, but it wasn't really a surprise. "You don't think we can sell her? Oh, it'll require just the right buyer, true, but there's a market for Wild Girls in her condition. It might just take a while."

"Then let me buy her," insisted Mister Thornback. Even I could hear he was getting desperate. Well, maybe only I could hear it. "I can afford it. We all know I was never going to retire."

"I told you, no," snapped Father Birch. "It's not about whether she can be sold. I won't allow Wild Children in this village. They are our sins given flesh, and by God I will drive them out." Then he looked at me, and I didn't like that look at all. I thought I had known how hateful Father Birch could be, but there was something in that stare I'd never seen. "I almost considered keeping this one myself. With that voice, looking like she does, no one will sympathize with her. Not even her parents. And everyone knows the kind of girl she was becoming. I could use her as an example."

I could feel Mister Thornback actually starting to shake when Birch continued. "But I told you. We won't keep any of them. Ever. You don't think villagers haven't tried to buy a donkey themselves once or twice? I convince them otherwise. I work too hard to keep this village pure. I'm not going to let Bray here finish the work she started as a human."

"Then you can give her to me after all, Father," Mister Thornback returned. I couldn't believe he wasn't getting angry. If anything he sounded more sad and gentle than ever. "She'd take forever to sell, and you want her out fast. Give her to me for the work of I've done, for my silence, for my loyalty to the village. And I'll retire. I'll move to Martz, or the capital. Our village will be kept pure."

The Mayor was starting to get it. I could see some sympathy in his eyes. Not for me, no, but for Mister Thornback. But it was Father Birch who was in charge, I knew. So we waited for his judgment. There was no sympathy in him. But… "Alright. I'll think about that. It's all the same to me as long as she's gone from here. I'd refuse just to save you, but it's too late for that. You've always been weak, Thornback. A good mind, but a weak heart. She's corrupting you already. Even if I got rid of her now, you'd be marked. We'll talk about it tomorrow, or the next day. The donkeys need to be trained and prepared for sale. When I'm sure she's biddable and won't run off on you and back to us, I'll probably let you take her and go. I'll just be purging all the corruption in one go."

"Thank you, Father," the teacher told him formally. Somehow the keys had ended up on the table. He took them and started unlocking my collar and manacles.

"Thornback, what are you doing? Are you crazy?" demanded the Mayor, but he didn't seem to be getting out of his seat.

"She has no dignity left, Sir. Give her this," Mister Thornback told him sadly. "Anyway, in her condition, what can she do? If she got away, no one would help her. She couldn't get very far. What can she do?"

"She can serve us drinks," muttered Father Birch, and the Mayor laughed.

As he took the metal bonds off of me Mister Thornback told me sternly, "There's no going back now, Bray. Do what they tell you. Do everything they tell you. This is the new life you chose for yourself, and if you get used to it then maybe I can pick you up tomorrow instead of a few days from now. Think about that, please."

I nodded. It was the first time anyone had really spoken to me. That it had been suggested I had any choices left, however small. It gave me something to hold on to as he walked off into the dark cellars, leaving me and the other Wild Children alone with our captors.

To them I might as well not be there. "He thinks he's protecting her. The fool." Father Birch groused as he lit a cigar. "He's letting her cloud his thinking. In twenty years he'll be dead, and she'll still be like that. Half girl, half helpless thing, reeking of sin. He's just putting off the inevitable. And for what? To coddle something worth less than the lazy little hussy she was when she was alive."

The Mayor just nodded. "Sympathy won't be his only weakness. I've seen what owning a Wild Child does to a man. It may take years, but she'll destroy every virtue he's got. You know it."

Father Birch just grunted. "It's too late for either of them. One way or another, they have to go. Maybe his way. I haven't decided."

And suddenly, I guess they realized I was listening. The Mayor barked, "You! Girl! What was your name? Bray! Our drinks are empty. Get us new ones."

It was the dumbest request I'd ever heard, but I knew he was just making fun of me. What was I supposed to do with hooves? So I steeled myself for it as I tottered over to pick up their tankards. Thank goodness for the loops. I was eventually able to hook them over my hooves. Of course they laughed the whole time.

And that – not just the laughter, all of it – was why I didn't feel bad for what I did next. It's probably why I was able to do it. It just all came together. I still had a choice, some kind of choice, however small. I'd felt so helpless with these hooves, but I was carrying their tankards anyway. Done something they figured I'd fail at completely. And I… I hated them. Okay, it's not noble. I wasn't really sure how I felt about Mister Thornback now, but I had always hated Father Birch, and he and the Mayor seemed like worse monsters even than Wolfgang. I had to do something.

I fiddled with the tap on one of the barrels uselessly. I think I could have done it, but I wanted them to see me fail and start laughing, and make sure they were sitting down again out of sight, not watching me. Then I called out to… to… it was weird. I was Bray, and she wasn't Violet even though it was the only name I knew for her. No time for thoughts like that.

"Hey! Come here! Come help me with this. I think, I really think I can get us out of here."

Of course they laughed some more at the ridiculous donkey noises I made. But she understood. She could only shuffle in the leg irons and she didn't look like she believed me, but she came.

"Well, I'll be," I heard the Mayor swear. "The expensive one's going to help her. Hind, what are you doing? No slumming with the cheaper merchandise!" That got him and Father Birch laughing again.

"A Hind is a deer, stupid," I snapped at them. Why? Because they couldn't understand, and I could say whatever I wanted. All it did was keep them off guard, giving me time to try something desperate.

"Half fill the steins," I whispered to Hind. She worked the tap and did as I asked, while I counted my way down to Wolfgang's special cask.

The spigot had been taken out. There was no way we could put it back, or even pull out the stopper. Hind was looking at me in shock. She'd realized what I was trying to do and that we couldn't do it now.

"Here!" I hissed at her. I wasn't sure how loud I was being. Donkeys don't whisper. They couldn't understand me, but I didn't want the Mayor and Father Birch realizing Hind and I could really talk to each other. "Give me the steins!" I wrapped my arms around them and didn't try to be fancy. Learning to use hooves could wait. "Find our mugs! I dropped mine. I bet none of us finished."

She still just looked stunned, but she nodded and started stumbling around in the dark room. Mug after mug was produced. They'd all tipped over when we dropped them, but they held a few drops here, a trickle there. Would it be enough? How strong was this stuff? What would it even do?

Then I heard a clip clopping in the shadows. The boy who had turned completely into a donkey was plodding over to us. I wish I could say he looked like he understood what we were doing, but he didn't. But he must have understood something. He was holding, awkwardly, kind of upright and in his teeth, one of the mugs. It must have been Wolfgang's. It was only half empty!

Hind poured an equal measure into both of the flagons. I kissed the donkey on the forehead, and Hind recovered enough to hug us both. It might already be too late. I heard a chair scrape and Father Birch shout, "What's with you, you hairy little tramp? Where's our drinks?"

"Coming right now, Sir!" I shouted back. I hoped it would at least sound deferential. I guess it worked, because they laughed long enough for me to hobble back into the room and clumsily put the flagons on the table in front of them.

"Look at that," mused the Mayor, taking his drink. "She had to get Hind to help her, yeah, but she did it."

"I don't like it. She's still too smart. They're all sinful, but this one is wicked."

And then I about fell over, because they drank the drinks anyway. In fact the Mayor mumbled something about, "Good stuff. We'll have to make Hind show us where she got it," and even Father Birch grunted something approving.

They kept drinking. They drank every last drop. Their steins were completely empty when they dropped them and threw themselves out of their chairs. And I learned, then and there, why there were no Wild Children over the age of fourteen. The Fountain of Youth was not for adults. Maybe it did mark us with our sin. Maybe that's what it did to adults, but… more so.

I don't know what the Mayor became. It was just ugly and even fatter than he was as a man, and it died right there in front of me. It couldn't breathe right, it seemed to crush itself. He wasn't done transforming before he stopped moving.

And Father Birch, I think – I think he became a dragon. Maybe. It was a monster. It had horns and plates and claws, but at the same time it was twisted and misshapen. He threw himself at me with those claws. At the very last moment, hate was the only thing he knew. It wasn't enough. All I had to do was fall on my butt out of the way. What hit the ground in front me could only twitch and scrape the dirt. After a few more seconds it couldn't even do that. They were both very, very dead.

I let Hind do most of the rest. Even if I'd had hands, they'd be shaking too hard. She was able to handle the keys. We got all the other Wild Children unlocked, and we told them what we could, which wasn't much. The Mayor and Birch had arranged it all, and they wouldn't be doing it again. Ever.

I tried not to look at the bodies as we all filed past them into the main cellar. They were still getting uglier. We had to help each other to get everyone with hooves up the stairs, and to push open the cellar doors without anyone falling down again. But we did it.

And then for a few minutes we lost track of each other, because we were all so grateful to be out of there. I plodded through the mess of the church and stepped outside into the village. The air was fresh. I could see the sun peeking over the trees. It was dawn. I ran a hand back through my hair as I felt the breeze on it, only I couldn't, really, because a hoof doesn't have fingers.

Oh, right. Hooves.

Crud. I was still a donkey girl.

ACT I, SCENE II

ASHES TO ASHES TO WINGS

I was dreaming about Wolfgang again. It was a forest I knew intimately. I walked through it most days when I was a child, when I was human. Now I ran through it on four hooves, and the trees were never where they were supposed to be. There was no time to worry about that. Wolfgang was chasing me. I could hear his panting, the soft patter of his pads on old leaves, like a dog – but he's a wolf, and wolves eat donkeys. There were other wolves, but they were shapes. They weren't important. There were other donkeys, but no one cared about them. Except, as happens in dreams, I was struck by a horrible thought. Would the shadow wolves eat the shadow donkeys? If I escaped, if I left the others behind, what would happen to them? Was it deliberate when I stumbled and fell? In dreams you don't think clearly, after all. But as Wolfgang loomed over me, with those grey eyes and that fanged grin I would never be able to forget, I stopped caring. All I could feel was despair. It was over.

And then he kissed me, and I woke up.

I wasn't actually that shaken up. Dreams like that aren't pleasant, but I don't get them much, and they've never had any hold on me. I was too content with what was to let what had been haunt me. And I felt pretty good that morning. It was hardly morning, really, but I liked to get up early. I slid carefully out of bed and put some clothes on. A fresh dress. It was very simple, but I liked the bright colors, the yellows and reds and blues Mister Thornback picked out for me. A sash to tie it at the waist. It took me a long time to learn how to tie a knot with hooves! Another sash to tie up my hair in a bow. That was really hard and took forever, squinting at myself in the mirror. It was one of the reasons I got up early, because Mister Thornback would have wanted to do it for me. Oh, and lastly, I put on my collar. They're not supposed to come off, but this one does. People would probably have fits if they knew Mister Thornback let me take it off at night.

That drew my attention away from myself and to my owner at last. I looked over at him, fast asleep on his pillow, and this morning for the first time I noticed how old he was. His hair wasn't white when I lost my humanity. Now it was, all of it. He still looked good, but just… old, and I'd never thought of him as looking old. It had only been a couple of years since I changed, hadn't it? Maybe five, tops? I didn't know. Wild Children don't age, so they tell me, and we don't get to celebrate birthdays. We weren't the person who was born that day. We weren't people at all. Again, so they tell me. But the upshot was, I didn't really know how old I was and I'd never known how old Mister Thornback was. I couldn't have been a donkey girl long enough for him to age this much. I knew I would outlive him, but… well, it had to be that you don't really look at someone you see every day.

I put it out of my mind and wandered off to the kitchen to make us both breakfast. Technically I was a servant, but it was understood that a Wild Girl in my condition – that is, without human hands or voice – wasn't any use for practical chores. I was determined to prove them all wrong there. I couldn't hold a skillet, but I could put it on the stove (Gas! Even after all this time, the conveniences of the capital were amazing!) and I could carry an egg in both hooves and crack it. You can do a lot without fingers if you're careful and practice.

So, eventually, breakfast was on the table. Mister Thornback didn't employ a maid. I think he could have afforded it, but he was always frugal. The sun was rising by then, and I knew the smell would get him out of bed. I needed to finish my plate before he came out for his and get to my room.

A room of my own was another thing I probably wasn't supposed to have as a Wild Girl, but the house, while kind of small, was still too big for just the two of us. So I got a room that was 'mine' and mostly we used it to store books. I had kind of ensured that my favorites ended up in there. I don't think Mister Thornback ever understood how much I loved having a room of my own. It allowed me to keep secrets. So before my owner could get himself into the kitchen to eat I was scurrying back into my room, shutting the door behind me, falling into my chair, and pulling my journal out of the desk. Oh, and adjusting my tail. I was forever adjusting my tail.

The journal was my secret. It was very important to me, writing down my thoughts, the events of the previous day, neatly and readably. It reminded me that I could write – a precious skill made all the more precious when you can't talk. Hooves instead of hands are a nuisance, a big nuisance, but it's just a nuisance. But becoming a Wild Girl had taken my voice from me, or at least words. I could only make noises like a donkey. Other Wild Children could understand me, but I couldn't talk to humans. I couldn't talk to Mister Thornback. He could only ever guess how I felt, but maybe someday he could read my journal and understand me.

Not today. It had to be a secret because Mister Thornback didn't like it when I wrote. It was more than a little strange. The pen I was using, which hooked onto my hoof, was something he'd made for me with great effort. And after a couple of sentences he'd taken it away from me again without an explanation. Or he thought he'd taken it away. Nothing in that house was hidden from me! I just had to keep it out of his sight. It was a strange thing to forbid, but he treated me so well, and in many ways better than anyone had treated me when I was human, when I was supposedly free. I wasn't going to think less of him for having a quirk or two, especially when I couldn't tell him how much being able to write meant to me now!

I was actually writing all those thoughts down when I saw the Dove Boy lower his head down and peek in my window. He was the first I'd ever seen.

Come to think of it, he was the first I'd ever heard of. But there he was, upside down as if it were the most natural thing in the world, pale and almost human. There was something about his skin, though, it was too pink and even. It took me a minute to realize that. What stood out first was his hair, because it wasn't hair, it was a mass of white feathers all sloping back. Then I realized that those white things peeking out behind him were his wings, and they were huge! And he had this grin. It made me think of Wolfgang, of course. But Wolfgang grinned like a wolf – a little superior, always confident. This boy's grin just gave the impression that everybody in the world was his friend.

I was in shock, which is the only excuse I can give for blurting out, "Are you a Wild Boy?" When I did I was embarrassed enough that the question was so dumb, but I felt worse when I heard the loud hee-hawing neigh come out of my mouth.

He looked shocked too, which for a second made me feel even more humiliated. My ears were probably hanging around my shoulders. But instead of laughing or something, he looked kind of sad. "Heaven's Mercy, sister, what did you do to get a voice like that?"

I didn't really understand the question. "I'm sorry?" I asked, trying to keep my voice lower. I stowed the pen away, too. I didn't want Mister Thornback thinking the braying meant I was in trouble and coming in to find me writing.

He tried again, with a soft stare and a softer voice. "You must know your voice was taken away, sister. What did you do to earn it? I've only met one other donkey with a curse like that, and he knew his sin clearly. He lied, not once, but all the time, and not in cruelty or for gain but simply to take the easiest path and be left alone, until... well, the rest is a secret it is only his place to tell."

This was already the strangest conversation I could remember. Not to mention that until that moment I'd had no idea Wild Children could be birds at all. "If I lost my voice because of lies, I can't figure out what they were. I don't know many other donkeys. Are you really saying that it's not just whether we turn into wolves or donkeys, but our sins determine how much we change? I haven't seen that at all, but-" I stopped and put my arms over my face. I was rattled. I shouldn't have been surprised at that. Other Wild Children always affected me strongly somehow, and I think they did the same to adults, too. I tried again. "Can we start over? My name is Bray. What's yours?"

"Mourn," he answered distractedly. The reason for his distraction became obvious very quickly. He twisted around and dropped through the window, upright now. I got an impression of just scraps of white cloth tied over him in place of real clothing, but he was stepping up to me hurriedly, taking my wrists and pulling them gently out so that he could look at my hooves. "No hands. No voice, no hands, but you're not a donkey. What did you do, Bray?"

Now I was starting to feel bad, and it kind of irritated me. "I told you, I don't-" I had to stop there, because I knew just exactly what I'd done, didn't I? "I helped a wolf lead my friends to rebel, and let him give us the Fount-"

I couldn't continue, because he'd let go of one of my hooves and placed his finger on my lips instead.

"The Fountain of Youth," he finished for me, and still he looked sad and concerned. I hadn't gotten a look like that from anybody except maybe Mister Thornback for a long time. "That is a lie, Bray. The Lord doesn't act that way. You're not a donkey."

I was getting more confused by the minute. "Listen to my voice, Mourn. You hear the words, but you hear the… noise, too. I'm a Donkey Girl."

He took a step back, and he was holding my hooves again and giving me that affectionate smile. The spell was wearing off, though. I was starting to wonder if all Wild Children were this strange. Did I treat people this way? Did they end up liking me anyway?

"But you're not meant to be. You mentioned wolves and donkeys. Did you think those were your only choices? This is not the body or the afterlife you were meant to have, Bray. I can tell that already. Kindness radiates off of you. I think you were meant to be a dove." He started looking around, and he dropped my hands and peeked out the window, and the way his head went every which way – I couldn't help but giggle. Physically he might not be much changed, but there was a great deal of the bird about him. "I can't stay. You know how adults are about Wild Children without collars. It's too bright out, and I might be seen. But be thinking, sister – did you deserve this? Are you meant to be a donkey?"

And he just leaped right out the window, and he… he flew. He flew away on huge, shining white wings, although I only saw it for a second before he was over the rooftops and disappeared.

Outside my room there were voices. No one sounded alarmed or angry. It was pleasant conversation. I knew Mister Thornback's voice immediately of course, and after a few moments I recognized Vick's as well.

It took me a minute to go out to meet them. I had a lot on my mind! There were other Wild Children besides donkeys and wolves? Whether they love us or hate us, everyone tells us that we were made into the Wild Children we are now because of the children we used to be. If there were more than just two possibilities, what was it about me that made me become a donkey? I had been content when I woke up that morning. Now I was just full of questions.

Of course, I've always been full of questions, which is why Mister Thornback kept me and sold Hind. I had been smart when I was human, and although I've heard that Wild Children get dumber when they change, the only people who really seemed to believe it were the ones who thought we corrupt every adult we get near. I certainly didn't believe that story. As a Donkey Girl I was still just as smart, and I took every opportunity to prove it.

So, of course, what I wanted was to get my questions answered, and the first person I wanted to ask was Mister Thornback. I can't tell you what a smart man he was, how much he knew. He was just a teacher, with no family or history, but he made a good enough living to own a nice house and me, because men who would never associate with someone of his class found reasons and ways to ask for his advice. But getting answers from him wasn't going to happen! How could I even ask the questions? I might find a way, but how would he react if I did?

So I'd start with Vick. Vick wasn't his name. His name was something eleven ridiculous words long, like any noble's. Mister Thornback called him 'Master Vick', and I called him – well, I called him 'ee-aw', but I thought of him as Vick. He was the Baron's son, and the Baron is important, so much so that he lives here in the capital and not on his own estates. He was a year or two older than I had been when I was human. Mister Thornback was Vick's teacher. The Baron, apparently, had a reputation. I didn't know what it was, but all the adults seemed to. It meant that he didn't want a stupid son, and I can tell you from experience that Mister Thornback would teach you everything you were able to learn, and then push you to learn a few things you thought you'd never master.

When I came in, Mister Thornback was giving Vick his instructions for the day. It was some kind of math project using different processes to prove a formula. Tough stuff, but at least it wasn't history. I'm no good at history at all. Then he turned around to leave, and they both gave a little start as they noticed me. How do you not notice someone who walks on hooves? I don't know, but the only Wild Child I knew when I was human had a talent for showing up without you knowing where he came from. Maybe I had it too.

Anyway, Mister Thornback put his hand on my head and leaned down and kissed my ear as a cover for whispering, "I think Master Vick may need some help with this, Bray," and walked out again. Does that sound weird? I understand most teachers don't leave their students alone much. Mister Thornback did it often. He'd go over a problem step by step with you for hours, but first he wanted to see what you could do without him looking over your shoulder.

Actually, Vick did pretty well. I pulled up a chair beside him and watched. I sat in on a lot of his lessons and spent hours reading Mister Thornback's books, and I was kind of sweating with this one, too. It wasn't just what you knew. It was what you could figure out. One time I moved his hand and made him scratch a minus sign under a plus, and later I did the same thing to insert a wobbly 'x' when he seemed to be foundering.

I was being pretty patient, and it kind of gave me something to do to get my own thoughts in order without really having to think about them. But I knew what would happen and after a while, when he finished the first proof, Vick lay back in his chair and gave a big sigh. He wanted a break. So, of course, he looked over at me and gave me a big grin, and kissed me.

Um, yeah. Vick likes me. A lot. A lot, a lot. So the kiss wasn't exactly a big deal. I felt bad about letting him, mind you, because it would upset Mister Thornback a lot of he knew. I could say that I didn't have much choice. Wild Children don't get to say 'no' too much, and I couldn't say anything anyway, right? And it's not really wise to hurt the feelings of someone who provides so much of your money. None of that would really be true, though. Vick liked me, and he almost treated me like a person, and aside from Mister Thornback, he was the only person who did. And he thought I was pretty. I'm not vain. I'm the opposite of vain. But there's something about Wild Children. Even the ugliest of us, with donkey faces and hair everywhere, are just totally adorable somehow. But when I was human I barely passed as cute, and I wasn't old enough to be pretty. Vick thought I was pretty, and he was rich enough that he had the most beautiful girls in the capital to compare me to. He lived with Hind, and if I were dressed like a princess and she'd just rolled in mud Hind would still be prettier than me. But Vick still thought I was pretty. On top of that he treated me like I was a person, treated me like I had feelings and they mattered. Maybe I was a slave, maybe I couldn't talk, but Vick thought I was still a person. Letting him kiss me now and then wasn't something I minded.

He put his hand on my head and started petting my donkey ears too, but all Wild Girls get that a lot. "I don't know what your Master thinks he's doing, but this one is going to beat me. And now I'm supposed to prove it again with geometry." He was cheerful despite the complaints. "How do you think I'm doing, Bray?"

"Pretty good, actually. I don't know how we're going to do this either. I know it's about the hypotenuse, though. X squared plus Y squared equals Z squared, right? We start there." No, of course he didn't understand. I was making the most awful noises. But we felt like we were talking to each other.

He got that I was talking about the test at least, and gave it a theatric look of disgust before leaning back again to look at me. "So how was your morning? I know, your mornings are always good, but you look kind of... I don't know, intense today."

I was, and I was glad he was giving me a chance to talk about it, because I wanted his help. And another reason why I liked Vick – he offered me his pen. Vick not only cares what a Wild Girl has to say, he helped me say it even though I couldn't speak.

Of course, writing with hooves is no picnic. I ended up holding it between both of them. The lettering was ugly and slow too, and I was tempted to just use some kind of shorthand. But for Vick, I went to the effort. 'Can we go to the library?' I wrote.

No, it's not an explanation, but it took me way too long to write that one short sentence and I wanted to go to the library. And Vick understood, like he always did, how frustrating it was for me that I couldn't communicate. "The library? You really are up to something, aren't you? Okay. I think I need to look up Pythagoras. I know I need to look up Pythagoras. I thought I was good at geometry, but I missed something somewhere."

So we packed up his books and went to the library. I carried most of them. It's how things are done. I had the collar around my neck, so I did the carrying. If we were in private I doubt he'd have let me, but Wild Children are expected to act a certain way in public.

That's why I needed him to go to the library. I could walk the streets on my own, although Mister Thornback didn't like it. Sometimes people stop you and say mean things. Adults tended to pretend they were compliments, and teenagers didn't bother. But nobody hurts you, because all Wild Children are really expensive and you get into trouble if you damage something that valuable that isn't yours. Now I sound like I'm whining! It's just that Mister Thornback really didn't like me to go out alone and he was totally being overprotective. I never had any real trouble, and I never heard of any Wild Children who did.

But the library was different. Not that it was dangerous. Are there any dangerous libraries? But they wouldn't let me in if I was alone. They didn't even allow in most poor people, and the kind of people who ran the library, they really believed that I was some retarded creature of sin. They wanted Vick to leave me at the door, but they weren't going to argue with the son of a nobleman. Mister Thornback brought me sometimes too, and they would argue with him plenty, but eventually they'd give in.

Despite that, I loved the library. I doubt that surprises you, so I won't explain it.

Once inside I helped Vick find a good book about basic triangle math, and a place to sit and read it. It was driving him nuts not to know what I was there for, but I wasn't entirely sure I knew myself and I needed him out of the way while I found it. I did find it, but I had to look all over. I couldn't find anything in Natural Philosophy, even in the Biology section. I wasn't expecting anything in Human Philosophy, but I looked anyway. History was an outside chance, too. I took a couple of books out of the Religion section and peeked into them, but other than learning every scriptural manuscript had a different origin story for us, and finding a lengthy article classifying us as demons, I didn't learn much. Big surprise there.

I found it in Alchemy. Of course, I had to dust off the books before I could read the title. I think the church has a fit if you practice alchemy in the capital. But alchemists were always learning strange new things and writing them down, so here was a bookcase full of their lore. The book? 'Wylde Children'. It was that easy.

Well, it was almost that easy, as I found out when I brought the book back to Vick and laid it down beside him and started to read. Mister Thornback has a couple of alchemy books, and at first I was fascinated. This one reminded me vividly of why I lost interest. It was so old that even if the author had been any good at spelling it would be almost unreadable. It was a manuscript, and the writing tended to wander. So did the narrative style.

On the other hand, it was filled with pictures that took my breath away. Donkeys were on the first page. Actually, they were about the first twenty pages. And there were wolves, right after. I found doves near the middle of the book. The rest… if the alchemist was correct, Wild Children came in every animal shape you could imagine. It was hard to tell the birds apart, but the eagle was easy to spot. In some lands, he said, wolves were rare and there were foxes or jackals instead. It was hard to be sure of anything. The book was old, maybe centuries old. He'd traveled around a lot and listened to people's stories, and most of the book was just hearsay, things people had told him. But he said he'd personally seen owls, and a jackal, and even animals he didn't know. He hadn't seen many because, he said, nobody had seen many. Even in the capital, back then, he'd only seen a couple of donkeys and they were all owned, slaves brought in from the corners of the Empire. There were certainly more of us now. And everybody, everybody, had a different explanation for how we lost our humanity. Most of them seemed to agree that we turned into something we were inside, but what made it happen, no two authorities could agree upon. And then I turned to the last chapter, and it was about dragons. Dragons. The author thought Wild Children could become dragons. He thought we could become anything. He said he'd examined the bones of a dragon in a village, and some of them were human bones.

The book hadn't answered my questions at all. It had just given me a lot more of them. But I was pretty sure nobody had ever mentioned anything but donkeys and wolves in our village. Why did we only have those choices? If it was based on who we were, well... I wasn't a wolf like Wolfgang, okay, but although Hind was my best friend after we both turned, we were nothing alike as humans. Why would we both end up as donkeys?

I hadn't even realized Vick was reading over my shoulder until I stopped reading and started thinking, and he turned a page for me. "This is amazing, Bray. Do you think any of this is true? Wouldn't you have loved to be a heron? You'd look beautiful in feathers. I've seen plenty of donkeys, and a pigeon once or twice, and the Archbishop yells at my father about hunting down the wolves about once a month. There's supposed to be rats and snakes too, out in the hills, but I think those are just stories. I thought they were just stories."

Of course, he was just interested. For me it was a little more important. Picking a pen up off a table by myself is hard, but I did it and I grabbed some of his paper and I wrote 'Should I be donkey?' He didn't seem to get it. I had to flip pages and point to different animals before he did.

"I don't know." I guess that was honest at least, although I was a little mad he was mostly just interested in the pictures. "Up until now I've only met donkeys. It's supposed to be something to do with your sins, isn't it? I guess you'd have to ask the Archbishop."

Oh, yeah. That was going to happen. A lecture on deserving my fate because I was inherently evil would satisfy all my curiosity. After I was beaten for being able to write and daring to ask questions. And then they'd never let me see Hind or Vick and they'd take me away from Mister-

I'm sorry. I stewed for a few minutes. Wouldn't you?

I got over it, though. I shouldn't have expected Vick to be able to help. I hadn't heard of any of this until a Dove Boy (did Vick call them pigeons?) stuck his head in my window. I didn't know it could happen. Did Mister Thornback have answers? If he did and he hadn't told me already, he wasn't going to. Which made me think he didn't. I couldn't remember him ever lying to me. Most of the things he said about Wild Children were what everyone else said. He believed them, he just didn't think that because we weren't people our feelings didn't matter.

Anyway, when we got back I found out we were going to see Hind!

Hind was my best friend. I've met several other Wild Children, but we're not encouraged to spend time with each other, and their owners are often strict. But I've known Hind since we were both human, although I hardly knew her at all back then. But she could understand me, and we came to the capital together, and we could talk to each other in ways we couldn't talk to our owners. Vick liked me, but he was human and the heir of a major noble title, and he didn't understand a word I said. That's not really friendship, and Mister Thornback was my owner, and, well, I guess I don't know what I'm trying to say.

Anyway, at the time I spent the whole carriage ride thinking about what I'd read, and what Mourn had told me. And about Hind. Mourn thought something had gone wrong for me, but he also thought we really were marked by our sins. Everyone seemed to think that. Did Hind deserve her transformation? I remembered her human self as someone who was content not to stand out much, just to let her pretty face get her through life. You could at least say her transformation was irony. Cruel irony, but also lucky.

Hind is beautiful. She's really, really beautiful. She has donkey ears and a tail, but that's it, and she'll never grow old, and she was never stupid. When we got to the capital Mister Thornback sold her because, well, donkeys just have owners. He picked her buyer carefully, though. She was worth a lot of money. Really, really a lot of money. He sold her to the Baron. Most Wild Children are servants - well, slaves really, but the idea is that, like the donkeys we are, we work for our owners. Hind was too special for that. For Donkey Girls like her, it's different. She became a pet. She was dressed up and shown off, she was taught to sing and dance, and she had to learn manners, really good manners. I think it was the best life Mister Thornback thought he could give her.

By the way, 'Hind' refers to deer, not donkeys. Humans aren't always smart either.

So we ended up in one of the Baron's sitting rooms. He and Mister Thornback sat in nice chairs and drank and talked. The idea was that the Baron was very interested in Vick's education and wanted constant updates. The truth was that he and Mister Thornback liked to talk to each other. I'm probably biased, but they might have been the smartest men in town. Vick would stand around at a distance for a while, because sometimes it's not much better to be a human child than a Wild Child, but eventually they'd let him leave. They hadn't so far, this time. Maybe they were talking about something interesting. Hind and I never really listen. We were interested in each other.

We were sitting on our owners' laps while they talked. I guess Wild Girls are considered decorative that way. And we studied each other. We were always aware of the differences. I liked the colors, but my dresses were plain and had no buttons I couldn't fasten. They're one layer. Hind... looked stunning. I never learned the proper words to describe dresses, but the pink and white were delicate and perfect on her. There were petticoats, lots of ruffles, laces and poufs and a separate bodice with ribbons. The collar of the dress was high, and her collar as a Wild Girl was sleek and elegantly engraved over the top of it. She was probably wearing makeup, but I couldn't be sure. It was that subtle. She probably put it on herself, too; it was the kind of thing she knew how to do. She would never have been able to put that dress on by herself. Even her shoes had little roses, real roses, a blushing pink, on them. They must have been cut fresh that morning. And little rose buds were in her hair, which was wound up in layers.

The way we sat, too, was so different. She sat on the Baron's knee, spine straight, hardly moving except to watch me. Mister Thornback kept me pulled up close in his lap with one arm around me, and he was always touching me, stroking my hair or my ears. The Baron hardly seemed to notice Hind, although, just sometimes, he'd touch the back of her neck with a fingertip.

To me, the big difference was our expressions. Obviously I was troubled and distracted, but most of the time Hind looked the same. She looked distant and sad. She was probably the best-treated Wild Child in the city and she was certainly devoted to the Baron, but it didn't seem to make her happy like I was. We knew all of this just from looking at each other. We weren't getting to talk yet, so we just tried to understand what we saw.

The Baron really is a kind and intelligent man, though, from what I've seen. I only started listening when I realized he was saying, "Let's get a fresh bottle, professor. I just bought one from the Marches, and I don't quite know what it is or if anyone will ever bottle anything like it again. I'd like you to try it, and we can let the girls stretch their legs for a while." It was, in a way, a code. He was letting us spend time together. He knew Hind was getting bored, and he knew she'd sit there all night doing nothing if she thought he wanted her to. I wasn't sure she realized he was doing it for her.

Anyway, we got ourselves a drink too, something a lot less expensive, and ended up sitting on the bar. Again we were watching each other. I'd have climbed up myself; I'm short compared to an adult, but I'm not tiny. But Mister Thornback would lift me anywhere without my asking. Hind couldn't climb up without messing up her dress and shoes, so the Baron lifted her as well. It was a little thing, but I knew she felt like little things were all she got. I wasn't sure how little it was. Men in the Baron's position don't help their Wild Girl find a comfortable seat, no matter how expensive she is. It's just not done. Hind should have known that better than me.

I worry a lot about Hind's happiness, don't I? She just looked so sad.

It's funny, but if we were human we'd never have been allowed real alcohol. It doesn't do much to Wild Children. Just another funny little thing, I guess. Even if it had, no one worries about keeping a Donkey Girl pure. They worry about protecting real humans from us.

So finally Hind and I got a chance to talk. She didn't have much to say. Well, she did, but I usually had to drag it out of her. Today I had my own stuff to talk about.

"Did you know Wild Children could be doves?" I asked her excitedly.

"I think so." She was surprised, of course. She was also kicking her feet. It's the kind of thing I noticed. She had to show off so much, she didn't get to do casual things like that. "I've heard the Abbot and the Archbishop arguing about it. The Abbot thinks they're angels, and the Archbishop…" She trailed off. She didn't have to finish. I knew what most of the church thought about Wild Children.

"Angels?" I was being quiet, but I didn't know how quiet I needed to be. My donkey neigh really carries, but nobody understands anyway. "I can see how someone would think that, at least. I met one! He just came right up to my window!"

"Really? What was he like?" She was perking up. It took a while, but I could usually drag her out of herself. This time I had strange news to help.

"He was weird. He told me things I didn't understand, then he wouldn't stick around and explain them."

"Well, what kind of things?" she asked. And you know, I wasn't totally sure?

"Well, he said there are more than just the wolves and donkeys we know about. And I looked in a book, and there are more. Lots more. Lots and lots and lots more. So why did we all end up as donkeys?"

"Because we were meant to be donkeys, Bray. It's who we are." That surprised me.

"You think I earned this?" I held up my hooves. "You think you earned this?" I wasn't mad. And she knew I wasn't. Hind and I are friends that way.

She smiled, but the happiness was gone. She looked so sad again. "It's not what we earned, Bray." I'm glad we were whispering. I hadn't heard her sound so emphatic since she was sold. "It's what we were meant for. It's not what we did before, it's how we live now."

"I don't get it."

"We were useless when we were human, Bray. What did we ever do for anyone? But now, I make my Master happy. Most of the time I don't have to do anything. But when he makes everyone else leave, even his family, and he wants to be alone, I stay. He doesn't spend time with me like Mister Thornback spends with you, but it's the important time. I'm a donkey because I was meant to belong to someone, and you're a donkey because you were meant to belong to Mister Thornback. I know I'm a little jealous, but every time I see you you're together… if he came over right now to get a drink he'd put his hand on your shoulder, wouldn't he? And you would both smile. You make each other happy. It's just what you were meant for."

I was stumped. I should have realized not to say what I was about to say, but I was trying to figure out if she was right. "That's not what the Dove Boy said at all, though. He said we were supposed to get our marks because of something bad we'd done. I'm not sure I believed that either, really, but he seemed to think…" I lowered my voice further, although I can't imagine why. "…that I could do it over. That it was a mistake. That it could be fixed." I didn't actually know that that was true, but that was what it seemed like, wasn't it?

"Turn you back into a human?" asked Hind skeptically. "That's never happened. People would talk about it."

"I don't think so. He talked in circles. He never answered anything. He said he thought I should be a dove. I think he meant I could change into another kind of Wild Girl somehow. He said he was sure it was a mistake."

"Bray, think about what you're saying! I won't let you throw your happiness away again!" This was her answer, and it was loud. Very loud.

Loud enough that the Baron and his son and Mister Thornback noticed, and they walked over, and Mister Thornback asked, "Is something wrong, Hind?"

I couldn't stop her. I didn't know whether to be mad or not. She thought she was doing it for me. She just told him. "She's been talking to some Wild Boy, sir. One without a Master. He's telling her crazy stories about making her something different. He's trying to take her away from you."

He just looked at me. He clearly didn't know what to say. I'm not sure what he was waiting for.

"Do you really think I deserved to be a donkey?" I asked him. It wasn't about the words. It wasn't even about the tone. Humans sometimes seem to get the idea. Maybe it's about how you say it. He got the idea, because he hit me.

Please understand, first, he didn't hit me hard. It was a slap. But it wasn't gentle, and it hurt, and he'd never hit me before, ever. He'd rapped my knuckles a few times with a ruler and there'd been the odd spanking, but that was all early on. Even back then it wasn't because I'd disobeyed him, it was because I was having trouble learning how to behave with other people. Other people hit their Wild Children, but he didn't. Which was why I started to shake, and I was about to cry. It wasn't about the pain.

Part of it was about the look on his face. He looked so guilty. Then he put his arms around me and he held me as tight as he could, and I held him, and we both cried. I can't explain, even now, how we felt and what we were thinking. I don't think anybody else really could understand, not even Hind.

Oddly I learned, then, who our friends were. The Baron and Vick didn't say anything. They just pretended it wasn't happening. We were doing something wrong, something we weren't allowed to do. Wild Children and their owners don't treat each other like that. It's corruption, I guess. No, I don't have to guess. It's the reason the church thinks we're evil, that corruption. But they liked me and respected Mister Thornback too much. They would act like it was a weakness we didn't have. And Hind was watching us, and she was jealous, but she was also happy. She thought she'd taught me something. She might have.

It didn't stop me. I'm not sure what would have. What I did next might have been stupid. If I'd been any other Wild Child, with any other owner, it might have been suicidal. I went up on the roof.

Does that sound stupid? I was pretty sure it was, even when I did it. If Mister Thornback found out I didn't know how he'd take it. If he were anyone else I'd be punished, and when I say punished, I mean I might not survive. If he were anyone else I wouldn't be able to do it anyway. Even after Hind told him what was going on he didn't watch me, or restrict me, or anything. He trusted me, and I was going to find the doves anyway. Yeah, I wasn't exactly feeling good about this, but at the same time I had to know the truth.

So, in a few days, when I hadn't seen Mourn again and wasn't sure when I would, I went to the rooftops. I knew where the stairs were. It doesn't snow much in the capital, and there are doors on a lot of roofs and nice, flat spaces. It was evening, and Mister Thornback was out. He'd probably be out until really, really late. I was hoping, anyway.

The morning we had met, Mourn said something about it being too bright, so I went out at sundown. I figured he might be out more in the twilight. It was never really dark in the city, though. Gas lamps in the street, candles and lamps in windows - that helped me. Without them I might have gotten lost or fallen off a roof.

Of course, after a few minutes of looking around and wandering from roof to roof, I felt a little stupid, but I felt a lot guilty and I wasn't letting that stop me either. I found a bridge stretching from one side of the street to the other. I'm not kidding, a bridge. There were boards across a lot of the gaps between close buildings too, and balancing on one of those on one hoof isn't easy. But it meant people actually traveled up here, so I kept roaming, kept looking up, trying to figure out ways onto the taller buildings. Eventually I did something really, spectacularly stupid. I stood in the last glow of twilight and yelled as loud as I could, "Mourn, please come and talk to me!" You know what? I got away with it!

My donkey voice actually came in handy there. No human heard a little girl shouting on the rooftops, they heard a donkey pitching a fit somewhere in the distance and they didn't care. It was still stupidly risky, but nothing happened except that I got exactly what I wanted. More or less, anyway. It wasn't Mourn, but a minute later I spotted something white in the air and a dove landed on the next rooftop. I guess she was cautious. I'm noticing I feel dumb when I meet new Wild Children. I was clomping around on hooves, and she almost danced on bare feet, she moved so lightly. She was beautiful too, older than me, old enough that she could really be beautiful, but she definitely wasn't human. It wasn't just the wings, or the feathers instead of hair. On one of her arms downy little white feathers ran all the way up past the elbow, and I could see them on her shoulder on the other arm and around her knees. She had this white dress on, even simpler than mine, and sort of rough and hand-sewn. I guess doves wear white.

"Sister, your voice is so sad." She stepped onto the roof I was on. "Mourn told us of a Donkey Girl with a cruel and capricious punishment, and you must be her. Other Wild Children don't come looking for us, so I am not sure what to do."

I was relieved it had worked, and surprised there were more doves, and really eager to get away from where I'd been yelling. "You could take me to him. He said a lot of strange things to me, and then he left, and I guess I have a lot of questions. And the stuff he said, I can't just go on not knowing more. You could also tell me your name. Mine is Bray."

"Bray," she repeated, and smiled, and it was like Mourn's smile, a little bit of pity and a lot of friendliness. "We receive such dumb names sometimes when we come back. I'm Egg, which isn't much better but at least it isn't cruel. We don't take strangers back to our nest, Bray, but we also don't turn our backs on those in need if we can help them. I think Coo will understand that. Love is the first virtue before God, and Charity is the second. Please, come with me."

So I followed her from rooftop to rooftop, working our way higher when we could because the buildings were getting bigger. Working our way higher when I could, at least. A slope of stinky, tar-coated tiles I had to creep up on all fours she could just flap her wings twice and seem to drift up. I thought we were actually headed towards the Palace and the big government buildings around it, but we didn't get nearly that far. We had to circle around a walled compound until I found a ladder leading up to the roof of what was unmistakably a large church.

That kind of freaked me out. I was a little hesitant to touch something like Egg with my hooves, but I did, and when she took hold of the rungs I asked her, "Egg, isn't this the cathedral? We can't go up there. This is the most dangerous place in the city!"

And she put her feathery hand on my hoof, and her smile was serene. No, blissful. I've seen other people besides doves smile like that, but only when they were in love. "This isn't the cathedral, sister. It's the church of the Abbey. We like to be close to God, and you're right, the Archbishop is a man who hears only hard words and keeps us away. The Abbot doesn't know we're here either, it's true, but he's not looking."

Once you've learned to tie a ribbon in your hair, climbing a ladder with hooves is a picnic. The church's roof was sharply sloped and harder to get around on, but we went in a window almost immediately.

Inside was some kind of attic. It was a nest. Egg wasn't kidding about that. The doves had built walls out of bookshelves for a little privacy, and little bird's nests of anything soft, lined with feathers. Actually, the attic was huge, since churches tend to be, and they practically had a village up here, with streets and walls made out of bookshelves and curtains and sheets of wood leaned up against anything. I only counted six beds though, and I never saw all the doves at once anyway.

When I stepped inside, Egg put her finger to my mouth and spoke in hushed tones. "Out of respect, please do not speak or touch anything until Coo gives you permission. I am sorry if it seems rude, but this is a place only for doves."

I nodded. Actually, I understood completely. And I was kind of awed. I thought Mister Thornback had owned a lot of books, but this place was packed. Most of them were scripture, or books about scripture. I saw a desk with a half-copied manuscript. Doves certainly did not live like other Wild Children.

There was actually more than one attic, too. It was too big to be one room. I was led into something like a chapel within a chapel, and I met Coo.

I guess she was meditating or something. It was more than just praying. They'd brought a little altar up here somehow and she was actually perched on it like a pigeon, her eyes closed, her hands folded in prayer and her wings folded strangely to match. Then she opened her eyes and stepped down and curtseyed deeply. "Welcome, sister. My name is Coo, and I am glad that Egg has brought you here. The donkeys of this city suffer too much, and we get so few chances to help them at all."

Coo needs a little explanation. She needs a lot of explanation, and I'm not sure I'm up to it. She was tiny. She was thin, and she was short even for her age, and her age was funny. When she'd become a Wild Child she must have been the youngest ever. I thought she might be eight, and most of us are ten or older, and even the ones who were ten when they lost their humanity are generally, you know, old for their age. Coo wasn't. She was a child. She wasn't lovely like Egg or pretty and elegant like Hind, but she had a certain ethereal quality to her. Just looking at her you knew that while she was physically young, she was actually old. I hadn't known how you spot an old Wild Child until that moment. They sort of become fragile, like some old people do, and Coo might have been made of glass. Her eyes could shock you, though. They were a pigeon's eyes, a garish orange, and seemed to stare despite her gentle expression.

"My name is Bray, Miss… Coo? I came to talk to Mourn." Really, I felt like I was talking to an adult. I'd forgotten I wasn't supposed to speak, but nobody mentioned it again. Coo just didn't seem to care.

"You would be welcome to, sister Bray, but he is out." She smiled, and it was warm. Egg and Mourn were friendly, but Coo loved you, in a tired way. "You may certainly wait until he returns, but he did tell me all about meeting you. Is he the only one who can help you?"

"No, not really. I just thought he'd be the only one willing to. He told me a lot of stuff and then left without explaining any of it. I just want to understand, and I had to find someone who could answer my questions."

If anything, Coo smiled wider. What I'd said seemed to make her so happy. "I can tell you now that everything he told me was true. Sister Bray, donkeys do not leave their homes. They don't go on quests, and certainly not for something as small but holy as the truth. Do you understand? The only donkeys marked more cruelly than you are the ones with no human body left, and there is a purity, a contentment in the animal shape. I know that sounds cruel, but I speak with them when I can. They are happier than most who seem human. Their afterlife works, and they learn in labor and duty and simplicity what they could not in life."

And then she laughed, although it was soft and kind of sad. "I am drifting. It is the habit of a preacher. We want to say everything." She reached out, and she took my wrists and lifted my hooves up. "Look at these, sister. I am saying you have already proven, just by coming here, that you were not meant to be a donkey. Your true afterlife was taken from you somehow. You spoke of the Fountain of Youth to Mourn, and yes, I have heard that story from other donkeys. From donkeys. Only donkeys, do you understand? And they only mentioned wolves. I only guide children who are likely to be doves to the other side, and even then I sometimes get… others. It is meant to be like that. The way you were brought over, that is not how it is meant to be. I wondered for a long time if somehow only donkeys and wolves were drawn to it. Now, seeing you, I am sure. It is some kind of perversion, and I promise you I don't use that word lightly or often."

This was really getting weirder, but at least unlike Mourn, Coo didn't talk over my head. "Now I just have more questions. What is the right way?"

"Have a seat." She urged me toward a stool Egg brought to us. "We do not sit well, but we do sit. Be comfortable. Have a drink. The wine is holy, but we think that's an even better reason to drink it." So I had a seat, and I had a drink. I even ate some kind of cornbread they brought me, trying not to stare too much at this dusty room laid out like a church or at this thread-thin little girl with the orange eyes and the calm, knowing voice.

Fortunately, Coo wasn't done talking. She looked really sad and distant for a while, although when she wasn't looking at someone she pretty much always looked like that. "I came over because I took my own life. I am grateful to God that he let time take my memory of why. I couldn't bear to live. That is a sin, though, sister. A crime. It is giving up, wasting a gift of great value. But God forgives, and when the angels judged me they said that there was too much of the virtue of compassion in me to condemn, and I was innocent enough to be sent back into the world and given another chance. I am… dead, but I am still here, earning my redemption."

That was, I have to say, the last thing I expected to be told. "I don't think it's like that for donkeys," I told her cautiously.

"I'm not sure it is." She wasn't offended at all, that I could tell. "The only thing I am sure of is that we are meant to be marked according to our sin, but also our virtue, and you were not. This is the afterlife, and we are allowed to live it on Earth. Beyond that I know nothing at all."

"That isn't true, Sister," Egg blurted out suddenly. "You've met the angels and been judged by them. We all have. You've spoken to them of God and our duty. And you delivered us to them, that we might have a chance to be forgiven. And you know the truth of God."

Coo practically glowed at her. "I do know the truth of God, sister. But that is my truth and it may, just may, be the truth for all doves. Bray here is a donkey, and the truth may not be the same. All the more so because she does not deserve to be a donkey."

I was a little comforted that Egg didn't seem to understand that any better than I did. I had more important answers to seek, though. "Coo, Mourn didn't exactly say it, but he sort of hinted that it might be possible to fix that. Is that true?"

Now Coo was studying me. She walked lightly, like I was learning Dove Children did, drifting rather than with the spring in her step Egg had. But she was pacing like a pigeon, and her head moved oddly. She did make it look graceful, I admit.

"I don't know if it's true," was her answer, and she was obviously thinking hard. "I think it is. You have not been properly judged, sister Bray,

I can see it in you. I know how to lead a child to the angels to be judged. I think that they would give you a better afterlife than this one. Perhaps not an easier one, but the one that you were meant for."

"Were you really judged by angels? Is that what would happen to me?"

And she told me the strangest story so far. "Beneath this city is another city. A city in a cave under the earth. A city of copper and gardens, inhabited by clockwork angels. They are strange, but they are the machinery of God and they can judge us. They are just, but they are also kind, as they should be."

I'm sorry. I couldn't believe that. "There can't be a city under the capital. It would fall in, or something. And even in church I've never heard of anything like that."

"I respect the men of the church. Even the Archbishop, who I worry sins in hate and pride, knows the truth of God, but it is not the same truth that I know. I fell into that city of copper when I ended myself. With care, with precautions, I can help another end themselves and come to that city for judgment as well. That is what I can offer you. I have led every dove in this city on that journey, and they will tell you that they have seen it and they came back to this world and were changed, even though you are right and such a thing cannot be. It is anyway. I agree with Mourn. I see how you treat me. You are kind, you are respectful, and you seek the truth. I believe the angels will make you a dove, but there is no guarantee they will let you return to the world at all. I am not offering you anything easy, but if you choose I will do for you what I do for any child I think must become a dove. I reserve it for lives soon to be over. Yours ended long ago."

"I'm not afraid, Coo. You're right. I've never understood, if I was paying for my sins, why I would pay for them like this. I can't even talk to Mister Thornback. To come back to him as someone that is really me, to be able to speak to him again, that's worth the risk I won't come back at all."

"You can't ever come back to him, Bray!" It was Mourn and he sounded, well, horrified. I looked back, and he was peeking in the door with a couple of other doves. "You will be made anew. Do you understand? Now, you're a slave. When you come back the angels will have set you free. You'll never see him again. No one who changes ever goes back, and if you wanted to the adults wouldn't let you."

I looked at Coo. She didn't say anything, but her head was bowed.

That ended the conversation right there, as far as I was concerned. That was a price I wouldn't pay. I returned home. Alone, most of the way. I wasn't feeling terribly charitable or loving towards doves at that moment.

After that I tried to forget. I just lived. Instead of looking for change, I looked for the happiness I had. I didn't have to look hard. I saw Hind often. I sat with Vick while he studied. I read books, and I ran errands, and I wrote in my journal. I belonged to Mister Thornback, and I was content with my choice. Time passed, and I couldn't tell you how much. I thought a couple of months, maybe. I didn't watch it go by and I don't know how long it was until the heart attack, when Mister Thornback started to die.

Do I have to describe that day in detail? I don't, and I'm not going to, but I guess I do have to tell the story of it. Our last happy moment was washing the dishes after breakfast. Mostly he washed, and I dried and put away. He was telling me about a man called Zoroaster, and how angry the church was about his ideas. He started looking like he was in pain, and then Mister Thornback put his hand on his chest and he fell over. I tried to catch him, but I didn't do a very good job.

He was still awake, but he was having trouble breathing, and he told me to go get a doctor. I'm glad he did. I couldn't think of anything at all. So I put his head down and I ran out into the street and started yelling for someone to get a doctor. I didn't know where a doctor was. Nobody would bring a Donkey Child to a doctor's house!

So I stood there and yelled, over and over, and nobody listened because they couldn't understand me. It was worse than that, even. The noise of me braying was making adults mad, and they were talking about getting the police. But a Donkey Boy told his owner that I was calling for a doctor and why, and there was someone there who knew who Mister Thornback was and where a nearby doctor lived, and in a little while the police came, but they weren't interested in me anymore and they came with a doctor. Doctors. Several. And they took Mister Thornback into his bedroom and wouldn't let me in.

I'm leaving things out, but nothing I want to remember. When the Donkey Boy told his owner what I was saying, she hit him for speaking out of turn before she did anything. That sort of thing. It was a very, very bad day.

The next day wasn't much better. People came and went a lot. They didn't let me into the bedroom. For two days, every time I tried to see Mister Thornback someone at the door would push me away. I went so far as to write a request on a piece of paper. It was just ignored. Nobody told me anything, anything at all.

Two days later the Baron and Vick came, personally. They went right in, of course. And a little later I tried to go in again, and they started to push me out, and the Baron started yelling – not at me, at them. He said that when he was on his deathbed they'd let his son in first, and then his Wild Girl, and then maybe his wife. I didn't like the word 'deathbed', but it was, and I knew it.

I'm not giving enough credit to the Baron. He was so angry, and it was for me and for Mister Thornback, and I couldn't be more grateful. But all I wanted was to see Mister Thornback myself.

He was awake and he seemed at peace, but he looked sick. He looked very sick. But I was with him and I kissed him and he put his arms around me and he held me. I couldn't say anything, of course. I probably tried, but it didn't do any good, so I don't remember what. I remember, after a while, he told me very seriously, "I'm sorry, Bray. I didn't think I'd have to leave you this soon. The doctors don't know how much longer I have, but I'm not getting better." He stroked my hair as I cried. "I've lived long enough. You won't be sold on the market. I'm making arrangements. They're not done, but all that's left is details. Master Vick wanted to buy you, right now, to make sure. He actually brought the money. The Baron knew that couldn't happen, of course. Vick is only a boy and he's going to need his reputation. But however your title is held, you'll see Hind every day and you'll be treated as well as she is. All that's left is figuring out excuses for the lawyers."

I cried some more. The doctors didn't like it, but the Baron wouldn't let them kick me out again. He let Vick do the yelling this time, and there was a lot of yelling, and I didn't care. I was being allowed to stay with Mister Thornback until he died. I got to be held by him until I could stop crying and accept that it was really happening. That we had days or hours or minutes. I thought a lot about the things I'd never get to tell him. Which of course is why I jumped up and ran into my room and grabbed my journal and brought it back to him. I didn't know if he'd be mad. I didn't get to find out, because a doctor just grabbed it before he could touch it. I don't know what he thought his reason was. There was a big argument about it. A big, big argument, with a lot of yelling and the Baron involved, but it didn't matter because the doctor had just thrown the journal right out the window like it was trash. Reasons didn't matter, and I wasn't listening. I had more to think about.

It was more important that they had let me stay, anyway. It let me think about what was going on, until I could think about what was going to happen. I had a choice to make. I waited until he was asleep again, though. I wasn't going to give up any more time with him than I had to, but I also had to make arrangements.

I slipped out. Vick wanted to hold me too, but I didn't feel like it, and he understood that my feelings matter. Which meant he also let me go off alone and didn't follow me. Which meant I was able to climb all the way up to the rooftop, and nobody cared anymore or wondered where I was.

I ran. I remembered the way. I made it to the back of the abbey's church and I climbed the ladder, and I threw myself through the window and ran around until I found Mourn and I grabbed his shoulders with my hooves. "It's almost over. Mister Thornback is dying. I won't have any reason to stay here anymore. I want to be sent to judgment. I don't care if I live or die, but I don't want to live as someone else's Donkey Girl."

"It's too late, sister." He looked sick with unhappiness. They all did, although I wasn't really paying attention to the others.

"Why?" I demanded. It was rude, but this was more important than manners. "I wasn't ready then, but I'm ready now. It's my life that's changed, not me. If I deserved it then, I deserve it now. Aren't you supposed to be devoted to charity?"

He took my hooves as if they were hands and held them together in his. He looked so sad I thought he'd be sick, or faint, or something. "We're not refusing, sister. We aren't able to help you. Yesterday, Coo was taken by the adults."

It took a moment, but believe it or not I was more worried about Coo than me, now. I didn't want to belong to another human, but if I couldn't stop it I would be taken care of and never beaten and would be with people who loved me, even if it wasn't enough. I would be one of the lucky Wild Children. Coo would not be, I was sure of that.

That was all I was sure of. I stopped being angry, and started being afraid, for someone else. "What happened? How did they find her?"

"They didn't have to find her." Suddenly everyone but me was sitting down. Coo was right, doves don't sit well. Their wings got in the way and they either curled up or their arms and legs went everywhere. They didn't care. They all looked like I did, like their life had been taken away. "She went to them. To the Archbishop. There was some kind of adult thing going on. A lot of nobles were there, and the Abbot, and the Archbishop, and she thought he'd have to let her talk. She flew down and tried to talk to him about God."

"She's always wanted to," mumbled another dove.

"He didn't listen," added another.

"She didn't expect him to listen," added Egg. In grief she didn't look like an angel at all, or beautiful. "She just had to try. If no one ever told him the truth then it was our fault, not his, if he believed in lies."

"What will they do with her?" I asked.

"We don't know," Mourn said. "They kept arguing about it. Doves are taken, sometimes. The adults either try to keep them as very fancy pets, or make them into songbirds. They probably want Coo to sing for them." That actually made sense to me. It was the last thing I'd paid attention to because my own is so much worse, but there really was something strange about Coo's voice. It was probably the reason for her name. There was a trill to it, a softness. If she sang I supposed it would be strange and beautiful. Well, maybe not. I didn't know, but it made perfect sense to me that adults would think that way.

"It doesn't matter anyway," Mourn went on. "Dove Children are never kept as slaves for very long. We don't survive. If they decide to keep her rather than kill her, she'll just die anyway."

"I hate that thought," Egg burst out. "Right now she must still be alive, locked up somewhere in the Baron's house, giving up hope. When it's all gone she'll just stop living."

"She's in the Baron's house?" I asked. It seemed like the strangest chance. "You know she's there?"

"That's where she was taken. The adults were gathering there, all the important ones. It happens a lot. And we know how nice the Baron is to you and his own Donkey Girl. She must have thought it was the best chance that she'd be allowed to speak. We never saw her leave, and we heard the Baron say he wasn't giving her to anyone until everyone agreed."

I didn't want to follow that thought through. I was so grateful that I didn't have to, that I wasn't made to offer, that someone asked instead.

"The Baron would give Bray anything," said Egg suddenly. "She could go get Coo out. Or help her pass on with dignity, instead of… whatever awful way she's dying now."

"The Baron wouldn't give her that," Mourn told her sharply. "He wouldn't get himself into trouble for her."

"No, he wouldn't." I didn't really know the Baron that well, but I knew enough to say that. "But I can get in and out of his house. Everyone there knows me, and no one cares if they see me. Right now they're expecting me. I'm not sure that means I can get Coo out, but I have a chance." Another thought. "The Baron's not even home. No one who works for him is going to question what I'm doing. They'll just think he let me."

I was terrified I wasn't going to be there when Mister Thornback died. Especially if this went wrong. I would never forgive myself. But I would never forgive myself if I let this happen to Coo when I might have helped. It wasn't enough. I was too afraid.

"If I save her, she can take me to the angels. I can be judged. I can go on to whatever I was supposed to go on to." I wasn't making a deal with the doves, I was making a deal with me.

"I can't speak for her, sister," Mourn told me.

"She would never refuse," insisted Egg.

So I snuck into the Baron's home. I didn't wait and I didn't plan. There was no time for that. I didn't really sneak either, I just walked right in. I told you it was safe for me to walk the streets. Wild Children are allowed out to perform errands, sometimes even to play. I couldn't recall ever going to the Baron's home without Mister Thornback, but it seemed like my hopes were true and my worries were false. No one noticed me. Or when they did, they were happy to see me and then didn't think anything more about it.

I went straight to Hind's room. The Baron was out. It was the best place to look for her. I needed directions. If I just kept wandering around the house, no one would get mad. They'd try and help me instead, and things would fall apart just as surely.

She was there. I hadn't actually been in Hind's room much. It was like a palace itself! No, more like a dollhouse. Everything was trying too hard to be pretty, so that it could be just like Hind. The bed had curtains and was probably fancier than the Baron's, and there was a lot of pink and red. There were cushions and toys. There was makeup and brushes and more clothes than fit in one closet. She had her own window on the garden, although it was barred.

My room was shabby and dusty and mostly bookshelves and boxes full of papers and laboratory equipment Mister Thornback never used. When he was gone, if I was still a donkey, Vick and the Baron would probably make sure I got a room like this. I would waste away and die, like a dove.

I didn't let myself start pitying Hind. She wasn't happy, but she wanted this life. It still wasn't right, but it was complicated and I didn't have time for complicated. I had to save two people who honestly, truly, couldn't live like this. Coo and me.

I was too busy looking at the room. She noticed me first. Her arms were around my neck and she was shouting, "Oh, Bray! They told me. Everyone's so upset. Even the servants." She looked at me, and her eyes were red, and I knew the only reason she wasn't crying was because it would mess up her makeup and someone would get mad at her. It was very, very hard not to think about how I wanted to save Hind, too.

"Are you here already? I know it's not over. Everyone's waiting on the bad news, and you couldn't have beaten a messenger. Master told me you were coming. There's been letters and a few arguments and everything. I... he talked to me about it, Bray. He wanted me to know you'd be taken care of, that you'd be here, with me. It's important to me and to Vick and to Mister Thornback, and he said... he said he'd see everyone else damned before he disappointed all three of us." She was babbling. She'd been trained for years how to put on polite faces, and she was about to start crying.

She was expecting me to be here, with her, at last. I was about to stomp on the only hope she had in her life. I would like to think I was only able to do it because, if I didn't, it was Coo's hope that would die. "I'm not going to live with you, Hind." I said it in a rush, to try and stop her from arguing. "The doves think they can make me something else, and I can be free. But one of them was caught. Her name is Coo and she's here, somewhere. I need you to help me find her. I have to get her out if they're going to help me. Even if they don't help me, I have to get her out. She's not a donkey, Hind. She can't live like us, and I don't want to be a donkey either. I know you think I should be one, but I don't anymore."

She didn't cry. She didn't argue. I forgot sometimes she was taller than me, especially in those heels they made her wear, but she looked down at me and said, "I think you were meant to belong to Mister Thornback, Bray. Not to anyone else."

We hugged. We probably wasted too much time doing that. But we understood each other at last. It was important. To us, it was.

Hind wasn't done surprising me. She'd just started. She did it next by letting go of me and telling me, "I know about the dove. With the news about you and Mister Thornback, I wasn't thinking about it. She's in the dance parlor on the third floor. It's not too big they couldn't lock the doors, and there's this big birdcage. I don't really know what they thought they'd put in it, but the dove is in there now."

I tried to think about this. I didn't know where that room was, but it wouldn't be too hard to find. "Alright. Do you know where I can find a key?"

I'm ashamed, now, to say that I'd just always figured I was smarter than Hind. She was a year older than me, but when we were human I was the smart one at school, and when we were donkeys she only seemed to live when I was talking to her or the Baron was giving her attention. She looked like the rest of her life she was half-awake, being taught to be a good little doll. But now she was looking at me like she was sad and disappointed that I didn't understand already. "You don't need a key, Bray. I have a key. I have all the keys." And she went over to her vanity and she took out of the box, well, a bunch of keys. A big ring of them.

"How did you get that?" I asked her. I was still being dumb.

But it made her smile. "Master wants me to be able to go anywhere in his house. Wherever he wants me, or even anywhere I want to go, without having to ask someone else for permission. I have keys to the doors outside, too. He knows I won't run away. He trusts me."

I didn't know what I thought and felt about any of this. And I was getting too close to forgetting about Coo. "Do you have a key to the cage?" This was starting to seem like I had a real chance.

She had to think for a moment and mess with the keys, but she shook her head. "No, I'm pretty sure I don't. Master just didn't ever think I might possibly want it. There are keys like that. To display boxes, the locks that hold up chandeliers. Silly stuff like that. I mostly have keys to all the doors."

There was still an obstacle, then. But it was already clear. I knew everything about Mister Thornback's house, and Hind knew everything about this one. "Do you know where I can find one?"

"Oh, absolutely. We'll get it from my Master's bedroom."

She grabbed my hoof and she dragged me out of her bedroom and through the halls. She never let go of my hoof. People gave us funny looks, but they were all affectionate. It seemed like everybody liked Hind, and she was smiling.

She had to unlock the Baron's bedroom door. I was right, by the way. His bed was a lot bigger than hers – although not as much bigger as you'd think – but Hind's bed was fancier. It was a nice room, but it really wasn't fancy. The furniture was good, though, and there was a lot of it.

The bed, unfortunately, was occupied. When the door opened, a woman sat up in it. She had to be the Baron's wife. I'd never actually met her. She didn't look happy.

"Your Master isn't here, girl. Why are you bothering me?" She sounded crabby. I was suddenly afraid that she didn't like Hind.

But Hind curtseyed. She hadn't bothered to finish getting dressed when I showed up, but it hardly mattered. Her underwear had skirts. More than one. She went down low and stayed there. I knew I couldn't match that. I probably couldn't do it without falling over. Hooves for feet and all. I bowed as deeply as I could, and just waited.

"You know I'm sorry, Your Ladyship. My friend Bray is here at last. I needed to get Master's extra keys so that I could get into the laundry room. I have a few dresses that will fit her okay. I thought we should be dressed to match when he got home."

The Baron's wife smiled. "When the Viceroy and Stephen and everyone will be waiting for him, wondering what the fuss is about." She softened, some of the displeasure bleeding away. "Thank you. That's a very, very good idea. I wish she were prettier, but it will help a lot. So this is Vick's teacher's little Wild Girl?" Now she was looking at me.

"Yes, Your Ladyship. Her name is Bray. That is why she isn't speaking. I'm sure what you've heard is true. She tries not to talk to people, because you would not enjoy it."

And the Baron's wife sighed. She looked tired and grumpy and much too intelligent, and she seemed to like Hind and dislike her at the same time, but she did not seem suspicious. At all.

"You know Vick can't buy her, girl. We can barely get the Archbishop to walk through the front gates since my husband bought you. And you, at least..." She didn't finish.

Hind just bowed her head lower. "I knew that from the start, Your Ladyship. The Baron does too. Master Vick is learning. But I also know that my Master will work something out. No one will say she's their Wild Girl, but she'll be here and your son and I will be grateful."

Hind was lying for me. How much trouble was this going to get her in? And it worked. The Baroness (was that her title?) was smiling again. "I try to be mad at you, but I can't. Alright, run along. Do the things I should have thought of myself. I suppose if you want I'll invite you to the High Tea next week. I know you wouldn't embarrass me."

Hind lifted up from her curtsey, although not completely, and actually smiled at the woman. "I know you won't make me go, Your Ladyship. That is something else I'm grateful for."

I guess that was funny. The Baroness laughed and lay back down, and while she messed with covers and pillows then I guess went back to sleep,

Hind dragged me over to a desk. I supposed we were also dismissed. From one of the drawers she took a really ridiculously big ring of keys, and we left the room.

That was it. That was the hardest part. I wanted to take the keys, but apparently I wasn't going to do this by myself. All Hind had to do was smile, and a guard would smile back, and we'd go wherever we wanted. She didn't test this on the guard at the door to the dance parlor. Instead she took me around to another, smaller door, which I guess was for servants. She unlocked it with her key, and we went in.

It was basically what I expected: A big, mostly empty room with a lot of decoration for show. In one corner was a stage with a big harp still on it and a gilded birdcage that went almost to the ceiling. Coo was in it. There was no food, or furniture, or anything else.

I thought the other doves might have been right. She was curled up on the far side against the bars, with her wings wrapped around her, staring at nothing. She'd looked frail before. Now she was gaunt and green. She looked up at us, but didn't do anything until Hind started trying keys. She found the right one almost immediately, too. By then the tiny Dove Girl was standing by the doorway.

She didn't seem about to say anything, so I did. "Coo, why did you do this?"

"For the same reason you did, sister." Her voice was very quiet. She looked awful, but she looked calm, too. I guess she was going to make it. "There are things more important to me than dying happy. I am nearing the end anyway. Remember, sister, we're not immortal. It may seem so, but we are not. I don't know how long I have been a dove, and I don't know how long I have left. But I am at the end, not the beginning, and I realized that I had put off what had to be done for too long. I tried to make our peace with the church. If God wants more of me, I no longer know what it is."

Doves were continuing to not make sense to me, but I was relieved she was alive to say things like that at least a little while longer. And there was one thing I completely understood. She'd done what she thought was right, although she was terrified and everyone else thought it was wrong.

While we were twittering at each other, Hind had been opening a window. We helped Coo up to it – she weighed nothing. I swear, she weighed nothing at all. And though she was shaky, the Dove Girl threw herself out into the air, spread her wings, and flew away.

The rest was even simpler. We went down back stairs and out into the garden, and Hind opened a little gate that led out into an alley. When we got there she hugged me, and we kissed each other on the cheek, because I didn't intend to ever come back. And I ran off.

I wasn't headed home. The streets weren't where I wanted to be, but the sooner I got out of that house, the less likely someone would realize Hind was involved in my disappearance. Getting up onto the rooftops was the only hard part, actually, and I found an old wooden stairway in an alley.

I was up, and I knew where I was going. I had to backtrack a couple of times to get there, since this wasn't the way I'd come before, but churches are hard to miss. I was up the ladder and in the window. I wasn't wasting any time. I didn't have any left.

I guess they knew I was coming. The doves were all waiting for me. Egg and Mourn took my hooves in their hands, and Mourn put his finger to my lips, and they led me back to the chapel.

There were books of scripture open, and bells and ornaments out, and incense burning, and lit candles everywhere. It was obvious they'd been praying. Coo hadn't been praying. She was sitting against the altar with her legs sprawled out, and she had her wings wrapped around her and a quilt wrapped around them. But she was smiling.

Egg led me to a little bitty stool, and I sat down on it because I guessed I was meant to. Mourn got out a jug and started heating it over a few candles they'd pulled together.

"Why did you come back to us, sister?" asked Coo formally, and smiled a little wider and added rather informally, "Not why you rescued me. That I think I know."

"My owner, Mister Thornback, is dying. He'll be gone very soon. I'm worried he might be gone already. Without him I have no reason to stay a donkey anymore. It wasn't who I am. I would like to try for something else."

Apparently, the jug was a drink. Mourn poured it into some ceremonial cups that probably only looked gold. When they gave me mine, I drank it. It tasted like berries, and maybe pepper.

Coo was watching me. "You refused us once, sister Bray. You embraced what you say was a lie. You can't just change your mind."

There was a weird, ritual atmosphere. It was some kind of test. Everyone was very quiet and calm, and so was I. "I didn't change my mind. I never believed I was a donkey. I refused to give up what I had, even to learn what I should have been."

"You gave up on the truth."

"Yes. The truth is important. There were things even more important. Without those things, the truth is all I have left to seek." I was starting to talk like a dove. I was more embarrassed about that than these accusations.

If they were accusations. "I cannot judge you for that. The angels may. No, they will. They will know if what you did was a sin or a virtue. They will know every other sin and virtue in your heart. Are you ready for that?"

I didn't feel like any more explanations. I was tired. "Yes."

Coo pulled her arm out of the blanket. She was holding a little box, a very ornate one. Out of it she pulled a little black ball, and held it out in front of my mouth. "The cordial you have drunk has prepared you, sister. Your soul is loose in your body now, and your eyes are open to new paths. This is the poison that will ease you off to the other side. You will die, but you will reach the city under this city and have a chance to live again."

I hit my head on something as I threw myself backwards. Maybe it was that, but the room seemed to be swimming. I staggered to my feet. Hooves. "Now?! I didn't mean now! I haven't said goodbye!"

The doves were in an uproar. I think Coo said something, but I didn't hear her. I ran. I slid down the roof. I managed the ladder somehow, although it fell over when I got to the bottom. I ran some more. I don't remember getting down to the street at all, but I do remember running down the street because it was so very, very strange. There was a family in a coach, and a black shape with horns crouched over them, arms around them. A woman was looking in a shop window, and somehow I could tell that she was hollow. If I looked back at the church there were white lights floating around it. There were people in the crowd, on the street, that other people walked through, and a boy lying on the sunny roof of a wagon watching me with the yellow eyes of a cat.

Like with the woman who was hollow, I suddenly knew I was late. I ran faster. People yelled as I bumped into them. That would have been trouble, but there wasn't time for trouble anymore, was there? I saw the front door of our house, and at the steps the figure in black with the blade in his hand. But he walked so slowly, and I ran, and hooves are faster than feet once you're used to them. A doctor had opened the door and stepped out of the way of the black figure without even realizing it. I pushed past them both and pretended it didn't feel horrible to touch it. I barged into the bedroom. Doctors were furious, and the Baron was gone, but I wasn't being polite anymore and it would take a minute before they threw me physically out.

All of that was stupid and unimportant. Mister Thornback was almost gone. He was awake, barely. But I knew I was the only thing he could see clearly, and to tell the truth he was the only thing I could see clearly. Everyone else was a sepia smudge. I walked over to the bed, and I put my hooves in Mister Thornback's hands, and I kissed him. Everything was upside down, but I still didn't have a human voice he could hear. So that was goodbye.

But not for him, if I had any say about it. The black figure stepped into the room. It was in no hurry, but it was raising its blade. I grabbed a jug of water and threw it at the thing. Of course it went through, but maybe that caught its attention, because as I charged at it the blade swung at me instead of Mister Thornback.

I woke up in a city under the city. If it could be called waking up. I was already walking down a path. A road, really, cobble-bricked and neat. It led in a straight line, towards what I supposed was the city center. Far overhead was the stone ceiling of a cavern. I was underground. Around me, most of the city seemed to be trees and parks with tall grasses and flowers in no clear order. But there were also buildings here and there topped by domes, all of it the shiny red-brown of copper, as were the walls that divided different parts of the city. It was exactly what I had been told to expect, although not when and how I expected to get here.

I was admiring the peacefulness of the place when I passed through an open gate, and walking beside me, as if he'd always been there, was Mourn. He looked at peace again, and his smile was so friendly and proud and warm. This part of the city was some sort of market. There were no vendors. Just booths lining the road, with jewelry and carpets and dresses with peacock feathers and astrolabes and anything else you could think of, sitting out. Some didn't even seem to have merchandise, just boxes full of money spilling over onto the street.

"You made it, sister. Here we'll find out who you are. I think you'll be a dove."

"I'm not sure of that anymore," I told him as we walked through another open gate. "It would be nice to have your virtues, but I don't seem to be like you in any other way. Although I guess I did take my own life, sort of."

This part of the street seemed to be part of a fair or, even simpler than that, a feast. On either side of the road and in the park beyond were tables laid out with foods I didn't recognize, and a few indistinct people moving among them. The smell was wonderful, I admit. There were even a few tables in the road itself, and I felt a pang of nostalgia as I stepped around one with breakfast food on it. I remembered sitting down to eggs and bacon, too often badly made with hooves, although Mister Thornback seemed to enjoy them.

"If not a dove, then what? You're not a donkey, or a wolf. You can't believe that." His tone was actually very friendly. There was the air that we were having a pleasant walk in the countryside, debating some tidbit of philosophy rather than anything as important as my future. If, being dead, I had a future.

"I don't claim to know. That's what I'm here to find out."

I think he liked that answer. He gave his smile to me for a moment as we passed through another gate.

"You've learned one thing, though. You've seen the truth here."

"The truth about what?" I was actually very distracted. Here, finally, we'd come to the real parks. Children laughed and played on either side of the road, in playgrounds randomly arranged and through clumps of trees between swing sets and slides. I couldn't see the children clearly. They seemed to shine, caught so brightly in the light that their features couldn't be made out. All I could be sure of was that they were happy and free. I envied them for a moment, then I was just happy for them. "The truth about the Wild Children? All I have are more questions. If this is where we're judged, why did Coo get here alone, and we had to be led?"

We passed through another open gate. I was sorry to leave that section. Now we seemed to be entering the city proper. On either side of the road were buildings, bizarre, fanciful structures of gleaming copper, with spires and swooping ramps and domes and a lot of other things I didn't understand.

"Because this is Heaven," Mourn told me fondly. This was what he had been trying to lead me to. This revelation. "It doesn't matter how you get here. If you get here, it's the right way."

I remembered the children playing. It certainly looked like Heaven should. "I don't understand any of that either. You have to die to get here and come back, so you call it an afterlife. But I didn't die to become a donkey. I just changed. But it's the same thing that happens to you, isn't it? Even if your way is better. Maybe it's not the best way."

We came to a gate, and this one was closed. It was the end of the road, leading up to the entrance of another huge, bulbous copper building. This one steamed from vents and made churning noises like I'd always supposed a factory would make.

Mourn stared up at the gate from beside me. "Then you will go no further, sister. This is the last gate, the gate of faith. You passed the others easily, but this one will only open when you confess your faith in God and accept his plan for you."

"Then I guess I go no further." I was sad about it, but that city was too peaceful a place to really get upset. "I don't know anything about God, or if he exists, or if he has a plan. I'm not sure I care either way. I have faith only in people, and how important they are."

And the gate opened for me, swung silently wide despite its huge, imperious bulk. "It can't do that. That isn't faith," whispered Mourn in shock. But he matched me, step for step, as I went inside.

From the chaos inside came a voice, and it certainly wasn't human. It wasn't animal either, so I can't think of words to describe it. It sounded fake, but fake like it wasn't a real voice. It also sounded warm and honest.

"It is the faith that is in her heart. She passes the test. She has passed all the tests, and I have agreed to judge her."

"She didn't learn anything, though." I understood he wasn't arguing against me. This wasn't how he remembered his own visit. This wasn't how he knew it worked. "She hardly noticed the other tests. They weren't tests at all."

"You will not speak again, dove. This is her judgment, not yours," the voice chided him. I could make it out now. If that had taken me a minute, it was because the inside of the building was crazy. It was all one room, but it was full of what I guessed was machinery. I'd never seen anything this complicated. It put the inside of the fanciest clock you could imagine to shame. There were furnaces, much deeper in. Huge pistons slammed from side to side above us, but hardly made any noise. Only this front area seemed safe. And hanging in front of us, from the machinery, was what I guess was meant to be an angel. It looked vaguely human in shape, and there were what I was sure were wings, but it was all made out of machinery and most of it was moving. I wouldn't have been sure it was alive at all, but it had a copper mask on what was probably its head, and that gave it a face. All be it not much of one.

The admonishment might have been a prediction. Mourn said nothing. It was my turn. I stepped forward. "I have come for judgment. I have been told that becoming a donkey was a mistake. I think it must have been. Can you give me my real afterlife?"

The clockwork angel was mobile. It slid around on rails hung in the air, and started peeking into drawers tucked into one wall. "Do you believe it's an afterlife?"

I had to be honest. "No. It doesn't make any sense to me. It's on earth, and maybe you die to get to it or maybe you don't, and it's only for children."

"Well, whether it is or not, it is something I can provide. You don't usually get two, but you qualify, and it is already clear to me that I would never have assigned you to be a donkey. Unless you requested it, perhaps. May I have your heart, please?"

Okay, that was weird, but it was also easy. I just pulled it out of my chest. It wasn't a nasty red gooey thing like the heart of an animal, and it didn't come out that way. It just came away in my hand. It looked like a soap bubble, a little pink, more purple. It shone and had little glittering spots on it. It shone very brightly, in fact, except where little chips of something solid clung to the surface here and there.

I gave it to the angel. A tray came sliding up with a pair of scales on it. He put my heart in one bowl, although that didn't seem to do anything. Maybe it just let him inspect it. While he did, I asked, "You said if I requested it. You can turn me into whatever I want?"

"I can give you any reward or punishment I choose, Miss Bray," the angel replied calmly. No, warmly. It was strange and formal, but it also talked like a friend. "I am your judge. I am taken with your heart, and with your honesty while you've been here. Your innocence is not perfect, but you still qualify. I am inclined to be very generous with you. Was there something you wanted?"

There was. It wasn't anything anyone had mentioned, but I had to ask. "I would like to give up my choice to someone else. There is someone I left behind, Mister Thornback. I don't want him to die yet. Make him young again. Make him a Wild Child. Whatever he wants. Or whatever you want. Just not a donkey, please. I don't think he would want that, and I want him to be alive and happy."

"I'm afraid he's already dead. The reaper is not that easily put off. You delayed him a few seconds, no more. But then, you're dead too, aren't you? Please give me his heart."

It was also in my chest, and it came out just as easily. It was very different from mine, though. It wasn't like a soap bubble at all. It was larger and like a pearl, sleek and hard and shiny, intricately inlaid in gold over a grid of iron, and… I'm probably not describing it very well, but it will give you an idea. I handed it over.

The angel put it in the other cup of the scales. It pulled a magnifying glass over its eye from out of the mass of machinery behind it. It pulled another four or five out over that. It studied the two hearts.

"This is not an innocent heart, Miss Bray. Very much not an innocent heart. It is certainly a beautiful one, to my tastes. I can see why you are fond of it. Many virtues, many sins. But I can only bring children back. If there is a child left inside here, I can only find out by cracking it open. Are you okay with that?"

That didn't sound good at all. "What do I lose? No – what does he lose? If that might hurt him, I'm not okay with it. I want him to live again, not risk whatever is left now that he's dead."

The angel smiled. That is, the mask smiled. I didn't know it could do that. "That was the right answer, Miss Bray." And it picked up Mister Thornback's heart and smacked it against a pipe, cracking it like an egg, and poured into the bowl another soap bubble. This one was a very dark purple, very plain, but it seemed to pulse. "He loses a great deal, but nothing he loses is anything you or he really care about. Memories, mostly. Pain. Yes, there is innocence here, although it was deeply buried. He would have made a strange and fine Wild Child, if he had found a way to come over in his youth." Huge wings made of twisting wheels flapped over my head as the angel turned around, slid over to the wall again, and gently, even reverentially placed the pearl that had been Mister Thornback's heart into a drawer of its own. "I will keep this. It is lovely for its own sake. One day he may come back for it."

The angel slid back again. The smile was gone. It picked up my heart and held it up in the copper struts of one hand. It looked very official.

"I have made my judgment, Miss Bray. You may need a new name. I will not leave you as a donkey, and your life is not done. I will return you to the world in a new body, and I will grant your request and bring the child you think of as Mister Thornback to life as well. There is payment, however. You have spent your reward on someone else. I cannot guarantee that you will ever see him again, or that you will recognize each other if you do. Also, you have asked for too much. We do not bring adults back, and you have asked us to give him not merely a different life, but an extra life. I only granted it because the request itself impressed me so. In payment you will not receive the body, life, and destiny you deserved. You must take a different one and try to make it yours."

I was changing. I'd been here before. I was dizzy, I couldn't think, I was giddy, I was drunk. I held up my hooves to rub my eyes, and I rubbed my eyes with hands. I had hands again. Hands sprouting feathers, more and more feathers. Not little feathers, long feathers. Wings, instead of sprouting from my back like a Dove Child, grew from my arms, long and pinioned in gold and scarlet and white. There were feathers on my head. I was, I thought, mostly human, maybe a little more than I'd been before, although my back was covered in feathers and it felt like I had a bird's fanned tail. I didn't dare look at my feet, but anything would be better than hooves anyway.

And something was missing. Something was welling up within me. I caught fire! More than fire, a burning glow shone along my feathers. At first I thought I'd consume the whole room, but it died down, became merely a flicker over my wings and hair.

What were my eyes like? I wanted to see my eyes. It was a silly thought, but I was giddy. I would have to wait.

It was just so much not what I was expecting. "I'm a... a..."

"Phoenix, yes," filled in the angel. He didn't need to. I knew, I just hadn't wanted to believe. "Do not think this is a reward. The destiny of a phoenix is often heavy, and we do not give it to children who are able to live easily and enjoy it. And you gave up a great deal. Had I been able to give you my first choice, I would have made you a unicorn."

That was too much. It shocked me. "I'm not a unicorn, sir. I don't want to seem ungrateful. I couldn't be more grateful. But I'm not a phoenix either. These aren't me any more than a donkey was."

It was unfazed. Of course, what could faze an angel made of clockwork? "You certainly were not suited to be a donkey. Did you find you could fill the destiny of a donkey, when you found that part of you that wanted to?"

I thought I understood that question. "I suppose so, sir."

"Then you may appreciate that no, you are not a unicorn, but a unicorn is something I feel you could have grown into. A phoenix is the same way. Your judgment is complete, child. I have no intention of changing it. Do you have any other questions before you live again?"

I did, and it terrified me. "Is this real? This isn't real, is it?"

And again, one last time, he seemed pleased. "No, Wild Child, it is not. This city isn't real. I am not real. He is not real." A finger made of interlocking copper supports extended towards Mourn. "In fact, you may meet him again and he will not remember this, because he was not here. But while this place isn't real, what happens here – that is very real.

Farewell, Wild Child. I think you should find a new name, but you are allowed to remain Bray if you wish."

I woke up. Again. I was lying on the floor of Mister Thornback's bedroom. I stood up slowly, groggily. I pushed myself up with hands, not hooves, and yes the hands were covered in scarlet and gold feathers. Had any time passed? The doctors were still in the room. Actually, they were cowering against the walls, and some had clearly run away because I saw a knocked over table in the kitchen and the front door was open.

I felt light. So very, very light. I hadn't realized a donkey body was so heavy. But something was way more important than that. Whatever Coo had given me was spent, and I was thinking clearly again, and it was time to stop being afraid and look.

The bed was empty. The pillow was still in place, the sheets had fallen as if Mister Thornback had just been in them. He was not here with me, but the 'angel' – already I was doubting that was what it really was – had been true to its word. I was alive, and I was no longer a donkey. Somewhere, Mister Thornback was also alive, and he was one of the Wild Children. Maybe I could find him. Maybe I could help Hind somehow, although I wasn't sure what would do that. Maybe I could do a lot of things. I felt like I had nothing but possibilities now.

My heart was so light that there was a thump, and flames burst up out of me, swam around me, and I leapt off the floor. The ceiling was no obstacle. I was too hot, and it simply fell out of my way as ash. For the first time, I flew.

I would come to love flying.

ACT II

PAIN CANDY

I hate the summer. It's not the heat, although I don't much like that either. It's the long days, and bright sunshine. Which is why I was stuck waiting for sundown in the most shadowy, overhung alley I could find, watching a street I wasn't dumb enough to walk out into during the day.

The city is huge and busy, and this narrow, sullen alley shrouded in darkness sticks off a main street. There were a lot of people going by, all the time. There were at night, too, but I can hardly see them then. At night humans were ghosts, hardly even people, which was pretty much how I felt about them anyway. During the day they were blurry, half-molded, but all too solid. That's why I never went out during the day. I could see them, and they could see me, and they'd like what they saw a lot less than I did.

So, you'd think I'd curl up and nap. Cats can sleep at any time, right? Pshhh, yeah. Watching a bunch of vague mannequins walk back and forth probably sounds pretty boring, too. What kept me from strangling myself were the others in the crowds.

Humans are dumb. Wild Children are dumb too, but some of them have good eyes. I have good eyes. All cats do, supposedly, but it's not like I've met any. I've heard we're very, very rare. Housecats are a dime a dozen, yeah, but Cat Children? I was the only one in the city, the only one who'd been in the city for a long time. If another entered, the whisperers would have told me.

Good eyes? Good eyes are animal eyes. Not many Wild Children have them. Those that do… let's say the humans don't like it. We see things they can't. Humans drift serenely through a world they know nothing about.

A thin human figure, wrapped in brightly colored fabric from head to foot except for an elaborate mask, was strolling down the street. What was it? I used to care. Now I just watched and wondered what the humans saw. None of them bumped into it. I could see doubt, an ugly worm, wrapped around a priest, sucking at him. Little black clouds like dust bunnies blew around in the gutters. A Wild Child walked past, his donkey face bowed, maybe under the weight of his heavy steel collar, more likely under the weight of the basket of fruit he was carrying in his shackled hands - which was the kind of stupidity I expected from humans. Come to think of it, a human owner was probably with him. I couldn't tell them apart. Humans aren't as real as they think they are. Wild Children – Wild Children are real.

But yeah, it was a slow day. Sometimes you saw stuff that was really strange. I was just killing time anyway. Summers were annoying. But after a while night fell, and things got a little darker. Dark enough – time to start my 'day'.

Now that the street outside was in shadow, relying more on street lamps than twilight, the alley was nearly black. That meant I had options. Out came my claws, and I climbed up a brick wall onto the rooftops. I didn't really favor the rooftops over the streets, particularly. When it got really dark I could go up and down walls, jump like a real cat, all sorts of things. Nighttime is my world, which is why the long days of the summer really irritate me.

Too much wasting time. I was up here to use my eyes. When I was human I read legends in books. Now I could see them. I was looking for omens, and they were everywhere. Golden motes fell around a building. A baby was being born there. Empty helmets were piled up on another rooftop. I didn't know what that meant. These were all kind of ghostly images anyway. Human stuff. I was looking for something specific, and there in the distance I saw it, lurid purple and glowing and huge. The sigil of pain. A Wild Child was hurting. It was so big too, and bright. I was really going to score tonight.

There are highways along the rooftops, for thieves and chimneysweeps and delivery boys and other human concerns. I hardly used them. I leapt from roof to roof. If I crossed a wide street I'd slide down a gutter and dart across. At night I could hardly see humans, and they could hardly see me. At night I could, and did, walk across busy streets all the time, and nobody noticed me. Which is good. The ears and tail are a dead giveaway for all Wild Children, cats included. Donkey Children could see me, but they certainly weren't going to point me out to their owners. So I was crisscrossing streets and alleys, shimmying up to race across rooftops, until I scaled a wall around a large, private estate with lots of yard. Must have cost a pretty penny this deep in the city, but Wild Children tended to be owned by the rich.

Who cared? I wasn't there for his gold.

It was so easy to find the room. I just looked for the barred window. It was on the second floor, but it was pretty dark by now and there was that nice garden wall to block the street lamps. Up I went, clinging to bricks like a fly, and squeezed between the bars. No human could do that, and donkeys are pretty wretched, but a cat can.

It was nicer than I was expecting. The bed was well made, the wallpaper was pretty, there was a toy chest. No kidding, a toy chest. Humans were messed up sometimes. And there was a Donkey Boy, curled up against the wall and chained to the bed, ruining his pretty silk sailor suit crying. Crying and crying and crying. He looked like he was six, but that was the godawful costume. I've only met one Wild Child who came over before she was ten, and most of us were a couple of years older.

He was crying so hard he didn't see me. Wild Children can, good or bad eyes. If a human was in the room I wouldn't have had to hide. She wouldn't have known I was standing there. I'd barely have been able to see her, now that it was full dark.

That made it easier. Most of my... clients. Yeah, clients. Or maybe 'patients'? They tended to be asleep, but he hurt, body and mind and soul, too bad to sleep. I crept up to him silently. I'd like to claim I walked like a cat, but any Wild Child could do it. This kid probably could, and he had a serious case of hooves. That was fine. By the time I was reaching for his face it was too late. They go into a kind of trance - I don't know why. I just had to hold his tear-stained face up with one hand, pry his mouth open gently, reach in, and find his pain.

Out it came, hard and round, sort of a dull purple. It was big. Like, walnut sized. I'd seen bigger, but not from children in any condition you'd want to look at. I couldn't resist. I licked it. God, it was bitter. There was a lot of hate in there, bitter and intoxicating. I ran my tongue over it again, got a good taste. Hatred, pain, shame, despair... the usual mix, but very strong, and the size of it was impressive. It would pay for a lot of sins.

My client was still out of it. He sat there staring at the wall dazedly, but he'd stopped crying. He'd probably sleep soon, and tomorrow he'd barely remember what hurt him so badly today. I could say it was a public service, but it wasn't. I took away his pain because it was valuable. The pain of a Wild Child? Oh, yeah. Alchemists would pay a fortune for it. Poor bastards. I had no use for their money, and they couldn't gather it themselves, being human.

Incidentally, human pain? Worth nothing. It's muddled and not very strong, and nobody wants it.

I was going to head straight to the Weaver. Straight to the Weaver. But I climbed up on the roof to get my bearings and I heard the wailing begin. Bain Sidhe. A Wild Child was about to die.

A soul would make this nugget of pain look like chicken feed - I'd be halfway to salvation. I was racing across the city before I even saw the Bain Sidhe herself. There's not much to see, just a skinny white woman in a lot of sheets singing really badly. She was solid though, and glowing bright. It was a Wild Child dying for sure. She doesn't usually come for humans.

So close. So close, less than a mile away. I might get there in time. I could run faster than a human at night. There wasn't much time. Those damn books I read when I was human said she wailed the night before. The truth is, you're lucky to get fifteen minutes.

Eave to rooftop, leap over a gap, down an outside staircase, across the street and up another one. Forget steps. I jumped up, clung, and jumped again. A roadway of weighted planks led me down an entire block before I had to jump down onto the top of a cart and speed through three twisting alleys, until I realized I wasn't going to find a good way up and scaled a wall with my claws alone. After that it was a straight line, barring a few more alleys to jump. I made it there before the wailing stopped.

It was an okay house - a little on the low rent side to own a Wild Child. Oh, who cared? I was in a hurry. The Bain Sidhe would probably be over his room... it was on the first floor. It had to be, with the barred shutters. Barred from the outside, of course, to prevent escape. I just opened them up and climbed right in.

The room was awful. It was a dingy, colorless little bedroom that was basically an oversized closet. Looking at it I hated humans, and I hadn't spoken to one in years. When I looked at the occupant of the cot, I hated them more.

He'd been beaten. Very, very badly. He was heavily donkey-like. Face, fur everywhere, hooves for feet. He probably couldn't stand up straight, although it was hard to tell. I could see a Reaper walking through the door. It was five feet away, I had no time!

Better not to think about the boy anyway. I hunched over him, opened my mouth, inhaled, and caught his last, hoarse breath. I closed my mouth over it then dived out the window and ran. Ran and ran and ran. You can't stop a Reaper, you can't talk to it. I didn't know if it would resent what I'd done or try to follow me, but I was pretty sure it wouldn't follow me far. I had hints of memories. I'd managed this once before. But it was a sin, and having the Weaver burn that sin away along with the others gave me only the vaguest idea of what happened last time. I'd gotten away with it then, though, so after a while I sat down on a chimney and coughed up the Wild Boy's soul.

Really, I didn't know it was a soul. Maybe it was 'essence,' like the alchemists talk about, or the potency of a final breath, or whatever. It was pretty. A little ball of swirling white, with faint shadows moving inside it. I felt sad, looking at it. Those must have been my own feelings, though. It wasn't just the cruelty, beating the boy to death. It was stupid, too. Donkeys are property, but even one that ugly must have cost a pretty penny, and some human had wasted it just to be mean.

Humans are so very, very stupid. But I lived in the night, and I didn't have to deal with them. I had to deal with things like the Weaver. I had a fresh soul and a lump of pain I could barely fit in my clenched fist. I was going to see the Weaver tonight. Right now.

Humans can't see what's going on around them, and that means there are parts of the city they don't know exist. My guess is they see run-down houses, cheap and decrepit tenements no one would live in, lightless back streets and thugs and poor people whose faces, funnily enough, they don't remember thirty seconds later. I would say that humans can't get to these areas at all, but they can. Sometimes I see one hurrying through, terrified and not realizing just how bad the danger they're in really is. Sometimes it's some teenage punk who just has to go to the worst part of town to prove he's tough and never comes out again. Sometimes he's less a punk and more an urchin, and if he's lucky he comes out a Wild Child.

Humans are pretty rare on these streets, anyway. Traffic's light, most of it things rather than people. I've just started thinking of them as 'others'. Do you want a description? How about shiny black bugs the size of oxes, with legs like stilts that hold them way above my head? A group of dancers whirling and leaping their way down the street who would look human, even beautiful, except they had no faces and none of them had the same number of limbs? Most of the things I see are more like ghosts, shrouded figures in layered robes and hoods who are a little transparent even to me. And some I'm pretty sure are demons.

There were times, when I was drunk, that I would try to make friends with one of the others. Some of them could talk, hold something resembling a conversation. I had a couple of close calls. As a cat I was halfway between the humans and the others, but stupidity could still get me worse than killed.

I had long since learned my lesson. I was only here on business. I guess I did almost see broken down houses with boarded up windows, but I saw them in the deep shadow of night, covered in gently glowing scrawls in random colors. Some of it I could read, some of it I couldn't. There were shops here. Bars. Restaurants. Do not, ever ever ever, eat in the restaurants. I was headed for the Weaver of Pain's shop. He was my business contact on this side of the city.

The inside of the shop is kind of a maze. Room after room in no order, never in the same pattern twice. Shelves and display stands with jars and boxes. They're labeled, but you can't read them because there's no lights. I could only make out that much thanks to my cat eyes. Cat eyes don't just see the world humans can't, they're also great in the dark.

I found the Weaver in the second room this time. He had a nice counter and everything. I think it was prepared just for me, because it looked very normal and I recognized some of the machines behind him. They were for me.

"Jinx! The stars are cold and have forgotten how to hope tonight. I thought you might be joining me." That's how he talks, and it makes him the most coherent and sensible thing I knew. As for 'he', he sounded like a woman tonight, so who knows? And... as for 'Jinx', yes. That's my name. I'm a black cat, and one day decades or centuries ago some human thought that was clever. Really, I don't remember.

The Weaver beckoned with one of its arms, and the mask it was wearing had a smile that was probably meant to be nice. Masks are very common among the others. Either they don't have faces, or they don't want you to see them.

I put on a little swagger. I was feeling good about myself, and the others usually respect bravery, as long as you're not obviously stupid. I leaned up against the counter and held out the ball of pain I'd gathered earlier. "I guess the stars were right. It was a good night. What can I get for this?"

Fingers as long and thin as wires plucked the pain out of my hand. He didn't taste it. He put it in one of his machines, weighed it, stuck it with a needle, did a lot of things I didn't recognize and couldn't see well. After a minute he came back and set it on the counter between us.

"Very pure, Jinx." His voice was a boy's now, but a squeaky little boy child's. "Or should I say, so corrupt as to be almost pure. Innocence and trust destroyed, a pain that, once distilled, could lead to madness. I wish to buy, and you wish to sell. I could offer you many things, but you cling to the thread of destiny tonight, don't you? You are steadfast in search of salvation. I can offer 0.87% redemption in exchange."

It was a lot. There must have been something special about this boy's suffering. He was offering to burn nearly a hundredth part of my crimes off of my soul for one night's work, and I'd been doing this so long I had no idea how long it was anymore.

The burning was going to hurt. It was going to hurt a lot, and I was about to make it a lot worse. I coughed up the soul again and held it out cautiously. "And for this?"

I could barely feel the soul, like it was made out of wind, but he plucked it out of my hand as if it were completely solid. "Oh, you wicked, wonderful kitten. Where did you get such a treasure? How did you get it here without someone knowing?" The little white ball wasn't put in a machine. The mask hovered over it, and it was passed from hand to hand to hand while more hands came out and stroked it, poked it, scratched it. The hands weren't all attached to arms anymore.

"I got it from a Donkey Boy." I was sure he knew everything I could tell him and more. "It had better be worth the rest of my sin."

"Not even close, Jinx, not even close, but yes, so much. We couldn't burn it all away in one night, not one night, you wouldn't survive. You'll need the pain you gathered just to pay for the sin of stealing this. You know that, don't you, Jinx? But don't worry, you're in pocket tonight. Mmmm, murdered senselessly on the crux of achieving its destiny. Lovely. I'll offer you this for it." He stopped drawling in an accent I didn't recognize and he laid a little bronze token on the countertop.

I almost pounded the counter in anger. The faceless spider-looking bastard. He'd been leading me by the nose! "It's worth more than that! It's the most valuable thing I've ever brought you! It's worth a bag of these!" I snapped back.

"Yes," answered the Weaver sweetly, still playing with its prize. "But you can only have one at a time, you know that. No credit, no account. One at a time, and this priceless little gem you've brought me will have dissolved into the aether by dawn. I'm sorry, Jinx, I thought you'd rather have this instead?"

He was laughing at me! Probably. It didn't matter if he meant to cheat me or not. I grabbed the token to throw it back at him and demanded purification. The things I see on these back streets have given me a glimpse of Hell, and I wasn't going there.

I couldn't do it. I could feel the little disk in my palm. I knew what it promised. I couldn't let it go.

"Is that a deal, then?" the Weaver asked in the voice of an innocent, boy or girl, I couldn't tell. The soul was deposited carefully in a fancy ceramic vase and set on the counter. Fingers like the tips of blunt knives pulled my hand open and set the disk beside the vase. The bargain was in front of me. It wasn't remotely equal. I was giving up months, years of gathering, risking my salvation.

I was about to open my mouth and accept when the Weaver changed the terms again. Maybe he planned it, or maybe he didn't know or care how I thought. He was pulling one of his machines over to the counter. It held a sort of metal gargoyle, all claws and fanged face that looked like it was screaming. Probably because it was studded with nails. The others have an idea of decoration that even I find hard to deal with sometimes. Especially since it's rarely just decoration.

"I believe I can make this one into a nightmare sentry." The Weaver's voice became silky as he adjusted things I didn't understand or want to understand. "Anger over an unfair fate, yes, he'll be strong, and if I keep his pain fresh, free will won't ever be a problem."

Again, trying to understand the Weaver is useless. But there were things I did understand. He wasn't lying, or even exaggerating. He might be understating. Inside that jar was the best part of a child who'd been beaten to death for no good reason. It represented my best shot at crossing the threshold and being saved. No, I couldn't lie to myself. I was going to trade it for a night in Purgatory. And in doing so I would give that child over to a hundred years of- I was still going to do it. It had been months, months since I'd gotten one of those tokens. When I realized that, my heart started to pound inside me. If I took this deal, I could go tonight.

I grabbed the vase. I was making myself stop thinking, refusing to make a decision, because I never made the right decision, ever, which was why I was here trying to trick my way into Heaven. That little bit of justification distracted me the few seconds I needed to get outside. I dumped the contents of the vase into my palm, and the swirling white ball was the only bright thing on this dark street. I knew what to do – I'm a cat. I blew on it and it unraveled. The shadows at its core dissolved, but the white lights it was made of simply drifted away into the air until I couldn't tell them from the stars.

"Jinx, my prodigal kitten," the Weaver said from behind me in a new voice, deep and bass. "I thought we understood each other. Didn't you want this? The pain, while delightful, isn't enough. In fact I'm going to have to put it away for you now. You know that setting that child free doesn't redeem you for stealing him in the first place, don't you?" He almost sounded convincingly concerned.

I turned around. He was inside his shop, of course. He hadn't stepped through the doorway. He never leaves, and might not be able to, and I don't much care. And he was holding out that damnable token. I had to have it. My hands were shaking already as I realized I'd given up my chance at it unless I did something… something crazy.

I had to pull out the stops. If I didn't get to Purgatory tonight, or tomorrow night, I'd go crazy. It was too close. I couldn't concentrate, but I tried anyway. What was I saving for emergencies?

I'd try to raid the doves.

Dove Children are very mystical or something. Read an alchemy text if you don't mind ending up like me. If you really, really don't value your soul, read a book on sorcery. As a cat I was a little more aware, a little more accepted, a little safer in the darkest, strangest parts of the night. As a Wild Child I was a much more attractive target. There are things in the shadows that crawled out of nightmares and drink blood. They'll take humans if they have to, but a Wild Child is so much tastier. And a dove? A dove is a feast. I have to explain these things to anyone who doesn't understand the others, or what I tried next won't make sense. Anything I could get from the doves would be valuable. I could sell a few stray feathers, even. The problem was, they wouldn't be valuable enough. The Weaver only sells tokens for a big haul. Usually I'd have to save and save to get one. It took weeks, and as I looked up at the church the doves roost in I started to shake again thinking about that. I couldn't wait.

But the doves were hiding a treasure, if I could get it.

A black cat in the middle of the night has a lot of advantages. The doves live in the attic of a church. How they get away with that, I have no idea. You'd think they'd be drowning in curious priests. If they couldn't fly they got in and out through the window at one end, which led straight into their nesting area. That was the bad way in, the way that would make a fuss. But even though church roofs go for sharp slants and lots of spires, I had no trouble clinging to the tiles and climbing my way around to a different window on the other side. The one that led to Coo's bedroom.

Poor Coo. She was the only Wild Child I knew of who'd been in the city longer than me. She was a god-botherer like all doves, but... eh. There's too much to describe. Right now what was important was that while the other doves slept in nests in one big room, they made her sleep in a bed in a room of her own. They weren't rejecting her. It was the other way. She was old, if a child can be old, and she didn't have much time left, and you could tell. They loved her too much, made a fuss if she stayed up all night praying, got her a bed and made her sleep in a place of honor. Which gave me my chance.

She even slept with the window a little open, so I was able to pry it up enough to get in without making a sound. There were no candles, only a little moonlight, and I was one shadow in a hundred, so dark I thought I might have grown fur. I was going to pull it off this time. Those dumb doves had sold her to me with their overprotective love.

I was confident right up until I got to the foot of the bed and Coo just sat up and looked at me. She wasn't surprised at all, and she could see me just fine. Coo has good eyes: bird eyes, a freaky orange, the wrong shape, but she can see as much as me and probably more. I was damned, this wasn't going to work!

"Good morning, brother," she greeted me. "Very early morning, but you do like those hours. You can pick any hour you like as far as I'm concerned if you'll visit more often. What brings you to me tonight?"

I wanted to hit her, but I couldn't. She was the oldest Wild Child in the city, but Coo looked the youngest. She's tiny and thin as a rail, and these days she was weaker and sicker than she looked. I was so god damn angry, but you can't hit Coo. And the worst part was that patronizing tone of voice, because it wasn't like that. Coo even loves me. She really meant it.

Which didn't mean she wasn't playing with me a little. "You know what I'm here for, sister," I snapped back. Blood of the damned, was I angry. "I want your pain. And no, I couldn't sneak up and take it tonight either. Can't you just give it to me?"

And she gave me that look, like I was a hurting child. But so was she. We all are, aren't we? Coo got to use that look a lot, and it made me want to grind my teeth. Anyway, I knew what the answer would be. Pity never made Coo bend an inch. "And hurt both of us, brother Jinx?" Man, did she sound tired. She didn't have much time left. "Pain is how we learn the lessons life must teach us. More importantly, it's my payment to God for my sins. I might give that up to help you pay for your sins, but you're not. You're trying to get around your fate, avoid your punishment, and redeem yourself without learning your lessons. You'll have to look elsewhere, brother. I won't help you hurt yourself that way."

"There is no elsewhere." It was so dark, I was so desperate, I was starting to sound like a cat and my hand gripping her bed rail trembled. "Nobody else's pain will do. I need a lot of it, tonight. Not just a lot, I need the best. You're old, sister, and you hurt. And I don't mean just in body. Let me give you a little peace. I can't take away who you are. Just a fragment of what hurts you the most."

Always that look, like I was completely transparent. I might have been. Like I said, Coo has good eyes. The best eyes, better than mine I was sure. Or maybe she was just smarter than me. "You're desperate tonight, Jinx. Why? I know why you've always wanted my pain. I don't like the way you steal it from the Donkey Children, but the pain you take from them…" She had to stop for a moment. Coo loves everyone, absolutely everyone, and just thinking about what I do made her sigh. "You take away the raw hurt of children whose burdens are greater than they can bear. You take away their chance to learn from it, but you help almost as much as you harm. There's no shortage of suffering out there, even if it isn't as… sweet as the doubt and regret and pity and fear of a Dove Child nearing her end. Why aren't you content with it anymore?"

She was too close. This wasn't going to end well. I almost considered taking it from her. She couldn't stop me, except with that expression. Unfortunately the expression was doing a really great job. "That would take too long. I need it tonight. Don't ask why. Coo, if you really care about me just give it to me this once." I was shaking again, pacing with tension. I knew I'd blown my best chance as soon as she woke up.

"I have to ask why." She was still arguing, but I was getting through. She looked worried. That was Coo's weakness. Because she loved me, loved everyone, she'd hurt herself for us. "Something has happened. You're older than you think, brother. Has your time run out? Why do you need salvation so-" And it all fell apart. It all fell apart in that look of pain and sadness in her eyes. "You're trying to get into that place again. Purgatory." She didn't have to tell me how she felt about it. I knew, and I knew I'd lost.

I also knew lying to her wouldn't work. "Yes."

She looked sadder than ever. "Jinx, you have to wake up. You think we're not human, but it's their world we're meant to live in. You live in dreams, and now you're trying to drown yourself in them. If you can't find your way back, at least realize how lost you are. The path of the Cat Children is strange, but you've left it, Jinx. I don't know where you are anymore."

Gritting my teeth, I spat back, "You know what? This is why I never visit you. I can put up with you wanting to keep your pain. But it's always a lecture, every time you see me."

If she had anything else to say I didn't get to hear it, because I was out the window and shutting it behind me. For a moment I thought about throwing myself off the roof. There was just no hope. Or... I'd take the long shot. I'd go ask the whisperers.

Humans can't do this, or at least not without a lot of help. It doesn't have to be at night, but it's a lot easier. You find a street, and it's easier if it's an alley because it has to be dark. It has to be so dark that you can't see the end. Not just in shadows, it has to be black. You start at the lighted end and walk towards the darkness. If you have the right eyes you won't walk towards the other end of the street. You'll walk towards the darkness itself.

I don't remember much about being human, but I think I'd read about it in my books. I'd have found out anyway because I've even done it by accident a few times. I usually don't go very deep. See, as you walk you'll notice that the way you came in is getting farther and farther away, but the darkness isn't getting much closer. You're just walking through shadows between two walls, and you're not in any place anymore, and you can hear the whispering.

I used to go see them, or at least listen to them, all the time until they started whispering about how dangerous it was getting. The whisperers know everything, absolutely everything. They whisper secrets all the time, and it's a little scary and exciting and fascinating to stand there halfway between the human world and somewhere else, hearing things you're not supposed to know. I still visited occasionally. They always told me about new Wild Children in the city, gave me hints about names and destinies and where they lived. I think they try to be helpful but don't know what we want to hear, because most of it is either useless, or doesn't make any sense. There's a lot of prophecy stuff. "In three days, on the hour of the sun twinned with the moon, the last cockerel will scratch the dirt off the stone of Azor." I'm sure a lot of it would have been very important to me if I'd had the slightest idea what it meant.

I hadn't been in a while, and I thought things were safe again. As I walked and the whispering began and hints of faces moved on the brickwork around me, I didn't hear any warnings. Most of it sounded like gossip about half the Donkey Children in town and how their owners treated them, and the rest was a babble about birds and a fountain catching fire. I liked it. If you were patient and clever and didn't walk too far, you could learn a lot. Tonight, though, I wasn't patient.

"I need a score!" I yelled at the talking shadows. "I need pain. Good pain, sweet pain, the best pain. I need enough pain, tonight, to buy my way into Purgatory. Where can I find it?"

Like I said, the whisperers are almost friendly. I would ask questions sometimes and they'd be answered, if I could understand the answer and if it was secret enough. The whisperers don't like talking about what you had for breakfast, they want to talk about broken hearts and murder and lies that will change your destiny. This got their attention. Suddenly, they were monomaniacs. I was surrounded by voices whispering about birds. "In the batless bird belfry bides the ancient maiden, sleeping-" Yes, yes. I'd gotten tips about where to find donkeys in pain a lot here, but if I asked they just started talking about Coo.

But one of the whispers was talking about something else.

"Two birds have flown, first white, then scarlet. They left behind the deer, the donkey, the princess of slaves, the beauty and beast, and her heart teeters on the edge of abyss, blackened but never tarnished."

Poetry, almost prophecy, but it wasn't about Coo. They were pointing me to someone else.

"Beneath the lesser throne she sits, lost in dreams but aware, perfect in body, sullied in mind, broken in soul, innocent in heart."

It sounded like Coo had a rival for the affections of the whisperers. To be fair they had a list of descriptions as long as your arm for me, too. I didn't get too excited about anything the others said. Everything was drama to them. But 'broken in soul' meant pain, and if they could lavish adjectives like that, this was pain I could profit from.

"Without going out to hunt the doe came to the Baron, and the Heart of the Hind was held in his hand, and sat at his feet, and slept at the foot of his bed. The dancing doll bleeds among her clockwork, Baron. She has lost her voice, though she sings still, only for you now. She is losing, not her laces, but her seams. Do not lose what you didn't ask for."

The Baron? Not once, but twice. They meant the real Baron. I knew he owned a Wild Girl. Hind… that was her name. The whisperers had a thing for this girl real bad. When the whisperers start talking about you, that's not a good sign. For her, at least. For me it sounded like I was being thrown a second chance.

I had never tried climbing the walls out of the whisperer's domain, and I had no intention of ever trying. I didn't run back to the human world either, I walked. The whisperers had told me too much about what was in the darkness on the other end of that street. Destiny was waiting there. Destiny isn't kind, trust me. It's a predator, and I didn't want to get its attention.

When the whispering stopped and there was trash on the ground and things nailed to the walls, it was another matter. I was up the walls and on the roofs in an instant. It was well past midnight, and nights are short during the summer. I couldn't mess this up. I had to do this tonight.

Fortunately, everyone in the city knows where the Baron lives. Even me, and I don't pay any attention to humans, really. There was an Emperor in the palace, right? Why was the Baron so important? These were things for humans to worry about. What I cared about was that he owned a Wild Girl, and the whisperers thought her pain was worth a trip to Purgatory.

Like I said, getting to the Baron's place was easy, and so was getting over the garden wall. Finding his Wild Girl would be harder. There were a lot of barred windows, because a house this rich attracts thieves. Too many people lived in this one building, or at least spent hours there every day. There were omens everywhere and I didn't know what they meant, and the ones I recognized were unhelpful. But it wasn't yet dawn, which meant even a rich house like this was mostly dark inside. I climbed up the walls onto a balcony and there was a door ajar leading into a bedroom. From there I just started to search. I figured if I tried to be quiet and keep out of the way I'd be safe. It was desperate and a little dumb, but the few servants moving around walked right by me and saw nothing, and that's what I was counting on. I peeked in door after boring door.

That is, until one door opened on a dollhouse. I saw this a lot in Wild Girl rooms, but never quite like this. This had to be why the whisperers called her a princess. Everything was expensive, and except for a few items of lacy clothing on the floor it was meticulously kept. There was a dress hanging on the closet door, and I'd never seen anything that elaborate, ever. There was enough jewelry on the dresser to send a thief into hysterics. There was a harp. A full sized harp, and although it was hard to tell in the dim light I would have sworn it was engraved in gold. None of that was any use to me, but it certainly got my attention.

I almost didn't notice the bed was occupied because it was so big. Once I did notice, I knew it was her, even in the dark. I'd have had trouble seeing a human. This was a Wild Child.

I crept up to the bed. I hadn't intended to get a better look, but I did anyway. With cat eyes, once I was close, I could see her clearly.

'Princess' and 'doll' didn't begin to describe it. Her hair was spilling out, half-undone, but had been tied up carefully before she went to bed, and a tiara was falling off of it. I wasn't sure how she'd gotten to bed. She was still wearing shoes, with more heel than I was used to seeing on a Wild Girl. They were sticking out from under a sheet, since she was laid out kind of awkwardly. I was grateful for the sheet, because it was pretty clear most of her clothes were the ones on the floor, and she obviously hadn't properly gotten ready for bed.

I could hardly tell she was a donkey. I could see the shape of the tail under the sheet, and she had the ears, but that was it, and her face... I'd been trying not to stare at her face. It first struck me that she was my age, which was dumb. Almost all Wild Children are. It's just that with the clothes, the hair, the room, you expected her to be older. She had that soft face, though, of girls our age, but already it was delicate, and you had to notice her lips, and she was just... pretty. Her eyes were closed, and I knew she couldn't have lashes that long and dark without some kind of makeup, and I couldn't believe I'd paid attention to that before noticing that she'd been crying. There was the redness around her eyes and the faint tracks of tears on her cheeks. Well, that was what I was here for.

I wasn't sure how long I'd been looking at her, so I kissed her. That's not as weird as you might think. A cat can draw pain from someone from their mouth. You can do it by hand, but the right way is to inhale it, to draw it out mouth to mouth. It's easier, or you get more, or something. I was able to convince myself with that excuse just long enough for my lips to touch hers, and then I was committed anyway, right? I admit I was starting to feel a little awkward about just how aware I was of her lips as I opened her mouth and started to pull, but then her pain rolled off her tongue and onto mine, and I kind of stopped thinking about anything for a minute.

Drawing out pain with a kiss worked. I couldn't just taste it, layers and layers of conflicting pains, with sweetness trapped amidst the gentle bitterness; for a moment I was her, standing on a balcony watching a bird, scarlet and lovely, that looked like it trailed fire as it flew away over the rooftops and disappeared. There was a feeling, a dull ache and a dread in her heart. She hated it, but I was only feeling it through her and I was hypnotized by it. For her it hurt, but for me it was only sadness, as sweet as the hard little ball of candy in my mouth.

As I stood back up again I let it fall into my palm. Pain doesn't get sticky or wet like sugar, at least. I couldn't afford to eat it myself. It was much smaller than I'd expected, but that taste had made it clear to me why the whisperers thought it would be valuable. The pain of Donkey Children was usually simple. I didn't even understand everything I'd just tasted.

I put the pain away in my pocket and gave Hind one last look. I couldn't help it; I was lingering. I'd been surprised at how pretty she was before, and now, with the taste of her heartache on my tongue, she was more than just a sleeping doll, she was someone I almost knew. It was the taste of her lips that was starting to haunt me though, and I was tempted to kiss her again, although I knew that I wouldn't be able to draw out more of her pain tonight. There was a deep wellspring of it in there, teasing me, but this wasn't about pain and definitely not about profit.

I would have sworn I'd seen more beautiful girls before, but they'd never hit me like this. Fortunately, while I couldn't say I had many morals, there's no class in kissing a sleeping girl, and cats are all about class, right? Mind you, during the day…

I was standing here with dawn starting to break, carrying a profit that would get me into Purgatory before the sun had burned the safe shadows off the street, letting myself get distracted by a pretty girl. It was a little harder to forget the sweetness teasing my tongue, but my hands were starting to shake again. I had all the motivation I needed to get out of there fast.

I was desperate. I didn't know if the Weaver closed up shop during the day. I'd seen others walking around in the sunlight. It wasn't safe for me to walk the streets with the sun up, though. It was peeking over the horizon, and humans could probably see me already, and I could hardly jump more than a real child and had to follow the highways along the roofs.

I got there. There's a certain murk in that part of the city. Narrow streets and buildings that lean over them kept the shadows lingering. I could see the unreadable signs and the pastel cobwebs on the Weaver's shop, and the door stood open.

I stumbled inside, gasping, and it was blessedly dark and still. There were windows, but they were painted over or maybe just coated with so much dust it did the same thing. It looked like the Weaver wasn't expecting me, because he wasn't in the next room, or the next, or the next. He had a couple of other customers, and normally I'd have avoided them and come back later just to be safe, but I pushed my way through the tangled labyrinth of identical shops until I found the one with the counter and the machines, machines everywhere, much more than he got out just to burn away my sin.

I wasn't interested. I wanted to talk to the masked stick figure standing among them. I wasn't in a good mood, either. I smacked Hind's pain down on the countertop and wheezed, "This will buy me that token, and you can keep the other Wilde Child's pain to take away the sin of stealing a soul. I've paid your price, now give." I was exhausted, and shaking, and I felt like I was at the end of my rope.

"Is that you, Jinx?" This morning his voice was a really little child's, barely understandable. It irritated me. "I barely know who you are. It's true that your balance of virtue is always erratic during withdrawal, but your constellations are severely misaligned. They have swung from the familiar spirit to the kitten of bad fortune."

Games and gobbledygook. Exactly what you get when you talk to one of the others when they're not expecting you. "I'm here for the token to Purgatory, Weaver. What I just gave you will pay for it, I know it."

"This?" asked the Weaver, picking up Hind's pain. He passed it between two or three of his hands before putting it in one of his contraptions. "A very average amount of pain, Jinx. And yet even as distorted as you are I foresaw no dishonesty in your statement. What makes you think it's worth so much?"

"I've tasted it. Taste it yourself," I growled.

"Yes, well, perhaps not." His voice had changed again. He sounded like some young dandy, drawling and full of himself. It was a voice that suited him. "We will see what the analysis says, however. Oh, my. Oh, my! Yes, how unusual. This really came from a Wild Child, my shadow urchin? I know you failed with Big Sister Dove, and I see that this is from a donkey. A donkey, really, Jinx? Where did you find one that leads a life like this?"

"I have no intention of telling you. Or going back, if I can help it." I had no desire to know why something like the Weaver wanted to find any Wild Child, and I wasn't leading him to Hind. "Is it worth a token or not? If it's not, I'll eat it myself." Yes. My shoulders were trying to twist at the thought of passing up a chance at Purgatory, but dreams of Hind's melancholy might get me through the pain until I was okay again. But I wanted the token. God, oh God who's forsaken me, I wanted the token.

"I suppose it is," the Weaver conceded reluctantly in the voice of a nagging old woman. "Just barely, but it's so unusual I can't risk passing it up by bargaining. Anyway, there's only one thing you want." Razor fingers pushed a bronze disk, too thin to be a coin, across the countertop. "Here."

"Where's the nearest door?" I demanded as I snapped it off the rough wooden surface. Already the shakes were easing, although not going away. I'd done it!

The Weaver just pointed. The door was tiny, like a broom closet. I didn't care as I stumbled over to it, and I didn't care that the Weaver laughed the whole time, changing in the middle from the cackle of a crone to the giggle of a schoolgirl who thinks it's cute. I just yanked open the door and handed the token to the overdressed thing I knew would be waiting on the other side, would be there because I had a token to give it, and I went in.

This is the part where I fail to explain what Purgatory is like and why I was so desperate to get there. It's not that I don't know the answer, it's that the answer doesn't make any sense, and might be wrong.

Purgatory is Hell, except you enjoy it.

The memories don't match either, and get muddled after I leave. I remember sitting atop a throne of skulls, laughing. I remember being chained in a raging fire, impaled on red-hot brands, and loving it. I remember wandering, buffeted by the wind, through a cloud of smoke, but I was one with the wind, and the embers writhing in the smoke were a symphony of color.

It may not make sense when you hear it, but it's like nothing in the human world at all. Any pleasure, any sin, any punishment, could happen to you at any moment and you'd like it. Have you ever wondered what the thief feels, as he sneaks out of the Sultan's palace? What the murderer feels, covered in the blood of his victims? You could find out, in Purgatory. But after a while you won't remember and you'll do absolutely anything to go back.

Except this time was different. The last thing I remember was some kind of club, with carpets and padded seats and a stage and a band, everything in scarlet. I remember a bottle of wine like I'd never tasted and would never get to taste in the world of humans, and being served by demon girls as beautiful as if they were still angels. But I remember not caring, because all I could think about was Hind, hidden under a sheet – no, her face, not as perfect as the demoness refilling my glass but somehow better – no, it was the feel of her lips – no, not that, the taste of her pain rolling onto my tongue. Yes. But more than the taste, the feeling it gave me watching a glorious fiery bird drift through the sky into the distance, and the ache it left inside her, the sense of being alone not because there was no one around, but because everyone you wanted was out of reach and always would be.

It was a feeling that I still felt when I walked out through another door in some part of the city I didn't know, watching the sun go down while not knowing how much time had passed. It didn't go away.

I kept expecting it to. I went back to my routine. Sleep through as much of the day as I could, hide through the rest, and when night came, I went hunting. I had to hunt. Purgatory was an itch in my head already. Something was wrong, and it hadn't satisfied me this time. It was never enough when you leave, but I didn't usually need it for a long time. Now I was antsy, dissatisfied, like it had been months since I visited.

And I couldn't concentrate. My very first score I found myself sitting on a rooftop, staring at the interlocking lines of a sigil of pain in the distance, and I realized I had no idea how long I'd been sitting there. All I'd been doing was drifting into that feeling. That feeling that I had nothing, because what I wanted I couldn't have.

I had to start saving for another trip to Purgatory. Everything I gathered, I'd keep. I was becoming pretty sure that cats live longer than other Wild Children. I had time to clear my head before working seriously to start burning sin again.

I was climbing out of a window holding a ball of pain, and I wasn't entirely sure who I'd gotten it from. My mind was drifting again, back to that moment when the pain rolled from Hind's tongue onto mine and I got lost in her sadness.

It irritated me, and getting mad about it helped. But I itched. I wasn't content. The next night, well, I was starting to think there was something about the summer. It was a bad time for the donkeys. There was another omen, and I followed it to a nice little house, not rich but comfortable. I climbed through a window that wasn't even locked, and there was a girl curled up on the bed with a pillow, crying softly. A Wild Girl, yes. She was still rather pretty, because there was nothing of the donkey about her face, but her hair had that coarse gray-brown and I could see how hairy her legs were. Still, she was pretty. She looked up and saw me, but it was too late, I was already there. I reached for her, and the memory was too strong, my mouth against Hind's, the taste of her pain.

I kissed this Wild Girl as her eyes went vague, in the way they always do, and I opened her mouth and I pulled out her pain, which rolled onto my tongue. It was a mild pain, not bitter but sour. For a few moments I felt it, that deep sadness of a life that was gone, of a new life that was difficult. It passed, and I let her go and stood up and put the pain into my pocket. It would sell well, probably, but what I was really thinking was that that wasn't what I wanted at all.

There were another couple of nights hunting, but I was breaking down. I was fidgeting, not so much nervous as not happy to stand still. I climbed through a window, and there was a human in the room who noticed and put up a fuss. Fortunately they noticed the window, not me. It was late at night, and the human didn't know I was there, and truthfully I couldn't tell you if it was a man or a woman or anything about them, just a vague shape in the air. But it was still sloppy and dangerous. I was losing it, and it was only getting worse.

I had to get to Purgatory again. I had to. I had to lose myself in the craziness of it, satisfy myself completely, set myself upright so I could function again. I didn't have time to do it the right way. Even when I did it I kind of knew it was dumb and I wasn't being reasonable, but the solution was obvious. I would go try Coo again. Thinking about doing it made me feel worse. I was shaky, and I almost fell off a roof on the way. I was still as silent as a cat when I climbed through the open window into her bedroom.

My timing couldn't have been worse. She walked out from behind a screen as I was getting my bearings, tying some kind of robe into place that left her wings free. She saw me immediately of course, and being Coo, instead of being alarmed she just lit a candle by her bed and sat down. And the crazy thing was, I wasn't angry at all. I felt better than I had since I left Purgatory.

She smiled, but it was weak. She was shaking, too. Just a little, but a cat can tell and I could see something, something shadowing her. I started to wonder if I was going to hear the Bain Sidhe outside any minute. Coo's soul… what could I get for Coo's soul? How could I sell it, if I saw those weird orange eyes when I held it?

"Good evening, brother. It's early for you, isn't it? It hasn't been dark long. Or has it crested midnight? I lose track too often." She smiled. She was happy to see me. Why would anyone, especially Coo, be happy to see me? "Come sit down, brother. You don't look well."

"I'm not going to sit down," I snapped at her. I sounded lame. There was no resentment in my voice at all. "You know what I'm here for."

She was looking at me. What did she see? There were other Wild Children in the city with eyes like ours, but not many and they didn't understand. Coo and I lived in the same world, almost. On the opposite ends of it, but the same. I saw mortality haunting her. What did she see, that she had such a strange expression? Sad, yes, but not as sad as she usually wore.

"No, brother, I don't. You're not here for my pain. Why are you trying to tell me you are?"

"Yes I am." I growled. Okay, I sounded angry now, and my tail was lashing. But I didn't sound angry enough. "I need it. I'm losing it, Coo. I've got to get to Purgatory, and damn you and your virtues and sins. I've just got to, okay?"

There, that expression of disgust. It hurt me this time, rolling my ears back… and then it went away. "No, you don't, do you, Jinx?" She smiled. It was a sad smile, because I was hurting. She was as easy to read as she thought I was. But it was still a smile. "You're free of that place. I'm relieved, brother. I know you hate to hear that, but I am. Why are you really here?"

Was she seriously trying to tell me what I felt? "I'm here for your pain. No… no, I'm not even sure you're going to make it through the night. Maybe I'm here for your soul. You won't be able to stop me from taking it. I've got to get to Purgatory. I mean it!" My desperation couldn't have been more real, but even to me that sounded like a crazy lie.

"Please sit down," Coo said gently, patting the other end of the bed. "I'd like to help you. You know I've always wanted to help you, but you didn't want anything I could give. Tonight I feel like you do."

Brimstone and quicksilver, she talked like a damned other. Well, except the others don't understand or care about you. Coo talked in riddles because she did both. I took a few steps closer. I didn't sit down, but I grabbed the metalwork at the foot of her bed, mostly so that my hands wouldn't tremble.

"If Purgatory can't help me-" She was right, damn her. It couldn't help me. It didn't last time, did it? "I don't know what can. I don't know what's different. I'm not dying, like you, but I swear I'm not alive anymore."

She thought about that. "You don't know what's different. Alright. Do you know what happened?"

This was why the other doves thought Coo was holy. Not because she'd pray morning noon and night if she had the chance, and didn't have the chance because she could always find something to do for someone else. It was because when you talked to her, she would worm her way in, gently and slowly; help you when you didn't want to be helped. It usually drove me crazy. Now I was wondering if she'd just saved my life.

"I know exactly what happened. The whisperers told me about the Baron's girl, Hind. Something's wrong with her, or right with her. I don't know. I kissed her to get her pain, and when I tasted it, it made me feel things that won't go away."

Coo looked thoughtful, in that deep and reflective way she does. I could see the shadows of her death dropping away from her. All that was important to her now was my pain and Hind's. I couldn't tell them apart anymore.

"Sister Hind has many pains, brother. If you met her during the day you would learn more of them. It is true that she doesn't suffer quite like the other donkeys do. I must confess to you, brother Jinx, some of my pain comes from her. She has learned the lessons I always thought children became donkeys to learn. In doing so she has taught me doubt, because God has not rewarded her. She hasn't passed on to salvation, or learned the peace that I feel following the plan he has for me. Abandoning her sin has made her suffer more. On reflection, I think the pain you share with her is loneliness. Who do you have, Jinx? You have me, but until tonight you've never let me help you. Who else is there? – Jinx? Brother, where are you going?"

I was climbing out the window, of course. "Don't worry. I know exactly what I need now." And I did. She hadn't quite gotten it, but she'd been close. Very close. Of course, she was upset. I think I heard her trying to argue with me from the window, but I was too far away. I didn't need to hear it. Coo and I had never agreed about anything ever anyway.

But now I knew what I needed, and I knew where I was going. I raced across the rooftops. I was focused. I trembled slightly, but it was mostly excitement, and I could think again because I wasn't fighting with myself. It took me hardly any time to find the Baron's mansion. It wasn't even all that far from the church. I remembered where the room was. I figured out that the window was barred pretty quickly and I didn't think I could get through them, but that was fine. There were other windows, and the humans inside couldn't see me.

Nobody saw me as I carefully opened the door to Hind's bedroom. I would swear there were even more clothes around than before, fresh gift boxes from wherever humans buy fancy clothes for young girls. Hind was still wearing one, in bed, fully clothed. On the table beside her was a bottle. I couldn't quite make out the label, but I didn't have to. She'd drunk a lot. That wasn't the same as if she'd been human. For a Wild Child, it would just help her sleep. Still, it was clear that she hurt, maybe more than before.

I could help her with that. I could take away the pain for a little while. Maybe I could keep taking it away, until she didn't hurt so much. Maybe I could save her, and she could save me. I was excited enough to think a lot of silly things as I bent over her and kissed her.

Her lips were just as I remembered them. Her mouth opened, and I didn't taste alcohol. I tasted the pain that slipped from her mouth into mine. It wasn't as vivid as last time, exactly. I didn't see anything. But I felt the same ache she did, and I didn't have to try and put a name to it anymore. I just let it drift over me. We felt it together. It faded away slowly until it was just a taste, a little hard ball of sweet and sour, strange and painful and wonderful. And only when the feeling was gone completely did I break the kiss.

She'd be blurry when she woke up, but she wouldn't hurt so much. I felt the same way. But I was recovering my senses and I didn't feel like I was alone. At least, it didn't nag at me anymore. It was just something faint and distant. I put the ball of pain in a pocket. I didn't want to use it all up. Maybe I would sell it, and Hind could save me in more ways than one. Maybe I would eat it myself, find somewhere quiet and suck on it and think of the girl who could feel this way. I spent a little time staring at her face, and it really did seem more peaceful now. I couldn't stay. I'm not quite invisible, and dawn would come eventually. It was just dangerous to linger.

I did wonder if what I'd done was best for her. I felt better than I had since I'd first caught that Donkey Boy's soul. I felt better than I'd felt before that, even. I'd needed this, but if it hurt her it really wasn't worth it. I was pretty sure I was helping both of us. We had both been losing our battle with this pain.

That was why I didn't go back the next day. There are a fair number of Donkey Children in the city, and I knew where most of them lived. The whisperers would tell me when a new one was brought in or when an old one died or left. No children ever became donkeys in the city, interestingly. The whisperers love to talk about transformations, but there'd be years between them and the only descriptions that made sense were doves.

The thing was, life was rarely good for Donkey Children. They couldn't make it on their own somehow. They never succeeded in running away, and almost never tried. Humans just kept them as property, and the donkeys put up with it. Not many of them liked it though, and there were times when a donkey would hurt, over and over, for a long time. Even if I harvested their pain there'd be more the next day, and the next day after that. Life wasn't good for donkeys, and for some of them it was worse.

So a long time ago I would pick one of the most suffering donkeys and keep going back to them, taking their pain every night. It was very profitable, but I found out it was very bad for them. Take someone's pain once, and their memory of the pain gets muddled and they're a little groggy for a while. Do it every day, and very soon they stop feeling pain, or anything else, at all. As bad as these children were hurting I might have prevented a couple of suicides, but it didn't do them much good when their life consisted of stumbling around in a daze, not noticing or caring if they were yelled at or struck or hugged or fed. I'd get a lot of pain in a short time, but overall it didn't do me much good, and I didn't like seeing what they became.

I sure as Hell wasn't going to do that to Hind, even if Hell was where I ended up because of it.

I thought I'd spend the next night hunting like usual, but I ended up spending it sitting on the rooftops looking at the stars, wondering what the things I saw around me were and how many of them humans could see. I wondered if I could ever explain them to Hind, or even if I'd get the chance. I just thought a lot, about everything. Seeing the children I take pain from was a grim task sometimes, and I didn't want any grim tasks that night. I felt at peace, just a little, and I wanted to enjoy it.

The next night I didn't feel at peace. I knew what it meant now. It meant I wanted to see her. It was too soon, though, and I was determined not to hurt her. I could go see Coo, but I could just imagine what a disaster that would be. Everything was a sin to her, and I didn't want to hear about how what I wanted was wrong. But I just got more and more antsy, and because it was the summer I'd already been up for hours before darkness fell. Around midnight I headed to the Baron's. I wouldn't take Hind's pain. Maybe it would be enough just to look at her. It was a little creepy, and Coo would have a fit about it, but I'm a black cat. Everything I do is creepy and everything I do made Coo have a fit. I had my own life to lead and, as soon as I got over the shock of all this, my own salvation to seek, on my own terms.

I knew the way now. The room I used to get in last time was brightly lit, but it was a mansion and there were windows everywhere. At midnight I could cling to a wall like a gecko and find another one. All I had to do was slink down a dimly lit hallway and ease my way into Hind's room.

Which was lit. She was awake, standing next to a mirror, doing something with her hair and singing quietly, and I didn't recognize the words or even the language, so it was probably from an opera. I could feel tears forming in my eyes and I couldn't remember the last time I'd cried. I hadn't even thought about what her voice would be like, but it was beautiful. I didn't want to wrestle the tears down though, because then I'd start thinking about the underwear she was wearing.

I didn't want to leave, and that was what got me. I hesitated, and hesitated too long, because black cats have reflections like anybody else. She saw me in the mirror and turned around, and she didn't seem to be embarrassed or frightened at all. She just told me quietly, "I haven't seen another Wild Child in a while. Where did you come from? What kind are you? You look like a cat. Are there really Cat Children? Oh, and please forgive me – what's your name? I didn't ask, because you seem very familiar for some reason."

I panicked. I'd like to say it was because this was dangerous and it was getting very, very likely some human would discover me, but when you panic you don't necessarily know why, right? I had to stop her talking, and I couldn't leave. None of that makes sense, but I wasn't thinking clearly. I just rushed right over to her and grabbed her arms and kissed her.

She didn't look afraid for even a moment. Mostly she looked a little sad, a little distracted, and I knew she was in enough pain she was hardly thinking about me anyway, and of course by the time she knew what I was doing she was slipping into that fog they go into when I steal from them. I really felt like I was stealing from her this time. It was too soon, and I could hurt her, but if I stopped now she'd remember everything, and I wanted it so bad.

A ball of pain slid from her mouth into mine. It wasn't any smaller than last time, but it tasted different. It wasn't the ache I'd expected, that feeling of having no one, not really. I hardly understood it. There was a sense of failure, not that she'd done anything wrong but everything wrong. Not everything, no. But when she did something right it was something that hurt her anyway. There were layers and layers and layers, and some of them felt familiar to me and some of them didn't, and before long I couldn't really feel them, just taste them like the strangest, most flavorful candy I'd ever had. I held it in my mouth for a while. I'd expected to share my ache with her, but I hadn't. But I still felt a lot better. This was wonderful. I'd gotten to see her awake and hear her voice too, but feeling what she felt for a few moments was better. Like Purgatory, it hurt, but I liked it.

She couldn't stand up on her own. Trying to ignore how close she was, to worry instead about if I'd hurt her, I walked her over to a chair and sat her down, and she seemed able to handle that. She'd recover. She was just a little more dazed than usual. It takes a lot more than being harvested twice in three days to hurt someone. And I felt so good, because looking at her I knew so much more about her. Not the details, what she did or what she thought, but how she felt.

I really, really had to get out of there fast. I ran for it. I didn't even take the pain out of my mouth until I was on top of the garden wall.

I never actually sold it. Selling Hind's pain to remove my sin would mean I was preying on her, or at least that's how it felt. I managed to not eat it, either. I just kept it close to me, and I avoided the Weaver's shop in case I was tempted. You never get to find out how much sin you have. The Weaver could measure it, but not in any terms that made any sense to me. I knew what kind of person I was, though, and that you didn't get turned into a cat for doing anything good. I had a lot to burn away.

I was able to think about things like that again for the rest of the night. I thought about going and selling the pain I'd gathered from the other children, but it would keep. It never went bad. I had places I hid things and I put it away there, but I kept Hind's pain with me, two spheres of complex, bitter-sweet emotion. There would be time enough to worry about my soul once I'd gotten to grips with what I wanted from life now.

That was the way I was thinking when I curled up and fell asleep at dawn. And that night, when it got very, very dark, I went back to the Baron's again. I didn't think about it. I would swear I didn't think anything. I just started heading that way, and I didn't have any words for what I was feeling. Not even as I snuck into her bedroom and saw her asleep on her bed, looking peaceful tonight, and lowered my face to hers.

Her peace was a lie. The pain that rose up from her mouth to mine was bigger than before. Most of it was loneliness again, and I understood it so well, having what you wanted right here in front of you and not getting it. I was kissing her right now, and she didn't know who I was or what I was doing. She probably didn't remember the night before.

When I realized all that, I realized what I'd just done. It was too soon. I didn't know what she'd be like in the morning. She would recover, but that wasn't the point. It was way, way too soon, and if I'd done this tonight I'd do it again. I was okay with taking her pain occasionally to ease mine for years. It might even be good for her, because she certainly wasn't happy. She was having a hard time dealing with it without my taking the pressure off. But if I did this again and again every night or two nights or three nights I wasn't sure exactly what would happen to her, but I was sure it would be bad, and it wouldn't take long.

I was serious about this. I wasn't sure what I was doing, or what the point was, but if I hurt her there was no point at all, even if I still saved myself. I had to take temptation away from myself.

The next night, as soon as it was dark, I went to the whisperers. I walked down a dark street until the voices started, until the walls were covered with shifting shadows that hinted at faces. I kept walking until I was good and deep and couldn't get out quickly if I lost control for a moment. I sat down against a wall, and I listened.

Time doesn't pass right where the whisperers are. If I sat here long enough days would pass, and listening to the secrets of people you'll never meet is an excellent distraction. It would let me cool off. I needed control, and the first step was to stop myself when I'd lost it.

It worked perfectly. The danger was that eventually it would stop being safe, but the whisperers would warn me. This time that was just what I was going to do, hang around until the whisperers started talking about what might find me. That might take weeks, plenty of time for Hind to recover, and hopefully I'd have learned a little patience.

I don't know how long it was. It was a long time. Days, at least. Sometimes I'd ask about Hind or Coo, and the whisperers would tell me that Hind was getting new shoes, but the cobbler didn't want to make them for a Wild Girl, only he was afraid of the Baron. Or they'd tell me that Coo had snuck out of her nest and visited some Donkey Child, partly because she thought her time would be very soon and wanted to help who she could first, but mostly because she was looking for me. Or they'd prattle about horns and "no one waiting endlessly in the dark" instead.

But then I asked again, "Tell me about Hind. How is she doing?"

And I heard, "Atropos sharpens her scissors. Baron, Black Cat, Bird of Fire, prepare your mourning veils."

And "A good deed never goes unpunished. Deer girl, Donkey Girl, princess of slaves, that will be your final lesson."

There was more, but there didn't need to be. Even for prophetic gobbledygook it was entirely clear. "How long does she have? What's going to happen?" I demanded.

"The end is not the final moment. It has its own beginning. The judgment of fate is already decided. The judgment of man looms."

"The child has given life to the child, and adults will take a life in exchange. Blame circles her like a vulture. There is no other prey to be had. Soon, she will be meat."

"Grieve, Baron. Your shield is pierced, and the child in your lap will take the blow for you instead. She has brought this on herself, but you will pay with sorrow while she pays with blood."

This was getting worse by the second. "What did she do?" My voice was getting screechy. My heart was racing and my ears were flat on either side, but I still didn't know what was going on.

"Two birds fled their cages. Both were named for their voices. The Hind that remained held the key. She prayed that her crime would be forgotten, but men listen to hate before Heaven. They know, and she will be punished. Her pretty face will stare blindly from a rubbish heap as the Baron buries her body."

Right. Coo had been caught and gotten free. It was the Baron's house, and Hind must have done it. And she'd helped someone else escape, too. I didn't know how long ago that had been, but it must have been a while. Someone still remembered? I didn't have to ask that. I'd just been told. Someone still remembered, and the blame had come back to Hind.

Beheading. The image of Hind's head staring- I was not going to think about that. Not if I could act.

"How long? You have to tell me how long!"

"Run. Run, and you have a chance. A black cat can get there faster, but a boy can get there in time. But both will get there too late. The headsman can be averted. Destiny cannot."

The Hell it couldn't. I ran. I could feel something watching me, and I prayed it was just the whisperers or my imagination, but caution could go to Hell, too.

I'd gone in too deep, and it took too long to get out, and when I started approaching the end I could see the entrance to the alley. It was bright, way too bright. It was daytime, and this just got a lot harder and a lot more dangerous. Humans keep Donkey Children as slaves. What they do to the rest of us is a lot worse. The Hell with that. I couldn't climb the damn wall!

I was thinking a mile a minute. It was a dark alley, that was why I chose it. I went back, I focused on the darkness, although there wasn't enough of it. Don't go in, just retreat until you can hardly tell it's daytime. My claws were working. It was a struggle, especially the overhang, but I got onto the rooftop.

It was bright sunlight up here, the middle of the afternoon, but you didn't see many humans on the roofs, and I knew all the bridges and highways and I certainly knew where the Baron's house was. I ran, boiling in the summer heat, and after a while my chest hurt from running so fast. When I got to the Baron's estate I leaped from the rooftop, just caught the top of the garden wall with my foot, and leaped forward again. I hit the ground on all fours, but rolled. I was enough of a cat even in the day that I didn't hurt myself. I found out I was still an excellent climber, too. Vines, windowpanes, deep bricks – there were enough handholds to make it to the balcony I remembered from my first visit. It led to a bedroom, and like most bedrooms it was empty during the day. Then I was out in the hall, and I hadn't been noticed yet.

The whisperers hadn't been kidding. Destiny was involved. There were omens everywhere, lines threading the walls. It meant I didn't have to search. I just followed them. I followed them at a run. Servants saw me and some of them yelled, but they didn't know what was going on and they didn't chase me. Up some stairs and around a few corners and I was looking at Hind's back as she leaned against a wall by a closed door. I thought she must be listening to what was being said inside. I could hear voices from here.

Even at noon I walk like a cat. I had to tug gently on her sleeve, which was the poufiest thing I'd ever seen.

She turned around, and again she wasn't surprised to see me, or at least she wasn't scared. She was curious and, well, maybe a little surprised, but not much. She even curtseyed. Earrings, laces, ribbons, the faintest dusting of rouge. I was finally getting to meet her and I had no time to stare. No time to meet her, either.

She snapped me out of it by saying, "I'm sure you look familiar, but I've never met a Wild Child like you. What's your name? You can call me Hind, but-" and she hesitated a second, and looked more worried, "You should go. My Master might let you escape, but his friends are all here and they have guards around, too. It's not safe for you."

"It's not safe for you either." I was gasping for breath. "They're going to kill you, Hind. And my name's Jinx." She didn't laugh, probably didn't see any reason to. We all have stupid names, and things were too serious.

She also wasn't surprised. "I know. I don't know how you know. They don't know it was me, but I'm the only suspect. Any judge would find me guilty because of who I am, and there's not going to be a judge. The Archbishop is demanding it, and everyone agrees with him. I'm going to confess. My Master can't save me, and if I don't give him the chance to try I can save him a lot of trouble."

I grabbed her by the shoulders and shoved her against the wall, yelling, "What are you thinking?"

She was so calm. I guess she felt nothing could make things worse. "What are you doing?" She was still trying to whisper.

I had to stop her from talking, and I had a really great way to do that. I took the pain I'd collected from her out of my pocket and pushed them all into her mouth at once. "These are yours. I shouldn't have taken them."

The taste of them stunned her. She was probably remembering things, getting emotions and pain back she'd forgotten. I didn't like it, but they were hers. I'd been indulging myself taking them. It was time to make up for that. The door was starting to open, and adults were saying loud things.

I yelled at Hind, still holding her to the wall, "Are you stupid? You're letting them think you did it! You don't even know me! Why would you do that? You're going to let them execute you because I stole Coo from a birdcage?!"

The door was open. There were men, adults, grown men, some of them old, watching us. They'd heard every word and they'd gotten a good look at me, a scruffy Black Cat Boy. I even heard the one in the really funny hat whisper, "Demon!"

That was exactly what I wanted them to think. I turned and ran. I mostly had my breath back, and I needed it. They were yelling, everyone around me was yelling, and suddenly there were a lot more guards and a lot fewer servants – and some of the servants tried to grab me, too. So I ran. At this time of day I was just a boy, maybe twelve years old, hardly anything more. I couldn't escape an adult guard. What I was trying to do was outrun the alarm. I ducked around corners and threw myself down the stairs. Everyone knew something was wrong, but by the time they knew they were supposed to catch me I was past them. Plus, I wasn't heading where they thought I'd head. I ran right back to that bedroom and leaped off the balcony. I had a little cat in me, still. Like when I'd jumped from the wall, I landed on all fours, rolled, and I didn't hurt myself. And I was lucky. They might be closing the front gate, but there were other gates, and a servant was bringing in bags of flour through one. I was through it while he was still yelling at me, and then I was in alleys. Alleys were my territory and they were full of shadows. I got away.

After a while I realized I wasn't sure it had worked, and I had to be sure. I thought it had, and the relief I felt was so sweet I didn't want any worry gnawing at it. I couldn't go back and check, of course.

For a moment I let myself be smug. I'm a black cat. It was perfect. They don't even like regular black cats. I didn't know what humans thought about Black Cat Children exactly, but 'demon' sounded about right. They'd believe anything, anything about me. They'd forget all about Hind. I was so much more satisfying a target. Well, let the city-wide manhunt begin. I could stay in places that weren't safe for humans during the day, and at night a soldier couldn't see me if I stood right in front of him. I'd be able to visit Hind again soon. She knew who I was now. I might even be able to really talk to her. She probably remembered me kissing her now, but we could get over that. I knew her pain, and something like that wasn't bad enough to notice.

I really had to make sure it had worked.

I had a way. I could find out anything, if I could understand the answers. I was already hiding in the alleys near the mansion. I just found one that was covered over by a flimsy roof so the other end was black as pitch, and I started walking.

Eventually the walls stopped being anything I could really identify. Soon after, the whispering started. I walked a little ways further until I was surrounded by unintelligible secrets.

"Did it work? Is Hind safe?" I asked the voices.

"The church sees a demon and the state sees a beast. They light their brands and charge away on the hunt, leaving the deer behind, accusations forgotten."

That was what I wanted to hear.

"The thread of Destiny has been plucked, but will not snap. Rather, it is the thread Atropos cuts soon to be severed. The deer, the doe, the Hind hounded by the cat, the donkey soul in a girl's body, she has escaped one blade for another. Destiny will reach its conclusion, will-ye-nill-ye."

That was not what I wanted to hear. It wasn't what I wanted to hear at all.

"Baron and Cat, noble and urchin, man and boy, the treasure you prize is tarnishing because you keep it in its case and never wear it. It no longer shines in the phoenix fire. The scales are tipping, and pain is too heavy, and love weighs nothing. Tonight she will escape you both, but not her own knife."

Damnation, damnation, damnation. That was way too clear. I couldn't go back during the day. But they said 'tonight'. As soon as the sun was fully down, I would go back.

I would have thanked the whisperers, but I didn't think they'd understand. I couldn't afford to run. Destiny was walking, and I didn't want to catch its attention. I wanted to hide Hind from it.

After a while the darkness overhead was some sort of sheet of tin. The light at the end of the alley was… street lamps. It was night already. I'd been wandering in the world of the others, and they don't understand time. I had to hurry.

Fortunately, since it was dark I was much more than a boy again. I sailed over the rooftops, untiring, as fluid as a cat, leaping over gaps, black and silent and unseen under stars I'd forgotten how to read the first time my sin was burned away. There was a beautiful girl waiting to be saved. Trying to think of myself as a romantic hero kept the fear on the edge of my mind. The whisperers didn't say I could get there in time, but they talked like it hadn't happened yet.

I was over the garden wall, up the mansion wall. There were lights everywhere. It was still early, and I'd been deceived by a moonless night. It just meant I had a better chance of being in time. I picked a dimly lit room. There were people inside, but they were vague enough I couldn't tell what they were doing, so they wouldn't be sure they'd seen me, especially since I was through and slipping out the door in two beats of my pounding heart.

I could tell Hind's door by sight now. As I grabbed the handle I suddenly realized she might have locked it, but she hadn't. I was inside, standing in that peculiar dollhouse. I didn't care. I only had eyes for the occupant.

Hind was sitting on the edge of her bed. For once I barely noticed her face or how little she was wearing. I noticed the knife in her hands. It was a kitchen knife, but it was plenty sharp enough to do the job.

There was no blood. She hadn't used it yet. If she'd been about to, having a Wild Boy enter her room had distracted her for a moment. There was no sign she'd been crying, but her eyes were too bright and there was no hope or happiness in her expression.

First things first. I darted over to her like only a cat can move and I grabbed the handle of the knife, wrapping my hand around hers. We were children still, maybe, but old enough that I knew I was stronger than her. "Don't do that!" I scolded her. It was stupid, but where do you start?

"I have to." The pain in her voice was awful. It wasn't hoarse, or loud. It was worse. It was quiet because she'd given up. I thought about kissing her pain away, but what would I do tomorrow? Anyway, I didn't want to anymore. I didn't want to steal anything from her.

Alright, I was emotional too, especially as she went on. "The Baron... my Master yelled at me, Jinx." Now her voice was catching and she was starting to cry. This was worth killing herself for? But I could remember her pain, the loneliness, the sense of failure. Yes, she'd just lost all she thought she had left. "They think I'm friends with you or something. They don't think I did it, but he's been humiliated. He's so disappointed with me. I think he might send me away." That did it. Tears everywhere, but they were better than a knife. In fact, she let me pull it out of her hand. I tucked it in the back of my belt. I really didn't want her grabbing it again.

I took her hand back, and she squeezed mine hard, so I put my other hand on the side of her neck. I wasn't Coo. What could I say? "I don't know much about humans." I was trying to use that soft, gentle voice. "But they don't send their Wild Girls away. It doesn't look like he hit you. He's punished you all he's going to, Hind. I don't know him, but you do. Is he the kind of guy who would get rid of you just because you embarrassed him?"

She thought about that. This was the most important question in her life. What kind of life did she lead that her owner didn't have to punish her, she'd punish herself instead? I knew how she felt. I knew it so well it was like talking to myself, which might be the only reason I was getting anywhere. I just didn't know anything else about her.

"No," she finally answered, and I was sure I'd talked her back from the edge again. Then she burst out, "But he took away my keys!" and she threw her arms around my neck and she started really crying.

All I could do was sit next to her and let her hold me and cry. I tried to hold her, but the truth was I didn't know where was safe to touch. I wasn't embarrassed, I was just afraid I'd offend her. I did the best I could.

Finally she was able to talk again. "I'm so lonely. She left, and I've disappointed my Master, and I don't know when I'll see either of them again." Yes. This was secret-telling time. This was the heart of it. I hadn't realized it, but this was what I'd been waiting for.

"I can come see you tomorrow night. I can come see you every night, if you want." She looked at me now, and it wasn't the look I wanted, but it wasn't the one I was afraid of, either. "I know you don't know me, but it's better than being alone, isn't it? It will be okay until the Baron forgives you, or your friend comes back." I hoped I was right. I didn't know what I was talking about. I was telling her what I wanted to say.

Apparently it was what she wanted to hear. "Alright." She still sounded miserable. "You'll have to stop kissing me, though."

I couldn't have been more embarrassed, and she knew it. She didn't laugh, but she smiled. It wasn't much of a smile, but I'd done it. She'd be okay. And she kissed me. It was on the cheek, but it was better than anything I could steal from her while she was asleep. "Please come back soon. Right now I have to sleep. I have to recite tomorrow morning. I didn't think it would matter, but now it does." She realized she was rambling. She was surprised to be alive, I guess. But she got to the point. "You need to go, but…"

I knew what she meant. "I'll never leave you, Hind." It was drama. I sounded like one of the others, but it made her smile again and that's all I cared about.

I felt pretty good, in fact, as I walked down the hallway. I thought the bedroom with the balcony would be a good way to get out. I wasn't in a hurry, and at night only locked doors could really stop me.

The lights were turned down, but there were still lamps in the hallways. So I didn't notice the omens until I got to the unlit bedroom. Softly glowing lines of all colors streaked the walls. They were threads of Destiny. They were still there. Alchemists were obsessed with finding ways to see them. There were ways, but they were all useless. Even if you saw them you couldn't read them. I didn't have to, because I remembered what the whisperers had said. I might have saved Hind for tonight, but Destiny couldn't be changed. I was only pushing back her death. It would still be soon.

Nothing I could do in the world would change Destiny's plan. How long could I even keep Hind alive? Could I stop an accident? Cure a disease? Would the next attempt come during the day, or in an hour? Sometimes people just… died, with no warning, and no one knew why.

Which was why I found the nearest dark alley and started walking down it. Eventually the darkness got deeper. The walls became… just walls. The whispering started. I tried not to listen to it, to look straight into the blackness ahead of me and keep walking towards it. If I listened I'd be able to pick some of the individual whispers out from the others. One of them might be about how Hind would die next.

Eventually, to my deep gratitude, they went quiet. The darkness ahead of me never seemed to move, but it was closer. It was watching me, but I was pretty sure it had been watching me already.

"Go back, Jinx. You don't want to do this."

It was a whisperer. They don't speak to you directly. They'd never called me by my name. It was still a whisperer. Whisperers know everything, and the others never lie.

So there was no use in denying it. "No, I don't. But I have to."

"Don't do this, Jinx. Come back to us. You don't know what you're doing."

"Will it save her?" I asked. My voice was tight. It was the only question that mattered.

"Destiny says no." The whispers were all a little different. There were many of them, following me I supposed.

But they hadn't actually said no. "I'm here to change Destiny anyway." I kept walking.

"This is suicide, Jinx," one whispered. "If you turn back now it won't save you, but you'll live much longer," whispered another. "Why are you doing this?"

They wouldn't shut up. "You're playing the hero, Jinx. You're hoping to redeem yourself."

That rankled. "No, I'm not. I want to save her." Talking to them wouldn't hurt more than ignoring them.

"We can see your heart, Jinx. We can see your soul. You've cared only for yourself. You refuse to do what is right if you can find an easy way. You hurt people all the time. You want to save her because you hope she'll love you."

They can't lie. "I also want to save her just to save her. I'm not going to live through this anyway, am I?"

"No. It's too late."

She would never be mine. Even if she lived, I'd be dead. And how do you stop Destiny? I stopped for a moment. Then I kept walking.

"You're not a hero, Jinx," they whispered. "You've been taking advantage of her."

"Then maybe I'll make up for that." I wanted to yell at them to shut up, but they wouldn't. Anyway, I was deep, deeper than I'd ever been before. In a place like this I might not be able to pass if I didn't answer.

"No, you won't," one whispered. "If you die now, salvation is beyond you. You're telling yourself you're doing this because your motives are pure, but it's a lie. You've added a new virtue to your heart, Jinx, but you've added a new sin as well."

"When you think about her, Jinx, what do you think of? You're thinking of her lips."

"Now you're thinking of her skin."

"Now you're thinking about the first time you saw her, the shape of her under a sheet."

The rest of the conversation you don't get to hear. Not you, not anyone, ever. That is, until one of them whispered, "Keep going, Jinx. It's too late to turn back now. We'll miss you."

That was the last thing they said to me, and the darkness was right in front of me, and I stepped into it and kept walking.

It was, not surprisingly, dark. It was a relief to get away from the whisperers. Coo said I was drowning in dreams. I was under the surface now, beyond the others. Nothing from an alchemy book would save me, but fairy tales might.

I was thinking wrong. Nothing would save me. All I wanted was to save Hind. No matter what kind of person I was, or why I was doing it.

So I ran. Fairy tales are about urgency, emotion. Willpower wins the day, and you only win by proving how badly you want it. Running was a good start, as hard and as fast as I could. I could see walls around me again, although they were much farther apart. I could make out that they were there, but not much more. It meant there was only one direction to run.

Until, ahead of me, something loomed. A wall, with a gate hung with a massive guillotine blade at the top. Above it was a face. I kept running, and as I drew near it boomed, "Those who pass must-" It didn't get any further because I kept running, ran even faster. It was going to ask me a riddle, and I didn't give it a chance. The blade slammed down, but it slammed down behind me.

After that I ran through cobwebs, faint strands that brushed across me. Annoying, but they weren't going to stop me, although they clung to my whiskers. I couldn't remember ever having whiskers, but I kept running rather than worry about it. I could see, up ahead but off to one side, an oversized but ornate pair of scales. Those were for the dead. They were no use to me, yet. The cobwebs were getting thicker, but I kept running, and as I passed the scales something leapt out at me.

I'll do the best I can to describe it. It made me wonder in the back of my head where I'd lived when I was human, because it had the head of a crocodile and its body looked like a hippopotamus, and I recognized both. Except that was just the beginning. Parts of it were hairy, or scaly. It was just the biggest, ugliest thing I'd ever seen, and those crocodile teeth were snapping, trying to bite me.

They were snapping behind me, though. Now I was glad I was running. It charged after me, but it was too ungainly, too misshapen to catch up. The strands of cobweb kept getting thicker, snapping as I passed through them, but it was no time to slow down and running had served me so far.

Until one of the strands didn't snap, catching me in the ankle and throwing me onto my face. Except I was a cat. I caught myself on all fours and was up and running again in an eye blink. It was harder now. I had to watch for the strands, duck or jump to keep from running into them, sometimes grab them so I could leap over. This was nothing a cat couldn't handle, and I could see black fur on my arms and legs to prove it now.

The thing fell farther behind and disappeared. The cobwebs thinned again, although they were still annoying. I kept a watchful eye anyway, and was rewarded for it. Every now and then one would be thicker, and I'd have to avoid it rather than break it.

Something else was up ahead. I saw a little pool of grey light, with an old man in it scribbling in a huge book. I knew this one. The book was full of names. Whether they were the names of the living or the dead, it wouldn't matter. If I found Hind's name, scratching it out wouldn't help either way. I was a cat, and it was probably a trap of curiosity, so I kept running and nothing happened at all.

How long was this hall? Why was it full of spider webs? I kept running. I didn't feel like I had done anything, but I wasn't trying to find Destiny. I was inside it. It was going to end badly somehow because that is what Destiny is about, but I would see my way through to the end.

That end was up ahead. Another pool of light, so faint that it could hardly be called such. The cobwebs were a net, too tangled to consider running through, too thick for me to hope to break, but I wasn't supposed to break it. That's what the old woman was for, sitting in a chair much too big for her, with a pair of scissors too big to even be called shears spread around one of the threads.

I stopped running. I'd arrived, and there was no point anymore. I was suddenly winded, although I'd been running fine for hours, if time meant anything in this place. Which it didn't.

"Atropos." I panted. "The whisperers mentioned you. I didn't think I'd see you in person."

"You are and you aren't, kitten." I stepped closer. She looked old, older than anything ever, gaunt and a labyrinth of wrinkles, and her smile was not friendly at all. "Nothing is what it seems through your eyes. You should know that."

I was gritting my teeth, but if I got too angry I might mess this up. This had to be the edge, the final gambit. "Then are you going to tell me that's not the thread of Hind's life, or that you're not going to cut it?"

"Oh no, this is definitely the thread of her life. I'm just waiting for the proper moment. Soon, now. You're not there to delay things anymore, after all."

That might be my clue. "You won't cut it until the right moment, will you? You can't cut it until then."

She smiled wider. "That's right, dear. The moment can't be stopped, but it can't be hurried either."

Then I had time, but not enough to waste. I leapt on the old woman, grabbing her hand, grabbing the scissors. I couldn't budge them. Her arm was immovable. My claws were out, and they wouldn't catch on her either.

She kept smiling, and now I realized how cruel that smile was. She knew what I would try, and that I would fail. "Sorry, dear. A little kitten like you can't hope to budge me. Or will you try to jam my scissors next?"

Another clue. It was a legend, a fairy tale, a children's story. They had to give me clues. I had to jam the scissors. I had nothing to jam them with. No... I had Hind's knife. It was still in my belt for some reason. I pulled it out, and then I threw it away. That was wrong. If I wanted to save Hind I had to prove how badly I wanted it. And let's face it, I wasn't getting out of here anyway.

I shoved one arm into the angle of the scissors and nearly cut myself open. They were sharp! My neck would have been more dramatic, but I knew it didn't make the slightest bit of difference. I did use my other hand to gently pull Hind's thread out of the path of the blades, just in case. The old woman let me. She had her sacrifice.

"Are you sure of this, dear? You're changing her story, and yours. Destiny won't like it. It will be a very bad end. This is one dream you don't want to wake up from." She actually seemed concerned.

I didn't say anything. I waited, and after a while I heard the scissors close, and I woke up.

I kind of woke up. I was already awake, really, but I'd been out of it from exhaustion, stumbling along automatically as I was pushed forward. I couldn't sleep anyway. Every inch of me hurt. I was bleeding around the edges of the shackles, and the ones on my ankles made it hard to walk. There were sharp twinges among the aches. They'd hit me too hard, but it wouldn't matter soon. I could see the machine, and the blade, up ahead. The collar was so heavy I could barely stay upright, and I was dirty, and I'd been drooling, and there was nothing I could do about it.

I could only feel the base of my tail. I didn't want to look back and see why. The guard shoving me along probably wouldn't let me, and the collar wouldn't let me turn my head.

They locked my hands and feet into place before taking off the collar. They had to, of course. Then they locked down my neck, but there was still that slot for the blade. I was almost looking forward to it, but... Hell. I was not looking forward to that.

115

I was too weak to struggle, but I felt a rush of gratitude when the priest stepped forward. The whole point of last rites was that anyone could be forgiven. Instead he started reciting a prayer to exorcise demons and send them back to Hell. I sagged in the stocks. Even my ears drooped. I had no hope or strength to resist anymore.

I could hear the blade drop.

God, it hurt!

I woke up again, and like the last time it was as if I'd already been awake. It looked like a dream. I was in a huge room made of copper, with strange machinery moving around in it. Some of it was familiar, as familiar as the jet black figure in the mask behind the desk. The Weaver of Pain. I was sitting in front of him in a chair made of copper, and just a little farther away was Coo, sitting in another chair. She said nothing at first, just watched me with those sad, orange eyes.

I had to know. "Where am I? Aren't I dead? I traded my death for Hind's."

"Yes you did, my errant night cat, and the trade was accepted. You are dead. Very, very dead. It is time for judgment, and I am your judge."

The idea was horrible, and although the voice was new and strange, the way it spoke was not. This really was the Weaver. "I don't want you as my judge!"

"That's not your decision to make, poppet. You are a very, very bad boy. You don't deserve an angel." A new voice, but this one was no more human than the last, slow and slurred.

I was silent for a moment. There was no point in arguing. I knew how this would go. There was one thing that really made no sense, though. I gestured hesitantly at Coo. "What's she doing here?"

The Weaver folded his hands. He had more than I remembered, even. "She insisted. It's not usual, but she demanded the right to argue your case."

And Coo spoke up. "He gave his life for someone else. Deliberately, knowing the consequences. He has earned salvation with that alone."

"He had considerable personal reasons to do it," countered the Weaver. I could only describe its voice as 'oily'.

"That makes it better. He was acting, not just dispassionately, but because he'd learned to care about others more than himself." She looked at me for a moment and gave me a small, wry smile. "Finally. I'm so proud of you, brother. I won't let you fall."

That was the Weaver, and this was definitely Coo. She looked so frail and weak, but there was an energy in her I couldn't remember. She was determined to save me. That was useless. I knew what kind of person I was.

"You don't make that decision, sister Coo," the Weaver reminded her firmly. "His sins are many. Do you expect one noble action to repay a lifetime of hurting others for his own needs?"

"I expect anyone to be saved if they were a good person at the time they were judged, no matter what kind of person they started out as," she returned. It was like a debate among scholars, except I was at stake. I hadn't the slightest idea what to say.

"A good person? The sin he was cursed for is still on his soul. He never learned the lesson he was made a cat for. If anything, he got worse."

"Then make him a dove," Coo told him gravely. "Give him to me. Let him earn redemption another way. If he can't cancel out his sin he'll become a better person in other ways, until his flaw drowns in his virtues. He can do it."

The Weaver was silent for a moment. Its mask turned to me, and the voice it used was gentle, affectionate, but authoritarian, like a beloved father. Not that I remembered mine. "What about you, Jinx? What do you want?"

I was surprised. "Do I get to choose?"

"You get to ask."

I didn't have to think. I wasn't sure I could. I didn't hurt any more, but I'd been through so much there was only one thing left to me. "I don't want to go back. Coo is wrong. I can't get any better than I am. Just let me wait here until Hind comes for judgment, and I'll go with her wherever. That's all I want."

"No," the Weaver told me sternly. "Thanks to you, Hind's lifespan is still undecided. It might be a hundred years before she passes to judgment. She will not be the girl you want to be with now. You won't even recognize her."

"Then let him come back with me." Coo was so firm about this, and I didn't know why. "He won't be with her like he wants, but he'll grow as she grows, and they won't be apart. When she passes, if they want to be together, it can be decided then."

"I don't give out extra lives, sister." The Weaver's hands were laid flat on the desk. If he hadn't been so strange looking it might have looked final. "In any case, my judgment is made. Are you ready to face your fate, Cat Child?"

117

I started to hang my head, but I remembered that whatever happened, Hind would live. "Yes. I'm ready for Hell."

And the Weaver laughed. "That's touching, my star struck kitten, but it isn't what I decided on."

It was very, very late at night. It had to be. She rarely got to bed early. It was a different room, with a locked door, but it didn't lack for luxury and there were fresh roses in vases everywhere. Hind slept in her new bed, drifting in the dreams of her sadness but not drowning in them.

A new room meant a new window, one that wasn't barred. The dove fluttered down from the clouded night sky and perched on the edge with grace no adult could hope for. Spindly arms had to work to pull up the sash, but she did, and folding her wings she squeezed inside.

She didn't want to wake Hind. That would spoil things. Tiptoeing up to the edge of the bed she reached out and laid a stuffed black cat toy in the crook of the Donkey Girl's arm. Immediately Hind rolled over, squeezing it against herself.

Just faintly, still sleeping, Hind smiled, and Coo squeezed back out of the window and flew away.

ACT III

FALLING FROM GRACE

It's much easier to be wise and patient and reasonable if it doesn't involve you. I never believed that I would live forever, because Wild Children pass like humans do. I think we often live slightly longer, but in the end God claims us like he does those girls and boys who are allowed to grow up. I look the same as I did when I was eight years old, at least after I was reborn as a dove. I have lost a little weight lately, but the truth is there was never much to lose. I knew, though, even as the years passed and I stayed the same, that those years were not limitless. I always lost track of the time, and I couldn't tell you even now the Lord's year that I was born or what this year is without asking a human. But I knew, now, that there was more sand in the bottom of my hourglass than the top.

And then came the day I couldn't fly. My wings wouldn't lift me, and I knew the end was getting close. Later I regained my strength, but I have fallen from the air twice since then, and only good fortune and my own tiny frame have prevented me from passing on by accident. Later, I wished I had. I would have died without doubts. The fear had hardly begun to touch me then.

Soon, although I couldn't tell you how soon, I began to lose my strength. My brothers and sisters made me sleep in a proper bed and would entreat me to stay in our nest rather than go out and do the dangerous work of ministering. Ministering. What a cruel joke that is. You see? Doubt. When I became weak I realized that just because I knew I would die didn't mean I wasn't afraid. The door was opened for doubt.

Until one morning I awoke, in a bed I didn't ask for in a room all alone, and I went to the window to watch the sunrise and I realized that I felt light and strong. The weakness had gone from me, and I had energy again. I knew that for a lie. The candle that burns brightest burns fastest. How long did I have? Days? A few weeks? No longer than that. It would be over very, very soon. The sunrise was considerably less beautiful.

Unlike humans or even most Wild Children, I had ways of being certain, or at least more certain. We are all different, marked according to our sins and virtues with the traits of the human child we were and the animal we needed to be. I had feathers here and there, yes, but the big changes were the wings on my back and the eyes of a bird. The wings were my blessing, because to fly is to feel like you are part of Heaven. The eyes were my curse. They are ugly, yes, but I was never terribly concerned with beauty because I had no use for it and never had enough to learn to value it. The curse was that they let me see things that I was not meant to see and still could not understand. The dreams of humanity walk the streets with them, and not all demons are bound in Hell. I have watched a spider the size of a coin weave a web across a busy street in maddening colors, insubstantial as mist except to the horse that got caught in it, which threw its master and fell on him. I watched the poor man die in agony and a Reaper come for him, because there could be no purpose for the spectacle other than God wanting me to understand the importance of my curse.

I was a fool then to think I understood what I saw. Understanding or not, I see, and all I had to do was find a mirror and look in it and there would be some hint of the truth.

But this morning I didn't go find a mirror. Instead I pretended to watch the sunrise and wondered if I knew anything about what God wanted at all. But since the day I rose from death as a Dove Child I have not been so weak as to let my fear paralyze me completely. What I needed was not more dream images to make me dwell on mortality. I needed confession and reassurance and to be shown the error of my fears, so I went out into the chapel where I expected I would find Egg.

My name is Coo. When Wild Children are reborn we do not keep our old names. Soon we cannot remember what our human name was. Humans think they give us our new names, but the names are always the same, some random and paltry word to link us to what we've become. But since the angels sent me back I had been Coo, and at the end I lived in the Holy Empire's capital in the very attics of the church of the Abbey of the Monks of St. Francis The Kind. I had spent many years helping lost children pass through death to find a new way as Wild Children, and the half a dozen doves that resulted were my brothers and sisters and thought of me as their leader. We were now, as far as I knew, the only Wild Children left in the city who were free. The rest were donkeys, living as slaves to the humans. That was one of the things I needed to talk to Egg about.

Egg was one of my sisters, and I thought she was the true leader. I gave advice and comfort. I knew the secrets of rebirth which I would let pass into the final grave with me. They thought I was wise because I was good at spotting lies and asking questions until someone saw the truth. Egg was as good a person as I was, and could make sure that everyone ate and keep track of where the most abused donkeys were and hear the talk of the city so that we did not become isolated in our bower.

She was in the chapel, praying as I had expected her to be. We never slept by any predictable pattern and if you were awake at dawn it was a good time to express your thanks to God for a new day. I knelt beside her before the altar then, but I knew I would not be able to pray on my own and I had no intention of deceiving either her or God by pretending.

"Sister, may I have your benediction?" I asked her gently. "I have a need to confess."

She smiled, and she touched my shoulder with the warmth and love that I expect from Egg. She was a very good person. "What sins could you of all children have to confess, sister Coo?" It was a joke, of course. I, like everyone, sin.

It wasn't enough of a joke.

"The sin of Doubt, sister," I told her, pressing my head into her arm. I needed to be supported for a little while. "My time is almost upon me. I have been wrong about too many things. I was willing to let them go, to take the answers I could find and have faith in them. But now death is watching me, Egg. I can't look in a mirror because it will be there looking out from my face. If I can be wrong about anything, if I can be wrong about so many things, am I wrong about God? About what he wants from me, about the fate of my soul? I have so many failures and so few successes. Even if somehow I am doing God's work, have I done it right?"

I was babbling, letting the panic that I had concealed come out into the open so that it could be healed. I wanted to have the truth explained to me, to be shown that I, like everyone who is in their heart human, was thinking with fear rather than faith or reason. Instead Egg stroked my hair and told me, "I don't believe that, sister Coo. You are nervous like we all are, but your faith will never waiver. It was you that showed me an angel and made me realize God had a plan for me."

She had been joking before, but not really joking. I was not allowed to have deep sins. I could hear the slight edge to her voice because I was used to listening for it. Too much of what was valuable in her was built on her faith, and too much of her faith was built on me. If she thought me faithful when I died that would be the bedrock a great person was founded on.

Whether I broke her faith or not, she couldn't help me. So I did what I had to do to ensure that she, at least, was undamaged by my weakness. I smiled and touched her cheek. "Thank you, sister. I will go think about that." And I was certain she did not notice any unsteadiness in my voice, see anything wrong in my face or the way I walked as I returned to my bedroom. I had an excuse to go out, anyway. When you're the priest there is no one to hear your confession but God. My solitary prayers were drowned out by my fears, so I would seek the prayers of others and go to church. It was something I did not get to do as much as I wanted anyway.

In a city the size of the capital there are several churches. The great Cathedral of St. George is the biggest and most beautiful. From the outside it is a towering and elaborately carved mass of stone and statuary and spires and stained glass windows. I had only had peeks, but the inside was said to be just as majestic as the facade. It is the official seat of the Archbishop, the highest spiritual authority in the Empire. He clings closely to the established policy that Wild Children are creatures of sin, sadly, and I would be in great danger there. In the many smaller churches, because of that dogma, I would be similarly unwelcome. However, the second greatest church in the city is the one we nested above, the central feature of the compound of the abbey. Technically the abbey was far away, and yet this was also part of it here in the city. I had always believed I knew much about God but little about the formalities of the church. I snuck into this church seeking reassurance that I knew anything about anything.

Getting in could not have been easier. I could fly and there was a bell tower, and in moments I was sitting on a vault support, hidden by it from the nave and its worshipers, listening to the gently chanted exchanges. It was comforting at least to hear the belief of others, to drift into the ritual and let thoughts of devotion and gratitude paper over my fears. I had died once by my own hand and been given a new life and a new body and a new purpose. I could concentrate just on that for a little while.

The services in this church were mainly for the benefit of the monks, and they were long and formal and elegant, which suited me. Which meant that soon the psalms began, prayers sung in glorious public chorus rather than chanted softly or recited from a lectern. They were lovely like they always had been, and after a few minutes of listening I forgot myself and joined in.

Had I done that in any other church I would have been lucky to escape with my life. My voice is not quite human, and it has a flutter and a pitch higher than an eight year old girl's should be. So after I wandered through well-remembered verses and melodies for a while, remembering years of prayer, I realized rather with surprise that the worshipers had stopped singing entirely. It was myself and the monastery's chorus, and I was being allowed to lead.

Churches reflect sound, and I was well hidden, a little girl with her wings drawn in sitting on a large outcropping of carved stone by the ceiling. I sang, and perhaps I paid a little more attention to my voice than to prayer, but I hoped that whatever the men and women who had come here to pray thought they were listening to they heard something that inspired them. If one owner staid his hand when punishing a donkey in the city because he remembered the voice of a child who was no longer human giving thanks to God, it would be a better accomplishment than decades of helping the donkeys learn to find purpose in their suffering.

The song ended. The preacher announced the hymnal page, and that next would be The Song Of The Sheep To The Shepherd. And they waited. It was deliberately chosen, of course. It was a song of thanks from the animals to Man who had dominion over them, to remind humans that they expected kindness from their steward. It was a reminder that I wasn't human, but it was also a way for me to teach humans that they have a responsibility to love us anyway. At least, it might plant the seed of that feeling. I could hope, and I let myself sing that hope.

This song I didn't get to finish. I was not prepared, because my eyes were closed and I was trying to think about the song, to put aside my doubts and pray for everyone for a little while. I was cut off by shouting, a man's voice yelling in Latin, which I read passably but was never very good at speaking. Shouting, and the tromping of heavy boots.

I crawled up to the end of the buttress and peeked over the edge. The Archbishop was standing before the dais face to face with the Abbot. They were both old men, but the Archbishop was older, perhaps as old as me. It was impressive that he was still fit and able. Regrettably he was as bitter as he had always been.

"Blaspheme, Father, blaspheme!" He was scolding the Abbot. "You've let some demon-blooded beast lead your service. I heard it at the doorway, so don't bother to deny it."

"Certainly, if you will also concede that you really must be watching my brothers and I closely if you were able to get here so fast. It's a flattering level of interest, given that we are not technically part of your flock." The Abbot replied with all appearance of serenity.

Some men's anger makes them seem foolish. The Archbishop's pride and slowly roasting wrath were intimidating instead. "I don't have to spy on you. There are enough faithful believers in this city that one would warn me if you made a mockery of our faith like this," he growled.

Perhaps no one but me could hear the resentment in the Abbot's voice. "Then while I politely inquire as to what brought you to my door, I can remind you that within these walls it is my definition of blaspheme that matters, and I don't extend it to the miracle of an unexpected song from an angel."

That had the Archbishop's teeth bared. Did the monks or the church guards they kept at the door or the people in the pews understand as they watched this, that these two men respected each other? Did these people see how they dressed alike in the stark robes of a regular priest rather than claim the costumes of their office? I did. Yet when they disagreed on what was holy, you would have thought these two old men would come to blows.

"It does not become any member of the clergy to use that word to be offensive. I know you don't believe those monsters shaped like pigeons are angels," the Archbishop snapped.

"What else are they?" The Abbot's pretense of calmness was fraying, too. They both felt so strongly about this. My Dove Child eyes could see their passions coiling around them as physical, sometimes animal shapes in a frenzy of colors. I try to ignore such things, but as men of power and faith they were both always surrounded by specters they were unaware of. "Our clerics have spent over a millennium debating the nature of angels and Wild Children as well. When I speak to a child with wings and an absolute devotion to the Lord and all of his creations, it does remind me of the scriptures."

"They remind me of the book, too." I'd heard this from the Archbishop before, almost to the word. Now this was a show. They couldn't convince each other, but they were arguing for the crowd. That was something men of authority did. "They remind me of the serpent who was not a serpent, who lied to Adam and tempted him. She had him expelled from the Garden of Eden and her children and his mixed with the true children of Man and infected us with the blood of demons, which we must stamp out wherever we find it. Wild Children appear many times in the holy writ, and never for good."

It really was all for show now. They had argued this many times, and it was theatrics that made the Abbot pause for a moment. Or perhaps he was trying to control his anger. That was very real. "The Testament of Nod has never been accepted canon, Your Grace. I know that it has been the center of many church decisions since the passing of the Line of Peter, but it is at best a book written by a demon, and thus suspect in every fashion. There are no other clear scriptural references to Wild Children, and the more likely the reference, the more harmless it is. God has not spoken on this issue, and viewing them as a man I have never seen evil in them at all."

"And that is why they are dangerous," came the answer. This was a new tone of voice. Harsh. The Archbishop was about to add something to years of debate, and I listened with care. That a man so devoted to God's word could be so full of hate was one pillar of the doubts that constricted me. So I paid very close attention. "They show you the face of a child, recite a prayer or seem obedient and respectful to their owners. Like the serpent in the Garden they corrupt with a show of innocence. Give a good and decent man ownership of one and you will see the darkness rise up in him. Have you met a man who didn't lose virtue from close contact with one?"

The Archbishop's mouth tightened, but he went on relentlessly. "You asked why I was so near? I was renewing the seals on the laboratories of convicted alchemists. It was a stark reminder that when they truly turn away from God and seek to pervert his natural laws on Earth they immediately seek out the Wild Children. Those are the books we burn, and the laboratories we seal up without entering. They believe universally that Wild Children are the secret to immortality, and that lure turns them to the darkest sin. Think about that, Father. Think very carefully. You have judged these abominations by their words. Judge them by their acts. They are corruption. They are unnatural forces given flesh."

I wasn't disappointed that the Abbot had no reply to that and let the Archbishop leave without rebuke. It wasn't that I understood that, even if they disagreed, those two men took each other's words very seriously. Heaven forgive me, I barely thought about that at all. The alchemists thought Wild Children were the key to immortality. I felt crushed by the fear settling upon me and compelled to find out more. I knew it was wrong, and might have resisted, but also… that argument had aired so many of my doubts. Why were we changed, if it only led to our suffering and to baring the evil that humans try to overcome? Was I made what I am because of God's will, or something darker? If the alchemists knew more, then that, too, I had to find out.

So when the monks had gently dispersed the worshipers and the front doors were shut, I flew down from my perch and landed in front of the Abbot directly. I had no fear of him, but he was a man of God, and even if I no longer knew who God was he deserved my respect. So I bowed my head and asked him, "Father, is what he says about the alchemists true?"

He answered me with the gentle eyes and voice of a man filled with wonder. "It should be me bowing before you, I think. It has been many years, Coo. I am honored that you are visiting me, and more honored that you sang to us today. When I realized it was a Dove Child it made me wonder all the more if you really are angels."

I guided him back to my question. "Apparently the alchemists feel differently, Father. What do they know that we do not?"

He was silent. I am sure my question troubled him. It wasn't like me, wasn't what he expected, but I couldn't stop myself from asking. And like my brothers and sisters, he trusted me, a child he barely knew. "I'm not sure. Most of them are guessing like the rest of us, reading bits from old books or listening to stories told by villagers. Most alchemists are harmless men who merely seek a different truth. Their worst sin is thinking a clever trick can evade God's will. I suppose you have never met one, because their practice has been illegal in the capital itself since well before I was born."

He wanted to stop there, but I was silent and he had to continue. "Because of that law, when we root one out here they are the other kind. Men bent on perverting natural law in any way they can. I have heard they are fascinated with Wild Children, yes, and their obsession with immortality is well known. I don't know what secrets they have uncovered or passed down to each other. When we find a place where something that unnatural has been practiced we close it up rather than risk burning it. I don't want to know what they know."

It was hard to be delicate, to not alarm him, and sound humble and pious as I informed him, "I do not have that choice, Father. I must find out what they know about my kind, however they learned it. Do you know where these sealed off laboratories are hidden?"

And like Egg, he trusted me. I wished, so very much, that they didn't. The question troubled him, troubled him deeply, but if I asked, he knew it must be for some good purpose. "The orders and the church itself are separate, but clerks are clerks first, and priests second. One of my secretaries will have a list of the places the Archbishop visited today. A copy will be left in the bell tower in an hour. These are bad places, the workshops of very bad men. I hope that you know what you are doing, sister Coo."

"I wish that I did, Father," I told him sadly.

But he just smiled. "That kind of honesty will protect you. I will say a prayer for you, just in case."

I kissed his hand then, and an hour later there was a sheet of paper with five addresses written on it in the tower. I looked at the first one and tried to decide when would be the soonest I could go there safely. I hoped that I would find answers, learn whether I was right or wrong about my purpose on Earth. I feared that instead I would find the secret of immortality. It was not a temptation I would be able to face.

Five addresses. I only needed one. After I visited the first there was no point in visiting the others.

It turned out to be an abandoned building on the edge of the city, the kind of oversized house and garden a well-to-do man would purchase, inside the walls but not so close to the center that the cost would be impossible. There were no guards, and none needed. Signs of quarantine by the church were enough. No one would try to buy the land or break in to learn its secrets. It might have been closed due to pox, or haunted by sorcery. The latter was far too close to the truth.

It was easy to get in, then, even during the day, and I didn't wait for the shadows of night. I flew straight there in the morning, keeping low to the rooftops but taking the risk that I would be seen and tracked. Reason was quickly deserting me. As for the house itself, a window on the second floor simply fell out of its frame as I tried to open it. My dove eyes showed me no strange marks, no omens or curses or portents, but something unnatural was rotting every beam and rusting every nail unless the house was simply incomprehensibly old. The floors might well have broken underneath me if I had not been as light as a bird myself.

I paid no attention at all to the house until I found my way to the basement stairs. In an abandoned house, they were everything you might expect: dank, dim, slimy with fallen cobwebs and who knew what. My feet were a mess, but the only thing that mattered was the door ahead of me and what lay behind it. Others might think that the elaborate designs in wax seals with their connected circles and funny words were sorcery. If anything they were the opposite, diagrams of the essence of God, his aspects, forces, and servants, designed centuries ago by men who lived their lives to research scriptural mysteries and intended to imbue this door with the essence of the divine to keep out... things. The unnatural. Demons, walking dreams, and the bizarre amalgams evil men would inflict upon the world. They were also intended to keep out Wild Children, and did not. Whether they worked on anything else was a question I could not answer, because I had up until now kept all the distance I could from this aspect of the world, knowing that too much of what I would see was a lie. Now I was about to walk into the center of it.

As I hammered the stuck door open with my shoulder, breaking the flimsy seals and scattering their fragments around the floor, I wondered if there really was any difference between these seals, the madness of alchemy, or the visions that accompanied every Wild Child's transformation I had witnessed. That was how far I had fallen, so fast, and it kept me from thinking too much about immortality.

The room was everything I had been afraid it would be. A human's eyes would have hardly seen anything through dim daylight that filtered down the stairwell. My dove's eyes were a bit more sensitive in the darkness, but that wasn't the point. I see things a human can't, and this room was full of them, and that meant the alchemist who worked here had been in deep and had truly abandoned every rule of God.

It might have been decades since it had been used, and the place was still awful. Awful and strange, full of things that made no sense, like a bathtub hooked up to pipes and surrounded by the kind of strange gears and levers and mechanical systems alchemists liked. I had not wanted to tell the Abbot this, but I knew a little about what they got up to. Any machine more complicated than a clock meant that Man was trying to infringe upon the realm of God, and whatever color it was to humans, to me the metal glistened raven black. Needles and surgical equipment were laid out among the books on the desk. Skulls lined a shelf, many of them quite bizarre. Against one wall slumped a mannequin as white as bone itself. On a shelf was a bottle full of what looked like fresh blood, so boldly visible despite the gloom that I knew it would have just seemed empty to a regular human, and in a jar on the desk I could see, through the ceramic, the kind of luminous crystal sphere I believed was the heart of a child because my eyes would show them to me when things were… bad.

There was more, a lot more. Worse, there were shackles scattered in corners or hanging from the walls that I had not seen at first glance because they were entirely real. My feathers were standing up on my head as I stepped into the darkness. Whoever had worked here had been willing to do horrible things for knowledge, or money, or power. I disliked the term, but… evil. The place felt evil, from the intangible pull as I passed what must be magnets on the bathtub, to a discarded rag by the desk stained with something that glistened. Still, I walked, very carefully, around behind that desk. I had to see what the books were about. Because… there were feathers on the floor as well. Just a few, hidden in corners, white and too big to be from a real bird.

The book was in Latin like most educated men favored, even now when the vernacular was officially sanctioned. I was able to read enough to not like what I read. The page it was open to was part of a procedure of some kind, a surgical procedure, and in the margins were scribbled notes in plain language. Next to a paragraph instructing that the subject be wrapped in hot, damp cloths from head to foot tightly enough that they couldn't move was jotted 'stopped struggling after two hours'. This was ghastly, and getting worse. I half-read parts about injections, not wanting to know what they really said, but then I got confirmation. A little further down was a paragraph explaining that there would be no body left because the body of a Wild Child wasn't real, and once the mortality was extracted, once every other element of the soul was distilled, the body would simply cease to exist. And beside it was marked 'no blood, no blood at all!'

I could see the word 'immortalis' in the next paragraph down. This was exactly what I was looking for, a book explaining the secrets of Wild Children and how to use them to never die. It had only taken hints of those secrets for me to know I would never be willing to read it, much less do anything it described. And I didn't have time to think further about it because something spoke behind me.

"Alex? You've come back for me? I knew you would. I'm so hungry, Alex."

It was the voice of a child, high pitched but neither boy nor girl and with an odd flutter to it. Fear, already a gnawing cold, drenched me like ice water and pulled my wings tight around my body. I turned around anyway. The mannequin against the wall was pushing itself clumsily to its feet, and I had been mistaken. Amidst all the strangeness in the room I hadn't looked at it properly, but it wasn't a mannequin, rather some kind of child. That is, it was a little taller than me and had the shape of a person, more or less, but there were no features. It was too thin and, though naked, wasn't boy or girl or anything, nothing distinctive except a little pit carved into its chest. There was hair, but it was wispy and translucent, more cloud than solid. The face was blank and smooth, but the eyes at least were alive. More than that they were eyes like mine, glaring orange and too round to be human, the eyes of a Dove Child. Wings were on its back too, except they weren't real, just faint suggestions painted in eye-teasing glimmer. They'd be invisible to a human with regular eyes, but I was sure the whole apparition would be. For a moment, I thought it wasn't real at all, just some specter, the kind of nightmare image my vision could trick me with sometimes. Its eyes convinced me. There was too much emotion in them, too much desperation and need.

"I'm sorry, but my name is Coo. Tell me how I can help you, brother, and then you can tell me what happened." I couldn't look into those eyes and not want to help it. As for 'brother' or 'sister', I was just guessing.

"I've been waiting for you." It whimpered as it staggered closer. It moved like a puppet, shambling and awkward. "It was all that was left to me. You love me, and you'll find some way to save me. Please save me. I'm all alone, and Uncle took everything."

That look in its eyes, focused on mine pleadingly, made it impossible to fear, although its words became so much more horrible when I thought about what I'd just read. I could only pity this poor thing, and I didn't retreat. As it threw its cold arms around me and clung, I hugged it back, held it as comfortingly as I could. "Who are you? What happened to you? How can I help you?"

"How long has it been?" I'd heard that tone from Wild Children before. We lose track of time. Decades, sometimes. "I'm Jay. How can you forget my name?"

It was rambling, half-lucid, and it wasn't going to like the truth, but the truth was what I had. "I'm not who you think I am, sister. And you've been down here a long time. This house- this house is a ruin. It may have been a hundred years, maybe more. Please, Jay, I need you to focus. What do you need? How can I help you?"

It was starting to cry. I could see tears forming at the corners of its eyes, inhuman but the only thing about it that seemed real and alive. "Uncle took it all," it whimpered. "He took my heart, he took my life, he took what made me human. He couldn't take the wildness, and it made him angry. I tried to get it back, but he'd already given some of it to you. Don't you have it? I need it back. I'm so hungry, Coo. I'm so hungry."

The words were rambling, pathetic, until it started talking about hunger. Those were too emphatic, too needy. One of its hands was fumbling between us and the other was looped around me, was holding me close. I was in trouble. I felt fingers, cold as ice, sinking into me in a way that had nothing to do with flesh.

"Brother Jay, what are you doing?" I yelped, half-falling back against the desk. I grabbed the hand that pressed against my front, pushing into me, and struggled with it. We jerked back and forth, but for a fight it was sad. We were both scrawny, sick children and we wrestled without any strength.

It went on long enough for the thing to whimper. "Your heart. I need a heart. You love me, Coo, please save me. I'm so hungry!"

A heart. Of course. I could feel, as I wrestled with it, the hole in its chest. I couldn't blame Jay. It wasn't quite a person. I wasn't sure it could make moral decisions at all, so much had been taken from it. But it was still going to kill me, because I could feel fingers brushing against something inside, something that was me, that wasn't physical and shouldn't be touched. And I was still scared, still terrified of dying.

I could also remember what I had seen walking into the room. We wriggled a little, rolling against the side of the desk. I stopped trying to push Jay away with one hand and instead reached behind me until I closed my fingers on delicate, glazed ceramic. I hoped it was delicate, and it was – one smack and the vase smashed open on the desk. I grabbed the heart it contained, which felt like a soap bubble that didn't pop, and tried to push the desperate white ghost attacking me away with one thrust.

As Jay staggered back a half-step I had an instant to look at the heart I held. It was wrong; small, grey instead of colored, and there were what looked like cracks in it. I have seen, in visions and during holy times and when a child was near death, other hearts. They were never like this. This was damaged, somehow. But I hadn't separated Jay's hand from my chest, and as it lunged forward again I could feel it gripping at my own heart, tearing at it. I had that instant though, and I shoved Jay's heart back into the hole in its chest.

Jay fell away from me and we both staggered a few steps from the edge of the desk. A white hand, delicate but too simple in shape to be real, clasped to the hole in the spirit's chest. But something clung to its fingers, hints of pink that slid off onto the gray and glistening surface of the heart. The pit in its chest was sealing up, but before it did I couldn't help but notice that the pink was patching some of the cracks. Jay had hurt me, taken something from me, but not killed me.

I felt weak, but those orange eyes were looking at me again and now they weren't desperate. They were sad and grateful and adoring, and had to be, because its slit of a mouth was hardly expressive at all. Most importantly it was the look of someone who could think.

I couldn't stop it as those arms wrapped around me again and I was pulled into another embrace. This one was tender, and that trilling voice whispered, "You saved me, Coo. Thank you. I trusted to love, and love saved me. I don't care how long it took, but I knew one day you'd come back."

"Brother, I swear we've never met. You called me Alex. That could be a girl's name, but it's not mine. I'm Coo, only Coo." I leaned against Jay, and it felt much more solid and less cold, and if its shoulders looked round and formless they felt right when I rested my head on them.

Skinny fingers stroked the feathers on the back of my head, and it murmured, "You don't remember, do you? That's why it took so long. You came over and you don't remember. You became a dove like me, and you don't remember who we were. That's alright, Coo. I'll always love you."

I was uncomfortably aware that I had no idea what my human name had been. It had been so long, it might have happened even before this house was sealed up. I wasn't thinking clearly. I was passing out, and it was obvious. Slowly everything went black.

"Thank you, Coo," I heard Jay whisper. "Thank you for coming back for me."

Then I really did pass out.

I woke up in my bed, in my room, alone. The room was dimly lit by a couple of candles, the fine white kind from the church below which my brothers and sisters kept putting in my bedroom despite my wish that they be used only in the chapel. I felt good, but too good. There was that strange energy still, that feeling that I was perfectly healthy, that I was really young, and I knew that would never be true again. I closed my eyes and was still until the fear flooding out of my heart washed over me and receded, making way for calm. To keep it from returning, I tried to figure out how much of the previous day had been a dream. I couldn't untangle it. Too much had happened, and most of it had been too sensible. I couldn't have dreamt the whole day, but there was no point where I could remember sleeping, or even giving myself a chance to.

No, I was thinking about it wrong. I had stepped into dreams while awake, not asleep. I had followed the lure of the unnatural and given in to the temptations of the things my eyes can see and abandoned what was real for a little while.

But of course there was a much simpler explanation still. I was the oldest Wild Child I had ever met. It was much more likely that as my body grew unnaturally stronger my mind was fading. It was an idea as scary as dying, because it meant death was reaching ahead, taking parts of me even as I clung to what was left. These were not pleasant thoughts, but I couldn't help dwelling on them and trying to pick out the truth as I slid out of bed. I stretched my wings as best I could in this confined space, because sleeping on my back always made them stiff, and took a few steps over to my mirror to groom my feathers.

Except the mirror was covered, hung over with a burlap cloth. I knew why I had put it there; I did not want to see the omens that would haunt my reflection. What I did not know was when I had covered it up. I couldn't remember doing so. I had just avoided the mirror as best I could. I considered for a moment lifting the cloth aside, but whatever I saw would only make me feel worse.

Instead I reached for the fine brush I used on my feathers, but beside it on the box that held my belongings was something that certainly had not been there yesterday. It was a flower in a vase, but I knew of no flowers in the world of Man that had lush and delicate white petals stained with purple hearts. Nervously I reached out a hand to stroke my fingers over a petal, and instead my hand passed through it, and flower and vase simply faded away until they weren't there. Which meant they never had been.

"You weren't supposed to touch it," a fluttering child's voice reproved me. I didn't want to look, but that was foolishness, so I turned around, and Jay was standing by my bed straightening out the sheets and the pillow, making it tidy. But those orange bird eyes were on me.

I wasn't going to fall in. "It wasn't there to be touched, brother. And neither are you." I could hear my voice shake at the finish. I was going to die, and first I was going to lose my mind. These were things I could no longer deny.

Its answer came in a wistful voice. "I found it in a cave under the city, where children played and gardens grew beautifully, but I knew a place like that can't exist and I couldn't stay. I could feel you slipping away while we were there. I suppose you're right, it wasn't real, and neither was the flower."

Then the chalk-white, inhuman child stepped forward. It moved naturally now, not like a broken puppet. I had a terrible urge to run away, but when it reached out I stood still. I could feel its fingers as they brushed lightly over my cheek. I could feel them, feel the pressure of them, and Jay didn't fade into nothing. I trembled harder, not knowing what to say, and slender arms wrapped around me and pulled me against a chilly body that still gave like flesh. "I'm not sure if I'm alive," Jay murmured to me, "but this is me, and this morning you saved me. It all happened. You're so afraid, my love. You're afraid of death and afraid you're being haunted by your own imagination, aren't you?"

And I thought, God, please help me, because she understands. Because she's right. Because with her arms around me I felt comforted, and I wasn't alone. "How do you know? You have eyes like mine, sister. Can you see it?" Was I going to cry? I cry sometimes, because I see too many tragedies, but not out of relief.

"I don't have to." Its arms tightened. It wanted to protect me. "I was dead for too long, and you were alive. I just have to look at you to know how old you've become, and I've waited for death too, helplessly knowing it was close by. More than that, I know you, Coo. When we were human I loved you, and nothing changed that."

I realized I was clinging to him, gripping his arms like a frightened child as he held me. I was a frightened child. Why pretend? I had lived for most of a century, taken on the responsibility of easing the hardship of my fellow children. My fellow doves, the donkeys we helped in secret, and even some of the priests of the city looked up to me like an angel. But I had never stopped being an eight year old child who ended her life because it was nothing but pain to her. I wasn't equal to these burdens, but this time I wasn't choosing to die, and I was afraid.

These are the uncontrolled thoughts you have as you cry, and I was crying soundlessly, letting tears fall on Jay's shoulder. It walked me gently back to the bed, and we sat down, and thin fingers stroked what had once been my hair. Eventually Jay spoke again, in the whisper of someone who wants to be gentle. "This may seem like a bad time, love, but can you do something for me? Let me be selfish for a moment?"

It was an odd thing to say, enough that my tears stopped and I nodded. I might have been afraid she would ask for something I wouldn't do, but I knew right then that Jay would never hurt me. So I let her ask. "Would you sing for me, Coo? When I cried, when I lay in my bed and my life was worth nothing, you would sing to me. I can't hear it in my head anymore, and I am as afraid of what I am as you are of what is coming."

I had been comforting children hurting and even waiting to die for a long time, and I knew how it was done. As my sadness and fear let go, I was being turned from them so that they didn't come back. I also knew that I did this with truth. Jay was asking for this now to make me feel better, but it was an honest request. For a few moments I held her tighter, and then I sat up straighter and let her rest against me, and I sang to her in a voice rough with tears and never quite human. I didn't know the title or what the words meant or if I was getting them right. It was just a lullaby I'd known as long as I could remember. It might have come from my first life.

After a while I ran out of words, and my arms fell as Jay rose, standing over me by the bed. I could barely see her mouth, it was so thin, but she was smiling and there was a peace in her eyes I could remember feeling myself, not long ago. I could only imagine her suffering, not alive but not truly dead, but somehow I had made her happy. Still...

"Sister. You're right that I don't remember my life when I was human, not really, but you weren't in it. You say we loved each other, but that can't be right. No one loved me. I would remember. It was the reason I killed myself. One of the reasons." I shivered a little. I was very thankful I didn't remember those reasons, but I knew that they were bad.

His fingers stroked my cheek again, and I was thinking of it as 'him' again because it was the kind of affection a boy gave a girl. Admittedly I was too young to have ever been the target of that, but I had seen over and over how romantic love would consume people older than me. Still, while Jay thought and I waited, I wondered about how much identity it had left, because sometimes I thought it was a boy and sometimes a girl.

Finally he answered. "We were cousins, not brother and sister. All you have to call me is Jay. You've done everything for me you have to. I'm not someone you have to take care of anymore. You've done that so long, I think it's my turn to take care of you." Which didn't answer anything.

"I still don't think I'm who you think I am." It just wasn't possible that there was someone who would show up from my human past after a hundred years, loving me in a way I was sure no one had. Jay was solid and could touch me, so maybe he was real, but he couldn't be right. "When I died and was sent back as a dove I changed a lot. How could you even recognize me?"

Jay wouldn't stop smiling, the soft, rosy smile of someone who was happy at last. "I don't have to know what you looked like. That's all shadows, like the sound of your voice. But I recognized you from the first moment. I know you and everything about you is familiar. And most of all I knew your kindness. It was what I saw most in you when we were real children. Even right now you're more worried for me than for yourself, aren't you?"

How do you answer that? My fear and doubts were quiet, but still there. At the same time I couldn't look at this faceless child, stripped of its humanity, and not want to save it. "It would be nice to think so."

"You are." I could hear the affection in his voice. That, and his eyes and the way he moved were alive, at least, and natural, although none of them were quite right. "You've been too long alone, hiding in the dark. You can't see yourself anymore." Awkwardly I realized I talked like that all the time, down to the way he started circling the room until he found an old lantern I never used and lit it with one of the candles. It did make the place much brighter. But as he walked back over to the end of the bed he asked, "You keep saying you died, though. I promise you, love, you're alive. More alive than me."

And that didn't make sense, but it was something else to take our minds off the worst. "How can you not understand?" I said, answering a question with a question and confusion with confusion. "A child who kills herself is judged by the angels, and sometimes they send her back as a dove. That is how it happens. Do you not remember when you changed?" It was something few of us forget.

That made him smile too, but it was an odd smile. I was used to people being hesitant to contradict me. He just wanted to be easy about it. "It's what I remember best." That, at least, didn't surprise me. "I lived with you and your father, my Uncle, after my parents died. I was always unhappy, and while the details are shadows I remember sitting with you one day because there was no purpose to my life, no value to it. You cared, but to everyone else I was a burden or worse. And when I explained all that to you, you asked me to live for you until I could live for myself again, and I knew that I would, and that moment - it was so intense, so powerful, I just became something else."

That didn't make sense. No, it could make perfect sense. Out there in the world no one knew how or why children became Wild. For me it was dying, and because I could lead other children through the same thing I assumed I, and I alone, knew the right way. But there were wrong ways, too many wrong ways, potions and curses and things that perverted the holiness of the process. Or so I had believed, because after all, we came back from the dead. This was our afterlife on earth where we earned our right to Heaven. And if I'd just fooled myself into thinking my way was the right way I really did know nothing at all. Worse, the other Wild Children had trusted me to know the truth.

Needless to say those thoughts shook me, until Jay leaned over the bed and took my hand in his and gave it a squeeze. "I don't know what you're thinking, but I know that you're worried you've done something wrong. You were always thinking about God, so maybe you're worried about Heaven. But I know you, Coo. I know your kindness. Have you really done anything but help people?"

He knew what to say, and already I was feeling better. I was afraid and full of doubts. But they'd been mounting for a while as my days dwindled, and he was telling me to look for something deeper.

Which I didn't have time to find, because Egg opened the door, rapping it softly as she did so and opening it slowly, which was all the privacy a dove ever expected and more than the others got. "You're awake, sister?" she asked, giving me her sunny, encouraging smile. Compared to Jay's, who had hardly any face, it looked distant and official. "I saw the light and I thought I heard you singing. You usually pray in the chapel. I just wanted to check on you."

Glaringly orange eyes would hide signs of crying, but not the redness around them, and my cheeks might be tracked as well. "I have been thinking about the past, and the future." I refused to lie to her, but I knew she couldn't share my burdens. "I am well, however. I've always known that we must go through pain to find peace."

And that was the Coo she thought she knew. "Yes." She smiled, delighted but trying to look as serious as the topic deserved. "That's true, isn't it? It's that way for everyone I've known." She wandered in carrying a bowl, and I smelled oats. Some food for me, no doubt. The others were worried about my body as I aged, but it was my soul I was worried about. Still, it made them feel better to take care of me, and my death would be enough of a blow to them already. So she walked over to the mirror and set the bowl on my dresser, but I stopped thinking for a moment because she had walked right through Jay.

Right through Jay. Like it wasn't there. It hadn't surprised me that Egg couldn't see Jay, but I had learned long ago a lesson other Wild Children with our eyes often didn't. The things we see are at least partly dreams. Sometimes they're all dreams.

But Jay didn't disappear, and although it looked surprised, it touched itself and it reached over to touch me, and I felt those fingers on my hand. I was dizzy, all too aware that I didn't even know if the things I could see and touch were true or alive anymore. I had another concern, though, that snapped me out of it. Egg was saying something which I didn't catch, but she was also starting to pull the burlap cloth away from the mirror.

"Please, sister," I told her abruptly and firmly to shock her into stopping and listening. "Let that be. When you're as close to the end as I am your reflection is no comfort. You may understand when you are my age, but I hope you don't."

It made her pause, at least. "You would tell me to face the truth, sister," she answered cautiously.

"I know what I will see, Egg. It is more a matter of taking some time to rest from it until I have the strength to face it again. You will tell me I look the same, but what I will see is not what you see." And that was all very true. She just didn't understand it.

"As you wish," she conceded, thoughtful. "I think that is something I should be glad of. I've never known you to do anything for yourself. Maybe it's time."

It was a strange thing to say. What did I want? "In that case, sister, and with regret and gratitude, can I ask to be alone?"

"Always." She bowed deeply before leaving, and as she walked out with that light and almost bouncing step she has, her smile was relieved and natural. She deserved it because she had shown she was wiser than I am, like I'd always suspected. But mostly I just cared that I was alone with Jay.

Jay who might not exist, as I was uncomfortably reminded when on her way out one of Egg's wings passed through its shoulder.

For a moment I stopped thinking of Jay as human at all. It was too easy to look again and see a bleached white doll, with a shape only a parody of human and nothing to distinguish it but terrifying orange eyes. Something I'd found in the workshop of a murderer who'd left behind the world of other men. Whether I'd even been there at all might be a figment.

As it walked deliberately around the bed to me I wanted to shrink back and be afraid, but there was such familiarity in those eyes. It wasn't that I knew them, but that they knew me, and as it sat down again and that jointed tube of an arm curled around my shoulders, it felt so good, so comfortable, and most importantly so solid.

That trilling voice, more childish than mine, reassured me, "I think she was right, love. When I needed to I lived for you. Now you should live for yourself. We were both scared there, but the truth is Uncle took my life and my humanity from me. If only you can touch me, I think it's because I'm here for you, not anyone else. Love saved me and love will save you. You've always believed in God, but I believe in love. And because I love you, I'm asking you to stop worrying about what's true for anyone but yourself."

I had known regret and helplessness and fear and anger and, lately, doubt. But I couldn't remember ever feeling so awkward. Jay could see right through me. Egg was kind to everyone, and she and the other doves wanted to take care of me because they thought of me as something better than I am. I was sure I wasn't the cousin Jay described and couldn't remember anything like it, but she knew how weak I was and she still cared. I thought about taking her advice.

Except, and I confess I felt a flash of anger as it happened, Mourn threw open the door at that moment, and Egg was behind him, and Mourn shouted, "Mother Coo! They've caught a Wolf Boy!"

"There's no time for me," I said out loud. Egg would think I was talking to her, but Jay would know it was for him, and probably for me. I slid around to the other side of the bed and asked sharply, "How long ago? Who caught him?"

"Some farmers, I think. They gave him to the city guard," he told me quickly.

"He's alive then, probably." The army would have killed him on the spot, and the church would have burned him. Humans don't like any Wild Children, but they hate wolves most of all.

"He is," Mourn confirmed, but there was something bad in his tone. "But mother, they caught him hours ago. He's already in the jail beside the execution square."

Which meant we couldn't possibly save him. The humans were going to kill him, and we couldn't stop it. What we could do is get my brothers and sisters killed or, worse, caught.

"I absolutely forbid any of you to go talk to him," I announced, with the hardest tone I could manage. The unexpected strength I felt as my end came near served me now. I was bullying them with the authority they gave me because if I didn't they would do what I was about to do, which was dangerous enough to be stupid. "All we can do is comfort him, and I will do that myself."

They wanted to argue, but my words silenced them for a few seconds, long enough for me to march over to the window and launch myself out of it into the night. And while my thoughts were full of a Wild Child about to die unfairly, there was a little room for the feel of Jay's fingers touching my shoulder and sliding down my arm as I was rising from the bed.

I got there safely, and I tried to think of it as a miracle but I knew, deep down, it was just luck. Even in the darkness the white wings of a dove are too easy to spot, and I was trying to sneak up to a well-guarded jail across from the cathedral. Somehow no one seemed to spot me, so I circled a moment behind the jail before landing on a windowsill on the second floor. I knew which window it would be. On the rooftop above it sat a figure wrapped in white singing quietly to itself, a figure humans would not be able to see. It meant death was coming for a Wild Child.

That made me feel a little more helpless, but I already knew how bad this was. Perching on a windowsill isn't easy, but I am light, much lighter than a human child, and I could crouch down and hold onto the bars for support.

I was looking into a cell, which didn't surprise me, and its only occupant was a Wild Child curled up against one wall, which also didn't surprise me, and the only furnishings were the chains holding the boy in place. So many chains, far more than were needed, but that didn't surprise me either. What did surprise me was that he wasn't a wolf. I could see how the humans thought he was, because he was very canine, but he was more yellow than grey and everything about him was leaner and longer. Looking at him tugged on my heart just a little more. He had been horribly cursed. There was enough human about him to stand up and not much more. I didn't want to know what this said about the person he was. Right now he deserved only what comfort I could bring him.

"I'm sorry, brother." I spoke up to get his attention. "I know-" I was starting to choke up. I had no peace inside me to get me through these counsels anymore. But I had to do what I could even if that was nothing. "I know it doesn't change anything, but I'm sorry."

I might have woken him, because he raised his head and looked up at me. His eyes were gold, no more human than mine, although much prettier. "Another bird," he husked. His accent was thick and strange, but at least he spoke the same language. "What are you sorry for? Birds are too special to care what happens to something like me. You have your adults well trained here. They'll clean up this mistake."

"You are from far away." It was a question, but I had to make it a gentle one. He was angry, and I didn't want him to stop talking.

"Yes. When I ended up like this you kicked me out. And when the birds kick you out, the adults do too. But in this land the adults didn't think that was enough, I guess. So in the morning off comes my head." There was bitterness in his voice, but I could hear the fear he was hiding under it. I felt it too, and I was going to live longer than him.

"I don't know what things are like in your land, brother." I tried to keep my voice from cracking so that it would sound warmer. Helpless. I felt so utterly helpless. "The humans here think of all Wild Children as monsters. At best they keep us as servants, and are not kind. Wolves or any child they think is a wolf they kill. I am sorry."

A hand reached up and touched mine. It wasn't the canine Wild Boy's hand. Jay was inside the cell somehow, leaning against the wall and watching us.

"You don't care what happens to a jackal, much less a failure like me," retorted the... jackal? And he turned his head to look away from me.

"I care," I answered. I was losing him, but I had lost when I started anyway. "I've never liked wolves and I've never met a jackal, but I don't think anyone should die like this. In our land the doves live to help the other Wild Children however we can. It isn't up to us to decide who is or isn't a failure."

Suddenly desperate, he lurched up against his chains and barked, "Prove it. Set me free, if you want to help! I'll run so fast they'll never catch me and I'll be out of your forsaken, hateful country!"

That was a line of thought I didn't want him following. Hope can destroy as well as save. "All I can do, brother, is help you make your peace with God so that you'll be ready. I'm sorry." I was.

He sank back against the wall again. "God? I've met my god, and he did this to me. Even if I made peace with him he would never make his peace with me."

"We are changed to learn a lesson, brother. My lesson was that it was up to me to make my life valuable, not throw it away as something I didn't want. If you want peace with God you only have to figure out why he made you what you are." I felt like I was lying to him. If I doubted all of this myself, what right did I have to lecture him in his final hours?

Worse, it wasn't working. He was angry. He almost sounded like he was barking as he shot back, "You birds really are the same everywhere! It's my own fault, is it? I spied on a conversation my little sister had with one of your messengers and insisted that they take me with her to see the Black Jackal. And for that horrible crime, when he breathed on us and remade us and she became a heron, I became *this*, a failed yellow cur, and was driven from my home and hated by everyone I've met. And now I deserve to be killed for it by strangers in an evil city where even birds are not respected. Yes, I see the lesson I was meant to learn now." His sarcasm hurt me, and hurt me worse because I couldn't make sense of anything he said. He was changed by a Wild Child who could act in place of the angels themselves? Children changed this horribly were always neck-deep in their sin, but his crime was nothing, and he talked like someone who was hurt and angry, not mean or selfish.

"I don't think it's your fault, or that you deserve this." I was resorting to what truth I could scrape together. "I think there must be some purpose in your change, some chance for redemption I want to help you find. I want to save your soul, because I can't save your life."

He spat contemptuously. "My soul is dust. The Black Jackal has spoken. When I die he will consume it and I will be nothing. There is no redemption. If you can't save my life, then go away."

"What is your name?"

It surprised him, but he was still angry. "Flea. It is one of the marks of my shame."

"Flea, please listen and believe me." My voice was shaking again. "If I could make them kill me in the morning instead of you, I would do it. If I could sneak inside and let you out, even if I knew I would die and there was only a chance to save you, I would do it. There are guards, and locked doors, and the keys are held by more guards. If I tried to get in I would die at the front gate. If that would only make you feel at peace as you go to your end, I would do that too. But it won't, will it? There are things I cannot change. Too many things."

I thought Flea might even be considering my words. He was silent for a moment, at least. I had just learned myself that there is comfort in knowing that someone cares. Instead it was Jay who spoke.

"I can let him out," he said quietly. I was stunned. It was something I didn't want to believe, because it had to be wrong somehow.

"I don't know if you can get through a cell door, but brother Flea can't. You'll need a key, and even if you can pick it up, it's carried by a guard and he won't let it go, even if he can't see you. What could you do?"

"The guard won't stop me." Its voice was grim – no, guilty, as it explained, "I'm still hungry, Coo. I'll eat him. I can eat all the guards if I have to. It won't be enough to fix me."

And now I was afraid, and angry. "You can't kill a dozen people to save one, Jay. You can't kill one person to save another. I would give my life to save this boy, but not someone else's. How can you think that?"

I was relieved when Jay put its hands to its head. The gesture looked so very human, and Jay wasn't talking like a human now. "I'm sorry, Coo. It's wrong. I know it's wrong. That's why I haven't done it. But I'm still hungry because there's still so much missing. I won't do it, but I can't help wanting."

I didn't have time to even figure out how I felt about that. Before Jay even finished I heard, "Who are you talking to?"

It was the Jackal Boy, and as I looked at him again I knew I'd lost any chance to help him. His eyes were angry, and confused, and scared. But they were also animal eyes like mine. If any eyes were Wild, not human, it was those golden ones.

"You don't see anyone else here?" He didn't have to answer. It was obvious. He should be able to see Jay but he couldn't, or hear him. Only I could.

"Crazy. Crazy crazy crazy," babbled Flea, eyes wide now. "No wonder you don't make sense! Go! Go away, leave me alone!"

He was shouting. We'd all been shouting, which had to be why the door was rattling and a man's voice was barking, "Who are you talking to, runt?"

They opened it too fast. There was a man, and he had a drawn blade and he was yelling, "Another one! They're trying to rescue their own!" because he had seen me. I turned and leapt away, flapping my wings, but it was much too late. Behind me I heard Flea yell, but there was a chopping sound and Flea's voice stopped entirely.

It was a nightmare. I was living in nightmares now, drowning in them. I had seen it happen to others with eyes like mine. Flea's death I was sure was real, and I had caused it. It was my fault. Was it? I couldn't tell the nightmare from reality anymore. I would do something I didn't want to do. There is a guardian against the nightmares that try to come to life. Someone who protects from them. His name is Jinx, and just knowing him meant

143

that I had been in too deep for too long. I would have to visit him and Hind, now.

I calmed down, a little, on the way. I felt very, very bad about Flea's death, but blame was not a black and white thing. Comforting anyone on death's door was difficult, and in prison like that… I had done what I could. And like a lot of my efforts to help my Wild brothers and sisters, it hadn't worked. How much had I just made things worse? Had I even known what was right for them?

I was heading to meet one of my failures and one of my successes now. No, that was arrogance. I had done almost nothing for either of them. But they both troubled me deeply.

The truth was that Jinx was a toy, a stuffed animal, a cat sitting on the bed of a Donkey Girl owned by perhaps the richest and most powerful man in the city. I believed that in that toy was the soul of a Wild Child with eyes like mine, who had gotten lost in the world of dreams. The world I saw through my eyes, the world Jay was a part of if she was really anything but senility and madness. It was only devotion to the girl Hind that kept Jinx in this world in any way, but that selflessness had saved him. I had always looked on it as the ultimate moral lesson. At the same time, he scared me. He was a toy that only I could hear talk, and he only acted in a world I knew was at least half a lie, maybe more. But he knew that world better than I and guarded his girl from it, guarded perhaps every Wild Child. There was a lot I didn't know. They were things I hadn't wanted to find out because I was afraid of getting lost like him. Now I was, most definitely, lost.

Jinx could not tell me anything about Wild Children, or about God, or about what was right. He could tell me everything about Jay and about my sanity.

Assuming I wasn't imagining Jinx as well.

It was late at night, and I knew Hind's bedroom window well. The Baron's mansion was large and separated from the city by a large garden. It was too well lit for comfort, but not enough to be dangerous. I thought it might be around midnight and Hind might not even be back in her room, but most of the house was asleep.

The lights were out in her room, but Hind was there alone, sitting on the edge of her bed. I opened the window slowly, making enough noise to be sure she heard me, and slid inside. I felt nervous.

Jinx was one conundrum. His girl, Hind, was another. Every time I saw her I had to face how wrong I could be. I had believed, still believed, that children become donkeys out of selfish laziness so that they could learn the virtue of hard work for others. Hind's story tormented me. She was surely the most expensive donkey in the city, prized by her owner. Her room as I stepped into it was a fairy tale, and her dress would have suited a princess, albeit one who liked to show off. She had the run of the house, her collar was an ornament rather than a restriction, and as far as I knew had never been beaten. Her owner doted on her, in the distant way of powerful men, and she ate well and had no shortage of gifts.

In return she had learned her lesson. With no threat of punishment she drove herself like a dog. She played his court games, attended to his every need and whim, honed herself from an average eleven year old girl whose only distinction was that she only had the ears and tail of a donkey into a poised and elegant debutante who glittered as she moved. She was everything a donkey was supposed to be. She lived for her owner, she hardly slept or paid any attention to her own needs other than those that kept her beautiful. She was selflessly giving to everyone, even people who had treated her badly, including me. And in return, every day, she endured humiliation and physical strain and the hostility of the upper class, who saw her as a shameful weakness of her owner. All for the occasional pat on the head and a chance to sit on his knee.

Hind tormented me. I couldn't help her, and her life was a testament that I did not understand God's plan. And now she was sitting on the edge of her bed, her face in her hands, crying softly as she did too often. She was as unhappy as any donkey in the city, maybe more.

I felt bad seeing it. And I felt worse because I realized I had done almost nothing to help her, ever. Only my need to see Jinx had driven me here tonight, and all I'd done was stare at her and stew in my own worries. I walked over as quietly as possible and laid my hand on her shoulder.

She looked up at me, and suddenly her arms were around me, squeezing so tightly I thought she would hurt me. She was stronger than she looked and much bigger than me. Everyone is. If holding me would help her, though, she could crack my ribs. I folded my wings over her shoulders and stroked her hair lightly while she sobbed. "Coo! Did he call you somehow? Is that why you're here?"

That was... odd. "No, but I'm glad I came. Tell me what happened, sister. You know I'll do whatever I can to help."

"He took Jinx! Jinx is gone! He took him off my bed!"

That was not good, but I didn't want to jump to conclusions. "The Baron took him? Why would the Baron take your stuffed animal?" I asked. I wanted to be gentle, but I knew I just sounded confused.

"No, Master would never do that." She whimpered. She was crying harder now. It was probably good for her, but it made her hard to understand. "Master Vick took him. I don't know, I don't know how, but he knows, Coo, he knows Jinx can talk and he just came in and took Jinx right off my bed."

Dreams. I was stuck in dreams, in a world where nothing made sense anymore. But I wasn't getting out and I couldn't let it stop me. Hind was the most blameless person I'd ever met. I had to help her.

"You can hear him talk?" I asked her cautiously. Hind has human eyes, and Jinx hardly talks to me. I wasn't sure he could see the world we live in anymore.

She seemed hesitant, embarrassed. I understood. I had never told anyone about Jinx, and there was no one I could talk to about Jay. Shyly she told me, "Sometimes, in my dreams. I thought I was just… remembering a boy I knew, at first. But when I'm sad, or scared, or when Master is angry, he talks to me in my dreams." She looked up at me, and I could see she was starting to panic again. "I can't lose him now. I don't know what Master Vick will do to him. Please, Coo. You have to help me!"

People thought I could help them, that I was special somehow. Hind was taller and stronger than me, knew the house, could mix with humans when they would try to kill me or worse. All I knew about Vick was that the Baron had a son, just one child. But she thought I could do this. If her owner had asked it she would have stood in front of an army and found some way to slow them down. She couldn't do anything for herself.

This was the only thing I was aware of she had ever wanted for herself. She lived entirely for others. If that had been the only reason it would have been enough, to let her have something just for her. I would do whatever it took.

"Where did Vick take him, sister? Do you know why?" I let my voice get firmer. She needed confidence in me.

She didn't know why, but she thought she knew where. Which was why I found myself tiptoeing down a quiet hallway, uncomfortably aware that my wings almost filled it and hiding was impossible, and that a servant could wander past at any moment.

There was nothing sudden, but I wasn't alone anymore.

"She has no one now," I told Jay passively. "Her friends are all gone, and she gives everything to someone who hardly talks to her, who thinks of her as this pretty and wonderful thing rather than a person. The only one who truly cares for her and takes care of her she's afraid doesn't exist."

I knew Jay understood me, because she said nothing.

"It doesn't matter if he's real. She has someone who's here for her, finally." I guess I must have lifted my hand a little, because Jay's slipped into it. There was no warmth to it, and she was too smooth to be skin and didn't give enough. But she was there, for those few moments. Vick's study had been just a flight of stairs and one hallway away, which was why there had been the ghost of a chance that I could get here.

I don't know why the door wasn't locked, but I left Jay behind and stepped in. The boy, almost a man, they called Vick was there. It was the kind of room only the very rich could afford, because there were cases filled with books, and a globe of the Heavens, and jars filled with I-didn't-know-what, and a couple of little braziers on his desk, and already I knew what was going on.

He looked up suspiciously when the door opened and pushed something under the desk, but his eyes widened when he saw me. No one could mistake me for human.

"A dove," he whispered, and the longing in his voice scared me. He stood up and Jinx was chained to his wrist; the chains were tarnished and the doll was held in strange seals, but the metal wasn't black yet.

He was too surprised to know what to say so I took the lead, praying that he wouldn't think about how helpless I was. He was half again my height, and the building was full of his servants. And God did not answer my prayers. I had always told others that he wanted them to answer their own prayers. Still, I thought I sounded quite confident as I told him, "You've taken a toy from sister Hind. Please give it back, sir. It is very important to her."

"Now? When it works so well? All I had to do was look out the window. And looking at you, you're surrounded by things I don't understand. With this I can do my work." He was too driven, and he knew what he had. This was getting worse and worse, and he was coming out from behind the desk and approaching me. If he got within arm's reach I couldn't possibly resist him. If I ran I couldn't possibly help Hind and Jinx.

I stayed where I was. Reason was my only weapon now, and whatever moral sense this young man still had. Keeping my voice quiet and firm, I explained, "I know what you're doing. You need to stop now. No one gets immortality. Those books tell you that you can have it if you're willing to do horrible enough things. Did anyone ever actually succeed?"

That stopped him, at least. I had gotten through a little. Humans were often surprised to find out Wild Children can think. "I thought of that. But I'm not doing this for immortality." He was staring at me, still. I didn't think it was because of whatever phantoms he was using Jinx to see, and I was certain I had plenty. He was staring at me, myself.

"I can see the same things you're seeing, brother. Rich men play with alchemy and no one cares because they just want to learn, but you've taken the first steps down a darker road. Living forever isn't worth that. What else could be?" As I said it I knew, in passing, that I had let go of that fascination myself. I didn't have time to dwell on it.

He was talking, and his face glowed. He was alive with desire, holding up his hands like he was on stage. "A bird. Not like you. A burning and beautiful girl, scarlet and gold and pink. I saw her talking to Hind on the balcony one day, and then she flew away. She looked so alive, so free. I didn't know Wild Children could be so perfect. I'm going to become like her and find her again."

The passion boys and girls, men and women, feel for each other is something I can only see from the outside. I had seen it save humans and Wild Children alike. It was going to damn this boy. "There are ways to make yourself cross over." It was a fact I hated. "None of them will help you. You must know that, brother. We're children, and you're almost a man. Have you ever met a Wild Child who was older than fourteen?"

I hadn't convinced him. I could see it in his face. I pushed again. "This is a mystery Men are not supposed to know, but it's been tried. If someone too old goes through the change, they die. Horribly. And even if you were young enough, we don't get to choose what we become. You don't want to become a donkey, or a wolf, and there are fates worse than those."

He still wasn't convinced. "You're right, I'm no longer a child, but I can go Wild. An adult can take that essence and become something stranger and more dangerous than the animals children turn into. I can become something like the bird I saw. Something out of a story. It took me a year of buying alchemy books that were supposed to have been burned, but I found the way. It's not like immortality, either. It's been done. Now I have this doll and I can see what I need to do. And I have Hind."

That was the chink. That one word, that name. "What would you have to do to her, brother? What do you have to take from her to turn yourself into a monster? You know her. Does she deserve what you're going to do to her? Can you hurt her, in cold blood, just to get what you want?"

For a moment it worked, too. Hind grieved me because she was, truly, a blameless innocent who had already suffered more than she would ever earn. But it fell apart just as fast because he was looking at me again, and he was too close. I couldn't get away.

"You're right. I won't hurt Hind," he told me with that spark in his eyes again. "A dove will work better anyway. Donkeys are hardly Wild at all. The essence of doves is stronger."

I had, at least, saved Hind. I wasn't sure I could save myself. He wasn't listening to reason, only to emotion. And then I heard a voice whispering to me, "I won't let him hurt you. I'll eat him first. Even if you hate me for it, I'll save you."

I was right by the door. If I tried to bolt, he'd just grab me. But instead I pushed it open all the way. And Jay was standing behind me, and I could see it in Vick's eyes. He could see her.

It stopped him cold. "That's not an omen. Its eyes – what is it?"

I didn't want him to panic. I wanted him to think. "That is what would be left of Hind if you used her the way you intend to. That is what would be left of me. Can you do that, brother? Could you do it to her, or to me, or to anyone?"

He was terrified, then horrified, and then it turned to pity. I was used to seeing into dreams, and I was used to Jay. He was seeing her fresh, and from his expression it was terrible. In the curve of my wing stood a spindly white figure taller than me but with less features than a doll. A child neither boy or girl, whose face was only a slit mouth and staring orange eyes. Even against the pale shadows of my feathers the blankness of her marked her as something that couldn't be real.

"No," he admitted finally. He sounded bitter, defeated, which meant he knew what he was saying. "I can't. Not even for a phoenix." There was seething anger in his face, but he didn't strike me. Instead he jerked Jinx out of his chains and threw the doll on the floor, and pushed his way past me and out the door without another word. He had made his moral choice. But I noticed that while he shoved my wing aside he made sure not to touch Jay.

Now there was nothing left but to pick up Jinx. He seemed undamaged, just a crude stuffed cloth cat doll, jet black with a creepy stitched smile and two red buttons for eyes. They didn't look like the eyes of a cat at all, but I knew they were. When you looked at them, they looked back at you.

I whispered to the doll, "Jinx? Can you hear me, brother? Are you alright?" Usually I had to wake him up. He didn't live in this world anymore. Unfortunately, neither did I.

"Yes," I heard him whisper after a moment. It seemed like the stitches that made up the mouth moved, but they really didn't. I didn't understand what Jinx was now. I was starting to accept it anyway. "I've never been bound like that. It's over now, anyway. Please take me back to Hind. I can hear her crying, even from here."

"I had a question for you first," I told him gravely. Then I looked over my shoulder at Jay, who nodded. She understood. I was being unfair, doubting that she even existed, and she forgave me without a moment's qualm. "I think I know the answer now, though. Vick saw her. What do you see behind me?"

"Yes, I see it. I don't think you need to be afraid. The alchemists call it a hungry ghost, but that's just a name. If a Wild Child splits, if they lose their humanity completely, this is what's left, but who they are follows the Wild half, not the human half. They're dangerous. They sometimes attack people, trying to get back what they're missing. But this one is under control, and I can see how it looks at you. You're in no danger at all."

My knees were wobbly. If I was imagining Jay I was imagining everything in my life anyway. It took effort to whisper, "Thank you. I've never trusted my eyes and I was afraid I was losing my mind."

"I understand," the voice of the boy in the doll told me. "As close as you are to the end, it's an easy thing to worry about."

Jinx knew how old I was. When he slipped away and became a doll we already knew my death was approaching. But that wasn't how he had said it.

But I didn't want to lead him. "Tell me what you see when you look at me, Jinx."

He hesitated. I had worried, trapped in a doll, living in the dreams of a sad little girl, that he would stop being a person. He still was. He was trying to be delicate, and when he spoke finally, his voice was slow and cautious. "I thought you knew, sister . If you saw yourself you would know. Death is hovering over you like a vulture. I don't think you have another day."

I was quiet, trying to take that in, and as the silence stretched he added, "I'm sorry, Coo." Yes, in the most important ways he was still human.

It felt like everything that was important was changing. I had to look back, look into Jay's orange eyes, see the grief written on its phantom face. "You didn't tell me." There had been guilt in those eyes. He knew.

He hung his head, and the grief in it made me feel sorry for him. I was dying, but the way it was hurting him seemed more important to me. "You were so afraid, Coo. We had so little time to be together. I didn't want you to spend it afraid."

I thought about that, and realized I wasn't afraid anymore, not really. This time it was me who reached out and took his hand. "I only have a day left. We'll take Jinx back to Hind because I won't let her suffer any longer, but after that-" I wasn't sure how to say it. "You said I should live for myself. I'm going to spend my last day doing that. And I don't want to be lonely. Will you come with me?"

I didn't have to ask, but I wanted to hear the love in that voice as it told me, "It's what I want, too."

I had to circle around and land on the rooftop from the back so that it wasn't too obvious from the street what I was doing. I wasn't sure what I was doing, or rather I wasn't sure why. It had been a long time since I'd asked myself what I wanted. The only things I could think of were embarrassing.

In fact, as I crouched on a roof peeking over at the street below, I was kind of thankful for the dim light because I was sure I was blushing. I was sure Jay would be able to see it anyway. He would be charmed, and I wasn't used to that either. He thought about me in a way that I wasn't old enough to deserve and he wasn't human enough to make sense of. I was also letting myself be silly, putting off the moment of what I wanted.

I leaned over a little farther and inhaled deeply. Dawn was hours away, but in a city as big as the capital there were always people on the streets, which meant there were other people selling them things. I had seen children, sometimes even donkeys, buying from these vendors. I had smelled this smell but been too embarrassed to admit how it called to me. But now I saw Jay, who didn't have to sneak or hide, walk up to the cart and take something off of it. He left a few coins, at least, that I had found one day. It was a little weird watching him climb the wall like a squirrel, but my eyes were on the trophy he held up for me, and as he came over the edge I snatched it awkwardly and held it beneath my face.

The smell was overwhelming, and I could feel how hard I was blushing. I was trembling with excitement over some kind of bread, cooked in grease and powdered with sugar and wrapped in a flimsy piece of paper. But I'd let embarrassment stop me from doing this for years and I wasn't going to wait a second longer. I bit into it.

It was delicious. It was richer, sweeter, than anything I could remember eating. It crunched slightly and tore like bread, but that was it for subtlety. It was oil and sugar and freshly cooked bread, and as I bit off piece after piece I forgot everything else and was happy for a few minutes.

In fact, I only dragged myself out of that bliss to pull off some and hold it out to Jay and ask him anxiously, "Would you like some? It's wonderful. It really, really is wonderful. Can you eat food?"

He was smiling, and looked as happy as I felt. His mouth was a barely visible line so I had to look really hard, but I could tell. He shook his head. "I don't think so, but when you eat it I feel something."

I didn't need to be told twice. I was letting myself be selfish, and anyway I honestly felt jealous for every second I was giving up of this. So I popped his piece into my mouth and started to chew, and let the world be sweet and oily for a little longer. It was okay when it was all gone because I couldn't eat any more, and the taste lingered. I leaned back a little and stared up at the stars.

How much of what I saw up there did humans see? Was the occasional lurid cloud that color because of the city's lights, and if an adult looked up would they see the shapes of them? I read books when I could, and I guessed that they couldn't see the faint lines connecting the stars, the shapes and patterns, the pictures they made. But you know I had never asked, and I just couldn't remember, years and years, decades and decades ago, what it was like to look up at the stars as a normal girl.

I lingered a little longer than I wanted because Jay was next to me. I didn't feel about him the way he felt about me. He was a ghost clinging to something alive, to the memory of some other person who was probably long dead. But he understood me and no one else did, and I wasn't going to spend my last day feeling alone. Being with him was just good, like the sweets had been good. I didn't have time to figure it out anymore so I wasn't going to try.

Unfortunately I was getting bored, and I wasn't going to let that happen either. Already I was remembering something else shameful and embarrassing I hadn't let myself realize how much I wanted. So I tugged on Jay's wrist and told him, "Follow me, okay?" and I ran over to the edge of the building and threw myself into the air, flapping my wings.

There was a park, just one park, in this city. When I saw the way the other Wild Children were treated I had lost all faith that people with power would be generous to people without. Despite that there was this park, a valuable space of land in a tightly packed city, with trees and flowers that anyone could visit. And then one day some rich person had paid to have toys built there, for no other reason it seemed but for children to play on. It would have had to have been someone very rich, someone powerful. I liked to think it was Hind's owner, that all that devotion had been given to someone who could be kind to children he didn't know when he had nothing to gain for it at all.

It's probably obvious what I wanted, and why I was kind of mortified by it, and couldn't do it when I had to take care of my brothers and sisters, doves and donkeys and, once or twice, children stranger still. I had to do it before dawn because during the day there'd be trouble. Even right now there were two children, still just young enough that they could have gone Wild, watching me. I thought they must have fallen asleep there by accident because they were a boy and girl, leaning together and holding hands. I wasn't the only person happy tonight.

Jay took a while to catch up with me by whatever mystery he does that. I walked off the path and let my fingers trail under bushes, and stared up at the black on black shapes of leafy branches between me and the night-time sky. I looked at the strange things that had been built in an open space for children, which I guess included me, to enjoy. They were simple of course, because the church and the nobles and I had all seen what complicated machinery could do if it was taken out of God's hands, and on that we agreed.

Fortunately I spotted Jay walking down the path then to keep me from dark thoughts I didn't want, and I smiled at him awkwardly and led him over to the craziest, simplest toy I had ever seen. It was nothing more than a raised plank. I sat on one end, and he sat on the other. I would go up, he would go down. Then he would go up, and I would go down. I giggled, then I laughed, because I couldn't help myself. Nothing so stupidly simple should be fun, but it was. I got bored of it pretty quick though, and told Jay, "Let's go try another one."

"Okay. How about that one?" He pointed, and I knew he'd read me somehow. I couldn't even figure out how to play with some of these toys, but I'd seen this one used and I wanted it the most.

So I laughed again and jogged over to it. "Okay. I think I know how we do this. I climb up, and you push me, okay?" I don't think he was able to laugh anymore, but when he said, "Sure," I could tell he was looking forward to this too.

This was also a very simple little toy. It was just a stick tied to one end of a rope, hanging from the branch of a big tree. I climbed up and stood on the stick, held onto the rope, and let Jay push me. And as I swung back and forth, slowly but a little higher each time, I knew the other doves would never have understood. Why would I want to do this when I could fly, spread my wings and be one with the Heavens themselves? But just a few feet off the ground, this was exciting. Forward and back, always changing directions, light in my stomach and the wind dragging my feathers around. I jumped off before I got bored, because I wanted that moment to be perfect. I was up high when I jumped, but I'm so light I landed easily.

Anyway, I had just realized something I wanted more. Because I'd looked up at the buildings as I was swinging, some of them rising above the trees, and seen a shape. I had never let myself play in this park before because it was silly and dumb and I had responsibilities. There was a place I had never gone because it was too dangerous, but what did I care about danger now? I was going to take away one more regret before I died.

The back entrances would all be locked, or maybe guarded. The windows were glazed, and there was no bell tower because this building was too glorious, too majestic. So I waited until the street was particularly empty, and Jay and I crept up to the front door of the great Cathedral of St. George. It was the most beautiful building in the city, terrifying and glorious with its spires and gargoyles and engravings. I had never been inside because that branch of the church would have killed even a donkey for setting foot in there.

It was so easy. The church was a public place, and there were little doors for people to use set into the huge doors they use for processions, and the little doors weren't locked. Inside there were candles here and there, but the building was dim. The services would start well before dawn, but we had hours until then. Hours when this beautiful building would be empty.

I was used to the open skies, but there was something about this soaring vault, going up several stories, that seemed even bigger. Everything was beautiful, everything was majestic. That vault could have been a rounded off dome, but instead it was threaded with interlocking buttresses. Every window was stained glass and every one depicted something different, something holy. Candles were arranged in huge, beautiful unlit displays, the only light provided by a dull shining through those windows that lit up their displays, and by elaborate silver candlesticks in sconces, in alcoves, on stands and on the altar.

Jay was hardly moved, but that was okay. I was moved enough for both of us. I padded silently up that enormous carpet, so red and so pristine, to the altar itself. Simple, tasteful. A stand for a book, some candles, and a cup, as it should be. The glory was what surrounded it; the icons on their screen behind it, the polished walls that glowed in the soft light, the gleaming wood and the pillars and everything. I was about to cry because someone had devoted their life to build this, maybe many people, because they felt as I did, that God should be something greater than us, something we should aspire to. This beauty asked us to be grateful and humble and care, to devote ourselves to each other rather than ourselves. So much of what I knew was wrong, and I had been plagued by so many doubts, but those feelings were right. I closed my eyes and took a deep breath, letting the subtle incense tease me, and I was comforted because no God who wanted these things could think less of me for taking this day to be myself, or for failing so often when I had no hope of success and tried anyway.

Then my comfort was shattered because someone growled, "I don't know what arrogance made you think you could come here, monster, but you won't get away."

It was the Archbishop, walking out of the shadows, old but not hobbled, given life by his anger and disgust. I was afraid, a little, but I bowed. "If I die here, Your Excellency, I will not regret it. Your cathedral is beautiful, more beautiful than I had dared hope." It was his cathedral after all. I didn't know who spotted me, but it was no surprise that he would confront me if I came.

"And it will take a month to sanctify it again after we've burned your body." This wasn't theater, or drama. He hated me. He kept his eyes on mine, and their color and shape was making his fury rise by the second. "What have you touched, monster? What have you stained with your evil?" he demanded, getting louder.

I kept my head low and respectful. I did not understand how a man so eaten away by hate could lead the church in this Empire, but I respected the devotion that had gotten him here even as I saw it losing its battle with something darker inside him. "I have not had time to touch anything, Your Excellency. And I have no more evil to stain it with than any other man, woman, or child. I know I have never been able to convince you of that however, and I don't expect to tonight."

"Not when I can see your eyes, no." His voice was husky, made throaty by his contempt. "People think the Wild Children are young and pretty. They don't want to think about the evil that has marked every one of you."

"Alexius?" That was Jay's voice. Behind me.

"Jay?" was the Archbishop's faltering answer. I should have been trying to understand the horror in his face, but I was too busy with my own sudden pain. This was not a confrontation I wanted to see. And what hurt worse, in that instant, was the proof that I'd been right. I'd known that Jay had to be mistaken, but it hurt to find out that it really wasn't me that he… I guess, she, had loved and waited for.

"How did you get here?" the Archbishop pressed. His voice was still shaking, but anger was overcoming his fear. And he turned on me again, too. "You let her out. You set that thing free to kill me and then tried to tell me to my face that you're not evil!"

I didn't know what to say, and Jay didn't give me a chance. "I waited for you, Alex." She was walking towards him, and her voice and her eyes were lost now, unreasoning. "Why didn't you come for me?"

"I did come." I couldn't tell if he was shaking now in fear or anger. My dove's eyes told me that something was moving inside him, something awful, but I didn't understand it. His hand seemed a lot less unsteady when he grabbed a candlestick off the altar it and brandished it as he accused, "I came in time to see what you'd become. I came in time to see you murder my father. In time to learn just how evil your kind are, and what kind of demon looks out of those animal eyes."

Jay seemed chastised. She looked scared and sad and guilty, but every few moments she would take another step towards him. "I was hungry, Alex. Uncle took something from me, and I needed it back, and you have it now. And… and he hurt me."

"Don't you dare blame my father!" the old priest yelled, and he hit Jay with the candlestick and I almost screamed. He hit her hard, across the face. It should have killed her, but she was already dead. It hurt her anyway. It wasn't just the pain. When she looked up again the misery in her face made my heart clench. What could I do?

And the Archbishop was still yelling. "You don't have the right to blame him for anything! He took you in, and he was a good man until you turned into that… that bird thing. And I had to watch as you twisted him, lured him, until all he could think about was his damned immortality. And even then, when he thought he had it, he made me take it instead. You couldn't twist him enough to do those things for himself. And then you killed him, ripped him open and ate him, and by God I shut the door and I sealed it so that you could never get out!"

Jay was crying, but when her tears fell they disappeared rather than hitting the floor. Her voice was just sad, sad and distant. She wasn't there anymore. She was turning back into whatever I had found in that laboratory. "I loved you, Alex. I thought you loved me too. Didn't you love me?"

And... he hit her again. That was his only response. It didn't have any more effect than last time, although now he was panting with effort and hatred, and her eyes were starting to stare, focusing on him without expression.

"Please, Alex," she whispered. It was ghostly, the last gasp of whatever I'd saved in her. "You have my humanity. Give it back and I can live again, and then you'll remember."

He raised the candlestick again. I threw myself in-between them, stretched out my arms to block him. It was absurd. It wouldn't do anything, and I hadn't been thinking. But I glared up at the Archbishop defiantly. I just wanted to stop him, not from hitting her but from dragging her back into her nightmare.

It did make him pause for a moment, but he just growled, "You're just as much of a demon as she is and you had to die anyway," and he swung at me.

I was thrown aside, pushed away and tossed to the carpet by Jay's arm. I had tried to take the blow for her, and she took the blow for me, stepping forward, but when it hit her she didn't budge. He might have beaten on the pillars of the cathedral for all the difference it made. But I didn't like what was in her eyes.

"I'm hungry, Alex." She whispered now. "So hungry. You have it. I can taste me inside you."

He started to lift his arm. I guess to swing again, but she caught it and her arm, skinnier even than if she'd been a real little girl, held his like an iron shackle. His other hand pulled at her and pushed at her, but it didn't make any difference. She was breathing hard and fast, both of them were, and she stretched out her other hand and grabbed his chest and pulled.

Something came out. Two somethings. Not a heart, because I had given that back to her already. It looked like a boy and a girl, their shapes blurry and melted, and they ran together and were one thing. The Archbishop couldn't scream, but he made hoarse noises of pain as Jay dragged them out. They came slowly, fighting all the way. And it was wrong. There was nowhere that what had been Jay and what must be the boy the Archbishop had been could be separated. They were one thing. Worse, they were corrupt, threaded with blackness that wound through them everywhere. It might have been hatred, but I could only guess at what the things I saw meant. It was evil. I knew that. It gave me the strength to move.

I threw myself to my feet, leaped back between the two of them. The Archbishop hadn't been able to move her, but I knocked aside Jay's hand and threw my arms around her neck and begged, "Jay, Jay, don't, you don't want that. Can you hear me, Jay? It's not what you lost anymore, it's something awful now."

I heard something collapse behind me and I knew the Archbishop was dead. There are things that you can't survive having done to you, and I had seen the shadows reaching for him as well. I had only saved one person, and maybe not her.

And maybe not me. Jay's hands closed on me, and like when we met she was gripping something that wasn't flesh and pulling on it. Pain shot through me, coming from my heart, but she only took a fragment of me. The shock of it made her wake up, and suddenly she was holding me like I held her. Jay was herself again.

"I'm sorry," I told her, and I genuinely was, even though I had no control over any of this. I hadn't wanted it to happen that way. "You waited for him and you wanted love to save you, and it didn't. But you can save yourself, Jay, I know it."

I wasn't thinking, and neither was she. We were just saying what we felt as she told me, "Love did save me, Coo. I just called you by the wrong name." For a moment my heart relaxed inside me. When she found out I wasn't Alex, when he hurt her, I had been afraid she'd stop caring about me, but she knew me so well maybe that couldn't happen.

And that moment ended, and my heart burst with pain again. I gasped and was having trouble breathing, and only Jay held me up. It passed immediately, but we knew what it meant.

Because of it Jay's face was full of grief, and her pain-filled orange eyes were inches from mine. "I've killed you, Coo. I killed you." She whimpered.

I had to stop her from panicking because it wasn't true. I shook my head and ignored another pain, sharp but not as bad, in my chest. "You didn't, I swear. You just sped up something that was happening anyway. I have no regrets. There's only one thing left I want to do anyway. Can you promise me you'll help me with it?"

I had her, and she swore, "I promise. Anything. Tell me now while we have time."

"You're still hungry, Jay, and what you lost is gone, isn't it? Take it from me instead. Maybe if I give it to you instead of you eating me for it you can keep it."

She didn't want to, which is why I made her promise. "I don't know what will happen. I know you'll die." She was begging me to change my mind.

"I'll lose a few minutes, then. I don't care about them." The pain in my chest, squeezing my heart, told me how true that was. If I looked behind me would a hooded figure with a blade be stepping from the shadows?

"It could be worse than that. You saw what happened to me. It could be worse than that, even."

And I smiled, despite the way I hurt, because she had to stop being afraid and understand how I felt. "It doesn't matter. Help me die the way I want to, and I want to die the way I lived. This is what I want."

There wasn't anything more to say, and after a few seconds all she could do was lower her face to mine. She kissed me, because it was the right way to do this. The last breath is everything. For her, it was more, it was her last chance for something she wanted. I didn't understand kissing, but I didn't mind. It was nice, being held, feeling her mouth against mine. And our lips opened, and I was falling. I felt it, vaguely, as we slumped to the floor. I felt drops of blood as huge, white wings burst from her back. Just a few drops, and they made me happy because blood meant she was alive. I saw eyes like mine, orange and round, watching my last seconds so I wouldn't be alone. And I wasn't, because when darkness hid those eyes I could feel arms around me and lips pressed to mine, the last thing I ever felt.

What would happen to me next, I still didn't know. No one knew, and no one would ever know who didn't follow me.

ACT IV

PASTORAL INTERLUDE, WITH FLAMES

"Something is coming. You should head back."

That was a Squirrel Child. They were why I was here, after all. When things were going well and we had more than enough food, we shared with the squirrels. Mostly pies, cakes – cooked foods, the kinds of things they couldn't get in the woods. Part of it was generosity. Part of it was family spirit. It could be your brother or sister or son or daughter who eats that pie. Either way, the kitchen at the manor was full of smiles when it was time to cook up a basket for the Wild Children.

But part of it was a trade. Somehow, the squirrels know things.

"Is that official, or can you see something from up in those branches?" I asked, cautious but mild.

Why did I have to be cautious? Because a few seconds later a Squirrel Boy was hanging by his feet upside down from a branch in front of me, waving his arms and trying to grab something out of the basket. It's hard not to like the squirrels, but they live for mischief, and most of them have forgotten what life is like outside their wood. They probably wouldn't lie about a message from their oracle, but taking anything they say at face value always struck me as unwise. Anyway, I thought this one might have been Jack Hickory, who changed a couple of years ago when Right and I first

160

arrived at the Manor. He was pretty unreliable to begin with. I couldn't be sure. For some reason squirrels all end up looking the same.

"Are you stupid, Sinister?!" demanded the squirrel. He had actually let go with one foot to get an extra inch of reach. "If you don't head back soon, you'll miss it!"

It occurred to me that if he did fall he'd ruin the whole basket. I wouldn't put it past the other squirrels to lick crumbs and sugar and marmalade off him, but it would still be less of a gift than we intended, so I lifted the danish off the top of the stack just a little. In an eye blink he was back up on his tree branch, his mouth full of pastry, and cheese smeared over his cheeks. I went back to laying everything out on the blanket. It was an occasion, so we tried to make things look pretty, although I'd watched the squirrels accept an offering from a distance and they were pretty much going to descend on it like starving vultures when they arrived.

"Do I want to miss it?" If he was going to be vague I had no intention of getting excited for squirrel games. "If it's a real message, tell me the whole thing."

"If you'll give me a strawberry," sulked the Squirrel Boy. They were his strawberries anyway now, so I had no qualms about picking one out of a bowl and throwing it up to him. Or rather throwing it hard, above and past his head. He caught it anyway, as we both knew he would.

"Alright." He sighed after he'd chewed it up, sounding aggrieved. "If you can't just take my word for it. The oracle said that something wonderful and awful – mainly awful – is coming, and when I saw you, and I guess I'm seeing you now, you'd have just enough time for you and Dexter to get back to the manor and play your part."

I couldn't help but be skeptical every time the squirrels made a pronouncement like this. "If it's awful as well as wonderful, why would we want to take part in it at all?" That was exactly the kind of question they liked to leave unanswered.

This time, they didn't. "Because if you don't it won't be wonderful at all, just awful."

Of course, the squirrels can be wrong, but that seemed like a clear enough message, and I'd been wasting time already. "In that case, you can keep the basket!" I yelled and set off at a run for the pasture. The squirrel laughed, but I was less than mortified by what a squirrel thought of my dignity when he didn't have any himself. Also, curiosity was starting to get hold of me, and I was a slave to it.

So was Right, and I knew just where to find him. He was watching the herds this afternoon, and I'd been sent to deliver goodies to the squirrels. We'd had a bit of a debate over who got which job. Last week we'd been moving rotten crates in the storage cellar when we found a moldy old book on animal husbandry. It had been pretty amazing. Old man Spruce had been happy to let us check the herds for signs of bot fly and eye worms. The book had been pretty technical, and probably no one else in the manor could have made sense of it, especially as damaged as it was, but we'd learned a lot and wanted to see if it could be of practical use. If I sound like I wished I could have been the one in the pasture, it really hadn't been an argument, more of a discussion. Visiting the squirrels was quite a treat too.

There was Right, holding open a sheep's mouth. I wasn't sure how he'd done that. Most people thought of us as interchangeable, and my twin brother and I just about know what each other are thinking, we're so alike. Still, there are some things he can do I don't understand. Presumably there are things I can do that he can't.

Right jerked his head to beckon me closer and called out, "Hey, Left! Come and look at this! I hope we have enough molasses."

The squirrel called me Sinister, and my brother Dexter. Right and Left were the names we were given when we were found. It was Miss Oakapple, the head cook, who started calling us Sinister and Dexter in the old language before the Empire came. I'm sure she just wanted us to have better names than 'Right' and 'Left', and everyone else felt the same way by then. So now everyone calls me Sinister and my brother Dexter. Everyone but us. I'm Left and he's Right. You can't just wish away a name that easily.

"No time. The squirrels have had some kind of message. We have to get back to the manor now or something that's coming will be worse than it is already."

I was amused by his expression. He was as annoyed and frustrated as I was by that kind of vague prediction. There was no sense ignoring it just because we'd never know if it was true, though, so we set off at a run, or at least the fastest run we thought we could keep up all the way back. We headed for the road because it would be faster and easier, which meant we were the first to see the wagons.

There were three of them, coaches really, piled with baggage and moving at a sedate enough pace. They were fancier than anything I could recall seeing before, and when we saw the livery we sped up, running hard the rest of the way. We were about to fall over when we passed the gate, but I was able to yell, "The Baron's here!" before Right and I dropped to our knees next to a horse trough.

We're not known as pranksters. Spruce was there like magic asking, "What did you see?"

"Three coaches. *His* coaches. Not just his symbol, his coaches," explained Right. I couldn't breathe. Anyway, that was all we had to say and old Spruce couldn't waste what little time we'd bought him. It took about thirty seconds before everyone knew and he was giving orders to whoever hadn't already figured out what they needed to do. I was touched that Millie, Miss Oakapple's niece, helped us drag ourselves out of sight of the main gate so we could get our breath back in the stables, and even brought us a jar of juice and some bread and honey. If things had been different I think she would have been sweet on Right, to tell the truth. She was as nice as her aunt, anyway. As we finished wolfing down the bread, she came back in her best maidservant dress and brought us our uniforms, such as they were. We had exactly enough time to pull them on and be standing by the front door with as much of the manor as could be spared to greet the coaches as they pulled through the gate.

I had never seen the Baron. He hadn't been to the manor in the time Right and I had lived here. He hadn't been to the manor in the time we'd been alive. When the Empire took this area, decades ago, the Baron had added it to his lands and built the manor where a village used to be as some kind of second home for vacations. Clearly he didn't take many vacations. No one who got out of the coaches was old enough to be that man. It was a very small group anyway, and most were clearly guards or servants.

Two were dressed much better than the others, however. There was a dark haired man, on the younger side, who was just well dressed. Nothing fancy, but the clothes were clean and the fabric gleamed. You could tell how rich he was. The girl was younger than Right and I, and I suppose she was beautiful, but it was like a statue or a painting was beautiful. She stood like a statue, absolutely still, and her dress had more pieces than I could count but still left her shoulders bare. I lost count just of the laces. Not only was she too still, she was pretty in the wrong way, dressed and styled like a woman when she was hardly more than a child. She couldn't be older than fourteen and might be years younger. Of course, then I realized she really couldn't be more than fourteen. She had big, long ears, grey and fuzzy. The Baron's daughter was a Wild Child?

I said Right and I could almost read each other's minds. He nudged me subtly and whispered, "Collar." Yes, there it was. We'd heard stories that

Wild Children were treated like monsters and kept as slaves in the heart of the Empire. I'd been skeptical, but there was no denying that collar. It was like an iron shackle around the girl's throat. Someone had tried to make it pretty with engravings, but it was an ugly thing at the core.

"It's alright," announced the man. "You can relax. My father's not coming." Nobody relaxed.

Old Spruce had been waiting to meet him of course, and bowed. He didn't have to fake 'humble and friendly', he was naturally good at it. "Master V-" was as far as he got before the young man took his hands and corrected him.

"Don't start. 'Sir Victor' will do these days." He did 'proud and friendly, but not too proud' quite well, too.

Then I found out Spruce had also missed the collar, because he bowed again and asked, "And may I ask Her Ladyship's name? We surely would have heard if she were your sister, wouldn't we?"

At a time like that I look at people's reactions. Sir Victor was trying to pretend there hadn't been a faux pas. The servants and guards with the coaches were either trying not to laugh or trying not to look angry. Spruce had noticed both, and I thought had seen the collar as well. I couldn't blame him for forgetting. There was a ring on the collar even, like a dog collar. Who leashes a Wild Child like a dog?

As for the girl herself, her face had been too composed to read, but for a moment it was sad. I might have used the word 'bleak'. Then it was gone again, and she was stepping up to old Spruce but still behind Sir Victor. She curtseyed, and it wasn't just formal, her head was bowed low. It was humble and elegant like nothing I'd ever seen before, although the elegance was kind of spoiled when as her hands came into sight; one of them was holding a ridiculous floppy black stuffed toy.

As sad as she'd been a moment before I would have sworn her smile, small and restrained, was honest. "Are you Mister Spruce, the estate manager? I am honored every time someone mistakes me for human, Sir, and it does happen often, but I am really only Hind, one of the Baron's pets."

Then she was standing again and back to being a statue, but the young man's hand lay on her shoulder and he added rather more warmly, "She's also your other guest. My father won't be coming, but Hind and I will be staying awhile. We're not quite sure how long, but I can explain everything after dinner, after you and the staff have had time to realize the sky isn't falling and relax." That hand rose to the girl's head and brushed back her hair. "She'll go out of her way to remind you she's not human, but please treat Hind as well as she'll let you. I don't think my father owns anything he values more."

Now everyone was looking at the girl, but if it bothered her she didn't show it. Anyway, they were all kind looks. Probably most of us felt bad for her. The collar made me cringe, and she acted like a pet, not a person. If I'd started to think she was pretty that put a complete damper on it. A glance at his face told me Right felt the same way. But there was that stuffed toy too, and now she wasn't bothering to hide it but was clutching it against her chest in both hands. No one was relaxed yet, but everyone was starting to unwind.

"We're honored to have both of you, your Lordship," Spruce was telling him now. "I'm keeping you waiting though, and you must be worn out from your trip. Would you like dinner or a bath first? Your rooms should be ready by now."

"Already?" Now Sir Victor was openly grinning. "With five minutes' warning? That's a relief. A bath does sound good, and Hind never passes one up." The three of them were walking up to the front doors, until suddenly Sir Victor changed course.

Right and I bowed as best we could and then tried to stand very still and look polite as he walked right up to us. He reached out and touched my furry ear, which I certainly wouldn't have put up with if he hadn't been a noble. But he was, and he could do what he liked, and if I said anything I'd get everyone in trouble.

"Wild Children? You have Wild Children out here? How many?" he asked.

Now Spruce didn't know what to do either, but he was sharp enough to take it easy. "A few squirrels in the little forest under the hills. We're not sure how many, and I think you'll take it well if I advise you very strongly not to go in there. As for Sinister and Dexter here, it's not quite that simple. When you meet with me later, your Lordship, I'll tell you the whole story."

Sir Victor was unflappable. "They can tell us themselves. Since you didn't know who's coming I'm sure you haven't assigned us servants yet. Dexter can wait on me while I bathe, and Sinister can wait on Hind. Would being attended by a Wild Child make you feel more comfortable, Hind?"

She smiled, and she was looking at us curiously too, rather than with the formal look she gave humans. I was sure this smile was honest because it wasn't much of a smile. "It really would, Master Vick," she told him. Now the smile, weak as it was, was for him too.

165

They were suddenly at ease, and the rest of us suddenly weren't. I was trying not to blush and trying hard. Right must have felt awkward enough, but I'd just been asked to bathe a girl, and she might not be properly a woman yet but she was obviously no longer a little kid either. Everyone else looked a little shocked too, but this was what the Baron's son wanted and no one was going to tell him it was inappropriate. So Right and I bowed again and stepped inside as fast as we dared to go make sure the baths were ready. Sir Victor and the girl kept watching us until we went around the corner.

The manor wasn't nearly ready, but a quick check with the maids told us that Sir Victor would have the Purple Suite and Hind would get the Scarlet Suite. They were on the northeast side of the second floor, on either side of the rooms reserved for the Baron himself assuming he ever came and used them. I was certain there would be lots of debate and second-guessing, but it was too late for that, and from my and Right's perspectives the essential fact was that in the servants' corridors behind the suites there was a cistern and boiler room. We wouldn't have far to go to draw the baths.

Other than the occasional cleaning chore I had hardly spent much time in the noble guest quarters. The white-tiled bathing chamber with its ceramic tub was prettier than I remembered. That was very likely one of the reasons it was given to the girl. I had hardly begun filling the bath when she walked in dragging a trunk I would have thought too big for her. She certainly hadn't dallied.

The Baron might not have visited in a long time, but this was his manor, and our job was to make it as comfortable as possible considering we were out in the middle of nowhere. I would do my part to treat our noble guests accordingly. So I put down the ewer I was using to carry the hot water and tried to take the trunk from her. "Your Ladyship, let me get that!" If she was a pet, I was certain we were supposed to treat her like a noble. She wouldn't let me take it, but she at least let me help her lift it up onto the foot of the bed.

The moment it was out of her hands though, she pulled that black doll out from where she'd half-stuffed it into her bodice and swept gracefully over and delicately shut the door. I noticed she'd done it delicately, because the moment it was shut she was leaning her shoulder against it in an entirely indelicate way. "Does the door lock?" she asked me curtly.

I didn't honestly know, but, "I think so. There should be a catch-" Our hands were both on the door latch and we found the lock at the same time, and flipped it.

It was something like snuffing a candle, or maybe lighting one. She was lying against the doorframe, and the poise, the unreadable expression was gone. First she pulled the stuffed animal up under her chin, and for a moment that bleak look was back, with empty eyes and a tight, pained mouth. It only lasted a couple of seconds, and then she was giving me a weak but honest smile. "Did they say your name is Sinister? First, please, I beg you, don't call me Your Ladyship, or Miss Hind, or anything but 'Hind'. I appreciate the sentiment, but my Master's men will be around, and I managed to convince him that he needed his best and most loyal and especially his most flexible back home. Do you understand? I know its three hundred miles or something, but rumors would get back home eventually. Anyway, we're both Wild Children. I get enough of that from the donkeys I meet in the capital. I'm not better than any other Wild Girl. My Master just paid more for me."

Unfortunately this was already as awkward as I'd expected, but she was at least acting like she was more than an oil painting. "Actually, my brother and I aren't really Wild Children."

Her eyes, the color of a dark lake, were suddenly more noticeable now that they weren't vacant and staring. "You have to be. Jinx keeps looking at you and he doesn't notice humans." As she spoke she walked around the bed and set her doll on the mantelpiece over the fireplace. I realized she was talking about the doll, because now that I looked at it it was just this plain black stuffed cat toy, but the eyes were red buttons and somehow they watched you. With that and the huge stitched smile, I thought whoever sewed it must have been some kind of warped genius and it was no wonder she talked like it was alive. It wasn't my place to tell her that it wasn't, or that she was being creepy, or argue with her about what I was. So I waited, and I was immediately rewarded because she wasn't done. With the doll watching the room she smiled at me again and continued. "I heard Mister Spruce say the same thing. If there's some kind of story, I'd like to hear it. You can tell me while you help me get undressed."

I had to help her get undressed. It was beyond arguing. There were laces on the back of her shirt just to start with, and buttons in odd places, and it was particularly tight around the waist and upper arms, and those were just the reasons I could see from here that two people would do a better job than one.

167

I would certainly end up in the same room with her while she was naked before this was over, but I wasn't going to completely give up on appropriate levels of modesty. "The bath isn't ready yet, Miss Hind. If I fill it while you take care of that, it will be ready at the same time you are."

She sighed, and I cursed myself. I'd called her 'Miss'. "It's just 'Hind', really, Sinister. I know you're trying to be nice, and everyone else here will want to be nice, but my Master's people are used to the court. If you'd called me that in front of a noble you'd have insulted every woman in the room by suggesting someone might one day marry me. The men, at least, would probably just laugh at you. I don't know what trouble there will be if people call me that here, but there will be trouble for someone, somehow. No one is to call me anything but 'Hind', okay? As for the bath, this outfit wasn't meant to be put on or taken off alone, and you'd end up helping me while the water got cold, and I really want to boil myself. And now I've just lectured you and I feel like an ass, which unfortunately I am." She put her hand to her forehead and looked guilty for a moment, and then restarted. "You can be shy about yourself, Sinister. You don't have to tell me anything. But please don't be shy about me, and please help me, because it really is hard to undress myself sometimes."

I was angry for a moment, but she wasn't trying to make me feel guilty. I was doing that all by myself. She was right, and I was wrong. So although I didn't exactly feel comfortable doing it, I stepped up to her as she turned her back, and started undoing laces and buttons. And, I supposed, I had to talk to her while I did it, or at least I should. "I don't mind telling it. And if I have to call you Hind, you can call me Left and my brother Right if you want."

"Wild Child names," she judged immediately. "Because of your ears." A few laces and a couple of tiny, awkward, hidden buttons, and the outer layer of her outfit was off, including most of the skirts. I realized she'd been making a joke, calling herself an 'ass'. Her long, coarse gray-haired ears were matched by a long tail just like them, which hung low and had a lot of black hair around the end. She was a Donkey Child.

I absently touched my left ear. It was longer than a human's but not much, and brown and hairy. And that was about it, really. "That's what they named us. They thought we were Wild Children at first. The only thing I remember is falling over on the kitchen porch in the rain. Before that, nothing. But the squirrels wouldn't take us, and no one had lost any children, especially not twin boys, so everyone just adopted us together.

Anyway, after about a year it became clear we definitely weren't Wild Children after all, because we grew."

"They promised me I would never grow up," Hind mused, although her introspective tone was kind of strained. It turned out there just wasn't any way to get that bodice off her but to pry it off up or down. We'd chosen up, and probably should have chosen down. "I didn't understand what that would be like. You're young enough to be a Wild Child, still."

"Just barely." I grunted as the bodice came off at last, leaving her hair a serious mess. There were more layers underneath, but everything left was looking much easier. "And we were younger than you when we got here. We're aging. When everyone realized that they started calling us Dexter and Sinister, and the wild speculation as to our true origins began."

She giggled a little. And she was, abruptly, naked. It was easier not to think about than I'd expected. The way she held herself, the way she was pretty, it was still more like a statue than a real girl. I didn't much care. Instead I was noticing how very pale she was. Was everyone like that down in the Empire? Sir Victor was, but not like this. And I was almost horrified by how much tailoring effort had been put into her underwear, of all things. It was the most frivolous waste.

Even if I wasn't ogling her it wasn't appropriate either to look at her or her underwear. I turned my back carefully, and she giggled harder. "You can fill the tub now, but you have to tell me if you ever figured it out."

"No, just a lot of guesses." I did feel better picking up the ewer and going out through the servant's door to get more hot water rather than standing in the same room with a naked girl, even though she didn't seem to care. I heard a little sloshing, and when I came back in she was lowering herself into the tub even though there were only a few inches of water yet. I was worried the fresh, hot water would burn her, but she didn't complain. She'd moved the doll, too. Now it was by the basin, still watching everything.

I also realized she could hear me as I went back and forth, so I just kept talking. "The parson thought we were possessed by demons or something, but it's not like anyone listened to him anyway, and he just disappeared a few months later. We think he tried to go into the woods. Miss Oakapple thinks we're the twins her grandmother lost when they were infants, finally given back by the fairies. When Brother Mordecai started dropping by to replace the parson he said he thought we were cursed. He says there are bad things up in the mountains, much stranger than Wild Children, and sometimes whole villages are destroyed. He thought we might be survivors.

That's the most sensible explanation I've heard, but it's still just rumor and guesswork. There've been weirder ideas too, but people dropped those."

"I'll bet," she said. I was pouring in another jug of water, so I at least generally had to be looking at her. I thought looking at her face would be the best way. When I did, I realized her eyes were red and there were tears running down her cheeks. Her voice had been perfectly normal.

"You're crying," I told her. She couldn't think I hadn't noticed. "What's wrong?" It wasn't my business and you don't ask questions like that of nobles, but she didn't seem to want to be treated like one. Anyway, curiosity.

"I haven't seen my Master in a week." Her voice was finally cracking. "I may never see him again. It's so peaceful and safe out here. Back home it's bad. Nobody knows it yet, but it's bad. I know he won't live through it. It's why he sent me here."

"I don't understand." I didn't. I couldn't have told you the name of the capital, even. Right and I had never been able to find a book on geography anywhere.

"The Emperor is dead." Now she was sort of hanging over the edge of the tub. She'd unbound her hair, and I could hardly believe how long it was. "Everyone knows. We've known for at least a year. But they were being careful because really, everyone knew he was just this crazy old man who would rather pray than make any decisions anyway. Viceroy Amicus and the court have been mostly agreeing on what to do for something like twenty years. And now the Archbishop's dead too, and without an Emperor to appoint the new one everybody's arguing about who the new one will be, and how to decide, and they've started to realize there's not going to be another Emperor unless something drastic happens. It's not like he had any children, or nephews, or cousins, even."

I felt cold. I was starting to wonder if I was going to cry, too. "You're saying there'll be a war."

She looked up at me then, and I just couldn't read her expression at all because there was everything in it, and her wet hand was holding onto mine. "No, don't worry about that. You're safe, the manor is safe. You may never even hear about it here. The court are a bunch of stuck up buffoons, but most of them are smart enough to know that the only real army belongs to Amicus, and Master runs it. If it came down to fighting none of them would win. It's all going to be a game, but it's not a friendly game anymore."

"Then what aren't you telling me?" I wanted to be gentle, but that was half a story.

She didn't want to say it. "...they poisoned my Master." The words finally blurted out, she sank into the tub, covering her eyes and sobbing. "He'd be dead, but we think it was one of the cakes and he fed them to me instead. I'd be dead if I wasn't a Wild Child. I was so sick I didn't want him to look at me, but no one died. I thought that was an even better reason for me to stay, but he wouldn't agree. I... I yelled at him when no one could hear, but he still made me leave." She might have been admitting to kicking a kitten, the way she said it. "He couldn't make the Baroness leave, but he packed us up and sent us here where we'll be safe. I don't want to be safe. I want to be with my Master." Now she was crying harder and she could hardly talk.

I didn't know who I was talking to now, and I realized even in the bathtub she was still wearing that collar. It wasn't some kind of leather strap or ornament. It was solid metal. "You're a slave. They really keep Wild Children as slaves down there. You really think he's your Master." The whole idea was revolting. I knew that in some places 'slave' and 'peasant' were just different titles, but she was a Wild Girl. The squirrels were children from the manor who changed and ran off. No, that wasn't even it. She acted like this was right, instead of just life.

She grabbed my hand again and smiled, but it was a sick smile. "People talk like that sometimes, who don't really know us. I talk to other donkeys sometimes, too. Mostly we just want our owners to be someone who deserves us. My Master deserves a lot better than me."

And I understood. This wasn't about what was true, or what was right or wrong. It was about Hind's feelings, and right now she was crying, and everything was black and white anyway. I wouldn't expect a squirrel to act like a human child either. Bluntly, it wasn't my place to judge this girl, and I needed to stop thinking like it was.

Instead I should do what you do when someone is crying, and gently try to change the subject. The only other subject I had available wasn't much better, but it was better. "I thought nobles try and poison each other all the time, don't they? It can't be easy to do. Look at how it failed this time."

Well, that had her down to sniffling, but she was shaking her head. She sounded cold now. Not irrational, but way too rational. "Do people think that? It hasn't happened in a hundred years. It was dangerous and stupid and it didn't work, you're right about that. But it means the gloves are off. Nobody's paying attention to the rules anymore. There weren't any rules really, but they've only just realized that. There won't be armies, but anything else might happen. People are going to die and Master is the biggest target."

I was still trying to find a better topic. "What's he like?" I admit, I was curious too. This man was our lord, and she knew him personally. All we knew was that when things were good he only took what we could spare, which might be a lot, and when things were bad food would come to get us through it.

The sniffling eased. "I can't tell you. I know most of his secrets and I guess that's part of it, but I just don't know what to say. There are kinder men, and smarter men, and I guess there are stronger men, but I've never met one who was so much of all three at the same time."

Again I couldn't let this be about what was true. This was about how Hind felt, and I was ashamed now that I'd felt like I knew better than her. "He doesn't sound like someone who loses when things get rough, then."

"No." I had her thinking again. Which meant I was relieved when she told me, "Could you get some more hot water? And then I want to be alone for a while."

I went and got more hot water, and I left through the servant's door so she could keep the main door locked. Talking to her had been getting to me. I could feel the doll watching me as I walked out the door.

Which left me a little at a loose end. Filling a bath wasn't hard, but talking to Hind had exhausted me. I was about to step out into the main hallway, and there was Right, so I grabbed his arm and pulled him in.

He was grinning. I wasn't. "So, what, did you have to scrub her back?" he teased. I'm not sure I can explain what it's like when you talk to your twin brother. Just assume that no matter what either of us says, we know exactly what the other means.

"No, it's not like that. I stopped caring, really. And she didn't care from the start. She thinks she's some kind of pet, so I guess it doesn't matter what she wears. And everybody has to call her 'Hind', and she was serious about that. It'll cause trouble if we don't. Did you tell Sir Victor everything?"

"Everything there is to tell." Like I'd explained to Hind, there isn't much. People make a lot of noise about not knowing anything. "One of those carriages? It was full of books, Left. He's got his own library, and he brought it with him. He says he might as well learn about the squirrels while he's out here."

I grunted. I wasn't sure how I felt about that.

Right was nodding. "I told him to take it easy. I saw the girl too. He seems to understand. He said he wants to learn about them because they're nothing like the donkeys back in the capital. He said those aren't wild at all."

"He was right about that. Like I said, she thinks she's the Baron's pet. She's grateful, even."

We were both thinking about that. "Well, what do you think of her?" Right asked me.

It was a good question. I was trying to put it into words. "I think that if the Baron keeps this place for vacations, he did the smart thing to send her. Apparently things are getting nasty among the nobles, and she's rather hysterical about it, but she's starting to unwind already."

"Sir Victor said something about that, too. But do you like her?" There wasn't any teasing or extra weight to that. If I liked her, Right would know he'd like her.

"I think so. She spent most of the time crying, and she's as weird as you'd expect a real Wild Girl to be but not in any way I would have thought. She's smart, though, and she tries to be nice, and I don't think she's spoiled at all. Even as upset as she was she treated me like she wasn't any better or worse than I am. What about his Lordship?"

Right grinned. "Oh, yes. He says he'll keep us assigned to him and Hind so that we can have free access to his library while we're not busy. And he said he mostly takes care of himself."

Now I was grinning, too. And that was how Right and I were introduced to the Baron's son Victor and Hind, his Wild Girl.

The next morning, we learned that the upper class likes to sleep late. We had bells and messengers ready and Right and I were sticking close to the kitchen, but there wasn't a peep. After a while Miss Oakapple decided not to wait. I was given a loaded tray, besieged with teasing questions about Hind's underwear from the younger members of the kitchen staff, and sent upstairs to deliver Hind's breakfast. I had no reason to believe she'd unlocked her door, so I went through the servant's hallway. I snuck into her bedroom as quietly as I could, and as I suspected she was asleep in the oversized bed, curled up around that doll of hers. I thought she was asleep, anyway. She didn't snore, or twitch, and I couldn't hear her breathing. I laid the food out on the dining table and left everything covered, and she still seemed to be asleep when I snuck out again.

Right's luck had been a little better. Apparently Sir Victor had been asleep too, but his library had been installed in his sitting room, although not in any order Right could figure out. By luck he'd found a copy of the animal husbandry book we had been studying, but this one was pristine, readable, and didn't have entire sections destroyed by mold. For me there was a book on architectural engineering. Stresses, baffling, and sound reflection were heavy reading, so of course I was enthralled. Right and I spent the rest of the morning curled up in a corner of the kitchen by the signal bells, reading. He was learning about multi-generation cross-breeding, and I was trying to figure out pages full of math. Sometime before whatever happened to us brought us here, Right and I had learned a great deal of math. This was the first time I'd run into anything so complicated it didn't immediately make sense, and I was figuring out what some of the symbols meant and how they were used, and nobody would be smart enough to just work that out from scratch. It meant that at some point I'd actually been taught these things.

For example, when I saw a couple of answers it was clear to me how the funny 'f' symbol was calculated, which meant I could solve most of the equations in the book, but I didn't know what it really meant yet so I wouldn't understand what I was doing. I was just contemplating that puzzle when a wooden ladle rapped me on the top of the head and then proceeded to do the same to Right.

"Boychicks," and that was the way Miss Oakapple talked sometimes, "if it were up to me you could spend the whole day buried in those books, but if the lord and his little girl up there so much as sniff that the service they got here wasn't the best anywhere I will see you two buried in the ground." She was kidding, but we only had to glance out the door into the yard to realize what she really meant. It was almost noon. The morning was over, and we weren't sure if our guests had even woken up!

"Should we draw a bath again?" asked Right. He was serious, and I suspected nobles bathed a lot too, but everybody else took it as an excuse to grin at me again.

"Bring the breakfast back and find out if they're awake first, and what they want," Miss Oakapple instructed us, and we nodded. That was a good plan.

"You take both books with you," I told Right. I gave him mine, and he nodded at that. It would just be better to leave them in the hands of the person who was visible to the owner and could put them back upon request.

Lake Gorse, who was a couple of years older, opened his mouth and his expression said it all – he was going to make some prurient suggestion about Hind. But he hadn't finished the first word when Miss Oakapple bopped him with her ladle, rather harder than she had us. Everyone understood. The joke had officially gotten old, and respect for both our guests was going to be the order of the day.

Of course, now that the subject had been brought up, I was a little nervous about what I'd find when I got back to Hind's bedroom. My guest had a doll with spooky eyes, a bewildering lack of concern for whether she was wearing anything, and a tendency to burst into tears when she knew no one could see. I immediately turned that around. If she was that unhappy, I should let her spend all day every day crying if my listening to her would help any.

But when I peeked into her room through the servant's door she wasn't in the bed. I knocked cautiously, and she didn't answer. Technically I shouldn't have done that since servants are supposed to be invisible, but it was pretty clear Hind would prefer to be treated like we were both people. I waited a moment and knocked again. There was no sound at all.

So I let myself in and I was almost certain, from the first moment, she wasn't there. Her clothes from the previous night had been folded and left by the door. Her clothes trunk had been opened and moved against a wall. She'd even made the bed, and sitting among the pillows was the cat doll. Carefully, I picked it up and moved it to the mantelpiece, trying to ignore its expression. If Hind had left her room the maids would want to get in here very soon, and I wanted to make sure no one touched Jinx. Then I collected the breakfast tray and dishes. They'd been used, but it looked like she'd eaten all of two pieces of toast and a single egg.

With everything piled up, I headed down the back stairs to the kitchen as fast as I safely could. I dumped the tray on the scullery, and Miss Oakapple was already lifting the covers and shaking her head in disapproval.

"She's gone out. She can't have made a fuss, or we'd have heard about it. I'm going to go find her, though," I reported. "You won't believe how tidy she is. She made the bed."

Miss Oakapple smiled widely. She did that a lot. Her life consisted of feeding people, and sometimes I thought she had the best job in the manor. "So she's a sweet little thing as well as pretty? She's not like those fool squirrels, that's for sure. Pity it's a waste. I'll send the girls up to strip the bed and see what we can send from her luggage to the laundry, but first-" She nodded behind me.

Millie was pressing a woven basket into my arms. "Here's the – Hind's lunch. There's extra in there for you too, and food for Dexter if you get a chance."

Hind, our guest – my guest – was just wandering around somewhere without anyone waiting on her. It was rapidly impressing itself upon me how important it was that I find her, fast. I paused to warn Miss Oakapple, "Make sure no one touches the doll, not even to clean it. She gets really intense about it," before rushing out.

I wasn't at all certain where to start. She'd had all morning and could be anywhere on the estate by now. We hadn't heard that she or Sir Victor were wandering around inside, so I used that to make a guess and checked the field out back first. It was a lucky guess. Even at a distance, a girl around my age with long hair and pale skin was obvious. I hurried out to meet her as fast as I could with the basket to burden me.

Hind was surprising me again. No one on the manor had clothes like that, true, but basically she was wearing a loose shirt and a pair of breeches. There were unnecessary ribbons, and I thought the breeches were rather too tight for a girl, but it wasn't anything like the fancy dress of the day before. She was even barefoot, and her hair had simply been tied back in a single braid stretching down exactly to the base of her grey tail. So exactly, I was certain it had been trimmed to that length deliberately.

She wasn't weepy either, or blank like a statue. She did look very serious about what she was doing, if I could figure out what it was. She would drift, with the kind of grace I didn't associate with donkeys at all, from one position to another, usually involving at least one limb stretched out, but she seemed to be perfectly balanced all the time. When she stretched one leg forward and bent her whole upper body flat along its length, then stretched her arms out further onto the grass, I found myself gaping.

"I'm sorry we didn't notice when you went out," I told her immediately. She might want to be treated like an equal, but she was still the honored guest. "I brought you lunch." And since she did want to be treated like an equal, I could ask, "What are you doing?"

She didn't quite smile like other people do. It was delicate, like happiness was something made of glass she might drop. That's a flowery way of describing it, but it's how I felt seeing it. "I'm training, which is why there wasn't any point in disturbing you. I've been riding in a carriage for a week, and I ate way too much of that breakfast you left for me this morning. I'm getting fat and flabby and stiff."

I was a little worried this would be rude, but, "I don't believe anything you just said, except maybe the part about the carriage ride."

She giggled, at length. I wondered if she'd trained that, learned to laugh like a harmless young woman. If she had it seemed natural now. She was a conundrum. "I don't gain weight easily, you're right. I watch it anyway. My appearance is part of my duty to my Master, and I have to be fit and flexible and practice all sorts of things I haven't had a chance to on the road. This is after I've been loosening up for an hour, too. I could hardly touch my toes when I started."

"It's been more than an hour, Hind. It's lunchtime." I pointed at the basket which I'd laid on the grass.

She actually looked a little horrified. "Oh, I can't eat yet. I won't be able to work out, and I'm not done!"

"You're on holiday in the countryside, and you just said you've been sitting in one place for a week. You don't have to keep yourself ready to serve at every moment. Take a break," I urged her.

"Yes, I do," she told me coldly. The look she gave me wasn't ugly, really, but it was hard. I'd offended her. And then it just disappeared. She didn't expect me to understand. "It looks like I spent the whole morning doing stretches, though. And working out without eating at all is bad for you, too. Tell you what. Help me practice my dancing and then I'll stop and eat. I'll even make up for breakfast. I guess I only felt like I was gorging myself."

"I can't dance. At all," I told her awkwardly. I actually felt kind of bad about it, suddenly. If she was weird, she'd obviously worked hard to be graceful and refined, and I was neither. "I don't think I can help you much."

"You don't have to do ballet," she replied with a grin – and stood up on her tiptoes. Honestly, without shoes, on the tips of her toes. I couldn't even guess how she did it, but it probably hurt and I was relieved when she dropped down again. "And I've seen country dances, and they're more complicated than most ball room dancing. Just let me lead. I'm not supposed to ever lead, but it will still keep me in the rhythm."

I didn't know what to say, but when she took my hand I didn't resist either. I wish I could describe what happened next. She seemed to float, and I felt like I was stumbling around, but at least I felt very quickly I was doing it in rhythm with her. It was easier than I'd expected to just try and match her footsteps, let her spin me around, and then, when I realized how it worked, hold my hand up and let her spin herself around or bend herself backwards.

I tried to stay involved, but I couldn't help but realize we were doing this in the middle of an open field in plain sight of everyone. People were staring, although soon I realized not as many as I'd feared. But up on a balcony on the manor Sir Victor and Right were watching, and Right was doubled over in hysterics. Of course I'd have laughed at him, too. He's my brother. And most of the people weren't watching us, they were watching her. I was sure no one who lived here had ever seen a performance quite like this. Although I didn't like how one of the older handlers seemed to be staring at her breeches. I glared at him, and I knew I was right because he looked embarrassed and stopped.

A little while later she was curtseying deeply to me, and I bowed as best I could, and she just flopped down in the grass beside the basket as casually as you could please. I did, too. I was actually tired, but it hadn't been that bad.

"You really eat well here, did you know that?" she chattered to me cheerfully as we both unpacked lunch. "We have fancier back home, yes, but not as much fancier than you'd think, and the cooking here is really good. And that's a mansion in the capital. Think about that." She ate a sandwich with remarkable gusto, and yet didn't make any mess that I could see.

"Everyone does some of the cooking, so I suppose we all share that compliment," I explained. "Miss Oakapple is in charge of the main kitchen, but that just feeds whoever's working at the manor that day. You can't see them, but there are houses behind every hill where most of us live. Not me and Right. We're part of the permanent manor staff. I suppose we just like to eat."

"I hope that doesn't get to me," she moaned dramatically, and patted her entirely flat stomach. Then she laughed, and it wasn't just a giggle. It was a little wicked, even. "Oh, lord, I sound just like Mane. She's Lord Margay's Wild Girl. She's like me, just ears and a tail, so she cost a lot." She didn't do anything as unladylike as pinch up her nose, but the look of disgust was clear. "I hope I'm not becoming that shallow. I know I'm not becoming that lazy. She's useless for anything but looking good. I bet she doesn't even know where Lord Margay's estates are, or where his money comes from." She grimaced suddenly and confided, "Now I'm becoming catty, too."

I reassured her, "I don't think you're shallow, and you're certainly not lazy. You seem to know everything about politics. I've just never met anyone who has to know about things like that and not how to bridle a horse or bake a pie."

She was grinning again, although like her smile it was kind of brittle, but it was a grin. "Do you think I can't bake a pie? I grew up on a farm. I look around, and this place is beautiful, but I can't believe you can let so much good land with no stones go unplanted. I was a human girl before I was a Wild Girl. My name was Violet-" She stopped abruptly. She looked sick. The squirrels never use their human name, or let us know who they were, and maybe this was why. She was starting to tear up and she was pulling her legs up and wrapping her arms around them and mumbling, "Don't call me that, alright? Forget I ever said it. I'm Hind now."

She relaxed again. Whatever saying that name had done to her, it was easing quickly. "I'm sorry about that. I just can't bear being away from my Master. When he has to go away and leave me behind, like if the army has to move, I get like this too."

It wasn't really a direction I wanted the conversation to go, since she seemed to have been finally relaxing. I was saved almost disastrously by the ball coming hurtling out of nowhere towards Hind's face. And to my surprise, she caught it. In both hands and it knocked her on her back, but she still caught it.

The ball is special. Balls of one kind or another are popular, but the manor was lucky. Ours was leather, which we kept fresh, wrapped around something sort of stretchy but thick that nobody knew quite where it had come from. You can use animal bladders, but they're wobbly and fragile, and this had lasted as long as anyone could remember. It was easy to blow up, and Right and I had cobbled together a sort of pump that would inflate it until it bulged so it was wonderful for kicking or throwing. It was a little solid, but not heavy.

And where the ball went, a bunch of kids soon came after. Most of them were younger than ten, and I supposed it was a quiet afternoon on the estate and there wasn't much work to do. One of them – Foxy I think his name was, which made me wonder if his mother actually wanted him to become a Wild Child, declared, "She caught it! She looks like she's made of twigs! Can she play with us?"

I couldn't remember the name of Foxy's sister, but she was wrapping her hand over his mouth and looking horrified. "You can't ask her to play with us. She's rich! She'll get dirty or something!"

"Actually Hind was just telling me she grew up on a farm, so I bet she can kick a ball as well as anybody. Would you like to give it a try? I danced with you, you can play ball with me."

She looked reluctant and sad for a moment, but she pushed herself up off the grass, and agreed cautiously, "Alright. I'm not sure I remember the rules."

"I'm not sure there are any rules. Don't hurt the kids and try and hit the post with the ball." I waved a hand at one loose group and suggested, "You'll be on their team, and I'll be on this one since we're bigger than they are." Not by much in Hind's case, but still…

So, we played ball. I was too busy to usually, so I had fun, and Right and I are kind of bookworms and it was nice to be the strongest, fastest, most athletic person on the field for once. Hind mostly looked confused, but she was smiling and she didn't act confused. Every time the ball came near her it got kicked in the direction of the post, and she never even used her hands. She scored a couple of goals too, and after one of them I had the satisfaction of pausing for a second while the ball was recovered and looking up to see what my brother thought.

Sir Victor had him with his arms stretched out and seemed to be measuring everything in sight. I would have laughed if I'd thought Right could see it from there. He hadn't gotten the easy job after all. He was stuck with the noble with the fascination with Wild Children, who thought he was one.

The game didn't last long after that. The ball came at me a little high, so I caught it with my hands, and although that's generally considered bad form I was feeling good and it was too near our goal, so I threw it as hard as I could down the other end of the field. Right past Hind.

And she kicked it. It was actually higher than her head, and she jumped up in the air and sort of twisted around and lifted her leg so high she kicked it back at me. And landed on her own two feet again like it had been nothing. Mind you, it didn't go very far and there wasn't any question of it scoring a goal, but all of a sudden none of the children wanted to do anything but crowd around her and ask her questions about the exercises they'd seen her do and why she wore so many ribbons and if they could touch her tail.

She looked even more confused by that, but when we went back to the manor she seemed happy. In a quiet way, I guess.

The next morning Right and I were holed up in the kitchen by the bells again. Unless our guests came up with different instructions, which they certainly might, we had concluded we'd start every morning this way while they were here. We were seriously considering sleeping here, but Miss Oakapple had put her foot down about that and said there were limits to responsibility and if Sir Victor needed a nightcap at three in the morning someone working night kitchen could bring it. I was a little more worried about Hind having nightmares and wanting company. She was cheering up quickly, but I was concerned she didn't trust anyone she saw as human and might not even trust Right if she started feeling bad again.

Right and I were discussing it in quiet voices, hunched up on pallets loaded with bags of flour. There are advantages to having a twin, and one of them is that it's very easy to make yourself incomprehensible to anyone but each other. If I told Right that she was 'bar Sinister', he understood that she was one of those people who didn't assume (and it would have been more correct if she had assumed) that he and I are more or less the same person. And if he replied that there was a three hundred year old vase in her room (which there is) I got that message, too. We'd made more than one reference to how she put on a face around adults like a porcelain mask. She might break down around me, but she'd been the girl she was maybe longer than we'd been alive. She could hold that mask forever if she had to.

Sometimes we talk and it's even less understandable. When he started going 'fwa fwa fwa fwa' I cracked up. He was telling me that Sir Victor sometimes forgets himself and talks like some stuffy inbred aristocrat. Knowing it all sounded like gibberish to the cooks and scullery maids walking past let us talk intimately about our guests, and I could confide that dancing with Hind had been rather exhilarating, and he could tell me that he had helped Sir Victor move boxes of philosophical equipment into his apartment. Apparently Sir Victor was completely convinced Right and I were some kind of Wild Children and was examining hairs from Right's ear under a series of lenses and even dousing them with chemicals, to compare to a bunch of old lists and try and figure out what animal we were. We could have been reading, but right now our guests were a far more fascinating puzzle. Just how to treat them was a debate by itself. They seemed to think of us as kid brothers.

Much earlier than expected Sir Victor's bell rang and interrupted us. Millie set the freshest food from the oven on a tray that had been waiting, and he went and carried it up. It was only a few minutes before he came running back down again.

"Miss Oakapple, can you pack up a basket for the day?" he asked her gravely, and then rather more excitedly told me, "We're going out and may not be back until supper. His Lordship just has to meet the squirrels." That got a lot of concerned looks, including from me, but Right assured us, "He knows not to go in. But he says they don't get Squirrel Children back in the Empire, and he would be betraying every man of learning in the capital if he doesn't try and learn whatever he can about them."

"He's going to learn what it's like to have acorns thrown at his head," Millie chirped, and almost everyone managed to resist laughing.

"Dexter, you look after him and the squirrels, alright, boychick?" Miss Oakapple told him worriedly, "There's too much that could go wrong there. When I was a duckling myself my best friend Frieda went over, and I'll never forget her and I hope she'll be playing games in those woods when I'm dead and dust."

I didn't have time to add anything myself. Hind's bell was ringing! I guess she wasn't going to sleep all morning again. "Fill everything sup, me!" I instructed Right as I grabbed the tray Millie was still filling. I hadn't meant to lapse into twin language, really. Everyone knew Right would tell me everything when he got back for dinner. Sometimes we just forget. As I tried to trot up the stairs as fast as I could without upsetting the tray, I heard Miss Oakapple saying something about being glad it was the responsible boys our guests had taken a shine to.

I thought about averting my eyes when I eased my way in through the servant's door, but there wouldn't have been any point. Her bath late last night had demonstrated to me that Hind still didn't understand modesty, or at least how it applied to herself. She had let me wait in the hall after it was filled, at least, and hadn't needed help with her clothes. I was mildly relieved to find she was wearing something this morning. It just wasn't much. She was peering into a mirror and tying up her hair in white ribbons on either side as she asked me, "I always thought I had too much hair for pigtails, but Jinx seems to like the look. What do you think?" The doll was sitting on a dresser not two feet from her hand.

"I'm not someone you should ask about hair," I admitted, and she giggled a little. As I set out her breakfast I pointed out, "It seems to me that you might as well try out simple styles while you're here. There's no one here who could make up your hair like it was when you arrived."

"Oh, we brought Sal with us, and she knows how, but I'm not going to ask her to." She left her hair hanging from bows on either side then, and started nibbling experimentally on one of Miss Oakapple's honey buns.

"And there's only so much I can do myself. Can you tie this up for me?" And with that she popped the rest of the little bun into her mouth, picked a dress up off the chair she hadn't used, and wriggled it on over her head.

It had laces going down her back. Way, way down her back. It certainly wasn't like anything any girl around here wore, but... "This is much simpler than what you were wearing when you arrived. At least it's a skirt." One that showed off her knees. Which, I realized, was why she'd been wearing the stockings already. I didn't understand the rules, but it seemed like there was a system to her clothing after all. She wasn't just trying to shock me. I was about to have that further confirmed.

"I don't wear pants much. Some Donkey Girls do all the time because it's practical, but I have to be ladylike even though everyone would laugh if you described me with that word." She rolled her eyes exaggeratedly and continued, "I can't really exercise in dresses, though. So I did all my warm-ups before breakfast. What do you think?"

We had everything tied up and fastened, including her shoes, and she was watching me curiously as she asked me to look at her. I decided after a moment of internal debate that she would prefer honesty.

"You look like a doll someone spent a lot of money on."

And she giggled again. "And out here you think that's a bad thing." I took it more seriously than she did. She was right. I was still trying to judge her by human standards. She was a Wild Girl, and she lived a very different life under different rules.

I was also, perhaps, forgetting that I was the servant here. She was eating again, so I waited a minute as she picked at the fruits and cereals and avoided the meat, then poured honey all over everything. When I thought it was a better moment I asked, "Did you have any plans for the day, Hind?"

"I did." Toying with me about her dressing habits had picked her up for a moment, but now she was serious again. At least it was a cheerful serious. "I'd like you to help me unpack some items from the carriage. I didn't think I'd need them, but the estate is so beautiful I have to get out my paints. Will you need to take the dishes back first? I could help."

Miss Oakapple would throw me in the oven if I let Hind do that. "No, as soon as we leave the room and turn our backs the maids will be in here. They'll clean and replace everything." When I said it Hind picked up her toy cat for a moment, then set it very carefully amid the perfumes and makeups she'd laid out on the dresser, broke off one of her long hairs, and wrapped it around his arm. Only then did she nod to me, and go, "Okay."

So I led her down through the pretty hallways for guests, through the rather plain hall for day to day storage, and into the stables. We found the Baron's carriages, and Hind figured out which one held her paints, and we dug around until we found her boxes. I made sure to pick up the largest and heaviest immediately so that the only thing left she could take from me was a little box with the paints themselves. Then we carried it all out back until she pointed at the biggest hill she could see, and we climbed it for her to get a better view. I erected her easel and laid out a few canvases while she mixed up her pigments.

Then for a couple of hours I sat down and enjoyed the sunshine and the breeze while she played around with a brush. It was, after all that preparation, a very relaxing morning. I had stopped watching every sentence we exchanged for weight, or worrying that she'd start crying again. Mostly she would wave her brush at something and tell me what a wonderful shade of green we had and how hard it was to match it.

I do remember when she chewed on the back end of her brush for a moment and told me, "I wish I were better. I'd love to do a portrait of you to take home with me. Or you and your brother – that would be even better."

"You practice these things every day. Wouldn't you be as good at painting as you are at dancing?" I regretted it after I said it. Not that it would upset her, but I was having to constantly remind myself that she was a guest and not just this strange girl who had wandered into the manor, and there were limits to how casual I should be around her. Friendly, but not casual. So I pushed myself to my feet, and pulled my hands back gravely and asked as politely as I could, "May I see?"

She immediately stepped away, but there was some reluctance in her expression and even before I walked around to look she was excusing, "That's actually why I'm not good enough. I hardly ever paint or do anything like that. It's not really a display talent. It's not something people can enjoy watching me do."

And I had to admit it, she was right. I liked the way she was capturing the colors of the landscape, but you could tell she was still learning. When she danced she could move like a fish. Then something made me grin. Correction, I don't grin much except at my brother, but it was a sly smile. "So you just decided you'd have fun and enjoy the scenery and play with paints for the morning?"

"Well, it's something I'd like to become good at eventually." She looked like she wanted to blush. I had caught her having a good time, and she didn't really feel guilty about it either. I was getting too casual with her again, but I felt good about that anyway.

It was time for lunch and we hadn't brought anything with us, so we started packing away her easel and canvases again, and I wrapped this one in gauze so it wouldn't smear despite the way she claimed she'd be humiliated if her Master saw how amateurish she was.

When we were in the shadow of the manor she started to get moody again. "I need to make up for that this afternoon," she speculated mournfully. "And don't tell me I don't, Left. You wait on me hand and foot even when I embarrass you. You believe in hard work just as much as I do."

She had disarmed me fairly well there, but I didn't want to concede the point. "I'm not the one on vacation." It was the best I could do.

"Collar," she reminded me, tugging on hers. "I'm never on vacation."

I was nervous about using this argument, but, "Don't you think your Master wants you to relax and have a good time while you're away from him?"

"Which is why he deserves for me to be in better shape than ever to please him when I get home." She wasn't joking, and it reminded me that I wasn't objecting to her dedication. It only bothered me because I didn't like that she thought of herself as property.

Then she surprised me again. She gave me her fragile smile and proved she'd been listening and thinking about everything I said. "I can split the difference. I'd like to work on my music this afternoon, and that can be fun if you're not being driven to prepare for a recital. Do you have a harp here?"

"I don't recall seeing one. There might be one in storage somewhere. There's a grand piano in the studio. I understand that they have to be professionally tuned, though, don't they?"

"It hasn't been tuned? Since the last time Master visited? No, don't even show me. I don't want to think about it. I'm best at the harp, but I can handle a violin or a flute passably."

"We have violins." Of that I was sure. "But I know they're in storage. We'd have to find one that fit you and restring it. I'm not sure how long that would take. I'll make sure one is gotten ready anyway, but if you don't want to wait we have plenty of flutes."

"She can have mine!" It was Foxy's sister. The kids were already watching Hind hopefully. It was a cheap wooden penny-whistle and not a flute at all, but as politely as she received it and as speculatively as she examined it I suspected she could play it too.

However. "She's a lady," I corrected the eight year old, earning myself a scathing look from Hind in the process. "She needs a fine metal flute." The watching children nodded. "There's at least one in the studio. I'll get us a lunch from the kitchen and bring both back out together."

So I left Hind trying to figure out what to do about a baby barely out of diapers pulling on her tail, stored her art supplies safely and hurried back out as fast as I could with a basket of food and a flute in a case. And then I and about a dozen children spent most of the afternoon listening to her play. The flute is a popular instrument around here, but instead of fast-paced and repetitive, she tended toward slow, intricately wandering melodies. I was impressed that anyone could remember one without a music sheet, and uncertain if it would be more or less impressive if she were improvising. It wasn't just children watching Hind as she perched on a hay bale in her frilly short dress playing on and on with her eyes closed as if breathing were something other people needed. A number of adults were staying much closer than need be, performing tasks that took much longer than could really be justified. I noticed windows opening too, and staying open. Miss Oakapple liked to tell stories about fairies. Hind was more like one of them than any Wild Child we'd ever met. Until you knew her personally, anyway.

While the guests and the more important people at the manor ate in the dining room, Right and I were able to linger over a meal ourselves in the kitchen and compare notes. We'd offered to wait table for Hind and Sir Victor too, but Miss Oakapple wouldn't hear of it.

"The squirrels wouldn't talk to him," Right told me. "More or less as expected. I explained to him that they're nervous around everyone who's not one of them, and he's an adult, a stranger, and human, and all of those make it worse. So, he starts walking into the trees, and of course a squirrel comes out and starts chattering at him. He kept it arguing for several minutes before it realized it had been tricked. When it was about to go he did the strangest thing." Here Right leaned close, and whispered to me. "He tried to catch its shadow. While it was turning around he takes out this knife and jams it into the ground right where the squirrel's shadow fell. It didn't work, and he said he didn't think it would, but it was something he wanted to try out of an old book."

"Well, so much for investigating the squirrels, I guess. I'd like to know more about them." We gave each other a special nod, because as plagued by curiosity as we always were the mysterious oracle that the squirrels delivered messages from was a mystery that nagged and couldn't be answered.

"He's not done," Right mumbled through a mouthful of cornbread. "I'll be getting up early tomorrow. He's coming up with a list of questions, and if I bring sweets we think I can get them to answer at least a few. And they'll let me close enough to the trees to see if I can get some hairs off the trunks."

"He sounds like he doesn't give up easily."

"He doesn't give up at all. He says he gets it from his father."

"That sounds like the Baron Hind talks about," I had to concede.

In the morning, both our bells rang at once, and we raced upstairs side by side with the breakfast trays. Hind wasn't dressed, but at least she was wearing some kind of dressing gown. She also pushed past me into the servant's hall, grabbing my arm and dragging me down to the corner, although 'dragging' isn't quite the right word. It wasn't rough. I didn't get the impression she was very strong. It was just insistent. She'd learned to beg with gestures rather than bully someone. So I peeked around too, and there was Right levering open the door to Sir Victor's study with his sandal.

But Sir Victor was pushing it open to assist and telling him, "Set it down. In fact, take a seat and eat up. You've got a long day ahead of you, and I want to discuss strategy."

Then as the door closed, Hind's tail gave a little twitch. It gave me the feeling that even when she relaxed, she was on stage somehow. She turned around and leaned against the wall, sighing theatrically, and then shrank away from it in horror because her dressing gown was now smeared with black dust. Servants' hallways don't get the same treatment the main hallways do, and these were hardly ever used.

She started to shrug it off right there, but to my relief thought better of that. Instead she started padding back down to her own door. "I was hoping we could watch your brother leave. I haven't met him properly yet. You hardly ever talk about him, and I wondered what he's like."

"Don't I?" No, I supposed I didn't. "It may be that I don't feel like I have to. If you've met me you've met Right, and vice versa. If our ears didn't tell us apart we'd probably have switched places already, and I'd be surprised if you noticed."

That got a speculative look and a wistful reply. "Really? That must feel like you're never alone. Someone always understands you. Now I just want to get to meet him more. For now I suppose I'll have to look ahead to my other plan for the morning. I saw a river when we were up on the hill yesterday. Is it big enough to swim in?"

"It's too fast," I told her regretfully. "But there's a deep water meadow where it spreads out a little further down, and we go swimming there sometimes. It's a good place to fish, too."

She looked galled. "I've spent too many hours sitting perfectly still. That doesn't sound like fun to me anymore. But I love to swim, and even back home I don't get to do it often."

I was thinking about taking her robe now so that it wouldn't make more of a mess before it was cleaned, which was why it hit me. "You didn't bring a swimming costume," I guessed with a certain amount of confidence.

"No?" For a moment, she sounded genuinely baffled, then when she figured it out she laughed almost the whole way down to the kitchen. We took the back stairs, because I thought she'd be self-conscious of the condition of her robe.

When I led her into the kitchens I might have set fire to a barrel of grease. Suddenly people were scattering, and Miss Oakapple was standing over me declaring, "Sinister, what could possibly have possessed you? You can't make a proper lady like Mist-" If Miss Oakapple weren't quick on the uptake she wouldn't have been head cook, and she saw our expressions. "Hind." She started over, changing directions with complete self-confidence. "The boys say you're as sweet as cream frosting," which was definitely not how I'd put it, "but I'm going to die of shame with a girl as refined as you seeing this mess. And before I die I'm going to strip the skin off that boy behind you for letting your robe get in a condition like that. I would swear that's real silk, isn't it?"

Hind was doing half the work for me. She gave Miss Oakapple a shy, flattered smile, making herself look like a little girl rather than a woman or a doll. "That was part of it," I told the cook. "When the dust got on it I wanted to take it to you right now, to be sure it was cleaned properly and wasn't damaged. But also Hind needs something to wear while she swims."

Then I had to stand there for a minute while both of them burst out laughing. But nobody else was laughing, and only a couple of the cooking girls were even brave enough to be peeking in through the door and windows. And eventually Miss Oakapple hurried over to us and put a hand on Hind's head and conceded, "Sinister is right, girlchick. If I let you go skinny-dipping within twenty miles of the manor, half the mothers in the estate will die of shock, and their sons won't be good for anything ever again." Then the spell of humor wore off and she told me doubtfully, "There's no way I can make something good enough for this girl to wear, Sinister. I've seen the things she wears. She's willing to get grass stains on a pair of pants that make me ashamed I ever thought I could sew."

And Hind put on the charm again with that smile. I actually didn't like it, I realized. She looked too much like a statue again. "If it were fancy or made of the kind of fabric I could wear to show off I couldn't wear it to swim, could I?" she pointed out impishly. "You don't have to make me beautiful, you just have to keep Sinister from blushing." And they were both laughing again.

I hadn't blushed once since I'd met her. Is there something wrong with just trying to keep things decent? I couldn't even say Miss Oakapple was an old woman and had stopped caring. She wasn't that old.

She still looked reluctant though, so I pointed out, "And who else would you let do it?"

That got her. "He's right, girlchick. I'm not the best tailor in the manor, but I'm the most important and nobody else gets to say they made clothes for someone like you. We can afford to lose a couple of hours. Girls, make sure all the boys are well away, and Hind can strip down and we'll get started."

"Sinister stays," Hind announced flatly. Miss Oakapple really did disapprove, but she wasn't going to directly contradict an order and she knew I had to wait on this girl no matter what she was wearing anyway. So I hunched up in my corner and tried to see as little as possible while Miss Oakapple and a few girls fussed and took measurements and fabric was cut and sewn together.

Hind was making friends rapidly, although she certainly didn't act the same way she did with me. But it wasn't long before Miss Oakapple was saying things like, "I wish I'd had a figure like yours at that age, Hind," and Millie was adding rather aggressively, "I wish I had a figure like that now."

Hind's reply, of course, was, "I only look like this because I have the time to exercise for hours every day, and I can only do that because I don't have to work, just show off. Or at least, showing off is my job." I tried to compare that comment to the girl I knew, who seemed to view her vacation as a chance to train harder.

I tried not to listen to the conversation about how Hind kept her skin smooth with oils, although I thought it was interesting that vegetable oils were better than mineral oils and much better than animal. And I certainly noticed when she explained, "Everyone is this pale where I come from, more or less. It was the whole opposite end of the Empire. I used to have a few freckles, but they went away. As for my hair, I don't know. I was afraid for a while it would turn the color of my ears, but instead it just gets a little more pale every year. Which makes it easy to dye."

There was hardly a pause to eat lunch. Girls swept in and out to carry food that had already been prepared to the rest of the manor while the tailoring went on. Apparently after they'd decided on about three swimming costumes, all of which seemed the same to me, Hind had convinced Miss Oakapple she could make a replacement house robe that would be wearable to Hind's standards. And they had to stitch it up before Hind could go back upstairs, because Miss Oakapple wouldn't let her wander even the back corridors in her underthings.

Eventually we were back upstairs, though, and Hind was putting on real clothing. They were again a shirt and pants, although it was hard to apply such simple words to anything she wore. I helped her tie a series of bows to make a simple ponytail acceptable, and she cheerfully talked about how she wished the bathing suit would be ready today, because she wanted to go swim now and instead she'd need to do some running to work on her stamina. So we wandered outside and ran into Right.

Something was wrong. He was sitting on a hay bale, not reading the animal husbandry book in his hands, but staring out dreamily over the meadow. It's something I could imagine him doing, but it was still wrong, and he didn't even notice us until I spoke to him.

"Right!" I greeted him, and he looked surprised and kind of distracted and sad when he saw me. "How did the squirrels go?"

"I'm not... sure," he told me vaguely. Right doesn't talk to me like that. He sounded like he was sick or he really, really had something on his mind.

Hind noticed, too. "It's a pleasure to meet you, Dexter," she told him with the kind of cheerfulness I only didn't believe because I knew her. "Are you really just like your brother? Are you as shy as he is?"

She wasn't teasing me. She was testing him. I wasn't sure if he passed or not. He did give us a grin and take her hand for a moment, and he even kissed the backs of her fingers clumsily. There was no passion to it, but I hadn't expected any. I expected him to react to her much the same way I had. "We're almost alike. He doesn't know how to treat girls, of course." And that *was* teasing me, which I'd expected, but it just stopped there. He seemed like he was starting to drift off again.

"Right?" I didn't have to say more than one word. It should have conveyed how concerned I was and asked every question I wanted to.

And again it kind of did, because he told me, "No, I'm okay. The morning was just odd, and I read some amazing things in this book while I waited for you and now I can't get it all out of my head. I'm going to go down to the pasture and see if some of it's true. I'll have it all worked out when I see you next."

So he slid off the hay bale and walked off, and again it was sort of like him, but it really wasn't like him. Not to mention that he'd left the book, and he wouldn't do that. Hind wasn't convinced either and told me, "He doesn't seem like you at all. Is he supposed to have that mark on his neck?"

I hadn't noticed, but I could see just a glimpse of something above the neckline of his shirt. Apparently someone else had heard us too, because I heard Sir Victor speak abruptly.

"They're tooth prints. I think one of the squirrels bit him. Would that make him act strangely? He's been like that since he got back, and he didn't take any notes."

"I could… ask the squirrels?" I was certainly going to do something. I just had to figure out what.

"I want to meet the squirrels too," Hind told me suddenly, stepping closer. "But I need to bring Jinx if we're going to see more Wild Children."

"I'll take care of that," Sir Victor said. He was above us, on a balcony. He went inside, and he must have hurried because a minute later he was stepping onto a separate balcony right above our heads. With great care he dropped the black cat doll right into Hind's arms, although she looked downright panicked while it was falling. Out in broad daylight I thought it would be less creepy. No, those red buttons for eyes looked more alert than ever.

"It's quite a ways. You might want to get something packed for supper," suggested Sir Victor from above.

"No. I want to find out what happened to my brother." I was starting to feel cold. A bite mark on his neck? I would find out why Right was acting this way and make sure he'd get better.

"And I want to help," Hind added firmly.

I don't know what his Lordship felt about that. We just started walking. Hind could keep up as good a pace as I could, although her shoes didn't look practical for walking. She wasn't getting tired any faster than I was, and we didn't stop to rest anywhere along the way. I think she spoke once or twice, but I didn't hear her, and she definitely tried to put her hand in mine once. I don't think she meant it romantically. However she meant it, I wasn't in the mood.

It had been later than I'd realized, and I hadn't pushed a hard pace because I was afraid Hind wouldn't be able to handle it. The sun was getting very low as we saw the trees ahead. Of course, there were no squirrels around. It wasn't that small a forest, and we thought there were only a very few. One child would change a decade, maybe, was how I understood it.

I knew how to deal with that. I walked right up to a tree that really marked the edge, which was bad enough in their eyes, and started to kick it over and over, hard.

"Hey! Hey! Hey! Hey!" chattered a squirrel, and sure enough one had just appeared like magic, scuttling out onto a branch nearby. "Get away from there! You're not a Wild Child. Only Wild Children are allowed into these woods."

Hind, who'd been hugging her doll tightly and looking rather scared, stepped up beside me. "I'm a Wild Girl," she told him.

"You're wearing a collar," he answered her snidely. "Do you even understand what the word 'wild' means?"

That did it. I hadn't expected anything would, but it made her angry. She was frozen in shock, but something like rage was filling her expression, which she wasn't bothering to hide it at all. I thought in a moment she'd actually be swearing at him. I was offended myself, but I couldn't let this get derailed.

"I'm not coming in, but I won't go away until you tell me about my brother," I barked up at the Squirrel Boy. I thought it was a boy. Most of them are young and have a lot of fur.

"Your what- oh, right, there are two of you, aren't there?" he replied dismissively.

"What happened to him when he came here this morning?" It's hard to keep a squirrel on topic.

"He didn't come here this morning. I haven't seen anyone but you two all day," the squirrel sniffed.

Squirrel talk. "Were you here this morning anyway?"

"...no," he admitted, and then changed track, asking archly, "What are you doing here, anyway? I told you, something's coming. Did you think it would change its mind? Did you think we meant that girl? It will be here any minute, practically. We weren't kidding about it being wonderful and awful, either. You ought to be back at the manor doing... something."

"Who was the Squirrel Child who met my brother this morning?" I demanded. "Was it her?" A Squirrel Girl was creeping out over another branch, staring at us anxiously.

But she spoke. "The oracle sent me. You have to go find your brother. You have to go find him right now, or he's going to die."

I stopped thinking. I ran.

I expected to leave Hind behind. I thought she wouldn't be able to keep up, or she'd lose her breath. I had lost my breath. I just kept running anyway. The pastures weren't far, but he was nowhere in sight. No, I knew my brother. He was with the cattle on the opposite end right now. In fact he was probably moving them into a new field, because the book had talked about that a lot. So I leapt over a fence and kept running. Somehow Hind was still with me, even in those shoes, even carrying her doll.

I saw the cattle, and they were in disarray. They'd been spooked, although they were calming down now. I didn't see my brother anywhere, but I knew he was there because I know him, and the squirrel's warning had me looking at the tall grass, and over there was a place where it was disturbed.

He was lying in the grass. I thought he was still conscious, but I wasn't sure. There was blood on his shirt, and blood around his mouth, and he was sort of staring, but his eyes were moving. There was churned earth nearby, and what had happened was all too obvious. He'd been charged by a bull. It hadn't gored him, but it didn't have to. He was broken.

"Right. Right, can you hear me?" I asked in horror. I wanted to pick him up, but I couldn't. I knew just enough about medicine and broken bones. He would die in an instant if I tried that.

"Left?" It was a question. He couldn't quite focus on me, and it was too dark; the sun had gone down, and the shadows were getting deeper by the moment. I could still see the mark on his neck. Cautiously, I pulled his shirt away a little – yes, a semi-circle of red, like someone had bitten him. I didn't think it was an animal, but Squirrel Children mostly had human teeth anyway, I thought.

Hind was shaking my shoulder. "We can make some kind of stretcher. We'll use our shirts. There's posts all over here, but I'll need you to pull up the thinner ones. I'm not very strong, Left." She was trying to snap me out of it.

I tried to snap myself out of it. "It won't work. There's not enough time. Even if we got him back to the manor, what could anyone do about this?" Your eyes are sensitive to strange things. He looked too flat, and if he was bleeding around his ribs they'd been broken too badly. I started getting to my feet. It wouldn't work, and we were going to try anyway.

The grass was the wrong color. Everything was the wrong color. Hind was looking up, and she gasped and started backing up until she fell over, and her eyes were wide like I hadn't seen them before. Then she shouted, "Bray!" No, it wasn't a shout. It was more like a squeak, but any noise seemed like a shout.

I didn't want to look up, but I did. Something was dropping out of the indigo sky, something glowing and brilliant, orange and yellow and red. As it got closer I saw spread wings letting it fall slowly, but they were wings wreathed in flame. To me it was hot, but the tall grass around us was starting to whither and brown and peel away.

It landed. She landed. It was a girl, and for a moment the wings deceived me. They were really arms, but they had feathers that made them wings, too, and made her look bigger. She was small. She hardly had any figure, and her clothing was nothing but a few scraps of white cloth tied around her in the important areas. Her skin was pale like Hind's, but her face didn't have any of that sculpted elegance. Still, looking at her my heart skipped a beat, because she had everything Hind didn't. Her eyes flashed gold and red and they were alive, seeing everything, full of emotion. In this case a growing sorrow and pain and sympathy.

My staring lasted only a beat. My brother was dying, and even this burning young girl couldn't distract me from him. I took a couple of steps towards the nearest gate, which had thinner posts we might use. I wondered, haltingly, if she could help us with the stretcher.

"I've... been called here to watch someone die again," the girl announced in a tight voice. She started to crouch down, reaching out to touch her fingers to Right's face, when Hind squeaked louder.

"Bray!"

"Hind?" asked the girl, looking up in confusion. They knew each other? I should be making the stretcher, but I couldn't move because I didn't understand what was going on anymore.

"Left, she's a phoenix!" Hind shouted at me.

"I'm the phoenix," the girl corrected her sadly. "There only gets to be one at a time."

She was. Instead of hair she had a glorious crest of feathers running from her hairline back to her neck, and down quite a lot of her spine that I could see. She had a tail of feathers, and although she had hands, much of her arms were either feathered or sprouted the pinions of her wings. They were all red and yellow, gleaming with liquid fire, and I could feel the heat from here. I felt bad, because my brother was dying, because she was younger than Hind even (although how, exactly, was I much older than either of them?), but she was beautiful because she was Wild in exactly the way Hind wasn't. I didn't think love at first sight was real, but if people looked at someone sometimes and thought they were this beautiful I could at least understand how they'd make that mistake.

There was something I was missing, though. I couldn't put it together, because I could feel Right falling away from me in the grass.

"Bray, you're a phoenix now," Hind repeated desperately. "You told me so. The power of life and death. You can save him."

"I don't think anything can save him," the phoenix replied doubtfully. "I can bring him – I can't bring him back." She looked agonized, but determined. "I can't give life or take it, Hind. If I do, it goes wrong. He'll wish he'd died. Do you want to do that to him?"

"You have to." Hind was starting to cry again. Come to think of it, we were probably all crying except Right. I felt so bad I couldn't tell, and I thought the tears were melting away off the burning girl's cheeks. "Look at him, Bray. Look at his face."

"I think he's too old." The phoenix, Bray, was whispering vaguely, staring down at Right. They were both giving each other the same look, like they'd met someone in a dream. "Not his body, his heart. It's almost covered over."

One thing was clear. I didn't know or care why she thought she shouldn't, but she could save my brother. I grabbed her by the shoulders, not roughly but getting down on my knees so she could see I was begging. Except for the eyes her face was human, and the eyes weren't animal eyes or bird eyes. They were eyes that shone with fire. It was just the face of a girl, but I could see the thoughts and emotions racing behind those eyes and it made a merely ordinary face striking somehow. Or maybe I just thought any chance to stop this from happening was beautiful. "Please, if you're really a phoenix, if you can save my brother, you have to. If you have to trade a life, take mine. I don't know how it works." I dragged her against me, holding her tight, and begged. "Please. He's dying right now in front of me."

She pushed me away. She wasn't any stronger than a girl her size should have been, but she was being gentle anyway. She looked into my eyes, and I don't know what she saw there, but she stroked her fingers down my cheek and she looked down at Right and there was that same expression I couldn't read.

"Stand back," she told us very solemnly. "Stand far back. You don't have to trade anything. Whatever happens, I'm the one who makes this decision and it will be my responsibility to fix the damage. But I have to warn you, when your brother comes back I don't think he'll be human."

I tried to step back, but I wasn't sure of my feet. Hind helped. She took hold of my arms and we staggered back, probably not far enough, but we watched. When I touched the phoenix her flames had died to a glimmer, maybe to protect me. Now she reached out her arms to take Right's face in her hands and the fire surged. It roared like a bonfire, but neither of them screamed.

I nearly did. I could feel the heat burning me instead of Right, but I gritted my teeth. If she stopped now just because it hurt me it would be too late, I knew it. I just knew it somehow. I was out of my head, so maybe I was wrong, but I held onto the pain although I could feel the burning crawling over my body. Hind could see it in my face, but she must have thought the same as I did because she didn't say anything either. And my brother, his body was burning to black char in front of me, but the ashes didn't fall away. Something was rising out of them.

I didn't get to see what. The pain was awful. My feet were twisting out from under me, my teeth were stabbing into my jaws, pain was jolting over me everywhere. Something was wrong with my hands. I could see my hands, and my fingers came to points, and in the light of the phoenix's flames they were blurry, but I couldn't make out the proper color.

Then it was over and I sat back in the grass, hard. I nearly fell over. The phoenix girl's light had gone out completely and even her eyes were dark. But my brother was sitting up in the charred and smoking grass.

He looked… different. He was still very clearly himself. Above the waist hardly anything had changed, but his hair was white and dense and curly and he had thick, short horns curling back out of it. There was a stretch of wispy white running over the backs of his forearms. His clothing was ashes, but it was hardly a problem, because from the waist down everything was fleecy white, down to large and very obvious split hooves.

He was a Wild Boy. Idly, I realized he looked just like a satyr. The old Hellenic stories that people liked to tell, even out here, were full of fanciful creatures. Right and I had found a book once that suggested very strongly that many of them, the satyrs and naiads and centaurs, were just bad storybook descriptions of Wild Children. I thought this was a pretty good case that the author had been right.

And myself... I had changed too. There was gray-brown fur over my hands, and I had claws, although at least I still had fingers. My legs bent backwards instead of having a proper ankle, and I had padded paws instead of feet. I could tell my ears had moved up because I could flick them and feel it, and that was a tail jammed in my pants. My teeth felt much too sharp.

But Right was alive, and people had thought we were Wild Children most of our lives anyway. They might as well be right. He was sitting up, and he and the phoenix girl were staring at each other face to face, touching each other's cheeks, and I couldn't blame them. I felt about the same way.

And then they kissed. Hard. My heart clenched in my chest, but I couldn't blame Right, because I'd felt about the same way looking at her up close. Not only that, but I didn't know what they'd felt as she brought him back from the edge of death. Even the bite mark on his shoulder was gone.

Hind was still holding onto me, and I managed to notice she was there. I couldn't read her expression as she looked at me. She wasn't letting me read it, but she wasn't hiding it so much that I couldn't tell she felt very strongly underneath the mask.

It was a terrible moment, really, for a crowd to arrive. Especially since a couple of them had torches and they were lighting lanterns because it was getting that dark. I didn't have to ask why they were here. People would have started moving the moment they saw the flaming bird in the sky. Sir Victor was out front with a heavily packed bag and a lantern that was already lit, but he dropped both the moment he saw Right and the phoenix kissing. The only reason it didn't start a fire before the villagers could put it out was because the grass was halfway ash already.

My brother and the phoenix had the decency to look embarrassed as they were caught kissing, and climbed awkwardly to their feet. They both looked a little unsteady and probably felt a lot less steady as Hind abandoned all dignity or grace and launched herself forward to wrap her arms around the golden bird's neck, hugging her and sobbing. "Bray! Bray, do you know how long it's been?"

"Not... really," she was answered hoarsely. "I can't keep track of the seasons anymore. I just go wherever I'm led, and I hope it takes me back to you sometimes."

"Bray?" interjected Sir Victor now. "It really is. You really are the phoenix, Bray?" He looked as stunned as any of us, but not as stunned as I felt. It was a bizarre, disjointed feeling. I had walked into someone else's life and been swept along in it, and I was no longer living my own. But that really was irrational. Whatever went on between those three, Right and I had our own lives and had to lead them ourselves. I staggered over to take my brother's arm so that we could just look at each other and what had happened to us and realize that, really, we hadn't changed at all.

Sir Victor was ignoring us anyway, and Hind fell away as he walked up to the phoenix girl. He held out his hands, and she took them, but he started pulling her up and lowering his head to hers until her fingers were suddenly in the way. She pressed her hand to his mouth, blocking it, keeping him at her admittedly tiny arm's length, and told him, "I don't wear a collar, Vick. I get to pick who I kiss." And then she threw her arms around his shoulders anyway, draping his back in a cape of crimson and gold feathers and hugged him tight, but she didn't kiss him and although he held her back he looked a bit stunned when she let go.

We all looked a bit stunned. The phoenix was walking, more like staggering, back to Hind and asking her in a confused tone, "Why are there two of him?" And she turned to smile shyly at my brother and then turned her smile to me.

In an instant her smile was gone, snuffed out. She almost fell over backwards, she looked so stricken. I looked down at my hands. What kind of monster did I look like now? But Hind grabbed her in both arms and told her, "No! He's not like that, Bray! I don't know why he's a wolf, but I know him and if you know one of them you know the other. You have to see them as the same boy and forget what kind of animal they are."

So... I was a wolf? From what I could see, that was about right. Awkwardly I freed my tail, and it was kind of short and scruffy. I looked at Right and he was looking at the girl, and I couldn't blame him. But she looked at him with a sort of dazed hope, and the look she gave me was cautious. It was controlled fear, but it was fear.

Miss Oakapple on the other hand didn't seem to be afraid of anyone or anything going on right now. Her arms were suddenly around Right and I, and she hugged us so tight she was lifting us off the ground. "Oh, my boychicks! Honest to goodness Wild Children now! A wolf and a sheep, I guess? Isn't this a night out of the fairy tales? Please don't tell me you're going to leave us now and run off into the woods!"

I had no desire to, and Right pointed out in a wobbly way, "I still don't think the squirrels would take us, Miss Oakapple. Maybe we'll get called away to the wild, but right now I don't feel like it."

Then Millie was beside us running her fingers through Right's fleecy hair, and Mister Spruce had finally arrived and was clapping me on the back, and everyone was pulling us back towards the manor and I was too tired to argue about it.

Only Hind and Bray were left behind, and only for a few moments. The Donkey Girl and the Phoenix Girl looked like they were whispering to each other, and then the phoenix took off, gleaming subtly again as she leapt into the air and flew into the deepening night. Very quickly even she wasn't visible against that purple murk.

The next morning Right and I were curled up on the flour bags by the guest bells again. No one seemed to notice us and we'd been sitting there for nearly an hour, I guessed, before Miss Oakapple suddenly stopped what she was doing and demanded, "What are you two doing here? Honey children, you can do whatever you want. Sinister, puppy, wouldn't you rather... be running free in the woods hunting down rabbits or something?" She sounded distinctly flustered. She realized even as she was saying it that she was being stupid, but she was trying to give us a choice.

I found it interesting that the suggestion didn't actually repulse me. It had a certain attractiveness to it. But still... "Not really," I told her in amusement, and looked over at my brother with his horns and fleecy legs and hooves, and asked him, "How about you? Dancing in the meadow playing the pipes sound good to you?"

Of course, I knew what the flicker of a vague look meant. It was something he would never have done before and was surprised that it seemed appealing, if only vaguely. "I'm in no hurry," he told Miss Oakapple while she sort of glowed down at us with affectionate confusion. "Our guests still need to be served and Sir Victor is most likely ecstatic that I've gone Wild now."

I nodded. We were both grinning. Well, almost. "Hind will be even happier, I think." She'd only opened up to me to begin with because she believed I wasn't human. Now I wasn't. I was looking speculatively at my hairy, clawed hands when Miss Oakapple's hands settled on both our heads and ruffled our hair lovingly. "Grey and white. I'll never get used to those colors."

As she wandered back to the ovens I glanced at Right and he nodded, just slightly. I couldn't see my own hair. It made sense that it had gone the color of my fur, what there was of it. His wasn't just white, it almost wasn't regular hair anymore. It turned out that Miss Oakapple had just been getting us breakfast, because she slid it onto the pallet between us and walked off clucking to herself, presumably trying to get used to having two Wild Boys about the place. Without exchanging a word, Right passed me his bacon and I pushed the bowl of dried fruit and grains and nuts over to him. I could have eaten it without objection, but I suspected I'd be in the mood for meat most of the time from now on. It was easier with my sharp teeth anyway.

Before long Sir Victor's bell rang, and Right picked up a tray of food and almost leapt up the back stairs. While his back was turned I caught Millie staring, but I knew, although it was a bittersweet thought, that she was out of luck. Even if any sort of relationship between a human girl and my brother was acceptable, I'd seen him with the phoenix last night. He was back very quickly looking solemn and thoughtful. I suppose he usually looked that way to other people, but I understood he was really thinking about something.

He didn't even sit down, just leaned up against the wall by me and explained, "Sir Victor isn't going to need me today. He isn't dismissing me, but he wants me to spend the day trying to find out how I've changed. He says I won't notice it at first, but we'll both be different now. Marked."

I thought about it. "I don't feel different. Not in any important way." There was one thing we both weren't saying. What had changed was that on the edge of our thoughts hovered a girl with scarlet and gold feathers and a look in her eyes that said she was alive and thinking about everything. I suppose that happened to everyone our age at some point, and I shouldn't make too big a deal out of it. It's just a question of who you fall for.

...of course, we were going to be our age for a long, long time now, weren't we?

That made me realize that time had slipped away from me. Anyway, Right and I didn't need to say anything. We could say everything in a glance as I grabbed the tray Millie had just finished preparing and headed up the servants' stairs myself. Hind may not have called and might well be sleeping in, but she had to eat something and as hosts we'd make sure the food was set out waiting for her.

There were differences, though, that I was already noticing. It's just that they were physical. I was sure I was the same person inside, but my back-jointed ankles made it easier to jump from step to step, crouched forward a little. Part of that was my spine, and I thought it really had something to do with having a tail now (which I'd had to cut a hole in my trousers to let out). My arms and legs still weren't quite the right length for it, but I'd have been at least as comfortable running on all fours as upright, and I kept wanting to grab things to push myself along.

I peeked through the door into Hind's bedroom cautiously, since there really was no telling with her. But she wasn't in bed and she'd even left her doll among the disheveled bedclothes. Instead I could hear voices from the next room, and I had great difficulty restraining my curiosity long enough to set her breakfast out on the stand. When I had, I crept into the sitting room quietly so as not to disturb her, only to see her standing on the balcony talking to the phoenix. They did not immediately see me, and spying on them would be even more rude than interrupting, so I knocked lightly on the doorframe and announced, "Breakfast, Hind."

"Sinister!" she crowed ecstatically, and in a swirl of skirts rushed over and grabbed my arm and pulled me out onto the balcony with her. It was a theatrical gesture, and I couldn't read her expression, or rather I couldn't tell if her enthusiastic happiness was honest or a carefully judged act. It seemed like both to me. But it meant that suddenly I was standing out in the sun a couple of feet from the phoenix.

"You two really need to be properly introduced," Hind explained in a rush. "Actually all three of you need to be introduced, but I'll do it one at a time if I have to. Sinister, this is my best friend Bray. Bray, meet Sinister. I trust him."

"My name is really Left, anyway," I admitted uncomfortably.

"A Wild Boy's name," the phoenix told me. "You can't let go of it, can you? It becomes your only real name."

This close, in the daylight, I could get a good look at her, and I gave up and let myself stare since I was going to lose that battle anyway. She was shorter than me and painfully young, just a bit over the edge of not being a little girl. Her eyes no longer flashed red and gold. They were brown, very plain, and that made them prettier. Hind was a donkey, but everything else about her was a made-up and sculpted princess, made lovely by poise and careful exercise and eating like a bird. This girl, with her glorious shining crest of scarlet feathers and her wings, was just alive in every way. I didn't want to feel like this when I looked at someone I didn't know, but I couldn't stop it. It just felt like I knew her already.

It made the look she was giving me hurt. She made no effort to hide her emotions, and she was being friendly and giving me a chance, but she had to do it because just seeing me made her nervous. She was too good a person to judge me because of how I looked, but it was something she had to hold back. Thinking about that made me ache.

Neither of us had said anything. Fortunately we had Hind there to smooth over the silence. "What does his heart look like, Bray?" she asked impulsively, and there was a definite edge of fascination as she added, "What does mine look like?"

And Bray, hiking her tail up out of the way, pulled herself up to sit on the railing and lapsed slowly back into casualness. She sounded a bit exasperated, as if she'd explained this a hundred times before. "I can't turn it off and on, Hind. I only saw his brother's last night. It was pink and violet and there was this shell of pearl creeping over it and I don't know what any of that means." She paused for a moment and added in distant reminiscence, "I met a girl way up north who was some kind of animal I didn't know. She had an animal's eyes, and instead of kicking her out her village made her their priestess. She could see your heart all the time and all sorts of things that weren't there. She was more than a little crazy, and mean. No, not mean exactly, just angry like you wouldn't believe, all the time. And strong. She was my size, but I bet she could have lifted a horse. It's only around here that people think of donkeys when they think of Wild Children."

I couldn't help it. Suddenly I was even more hooked. "You've been a lot of places." I wanted to know more, needed it worse than I could describe.

"I just end up in them. It doesn't matter where I mean to go, I turn up somewhere strange, somewhere I think I'm needed, although I usually can't figure out why. I don't think I do it right very often." Suddenly she was looking at Hind, and they reached out, linked hands and squeezed tightly. "The worst part is, I can't see my friends. Every once in a while I get pulled back to the capital and can visit Hind, but even if I try, most of the time I can't. I certainly didn't expect to run into her here without the Baron."

I immediately wished she hadn't said that. The tears were forming in Hind's eyes already. I took her other hand and Bray and I just stood there on either side of her for a moment. After giving her that time to get over the shock I told Bray, "He sent her here to be safe for a while. Apparently politics are getting ugly in the capital."

"I'm well out of it, then," she told me grimly, and at least those earth-colored eyes were looking at me now. "All I could do for that place is burn it down. I don't miss it at all."

"Was it that bad?" There was a lot of emotion there, and I wanted to know more about her. Then her expression changed, and I could tell she didn't want to talk about it. At least, not to me.

Hind seemed to be recovering quickly. She had taken her hands from ours and reached them up to hold my cheek and jaw and said, "She lost the only thing that was keeping her there."

They were both looking at me, but they were talking to each other. It was like twin language in miniature, a conversation about me I couldn't follow. Bray, at least, didn't have anything more to say. She leapt to her feet and threw herself off the balcony and soared up into the sky as if it were as easy as playing hopscotch. It was only Hind tugging gently on my elbow that kept me from staring at those shining wings. Instead of resenting being pulled away, I was grateful. I didn't like this. I had no control over myself at all.

I arranged the place as best I could and listened to Hind chatter as she ate, and I'm ashamed to say I didn't remember anything she said, although it was nice to see her so relaxed and unguarded. Cleaning up was useless, really. The maids would do a better job shortly. I was just trying to make things easy for them. I didn't get much chance, because Hind would pull me aside every couple of minutes and put something sweet in my mouth for me to eat. It wasn't appropriate, but she didn't even seem to understand what was, and I would put up with worse to see her like this.

Eventually she decided that since she was already in a dress the best thing we could do was go on a long hike. She wanted to see the estate better and felt that her plans to go swimming had been derailed. We would need an easily carried packet of food. I went downstairs to the kitchen, and Hind insisted on coming with me, so we took the main hallways and I at least convinced her to wait outside the door so she wouldn't embarrass the cooking staff.

We were walking out the door when we ran into Right again and I started paying attention to the world around me. He was sitting on a barrel against the wall, chewing on a stalk of grass and staring off at the horizon. I knew exactly how he felt. The grass stem wasn't just something to toy with, either. He was slowly eating it, and while I felt no urge to do that I empathized with the strangeness of it for him. It must be like finding out you want to walk on all fours.

"Miss Hind wants to go hiking." I held up the wrapped bundle of food. "Want to come with us?"

He had to think about it. I could tell he wasn't going to agree, but I'd helped him make up his mind. He slid to his hooves and told me what he'd decided. "No. I'd like to meet her better, but I can't just do nothing all day. You have to take care of Hind and I need to find something useful to do. I'm going to head back out to the pasture. I never really got to finish checking out the herds."

"I'm used to taking care of someone else," Hind told me with a sort of wistful slyness as we watched him set off, hands in the pockets of his breeches. He didn't seem to care about a shirt anymore, and until now I hadn't even noticed. "You really are exactly the same. I can see it now. If I weren't here you'd have found some other work to do."

I thought I'd lead her down to the river, so we skirted around the back of the manor. I was getting my thoughts in order again and starting to look around and notice things, only to have it yanked out of my hands again. Because when I looked up, I noticed was the phoenix up above me, talking to Sir Victor.

I could hear them clearly. I almost didn't understand why I hadn't noticed until I looked right at her. "No, Vick. You only think you want this. It would be something horrible, and even if you understood that I'm not going to do it."

"But you can?" he was saying to her curiously. She was crouched on the railing, perched on it exactly like a bird, and I thought she must have weighed next to nothing to balance like that. It would explain why she could fly, but only replaced one mystery with others.

He had his hand out and touching her cheek, and she didn't seem to mind, but I didn't like the look on his face at all. I felt bad looking at her like that, and I was hardly older than she was. He was a grown man, and he just didn't seem to notice her age. Of course, she might be older than him. She might be much older than him. But she'd never grown up, and he had.

"…I think so," she answered him. She said it reluctantly, but she also held her hand over his, if only for a moment, before pulling them both away. "I know that you're right and it can happen. I met a dragon, and he wasn't a child at all."

Sir Victor's expression of fascination, his hunger to know more, must have been the same as my own. "So you're not the only special child either. There are other legends," he pressed.

"Yes," she admitted. He was making her remember things she didn't want to, and suddenly I didn't want to know more at all. I wasn't willing to make her have that look on her face. I wasn't the one asking, though. "There are other monsters. That's what most of us are. He was the worst, and he wouldn't burn. There was nothing I could do but fly away and hope he'd go back to sleep for another century or whatever. There are more. I think I've met all of us by now, and we're only a handful anyway. One was a patchwork child, and they... were so miserable, and nothing could kill them. They'd just switch to another child while the first one slept. The... I guess she was a manticore, and she could die, because I killed her. I thought I had to. She'd killed so many adults already. I had to stop her. I'll never do that again. There had to have been another way."

Sir Victor's arms went around her then. She hadn't been crying, but I honestly hoped she felt comforted. He still looked curious, and I understood that, but I wasn't at all. I promised myself that if she ever learned to trust me like she seemed to trust him I wouldn't ask about her travels after all. If she wanted to forget, I would let her forget. For now, Hind and I started walking again. I didn't quite know when we'd linked arms, but we were thinking the same thing, about a girl who seemed more like a girl and less like a phoenix by the minute.

After a while we were just walking. There are a lot of hills around the estate, but only the one little forest. Otherwise it's just the occasional clump of trees, and once you're out of sight of the manor there are lots of farms laid out in no particular order. I tried to keep Hind out of them, but she could be remarkably interested in a pumpkin on a vine, or a leaf full of aphids. She set a good pace and I thought I was getting tired before she was, but we stopped for a few minutes to dip our feet into the river and then a few minutes after that because she wouldn't put her stockings back on until her feet had dried completely. Personally I didn't think I'd be wearing shoes of any kind ever again. My feet had tough pads, and it didn't seem to matter anyway.

Towards the end of the afternoon we wandered past the pastures. I couldn't imagine a bunch of cows were exciting, but Hind seemed to like everything and there was a good chance she could meet Right properly. The animals were nowhere to be seen, though, until we finally found them all together. The herd was arranged in a sort of ring, or maybe just a mob, surrounding and looking inward. At the center were Right and Bray. They were talking, but we were too far away to hear about what, and it wasn't my business to know. They both looked happy, though, and they kissed. It was quick this time, not touching in any other way. They looked very shy and flustered about it and almost immediately she took off, scattering the animals a little as she circled once and flew back towards the manor.

To add insult to injury, as I led Hind up to my brother the animals hurried away from me. They weren't really afraid, but all I had to do was start walking towards one and it got nervous and kept its distance. It was an obvious side effect of being a wolf and so trivial it seemed silly and boosted my spirits considerably. Enough that I felt bad interrupting that peaceful, hopeful look on my brother's face.

He looked just as happy in a calmer, more studious way when he saw us. He'd noticed the nervousness of the animals too, and like me it amused him. To my further amusement he was also holding a set of pipes in his hand. It was Hind that spoke first, giving him a very warm smile. "I haven't properly met you yet, Dexter, but I feel like I know you because I know Sinister." I wondered if he could see the nervousness that hid behind that smile. I could, because it was too convincing.

She held out her hand, and he took it and squeezed for a moment, then let go. She was relaxing already. "I've been finding myself," he told me enthusiastically. "It's all little things, but they're there. Can you back up for a moment?"

It was about the animals, of course. I let go of Hind and took quite a few steps back. I had never seen such a crowd, the cows and the sheep all mixed and not caring, and even a few horses. I had no idea how they'd gotten out here, even. Hind started to follow me, but I held up my hand for a moment and she stayed where she was.

Right held up the pipes. "At first I tried these. You know. I just wanted to see just how true the stories were. I didn't suddenly magically learn to play them, and it was pretty bad." Hind giggled and nodded. Apparently it was an experience she understood.

"It worked anyway," he admitted, looking both flustered and proud. "I figured out pretty quickly it wasn't the pipes. I just have to get their attention. Watch this." And he leaned forward a little and patted his leg loudly a couple of times.

There was a migration. The animals just drifted in, staring at him, although the ones nearest me were hampered because they still didn't want to get close. He reached out to a cow, which is not the most cooperative animal in the world, and lifted up its chin and the cow just raised its head as far as it could go. For a few seconds anyway, before shaking its head free and giving him what I imagined was a reproachful look.

"It looks like you get to keep the animal husbandry book," I told him enviously.

"I never was able to do anything like that when I changed," Hind was remarking in surprise, peering around her in delight at the sheep hemming her in on every side and nibbling at her dress. "Becoming a donkey is a punishment, not a reward."

"Maybe you just never learned what the good side was," Right told her, and the look of gratitude that flashed over her face for a moment astonished me. He glanced at me then, but of course he didn't need to. I was already realizing that there would be good things and bad things for me too. Looking around, Right remarked bemusedly, "Anyway, it's showy but it's sort of a parlor trick. They're a little more cooperative, but only a little. Mostly they just follow me around and stare at me if I let them."

Hind giggled a little, and it was much the same sound she made whenever I tried not to look at her undressed. So we ended up arm-in-arm-in-arm, heading back to the manor for a late supper. It was Hind who grabbed us, of course. Right and I aren't that demonstrative. I imagine we made quite the sight, a Donkey Girl storming over a hill dragging a tired wolf and ram on either side of her.

I thought Right must have had a chance to talk to Sir Victor, because the next morning he didn't even bother trying to wait to be called. He walked out into the yard and he had our books again. If the animals were going to come when he called, it didn't surprise me he wanted to learn everything he could about taking care of them. My thoughts were even starting to stray back towards higher math. I was taking the architecture book from him when the phoenix dropped daintily out of the sky next to us.

We both sort of stared. All three of us sort of stared. "Hi," she greeted us with a little smile. "I wanted to see the two of you side by side for once. Anyway, I'm not a rooster. I can't spend all morning crowing at the sun and not get bored."

She was just saying something to say something. I wasn't even sure I could do that. Her brown eyes, amidst the white of her face and the barely visible freckles and the wildfire mane of feathers, were moving between us, studying us. I didn't know what she was thinking, but she was getting more out of this than we were. Quickly, though, her eyes drifted more and more back to Right. I tried to ignore the ache it caused in my chest, because there was something so hopeful and relieved in the way they stared at each other. It was weird and sudden. I wasn't sure it was right, but I was just hoping it would work out somehow for them.

As casually as I could, I told her, "I'd like to stay and let you talk to us both, but I need to go inside and wait for Hind's call."

"No you don't!" came a decidedly smug call from behind me. We all stared, even Bray, dumbfounded as Hind emerged from the kitchen door holding a big tray of food. "I'm bringing you breakfast today, Left." Behind her I saw the kitchen girls staring with the same confusion out at her. They probably hadn't had the guts to tell her 'no'. She could seem very important and make you forget all about the collar around her neck and what it meant.

Her real intent became clear almost immediately. As Right and I picked up a couple of buns out of a bowl and nibbled on them thoughtfully, Hind was pouring syrup over an already frosted pastry and holding it up in front of Bray's mouth. I thought Bray wanted to argue, but knew what this meant to Hind. Unlike the Donkey Girl, Bray wore her feelings on her face. She bit in.

And for a while we ate. Hind had a few bites, which I was getting used to, and at first Right and I just tried this and that. Miss Oakapple laid out an excellent spread for her guests and we had a chance to see how much our tastes in food had changed. It turned out not much, although I really kept coming back to the meat and eggs. But Bray, after she got started, ate like she'd been starved. The tray was almost empty when Right pointed out, "You probably don't get food like this often, do you? I know the squirrels mostly eat nuts or something, and I think I could live on grass now if I really had to. What do you eat when you're traveling?"

There was a pause, and I was realizing Bray was trying to find a way not to answer the question, but Hind had realized it first. "You can write a book about her and fill in the margins with love poetry later," she told Right, standing up and brushing off her trousers. "For now I have an idea. Go get that ball."

Right actually blushed. So did Bray. I almost did. Hind giggled quite a lot as Right ran off, and I was starting to wonder if she was drunk. She kept watching Bray's face, though, and instead I wondered if this was just a different kind of show to make a different kind of person happy. Then an unpleasant thought struck me. Bray had talked about being forced to wander. Hind didn't have much time, and maybe she didn't want to waste any of it.

I also thought Hind might have planned this game from the beginning, because she was wearing a blouse and trousers. Of course, being Hind, she'd managed to find a way to make that combination immodest. They were both so tight I thought she might have had to have them sewn on around her, and I wasn't sure how she'd put them on without help. I was a little surprised I was getting so used to her already I hadn't noticed until now. I hoped nobody else was noticing.

I didn't have time to worry about protecting Hind from stares because it hadn't taken Right long to find the ball and come trotting back up with it. We were all giving Hind a quizzical look, and finally that mask of confidence started to crumble. She looked a bit abashed and told us, "We're all Wild Children now. I'm just a donkey, but I think I can keep up with the three of you. I just want us to play a game together."

"I don't know the rules!" squeaked Bray in alarm, but she was already recovering. She reached out and took the ball from Right and was already turning it over and tossing it up and down a little to marvel at its lightness as she told us, "You'll have to tell me how to play."

"There aren't really any rules, or none you'd be willing to break," I told her. "You see those two posts? You take the ball and hit the other side's post. Kicking is preferred." And there was a glint, a real glint, a flash of impish gold over the brown for a moment. She thought she could do that.

"Then you and Sinister will be on a team," Hind instructed us, "And me and Dexter will be on a team." It was a blatantly obvious attempt to let us get to know each other, but she covered well by calling out to the children already starting to gather, "Do you kids want to play?"

They stared at her as if they were stunned. I looked around and was uncomfortably aware that some of the men were staring at Hind too, but there was nothing I could do about it. Or maybe it was just that all four of us together we made a very strange sight.

Hind's team assignment might have been prescient. She couldn't kick very far and didn't seem to have great aim, but the ball just couldn't get past her if she was anywhere near. There was no angle too awkward for her to hit it. Right seemed stronger, more confident than I remembered, and held up well too, and I learned very quickly that his hooves could launch a ball with the power of a catapult. Bray on the other hand wasn't any good at all, although she didn't seem to mind. Missing the ball or having a goal blocked never frustrated her. And somehow I was the best player on the field. By a good margin. I couldn't kick above my head like Hind could, but it just wasn't hard to be in the right position if the ball was ever coming towards me, and I ran much faster than I thought I used to be able to. Kicking the ball with a paw didn't seem to hurt, and I was pleased by how strong and accurate these backwards-bent legs seemed to be.

So for a while, we played. We didn't keep score or care how long it took, until eventually Bray was clinging to both Right's and my arms and panting desperately for breath in-between wonderful laughter. My brother and I were at least smiling, and Hind for a moment was unguarded, although I wasn't sure I understood the way she was looking at her friend beyond a certain affectionate concern. She seemed pleased.

People were still staring. A lot of people were still staring. The little children almost immediately began clapping, although I wasn't quite sure what for. I thought all four of us felt about equally awkward. When Bray tugged on one of the sashes of cloth she used instead of clothing, though, Hind fastened onto it like a magnet.

You couldn't really lock arms with Bray thanks to all those feathers, so she eased up and took Bray's wrist in her hand and told her quietly, "Listen, would you like some real clothes for once?"

"I don't know how long it would last, if we can find anything," Bray answered her anxiously. Hind started to lead us back towards the manor, and getting out of the spotlight and a distraction seemed good for the Phoenix Girl's comfort. "Anyway, I can't wear any of your clothes. My wings and tail get in the way."

"Which is why you need something made especially for you," Hind answered her, which is why I wasn't surprised at all when we were led straight back into the kitchen.

The staff didn't even run away. They just stared until Miss Oakapple noticed the silence and emerged from the pantry and nearly dropped the pickling jug she was carrying. "A phoenix in my kitchen," she babbled helplessly. "I don't know if this is the proudest moment of my life or the most ashamed. Dexter! Sinister! I keep telling you, you can't bring the likes of them down into this mess!" It was a mark of how out of sorts she was that she picked up a tablecloth and draped it over a pile of fresh sheep parts. She didn't lose her balance easily, but apparently she had.

"Actually Miss Oakapple, I needed a very big favor," Hind told her, suddenly formal and elegant and ladylike. I think everyone but me forgot how she was dressed. She curtseyed like a princess. "My friend needs clothes. Nothing fancy. But you can't find or steal clothes for wings like hers. They have to be made special."

Miss Oakapple is no fool and I thought she knew she was being baited with honey, but that was a game she liked to play and she didn't mind having it played on her. "I wouldn't – no, I can make her clothes, girlchick. And you, you really are a little chick, aren't you?" she asked Bray dizzily.

It was an attempt to be nice, and that's how Bray took it. She giggled and tried to curtsey too. "I'll take anything, but only one set. I can't really carry much with me."

"We'll make you a tunic and a pair of short trousers, then," Miss Oakapple decided. "A real skirt would be just no use at all to you, would it? And if the shirt ties on around the shoulders the wings won't be any trouble. Alright, girls get the sewing things; boys, get out!" Here for a moment she did hesitate. "Hind, honey, I hate to ask a lady like you to work in a kitchen even a little, but I might need your help with this. I need someone who knows what you have to do to fit a Wild Girl."

I was already on my way out before I saw Bray begin to fumble awkwardly with the rags she wore. I'm ashamed to say my brother didn't leave until I gave him a good yank.

So for much of the afternoon we sat outside. We hardly talked at all. We had too much to think about. I realized, and I think I really might have blushed when I did, that I'd been wagging my tail on and off all day without noticing. And Right caught himself eating hay. We didn't feel different, but the animal acted for us sometimes. We were just getting back into our books again when Bray came out. The shirt and shorts were simple, hard-wearing line, and the shirt was loose and gave a bit of a skirt, and she seemed delighted to have modest and practical clothes again. Apparently wherever Hind had gotten her indifference to appropriate levels of dress, Bray hadn't picked it up with her.

That made me wonder why Hind hadn't come out. I thought I'd better leave my brother a minute to admire Bray alone anyway and eased back into the kitchen, but Hind wasn't there. When I asked, Miss Oakapple just admitted, "I don't quite know when she left, boychick. You can all disappear like fairies when you want, I'm learning that already."

Given the hour I thought she might have wanted a bath before supper, so I put together a quick tray of food for her and trotted upstairs. I eased into her room. She wasn't there. The bed was made and there was no mess of clothing or anything in the bathroom, but she tended to pick up after herself. I set out her food and waited for a little while.

When I woke up the moon was out, and I found out I'd been sitting on the edge of the balcony, and I thought it was typical of Hind that she hadn't woken me. I stared up at the moon muzzily for a little while, wondering if as a wolf I'd start howling at it or something. It didn't seem to happen. When I woke up again it was almost sunrise, and I was abashed to realize I'd spent the night in her rooms. Not that it meant anything or Hind would care, but still. I crept back through her bedroom to the servant's door.

But the bed was empty. Empty, and made. The food hadn't been touched. Nothing had been disturbed since last night. Jinx wasn't here and, I remembered, hadn't been here when I brought food up the night before.

I tried to remind myself that I should ask around before jumping to conclusions, but I couldn't convince myself. Hind was gone.

I was upstairs, so the first thing to do was to check with Sir Victor. It meant waking him up, but this was important enough. I hoped. Knocking on the door to his apartments didn't do anything. Of course, I was a servant and I wasn't supposed to knock, but I wasn't supposed to wake him up either. So I crept through his shadowy study, only momentarily distracted by the books piled onto shelves and the equipment scattered over every flat surface, and knocked on his bedroom door instead.

Since the door was open when I knocked I could see very clearly as he lifted his head from his pillow and looked at me. He didn't immediately yell, at least long enough to tell him, "Hind is missing."

"It would be entirely like her to get up early to practice her singing while no one was around." His voice was blurry, but he sounded like he was taking this seriously.

"She hasn't been in her rooms all night, your Lordship. I was waiting for her with supper and she never arrived. And she took her doll."

He thought about this for a moment. "Then she knew she wouldn't be back tonight. It's possible she spent the night outside somewhere talking to Bray. They're very dedicated to each other." I didn't have to argue against that. After a moment of thought he continued, "It's not all that likely, however. More importantly, we can't take that chance."

He sat up, swinging himself around to the edge of the bed immediately. Even as he stood he was grabbing yesterday's clothes, too impatient to wait for new ones. I was trying to figure out what I should do next, but he took that responsibility away from me by walking over and laying his hand on my head. "I'm hoping we'll find her sound asleep in the conservatory, and she'll be apologizing to everyone the rest of the day. But whether she's okay or something has happened to her, I'll make sure every inch of this estate is turned over to find her, and then turned over again. Go find Mister Spruce and tell him to meet me in the planning room. Then I suggest you and your brother find Bray."

That was sound advice, and I wasn't going to waste any time. It was all I could do not to run through the halls and leap down the stairs. The few seconds I gained wouldn't make a difference, especially not if I broke my neck on paws I was still learning how to use. I still hurried. Actually, breaking into a run was all I could keep myself from doing, and I caught myself dropping to all fours to lope a few paces more than once.

The problem was I didn't know where Mister Spruce would be. It was dawn and everyone was either asleep or already working, not wandering the halls. When I reached the top of the stairs in the entrance hall I realized that there would be a number of people in the kitchen who might know where he was and could spread the word anyway. That made sense, but as I hit the carpet on the first floor I heard Mister Spruce's muffled voice, and followed it.

I found him standing at the front door checking off items being unloaded from a cart. He hadn't seen me, so I hurried up and touched his elbow to get his attention and explained things as fast as I could. "Hind is missing. Sir Victor knows and is going to meet you in the planning room to discuss a search."

Old man Spruce's face looked very bleak. So did the carters'. He turned to the nearest one, who was one of the Maple brothers, and instructed him, "Sir Victor will want this orderly. Go bring in everyone whose job can wait a day or two. Leave everyone in the fields and make sure at least a few people remain in the stables and tell as many of the older children who want to help they can join in." He wasn't panicking, but I could see the pain in his face as he told me, "Tell the kitchen staff. Miss Oakapple will want to set the maids to looking inside immediately and I'm sure that's where we'll find her, but they need to gather by the planning room first."

"After that Sir Victor wants me to find my brother and the phoenix," I added, and he nodded. He seemed to think that was good sense as well.

Whether he did or not, I wasn't going to wait around if I had an out. I jogged as fast as I could through the back hallways into the kitchen. At this hour Miss Oakapple was just getting up, but the morning's cooking had started long since. The kitchen never really goes to sleep. Still, even though I knew what she was taking out of the oven was her own breakfast, I grabbed her wrist and told her quickly, "Hind is gone. Spruce says to get the maids together and have them wait outside the planning room for directions from him and Sir Victor."

She dropped her baking pan. To my surprise I caught it, and was immediately grateful for the fur that kept me from burning myself before I could shove it quickly onto a cutting table. "Hind is gone," she repeated in shock, but she recovered quickly. Suddenly it was her hands on my shoulders, and I thought I saw tears in her eyes even as she tried to reassure me, "I bet she's turned her ankle out in the fields or locked herself in a broom closet. I did that once when I was five. We'll find her. But you forget the rest of us and go get the bird girl now."

"That's what Sir Victor told me to do too."

Miss Oakapple was recovering already. I was shocked by just how much she seemed to care for Hind, but she was a very hard woman beneath the sweet attitude, and I knew it. Still, her voice was more than a little emphatic as she agreed, "Smart man. A Wild Child will find a Wild Child. You can do things we can't."

I wished I knew what those things were. I didn't have a dog's nose. I'd tried following scents already with no luck at all. I bolted anyway. I would find Right first, and then we would find Bray and somehow she would find Hind.

But Right wasn't in our room and he wasn't out in the yard. Since Sir Victor had set him loose he might be anywhere, doing anything, at any moment. He wouldn't have gone far from the manor without telling me though, so I started crisscrossing the major rooms.

When I poked my head into the planning room Sir Victor was telling old Spruce, "Put that out of your head. If something really has happened to Hind my father will be furious, yes, but he doesn't take revenge against anyone who's not at fault. You won't be blamed, and the manor won't be blamed. I would make sure he saw you as the people who tried to find his Wild Girl, not the people who lost her, but I won't have to. It's just how he is. And we're all hoping it won't come to that anyway."

That... was a problem that hadn't even occurred to me. It slowed me down for a moment and made me think again. Which is why I headed up to the third floor to the solarium, because I only had to think for a moment to know how my brother thought. There's a wide rooftop patio that juts out from the main building there, and he was standing on it looking up at the sky. Thinking about Bray, I was sure.

He only had to see my expression as I pushed my way through the glass doors to know something was bad. "Hind is gone. Sir Victor wants us to find Bray," I explained as fast as I could.

"She's up there." He pointed up across the roof. And she was. There's a short tower with an open room on that end of the building. I realized, looking at it, I had no idea how to get into it. There was no doorway into it from the attics. The manor was big enough to hold a few secrets. Over the ledge of that open room I could see the rising sun shining on gold and scarlet feathers, and I probably had the same expression on my face that my brother did as I looked at her, but we both knew there was no time to stare.

I glanced at the roof. We were proud of the tiling and the sturdiness of its slope that kept even the worst snow off. "I can't climb that. I'm not a squirrel," I told Right in frustration. We could see Bray, but we couldn't get to her!

"I certainly can't," he agreed, tapping a hoof on the stonework. "I don't think we have to, though. She says she sleeps light." So he lifted his fingers to his mouth and whistled as piercingly as he could. I realized, absently, with my teeth I probably couldn't whistle at all anymore. I'd figure that out later. Worry for Hind was making my thoughts scatter.

But it worked. Bray sat up and looked around, and when she saw us she fluttered over, landing on the nearby rooftop. I wasn't sure she could climb it either, but she was light enough to stand on it. "What's wrong?" she asked us. Our worry had to have been pretty plain.

She was looking at Right, but he looked at me and I told her, "Hind is missing. She didn't return to her room last night, and Jinx isn't there either."

She thought about that for a moment. "Then something's wrong. Someone either knew not to leave Jinx behind, or she left herself. She hasn't just gotten lost." That was what I had been trying not to think, and we were all suddenly very grave.

"Sir Victor wants the three of us to search on our own. Everyone seems to think we can find her somehow," I told her. Right's pained expression reflected how I felt about that. I hardly felt any different from when I was human. I didn't think I could achieve any miracles adults couldn't.

"They may be right," Bray told me cautiously. "I am drawn to people sometimes. I wish I could say it's likely that I'll just stumble over her because of fate, but it's not. But I can fly, and you know where her favorite places are, and even out there searching I think Right can find both of us if he has to."

"And whether we can do a better job than anyone else," Right added, "we're going to try." I felt so grateful I wanted to hug him, but I couldn't make myself do it in front of Bray.

There is nothing else to say about the rest of the day. Nothing but frustration and worry. I checked the river and the lake first because she'd wanted to go swimming. All it did was give me terrified images of her drowning and her body hidden at the bottom. But there was no sign of her at all, and she'd at least have left Jinx by the shore. I climbed hills that let me look around at the farms, and she wasn't anywhere admiring the fields. I went back to the manor and dug through the storage rooms until I found the ball, and she wasn't trapped anywhere.

Bray had been right about one thing. She, Right, and I kept running into each other. The estate was huge, but we crossed paths several times. When I had dropped by the manor then, I left with an extra-large sack on my back full of food for all three of us and headed to the last place I could think to check, which might have been the first place I should have gone. There I met Bray and Right, who'd arrived just before me. It was the burned-out spot where Bray had transformed us both. Hind wasn't there either.

We tried to compare notes, but we already knew where we'd checked and that we hadn't seen her. We weren't going back to the manor tonight. We'd sleep in the field and start looking again as soon as the sun was up. That was why I'd brought the food. But the truth was, there was nowhere we could think of to check that we hadn't looked already.

If there was one thing that had changed, it was that it was surprisingly easy to sleep on the grass without a bed. While I curled up almost like a dog, I kept looking at my brother with his hair like fleece and his horns, and the striking flame-colored bird whose anxiety had her glimmering in the darkness. And they were looking at each other, and at me. Eventually we fell asleep anyway. I thought Bray fell asleep first, because I remembered her fire went out.

I woke up with a start with the sun just rising over the woods – and at the same time so did they.

"I had a dream," I explained haltingly, and I knew from their look that so had they. But I had to explain it just to be sure.

"I was seeing something. But not through my eyes. It was like I was looking through lenses, perfectly round," I described.

"With black crosses in the middle," added Right with the expression of someone working out a puzzle.

"Jinx's eyes," Bray told us, even as I was coming to the same conclusion. Even though it made no sense, it was obvious.

I supposed I had to tell everything. "All I could really see was Hind. Her clothes were torn and her eyes were red, but she didn't seem to be crying. She was just standing there, and everything else was shadows."

"And one of those shadows hit her. More than once," Right filled in, in a horrified tone.

"And she just didn't do anything. She was obviously awake and she wasn't tied up, and it looked like it hurt. But she just let it happen," I added.

"Yes," Bray agreed mournfully. "I don't think Hind would lift a finger to save her own life."

I thought she was right, and if we'd all seen it, somehow through the eyes of a doll, it had to be real. That someone was hurting Hind that way made me cold inside. I couldn't bear it, but I couldn't think of anything I could do. Right looked just as helpless, although he didn't really know her and I think it didn't hurt him as much.

It hurt Bray worse. Her face had something of the bleakness I'd seen on Hind, but her eyes were never empty and they were starting to shine bloody and golden again. "Someone has kidnapped her," Bray concluded. "She's alive, but they're willing to hurt her. I have to find her now." Those eyes, suddenly, were riveted on me. "The squirrels have an oracle."

"Something like that," I admitted. "But they won't let us talk to it and they won't talk about it and they won't let us into their forest."

"Then we'll find it anyway. We can be polite or we can save Hind."

I didn't have to think about it. Neither did Right. "The forest is over there," I told her, climbing to my feet and pointing.

I thought she would fly ahead, but she didn't. Right and I ran most of the way when we could. Bray would fly, then land and run with us, then fly again. When we saw the trees ahead of us we stopped running, but Bray kept walking and we stayed alongside her. Needless to say, before we'd reached the shadows of the first branches a squirrel was on one of them with back arched and tail raised.

"Hey! You can't come in here! And we're sure not letting her in here!" it barked at us.

"May I ask a question of your oracle instead? Then I won't have to come in," Bray asked. She stopped, so we stopped, but she was tense.

"No," the squirrel snapped. Which was what I knew they'd say.

"It's very important," Bray continued, grave and polite. "My best friend is in trouble. We think humans have taken her and are hurting her. We just want to know where she is. She's a Wild Child like us."

"So?" asked the squirrel dismissively.

So Bray started walking again.

"Hey! Hey!" the squirrel barked. It didn't feel very animal, but it was scampering back and forth on the branch and its voice was screechy like, well, an angry squirrel. "You can't come in here! She really can't come in here! Go away, fire bird! Go burn someone else's home to –" and as Bray came level with the first tree trunk it did something I didn't expect at all. It made this horrible noise like a bird of prey and it leaped at her.

I had just enough time to think just enough. It was all very, very plain. I stepped in front of Bray and reached up and I grabbed the squirrel's arm and belly. It was already moving fast through the air. I completely ignored its pathetic claws and kept it going, heaving it forward faster in a new direction at a tree trunk.

It could not have looked more surprised, but it didn't exactly hit the tree. It twisted around and managed to catch the trunk with all fours and drop to the ground. Bray just kept walking, and I'm not sure whether it looked more scared of me or of her. It didn't attack again and instead ran straight off into the woods.

Bray immediately turned. "That way," she said, pointing after the retreating child. "I'm sure he's heading straight to the oracle."

It made sense to me. We started walking that way at a good pace, but calmly, watching the trees. They really were very ordinary trees. It was the largest stand of them in the area, but trees were trees, and a carpet of old leaves and the occasional log or bush was no different than anywhere else. Pretty soon, though, a Squirrel Boy was sliding down a trunk and stepping up in our way. I saw a girl and what I thought was the first squirrel, who I just couldn't identify at all, watching from the branches.

I felt sorry for the boy standing in front of us. He looked like he was trying to be brave and he must have been sent to do this because he was the biggest of them. He still wasn't as tall as me. And when he held out his hand Bray didn't stop walking for an instant.

"You have to leave! Now! You don't belong here! And that thing isn't allowed here, ever!" It was pointing at Bray now. They seemed to have quite a thing against her. I would have thought they'd hate the wolf most.

Right was gritting his teeth at the way they talked about Bray, but he held up his own hands and tried to step in front of Bray, explaining, "We're desperate and we need an answer from your oracle. Let us talk to it, and we'll leave. Or just ask the question for us, and we won't even have to come any closer. We don't-" He didn't get any farther. He hadn't stopped walking because Bray hadn't stopped walking, and the squirrel hit him in the face.

It probably surprised him more than it hurt him. That first punch had been thrown in fear and hadn't been very hard. It had also been just a little too far away for me to intervene, but by the time the second fist was swinging, rather more forcefully, I was there. I grabbed the wrist and yanked him off balance. The squirrels were nothing if not quick and agile, and even as he was falling he was getting his feet back under him and grabbing my arm too, and he sank his teeth into my wrist. Or at least that was the general idea. He had hardly begun to bite me when I pulled my knee up into his descending stomach. It took the force right out of his bite, and I threw him at a bush to wheeze.

They couldn't react as quickly as I could, but the squirrels were pretty fast. The other two were leaping out of their trees at me. I was glad they were attacking me and not my brother or Bray, and I was even more grateful they were so bad at it. All I really had to do was duck forward, which I had just enough time to do, so that they hit each other and not me. Then when they fell to the ground I hooked a foot into first one and then the other and booted them out of Bray's way. The boy squirrel was up by then, and only a flash of movement let me see him coming. Both his hands were outstretched, I supposed to grab or tackle me. I just stepped in and grabbed him instead by the face. Being brought up short that way jarred him, and I swung him down and smacked his head against the ground. It was soft earth, so that wasn't as bad as it sounds, but it still disoriented him for a few seconds. I watched him and his friends carefully anyway as Bray and Right kept walking.

After a few seconds the squirrels got to their feet and went running off again. All in the same direction. My brother and Bray adjusted a bit to follow them – it's easy to get turned around in even a small forest. I watched for a moment, but I wasn't really watching. I was listening to myself. I was hearing the growl that had started in my throat. I felt excited, alive, alert. I was not, was absolutely not going to be the kind of person who enjoyed this. Reminding myself of what I'd seen in my dream the night before was enough to make it all very grim again, and I loped out ahead of the other two with a proper solemnity. I was defending two people who couldn't fight for themselves – three, really. Nothing more was justified.

We must have really spooked the squirrels last time, because it was quite a while before we saw another. When we did I knew it was far more dangerous than before. It might not have seemed like it, just a little squirrel sliding down to a low branch and heaving an apple at us. That was something we couldn't do much about, though, and I had to make them think it was a bad idea before we were facing rocks from every direction. One apple gave me a chance to do that. I grabbed it right out of the air and threw it back, much harder than the squirrel could have. The apple bounced off her forehead and knocked her off her branch onto the ground. That was fifteen feet, but she was on her feet again almost immediately and scampering away. I figured squirrels weren't going to be hurt much by falling out of a tree.

And she'd run in exactly the same direction. They were leading us right to… something, without knowing it.

We soon found out that 'something' was a sort of village. The squirrels didn't have much. They'd built nests of rags and twigs, and some had little lean-tos, and I saw haphazard platforms on convenient branches. There were a few baskets and pots. Everything seemed to have been scavenged from the manor. There were actually more of these little makeshift homes than there seemed to be squirrels, and I got a pretty good idea of that because here was their last line of defense. Five of them stood against us, not including the little one that had thrown the apple before and wasn't here now. And that seemed to be it. Three of them were the boy, the girl, and the one I couldn't place that had attacked me before.

Right was starting to spread his hands and step forward and say, "Please-" when, as I expected, they all rushed us at once. They weren't here to talk.

The first thing I had to do was make sure that none of them went after my brother or Bray. I had to move fast, faster than I could really keep track of. A kick sent one of them rolling away, and I was able to grab the squirrel on the far side who was diving at my brother's legs, and swing him like a club at the three coming at me. He wasn't an effective weapon, but it threw them off-balance and made them pay attention to me and only to me.

After that, for a minute, it became very focused. I only had time to notice teeth and feet and claws coming after me, to lean out of the way, to push one squirrel into another, to swing my elbow against the top of one's head. I knew how it would end. If they were squirrels and I was a wolf, it hardly mattered how many of them there were. When the last threat passed and I could notice more than what was coming at me again all five of them were lying around the little clearing whimpering. One of them started to push himself up, and I couldn't help it. My eyes were there, focused on him, watching him for danger, and he gradually lay back down again. They looked terrified.

Then one more squirrel came out. This one was a girl, older than the others, and her eyes were a black that filled the whole eye from edge to edge. She looked scared, too. Scared witless, but she stood defiantly, pointedly in front of a box laid out against the roots of the biggest tree. I hadn't even noticed it before. It was just a sort of cabinet, hand-made from bent planks of wood, covered in moss and badly stained. We really would never have found this place or paid any attention to the box if the squirrels hadn't led us here.

"I will not let you touch the oracle," she announced coldly. She was trembling. She tried to talk to Bray, but she kept looking at me.

There wasn't much else to do. I started walking over to her to push her aside, hoping I wouldn't have to hurt her to make her stay away, but Right rushed in front of me and held out a hand to me and to her.

"No! Listen, there's been too much fighting." He was protecting her, but he was addressing her, too. "What did it get you? He won't touch your oracle. I won't, either. We wouldn't know what to do with it. But the phoenix has a question. Look at her. How can you deny her anything? We're just a sheep and a wolf and some squirrels. She's got to be as special as your oracle is."

I thought they'd made the point fairly well that they especially didn't like her, and in fact the Squirrel Girl replied, "You don't know what she is, do you? Fire is pretty, but it destroys everything." I was amazed she could stand, she looked so afraid. At the same time she at least seemed to be listening.

"That's why I try not to use it," was Bray's reply, and her voice was haunted.

"Do you succeed?" challenged the squirrel. The others were still lying around making pained noises, and I glanced at them occasionally to make sure of it.

I didn't want Bray to have to answer that and neither did Right, which is why he changed the subject. As gently as possible, which wasn't very, he told her, "Does it matter? You've made your own point. If you somehow manage to hurt her you might burn down the forest. What has any of this fighting done but made the whole thing worse? We would have asked our question and left with an answer and never even have come in. We're doing this to save someone and we can't go away without it, but if you can give us an answer now we'll leave."

I really thought she was going to faint and I didn't know who she was more afraid of, me or Bray, but the squirrel held her ground. "I can't," she told Right desperately. "I can't help you. I won't be a part of this. I won't help it in any way."

"Then at least let me make this a little easier," Right told her. He walked up to her very slowly, reaching out his hands. She almost looked grateful as he took hold of her upper arms, lifted her up and pulled her out of the way of the box. "Now there really is nothing you can do," he told her calmly, "and there wasn't any more fighting." He gripped her arms so tight it must have hurt a little, but there was no 'almost' anymore. She stared at Right like he'd saved her life.

And Bray gave him a look that was almost as relieved and admiring. She didn't look at me, but there was a moment of hesitation, a grimmer, sadder look on her face that I thought was the one she didn't want me to realize was meant for me. I felt ashamed, because I'd just beaten half a dozen children younger than me senseless and that was nothing to be proud of. I hadn't been able to find any other way, but I hadn't seen any other way to deal with this last squirrel either, and Right had.

But it had gotten us here, and whether it was polite or whatever it meant about me as a person now, no one was really hurt and maybe we were a step closer to saving Hind.

So with me watching the fallen squirrels and Right holding what I guessed was their leader, Bray picked her way across the clearing to the sprawling tree root and opened the awkward little door of the cabinet. Inside was just this doll. Even 'doll' was the wrong word. It was an effigy, less than a scarecrow, a bundle of hay and sticks tied here and there with twine in the vague shape of a person.

Not much of an oracle to look at, and Bray just picked it up and turned it over in her hands for a moment. Then for a few more seconds she was very still. Before she moved again the flames started, flickering around the edge of her wings, lighting up her eyes. She dropped the doll, and it had already caught fire at the edges, and although Right and I started moving to put it out hay just burns too fast. The whole thing was burning before we'd gone a few steps and my only consolation was that it was also burning too fast to set fire to the soggy tree roots it had landed on.

The squirrels weren't consoled. They were all screeching and wailing, and despite the beating I'd given them they were all back up on their feet and running off in every direction. Bray hadn't seemed to really notice any of it, although her expression was so dark and hard she might have. She was very, very unhappy.

"Did you see something?" Right asked her cautiously. He'd let go of the dark-eyed squirrel, and she'd run off like the rest.

"No," Bray told him. "No visions, no sudden flash of inspiration, no knowledge or prophecy. I know where Hind is now, more or less, but there was nothing to it after all. I just put together things I already knew and now it's obvious."

"Where?" I asked impatiently, "Is there any reason not to go now? Do you know what we'll have to do to free her?"

"There's nothing you can do at all," Bray told me – told both of us. "Nothing that wouldn't make it worse. This is about me, and it always was, and I just didn't realize it."

I was about to say something, but she didn't give me the chance. She looked at me directly now, and while it wasn't the look I wanted from her there was warmth and approval in her voice as she told me, "You can stop worrying. I can save Hind and I'm going to do it now. She'll be fine."

Right and I had talked to squirrels, though, and we knew what was unsaid in that sentence. And she seemed to be thinking as fast as we were because now she looked at Right and told him, "I'll be fine, too. It may take some time – it may take years – but I'll come back and I'll find you both. I can save Hind right now, but that's the price. Anyway, I'm going to go and you can't stop me. I can fly and I won't let you follow me."

We didn't like it, but Right told her grudgingly, "Alright."

"I'll miss you both, like I miss Hind." It wasn't me she was looking at. The look she was giving Right and the look he was giving her – I thought they wanted to kiss, but they didn't want to do it in front of me and hurt my feelings.

So I turned my back and stared at a tree and I honestly don't know what they did or even if they said anything quietly to each other until my brother's hand squeezed my shoulder and he told me, "It's okay. She left."

We walked side-by-side out of the forest. We didn't see any squirrels. We didn't see anyone on the way back to the manor and we weren't walking fast, so it took a long time. We didn't talk to each other. We each pretty much knew how the other felt.

Still, I couldn't help but feel relief when I saw Hind sitting on a basket at the top of the hill she'd used for painting. Someone had ripped her clothes and broken the laces and buttons, but hadn't actually destroyed them, and she seemed to have tied most of it back together. It had been one of her plainest dresses anyway, I could tell. Jinx sat in her lap and she was trying to wrap her long hair up into some kind of bun, but obviously wasn't satisfied with doing it any simple way. At least, until she saw us. Then she just jammed some kind of long pin into it to hold it in place, scooped up Jinx in both arms, and started walking down the hill to meet us. She looked quite calm and didn't seem to be hurt, but I could see how tightly she was squeezing the doll and that gave lie to everything.

"I'm sorry I made you all worry," she told us quietly with her mask of doll-like politeness, "but I'm about to make it worse. I wasn't ever really in trouble. It was Bray, all along. Can you two help me save her? I'm not sure I can alone, and anyone who does is going to be in a lot of trouble themselves, and there's no one else I can ask for something like that."

"We don't care how much trouble," Right told her flatly.

"It will be a lot," Hind insisted. "The rest of the people here should be okay, but-"

I put my fingers over her lips. I certainly wouldn't do that to any other girl, but Hind had no grasp of modesty anyway and she hadn't understood. "We don't care," I repeated. "If it will save you or Bray, we'll do it."

The mask cracked, and while she didn't exactly start crying or have any readable expression, her arms flew around both our necks and she squeezed us tightly. Then she started talking.

"The first thing you need to know," Hind explained calmly as we sat on the hillside, "is that it's Master Vick who's holding her. I can't ask anyone from the manor to oppose him. It would destroy their lives. Are you sure you want to do this?"

"Yes," Right and I said, at the same time and in the same tone. We had to be firm about it so she'd stop arguing with herself.

"...alright." She continued very quietly after a moment. "I'm sure you think I was kidnapped. Bray seemed to. I wasn't. Master Vick asked me to come with him and he asked my permission to beat me. He didn't tell me why. I didn't ask, and I should have."

Right still didn't quite understand her, and I hoped she didn't see the look I gave him so he wouldn't ask. To me there really wasn't any question how Hind would have responded to something like that from her owner's son.

"He only told me why he did it when Bray arrived. It was such a simple plan. If he hurt me, he knew somehow she would find out and she would find me. And I guess it worked."

I nodded. It had. Maybe he'd just had faith in the phoenix.

"And once she arrived he said she'd do anything he wanted to make sure I was safe. It wasn't quite true, I guess. I tried to tell her that I wasn't in any real danger, and not enough to risk herself for. And she wasn't exactly cooperating with him, but she let him put those things on her, which was enough for him to tell me I could go."

"Things?" asked Right about a half second before I did.

"He had these shackles, and a collar. He said the hardest part about taming a phoenix was figuring out how to hold her, since she would simply burn through or melt anything he bound her with. But these were made out of some kind of black rock and he thought that would do it." Her voice was becoming very cold again, very matter-of-fact.

But then, I suppose so was mine. "Obsidian, I'd guess. It's a volcanic rock and it's very hard to melt."

"And if she tried she'd burn down the manor in the process, and she won't do that," Right added. "The same with melting her way out of a wall. She's somewhere in the manor, isn't she?"

"Yes," Hind acknowledged. "I can show you the way. We can't go in the front way, but I have it all worked out. He just let me leave because he knew I wouldn't say anything. He knew I was completely trustworthy and obedient."

Again her face was too cool and composed, and that told me everything I needed to know. I reached out and squeezed her hand, and after a moment Right did the same. "He knew wrong," I told her so she'd know she'd done the right thing.

But she didn't need reassurance. Her brow furrowed just a little, and although she didn't look at either of us directly she started talking again in a very flat, grim voice. "Yes, he did. I know where he is, I know how he thinks he's protected more or less, and I know how to get in and out. And I stole this." She took out some kind of metal flask, like people put alcohol in sometimes.

"It's something he took from Dexter," she explained when we didn't have anything to say about it. "While I was picking up my things and leaving, he poured a little of this on Bray, and it worked like some kind of drug. It made her weak and a little crazy. She didn't have to drink it. We'll splash it on him, and hopefully that will give us time to use these."

And out of the box she'd been sitting on she took a solid iron hammer and chisel, which I supposed had come from the smithy. "I don't know anything about obsidian, but if it's a rock and not a metal we can chip it off. We just have to keep him immobilized long enough for one of you to break her out of those shackles. If we can get her out of the manor she'll fly away and that will be it. There just won't be anything else he can do."

"You've thought this out," Right observed, sounding a little surprised. I should have been surprised, but I wasn't.

"Yes," she agreed simply. "He's mostly relying on things that don't matter to us, like the manor staff not wanting to get involved. We won't get them involved. And he's relying on me." I thought about Miss Oakapple for a moment. No, we wouldn't make them choose.

Then she surprised me, too. "I'm not going to rely on anything. All we have to do is get Bray out of the manor. We can even get the shackles off later, if we have to. If we miss with whatever that drug is or it's not strong enough, there's still three of us and one of him. I think you're stronger than other Wild Boys I've known, but if you're still not enough I promise you that he's not expecting a knife in the back from me."

And to my horror she pulled out a knife. It wasn't even a kitchen blade, it was a slim but actual dagger and I wasn't sure how she even carried it in her clothes safely. "If I possibly can I want to save Bray without hurting Master Vick. But I've faced the possibility that we won't be able to save her without killing him, and I've accepted it."

It was the most coldblooded assessment of what might have to be done I could imagine, and that was how she explained it to us, with a calmly emotionless face and tone. And I knew, from Hind, that meant it was a lie. At least, pretending that it didn't bother her was a lie. I was sure she'd do it.

"It won't come to that," Right told her very grimly. "I won't allow it to. No one is going to die. Sir Victor is not that bad a man. We will save Bray, but we won't have to kill him to do it."

But Hind had made me face the same choice. If we did have to, I would. I would pick Bray's life over the life of the man who had imprisoned her.

Still, my brother's words had comforted Hind a great deal, and while it was barely there, she did smile, and the hug she gave us was almost crushingly strong. "We don't have time," she told us before she let go again. "We have to go now. I have no idea how he thinks he can get her to accept a collar, and we can't give him time to try."

Right and I nodded. We didn't know what else to say, so Right took the hammer and chisel and I took the flask, and Hind put the knife away again.

She led us, a silent company of three, back to the manor. The search had apparently ended and everyone knew Hind was okay. At least when people saw us they smiled and waved, and she would smile and wave back.

What she led us to was a tightly shuttered and locked door, set in the ground on one side of the manor house. I had seen it before, but I hadn't the faintest idea what it connected to, and it wasn't really a proper door. It was more like a closed up coal chute. "They're down there," Hind explained. The door was barred and there was a padlock set into the bar, but the door was old wood and a few blows of the chisel let us pry it off. Underneath there really was sort of a coal chute, but it was a big one and the slope was gentle, and it was easy for us to climb down even with Right's hooves. We let him go first just in case. What stunned me was how far down it went. Eventually I realized we were below the storage cellars. They were stone-floored and there could have been something underneath them, but I'd never heard about it.

Near the bottom, where it opened into a badly lit room, there were a bunch of marks on the walls. At least some of them I recognized as Hellenic lettering, although I certainly couldn't read it. A lot of the rest looked like mathematical diagrams. I was curious about them, but Right had already passed them and was about to drop into the room, so I wasn't concerned until Hind suddenly announced, "I can't go past those."

"What?" Right and I asked at the same time. Yes, we do that sometimes.

"Those signs. I can't go past them. I mean, Jinx can't go past them. They're to keep out... things. Things like him." She looked horrified. She looked like she was panicking, and I'd never seen her like that. I could see white all around the edges of her eyes.

"Can they really keep out a doll?" Right asked.

"You don't have to come. We'll do this without you," I told her gently. Whatever her attachment to that black cat toy was, it was fanatical.

She was breathing heavily, but in seconds she started to return to normal. "While we're in there, past these marks, he'll just... be a regular doll." It was obvious to both of us that the thought scared her witless, but before either of us knew what to say she concluded, "I have to save Bray. Master Vick has gone crazy. I don't know what he'll do."

We didn't really have anything to say to that, so Right dropped down into the room below, and then I did, and finally Hind. When her feet hit the floor the only sign that she'd panicked was that she was squeezing Jinx to her chest so hard I thought she'd be more worried about tearing the seams.

We'd landed in some kind of little stone room with a table and a few empty shelves. There were a couple of freshly filled and lit lanterns to keep it from being too gloomy, and some sunshine was coming down the chute now. That was it, except for a couple of corroded but serviceable metal doors – one up a short flight of stairs and the other set into a different wall.

Right pointed at the stairs. "You know that old doorway behind the lumber rack?"

I did. "I never thought about it before. I didn't think anybody'd been down there... ever. What is this place?"

Cautiously, Right opened the other door a little and peered through it. He beckoned to me with his hand but didn't say anything, so I padded up to him and looked through the gap. We might have to be quiet from here on through.

What I saw was a short hallway with another door on the end. The hall was lined with doors, solid metal with barred grills. "This is a prison." I was nonplussed. "There's a little prison under the manor. The Baron built this place, so he must have put it here. Why would he put a prison under his vacation home?" I asked Hind.

Looking back at her I saw tears forming at the corners of her eyes, and her face looked tight. I had asked a question, like Victor prying into Bray's travels, that shouldn't be asked. "We don't have time to worry about it," I told Right.

"No, we don't," he agreed, and started creeping through into that hallway. His hooves actually didn't make much noise, but the stone was roughly cut anyway and largely covered in dirt.

Something moved. I couldn't tell what, and that was why I grabbed Right by the shoulder and yanked him back into what I suddenly knew was the guardroom. But Hind was throwing herself forward in front of us. All I could see was shadows shifting and suddenly she stopped, although not completely. It looked like she was being held by something, and she twisted and jerked a little but couldn't get free. It's just that there was nothing to hold her.

"Is that... the squirrel's shadow?" Right asked. Yes, much of Hind was darker than it should be, and I could see in the bad light the silhouette of a tail flicking across the floor. For a moment my brother and I just stared, fascinated. I had too many questions. How did that even work? What could we do about it?

Apparently nothing. "Just keep going!" Hind grunted, still struggling with its grip on her. "It's a stupid trick. Someone told me about it. It can't hurt me, I swear, and I'm the person least able to help Bray anyway."

I didn't want to, but what exactly could I do? And Right was already pushing forward into the hall, so I followed him. We glanced worriedly into the little cells on either side, but they were empty and there was no sign they'd ever been used. That left the other door, which Right pushed open with considerable trepidation.

I'd expected a torture chamber. Instead it was a sort of laboratory. There were a few tables that looked so old they might always have been there, and a certain amount of equipment, beakers and tools and bits of metal, were scattered over them. A few books here and there. A couple of lanterns hung on the wall, but the light came from four tall, ornate candlesticks – and from Bray.

She was at the other end of the room, and like Hind had described she was wore shackles that fastened her wrists together and another pair that fastened her ankles, and a heavy collar around her neck that seemed to have no purpose at all. All were made of a shiny black rock instead of metal. The room might have originally been a torture chamber after all, because a metal chain connected the ankle cuffs to a ring in the floor.

Bray ignored all of them, standing up straight and looking up at Sir Victor, who stood over her. He was a lot taller than her, but she looked calm. Her eyes shone gold, and light gleamed from her feathers without any sign of real flames.

He in turn was stroking the feathers she had instead of hair and telling her, "You don't understand how the years pass. None of you seem to. I won't let you leave me again. Will it be a decade before you come back? Two? I'll either take you home with me like this, or leave with you Wild myself."

She was just giving him a sad look and not saying anything. But then she saw me and Right and she shook her head quickly. "Oh, no. No, no. I didn't want you here. Please, just go!"

Which made Sir Victor turn and look at us too, and Bray's expression behind him was obvious. She was terrified for us. He just looked resigned and maybe a bit curious. "Dexter. Sinister." He greeted us with a nod. "I wish I could say this was pleasant or a surprise. I was hoping to keep you out of this too, but I knew the phoenix would draw you to her somehow. She makes us all dance like puppets, and is made to dance herself." I thought that was annoyingly poetic, but the look he turned back on her for a moment made it clear why he spoke that way. There was much too much emotion there for someone keeping a girl in chains.

"Anyway," he continued, stepping away from her towards us with a guarded, careful walk. "I don't know what you think you can do. I guess I shouldn't be surprised the shadow thing failed me. It was just something I wanted to try. But really, you're two boys and that hammer doesn't count as armed. Nice thought, by the way. I knew you two were smart. Be smart enough to walk out of here, because I very much don't want to hurt anyone, especially you. This is between myself and Bray."

"You know we're not leaving," Right told him flatly. He was also stepping forward.

"I know-" Sir Victor agreed with obvious regret, and that was what I wanted. He was talking to Right and ignoring me. I simply shook the flask Hind had given me, and the liquid inside of it sprayed out, quite a lot of the stuff getting on Sir Victor.

It just didn't seem to do anything. He even dabbed at some of it with his fingers and sniffed it thoughtfully. "Ah, yes. Also clever. It makes me very glad you haven't had a chance to read as much as I have. No, this essence does nothing at all to humans, as much as I wish it did." And then, quickly but quite casually, he pulled out a knife and threw it at me.

Except it wasn't at me. I had a split second to decide, and I realized it wasn't going to hit me, and trying to catch or knock away a knife in the air was a bad idea. It was one of the stupidest decisions I'd ever made. The knife hit the floor behind me and stuck point-first in the dirt that had covered most of the bare stone. The blade barely stood up, but that seemed to be all it took, because I couldn't move. I couldn't even struggle like Hind had. I had been pinned in place, and because I'd been looking at the knife I could see out of the corner of my eye that it was sticking out of the middle of my shadow.

"But that did work," Sir Victor continued, watching me with mild surprise and fascination. "At least, it worked on a Wild Child. A lot of what people call alchemy is just listening to old wives' tales until you find one that's true." He turned his attention back to Right and added briskly, "As for you-" and turning, he slapped Bray across the face.

The blow was at arm's length and it looked like he hit her pretty hard, but it was just a slap. She hardly whimpered, although it must have hurt. Right, though, made a noise I guess must have been something a sheep made, and bolted straight for Sir Victor. Except that when Sir Victor reached out for him, my brother ducked under his arm and ran right past him. Instead he swiveled sharply and planted himself in front of Bray. It was a noble and protective gesture. I just couldn't figure out what good it was going to do.

"I don't want to fight you, but I won't let you hurt her either."

It was Bray who replied, scolding him desperately, "He's not going to hurt me. Don't you get it? He doesn't want to. He's just trying to make me burn him!"

Then what I'd been afraid would happen, happened. Sir Victor turned around, grabbed Right by a horn, and threw him against a wall. It couldn't have hurt that bad, and Bray whimpered louder than my brother did.

"Yes, and her patience and self-control are remarkable," Sir Victor explained, calmly and gravely. He sounded like a teacher with a very unfortunate duty to perform. "She doesn't have a lot of weaknesses I'm willing to use against her, but I think I just found one." Right was pushing himself back upright, and whether he was going to fight or not he didn't get a chance. Sir Victor punched him in the stomach and then cuffed him across the side of his head with a fist.

My brother fell down, and as he did Bray yelled, "Not again!" The fire was suddenly burning, rising up off of her like a halo. I could feel it from here. That was obviously what Sir Victor had been waiting for, but as he turned around and stepped back up to her, she somehow strangled it back. There were flickers, but that was it, and I didn't think they'd do him any good. He looked angry. The two of them stared into each other's eyes challengingly, and then he took her head in both hands and leaned down and kissed her.

It didn't make her burn again, but it got my brother staggering up and Right threw himself at Sir Victor's legs, only to be kicked away. I stumbled forward automatically towards my brother as he fell, and realized I could move again. I was no longer pinned. For an instant, I glanced back.

Hind stood there holding the knife in one hand, with Jinx tucked under her arm. How she got free I didn't know, but the seam of his mouth had come undone and stuffing was starting to spill out. One of his red button eyes had come off too, and she was holding it up, peering at the room through it like a monocle.

I think she misunderstood my stare. "He can be fixed," she told me, although her own voice cracked. "There's no more tricks. Do something!"

Sir Victor heard us, of course. He, Bray, and Right all stared at us. "Hind?" he asked in shock. "How can you do this to me?"

"She doesn't love you and she's not your donkey," Hind spat back. She was trembling. I hadn't realized she even had limits, but she was hitting them.

"You can't side with them against me," he continued. He didn't seem angry. He just couldn't believe it. "What will my father say?"

"He'll forgive me or he won't," she answered, and the shaking of her voice was very plain. "He's my Master, not you."

More of this and she was going to break somehow. So I grabbed a candlestick. It was as tall as I was and made of metal, and I thought it would make an excellent staff. And I was a wolf now. I had to hope it was enough. "Stop this now," I warned Sir Victor, although I knew it would be useless. "They don't want to hurt you. I don't care."

Bray looked sick, and I started to realize how arrogant I was as Sir Victor studied me calmly and walked with the kind of careful deliberation Hind often used, over to a table. What he pulled off of it was a sword. It was shorter and thinner than I thought of a sword, but it couldn't be called anything else, and he drew it from its sheath with easy grace.

"I invite you to think about my title, Sinister," he explained as he walked slowly towards me. "I have, in fact, been trained as a knight. At the time I thought it was stupid. Eventually I realized it wasn't. If it helps, I really will try not to hurt you permanently. I don't think you boys understand how much I admire you. But I won't let anyone take Bray away from me again, either."

My best hope was to surprise him. If it had been some kind of real staff instead of a candlestick with a heavy base I might have ended it there, but it was the slightest bit too slow as I swung it at his head. He managed to catch the end with his sword and then his arm, and push it away. I wasn't strong enough. I was stronger than I should be, but he was a grown man and if it came down to strength I was going to lose, and in the next instant I discovered he really knew what he was doing much better than I did, because the point of that sword was heading for my arm.

It was way too close, but speed mattered as much as strength. No, more than strength, and I was faster than he was. I saw the point coming and I turned, and as I did I smacked him across the ribs with the other end of the candlestick. It didn't do much good, but it separated us.

What followed was kind of like dancing. I could barely hope to attack. When I did he would either bend the blow aside or step back out of the way. I thought it was close. But he just kept doing something that surprised me. The blade, usually the tip, would come at me from some direction I

232

didn't expect, and I was always ducking back or using the candlestick to knock it away. And those were close, too. The only thing that saved me was that, always, I could just see it coming in time to figure out how to escape, if only by an inch.

"Sinister, Hind, please! Take Dexter and go!" yelled Bray shrilly. "I won't change him, and he can't keep me forever, and he's not going to hurt me. Even if he did, I think if I die by violence-"

She stopped herself, but she'd gone too far. "The phoenix rises from its own ashes," quoted Sir Victor. I was already stepping forward to swing, but I'd had to back up too far. He was turning, and it was obvious he was going to stab Bray with his sword and when the fires saved her, however it happened, they would consume him as well – and I guess he thought they would turn him like they had us.

But Right had recovered, at least enough. He pushed himself between Sir Victor and Bray. Whether it would work I couldn't say, but it made Sir Victor hesitate. He really just did not want to kill us.

I didn't have to kill him. I hit him in the side with the base of the candlestick. He spun again immediately, but it was too late. He was bent a little, slowed by the pain, and maybe I'd hurt him. He couldn't stop the next blow that took him across the shoulder hard and knocked him halfway to the floor. Or the one I drove across his back that flattened him completely. I heard the sword clatter on the floor. I heard sharp smacks of metal hitting metal hitting rock, which then shattered. Right had not been wasting time. Bray was still wearing the cuffs and the collar, but she could move. The obsidian, I guess, broke easily even if it didn't melt.

He must have been in terrible pain and I had probably broken some ribs, but that didn't stop Sir Victor. He looked up at me with that same grim, methodical stare, and then turned his head and looked at Bray and started to push up. Whatever he was going to try, I didn't give him the chance. I hit him good and hard across the top of his head and he fell down and looked too dizzy to try again.

I heard Bray whimper in horror, but I didn't take my eyes off of him. "I'm not going to kill him," I told her and told myself. "Whatever happens, I won't kill him. I'm not willing to do that and I don't have to."

There was a metal noise. I was watching Sir Victor for any sign of movement, which is why I didn't see it in time and was too shocked to act in the split second I had. Right drove Sir Victor's sword through the man's back. The blade went so deep it probably came out the other side. No, I knew it did, because there was blood, a lot of blood, spreading out underneath him. He was very still.

I looked up at the glare of fury and anguish my brother was giving the corpse and heard Bray sob, "Vick!" She was crying, and she stumbled forward, and despite the blood she wrapped her arms around the body and pulled its head against her. Tears trailed down her cheeks and she held him like he was a family member, not a man who had kidnapped and chained her. And the look she gave Right was one of fear. Horror. No, betrayal.

But the anger was gone from my brother's face. He looked calm in a sad, accepting way. "He would never have stopped. Ever," he told Bray, although I wasn't sure she was really taking it in. "I knew you could never forgive me for it." I understood that, and neither I nor anyone else knew what to say as he walked out through the metal door and pulled it loudly shut behind him.

And Bray was staring at me now, and there wasn't any fear in it at all. "It was you I was looking for," she whispered deliriously. "Not him. It was you, and I didn't want to see it."

"I almost killed him," I told her. I knew too well how my brother felt. "I wanted to when he tried to kill you. I thought he deserved it. He didn't know you'd survive, or what would happen."

"But you refused," Bray contradicted me quietly. "You wouldn't bend. There are things you will never, ever do." It was like she was reciting things she already knew about me, but to be honest, as worn out and emotional as I felt, she had to feel a hundred times worse.

"He's leaving," I told Bray, and Hind too I guess, looking back at the door. "He won't come back. He'll leave the manor. He's my brother. I have to follow him."

Suddenly Bray bowed over Sir Victor's body again, squeezing it as more tears came, but she told me hoarsely, "Find him. Find him, and I'll find you. I promise, I'm coming."

I was already starting to move, reaching for the door, but I had to stop for a moment as Hind declared solemnly, "You both have to leave. All three of you, as fast as possible. The people here can't stand against their lord, and we can't ask them to. I will take Master Vick's body back to my Master."

We both stared at her, shocked all over again. "You have to come with us too, Hind," Bray pointed out. It was, well, obvious.

But Hind's look was patient and sad. Between just us she didn't have to pretend, and there was grief in her expression and it wasn't for the dead man. "My Master's only child is dead. Whether he needs someone to punish or someone to still be with him, I will be at his feet."

It was the way Hind lived her life. Neither of us could stop her, and even to try would be to tell her to be someone else. I exchanged that look with Bray, but the phoenix girl, glowing gently, was giving me another look. It was the look she gave my brother when I thought she wanted to kiss him. Now was not the time. Probably that time wouldn't be soon, and if it came she would have to face her feelings for my brother, too.

But it was a promise that gave me hope, so I could walk out that door and try and figure out where my brother would have gone.

ACT V

WHAT HAVE I BECOME?

I had to go through back streets to get past the crowd. There was a lot of yelling and a few people were holding brooms or shovels or tools from their craft, the weapons that are always at hand, but there wasn't any violence and nothing had been thrown yet. But it would happen. By now the crowds knew that there was nothing the government could do to stop them. What was left of the government.

Father Gabriel was going to do something. I knew why, of course. Someone had to. I did not know what he thought he could do, but my heart was calming as I eased past a church guard into the jail. I had faith.

My teacher and patron was standing by the front door with a couple more guards. I was not at all surprised they'd insisted on escorting him to the jail. It was right across the plaza, but that plaza was packed shoulder to shoulder with a mob that would soon become a riot. He looked calm. Nothing ever really seemed to make him nervous or angry. He was, I knew, a man God had blessed with the ability to see with unveiled eyes, and very little ever surprised him.

As I slipped up behind him, prepared to wait on his convenience as was my place, he finished the fastenings on his formal regalia for high ceremonies and settled the half-miter on his head. He would never claim such finery in his day to day life, but I could see his purpose. He was about to step out there, and when he did he wanted the crowd to see the church as much as a man.

As he reached for the front door the guards turned to follow, and he waved them back. No one said anything, but there was a momentary battle of wills visible in their expressions. They did not want to let him go out there unprotected, but his stare didn't budge, and they settled back in their places. Only then did my teacher look back at me.

"Elijah," he said in hushed tones, although with the noise outside I didn't know who he thought would hear. "You may come, but stay well behind me. These people are afraid, for good reason, and they need to be calmed."

Which meant it was just the two of us who stepped out into the plaza. It was terrifying, enough to make cold gnaw at my muscles, but I had faith, and the fear passed. Already I was seeing how he had chosen well. The crowd was paying attention everywhere else, and the few near the jail's entrance stepped aside for two clergymen, letting my teacher climb the high stairs to the broad platform the church reserves for punishing the most terrible crimes. As he crossed that to stand at the edge above the crowd, there was time for them to notice him, to begin to turn and look and wonder.

"I am supposed to tell you to disperse, to go back to your homes and respect the law." His voice carried. It was something they taught you for preaching, and he was very, very good at it. They could probably hear him at the back of the crowd, but he didn't sound like he was shouting.

"If I did, you would not listen," he continued solemnly. "And you would be right. You are here now because the law has failed you, aren't you? The law has failed you because the people that make it have failed you. Which is why you are here, scared, asking for answers. You deserve them, and it is the church's place to give them to you. Ask."

Someone yelled something. A number of people yelled things. I couldn't make out any of them, but Father Gabriel seemed to understand. He paused before answering, and in his gold-embroidered cape, his robes and a hat kept for ceremonies because it belonged to men of higher rank than him, he sat down with the effort of an aging man on the edge of the platform. I stood at the back and watched. Aside from the questions, the shouting had stopped. The riot was on hold.

"You leap straight to the most important questions, don't you?" my patron answered. Even speaking to a crowd, the warmth was obvious in his voice. "That is good. You know that we are all at the mercy of big events outside our control and you've learned not to trust rumors. I will tell you the truth, as much as even the church knows. Yes, the Emperor is dead. He has been dead for some time. Will there be a new Emperor? Yes. There will be an Emperor, or a Regent , or a succession of Viceroys. And yes, the Baron is dead. Both of those things are true, not rumors. Archbishop Alexi is dead as well, but you did not have to ask because the church does not keep secrets like that. They were all good men, and you are afraid, because they were the three most powerful men in the Empire. Now only Viceroy Amicus is left, and you are afraid he can't keep control. I won't lie to you and say he can. But he is a good man too, and there will be no starvation and no armies in the streets until new good men step forward to help him lead."

He paused for a moment then, and new questions were already being yelled out. It wasn't just a pause, it was a hesitation, and his tone was grim when he answered. "You want to know how they died. You've heard stories, and some of them are terrifying. One of those stories is true. His Excellency Alexi was murdered by a Wild Child, in the night, in the cathedral itself. It was an invader that he confronted and drove away at the cost of his life. The Emperor died in his chambers in private and we do not know what killed him, but there was not a mark on either his body or the Archbishop's. For Alexi at least we had witnesses who could tell us what happened, and their stories are like a nightmare. The Baron died by more prosaic means, by a blade. Who wielded it we don't know. Everyone who claims to have seen the event tells a different story, and yes, the Baroness has abandoned the city entirely, like many other nobles. It may simply have been an assassination by his enemies. He was a man who would give anyone a chance, high or low, sinner or saint. He left himself vulnerable."

There was another pause, but no answer from the crowd. When they did not immediately have any more questions Father Gabriel continued. "As I said, I am supposed to ask you to disperse out of respect for the law. That would be foolish. I am going to ask you to decide for yourself if you should return to your home or not. Put your fear aside for the moment and ask yourself what is the right thing to do. Some of my colleagues say God is punishing this city, and I agree, but he is not punishing us as a whole. Do what is right, and peace will be restored. Fear is distracting you from the goodness in your hearts, and it leaves you vulnerable to sin. There are many temptations to sin in this city. The nobles turn their face from the people. My brothers in the church are good men, but they are also afraid and they sin by forgetting that it is their job to lead you to good. On every street corner you will find a house of strong drink or ill custom or a Wild Girl flouting God's law and watching you with the eyes and heart of a beast. Archbishop Alexi died to protect you from temptation, but one man can't change everything. It is you who must turn away from fear and away from temptation and do what is right. You are scared of the riots. If you decide, right now, to go home and live in peace, there is no riot. If the guards are away and a shop is abandoned and you decide not to steal from it, there is no looting. Even the lords who think they have power over you must follow if you lead. Decide for yourselves what to do next. I know you will choose virtue, because I have faith in God, and I have faith in you."

And with that he pushed himself to his feet, and I rushed forward to take his hand. I hardly needed to because he wasn't really that old, but I was in awe. The crowd stayed quiet. People were talking to each other, not shouting. At the edges they were already walking off. His faith had been justified, and the people had chosen peace rather than chaos. Today.

"That was amazing, Father," I told him quietly. I had intended to support him, to lead him back inside, but I didn't need to. There was no sign that he had been as shaken and terrified as I had been even for a moment. "But it won't last. There will be another mob tomorrow, and the next day." But I didn't know as well as him, so I asked anxiously, "Won't there?"

"There may be," he answered, and still he wasn't worried. "If there is we will speak to them again. They are surrounded by fear and uncertainty and sin on every side. We will calm their fears, show them the true path, and take away their temptations. Every day. In the churches, on the streets, in the pulpit and in the confessional. We will take back the city from sin. In a way I am grateful to this crowd, because now everyone has seen that it can be done."

I was reminded at that moment, very definitely, why I did not deserve the honor of being this man's secretary. He held no high rank in the church, because he had never sought power. But everything Father Gabriel touched was changed. He had picked me out of a crowd of other young men who I could not see were less than me in any way, and let me be his assistant and watch as he did his work.

"And speaking of the confessional," he continued, giving me a sudden look, "I can still smell the oil, but you are officially ordained now. I need you more than ever, but so does the flock. Take your turn in the confessionals tomorrow. These people need guidance." It might have been a dismissive statement, but it wasn't. He looked back at the doors to the plaza we'd just left with fondness.

"I can't do what you just did, Father." That wasn't humility, false or otherwise. It was fact.

"Eventually you'll learn to," was his serene and confident answer. "But the confessional is not the same. There, souls are laid bare. They will come to you and they will expect punishment or absolution. Instead you will open their eyes, and they will do the rest."

The rest, he didn't have to say. He thought I was ready. I had faith in his judgment.

For everything else I did, but not this.

"Tomorrow afternoon you'll realize you were nervous for nothing," he continued when I didn't respond. "For now, how is the book collection going?"

"That's why I came, Father. This is the last cart. The capital is so large I may find more collections, but I believe I've covered every library in the city, public and private, that isn't deliberately secret – and I found a few that were. Would you like the names, Father?"

He shook his head. "No, Elijah. It is not my place to punish sinners, only help them walk straight again. Opening their eyes is easy. Removing temptation is the difficult part. The word says it all, doesn't it? It clouds the vision, lies to you about what is important."

"As for the books," he added, "burn them. That was the point."

I bowed and went to do just that. There were a lot of books. I had spent the last two weeks scouring the city to find every book of alchemy and heretical thought it contained. It was my final task as a mere clerk, as a novice, before my birthday and my ordination. I had started training young, and I'm sure Father Gabriel's approval had a part in my being confirmed as soon as I was eligible, although I was just as sure he hadn't taken any action to ensure it. I was not the only person in the church who trusted his judgment.

So on my birthday my brow was anointed with purified oils and I received the Laying On Of Hands. It was a sacrament passed down for over a millennium, linking me to the original apostles. Spiritually and temporally I became a priest, although my work hardly changed. I was young to be ordained, but it happened. No one is allowed to enter the priesthood finally and irrevocably until we turn fifteen, however. There were practical reasons and mysteries associated with that coming of age, but Father Gabriel, as his fingers touched the oil to my scalp, explained the most important reason which was neither secret nor anything the church wanted to admit. That birthday meant you were safe, that you could not be taken away from the church, the priesthood, or humanity. At fifteen, you were too old. You could no longer be cursed and become a Wild Child.

Was that three days ago? Four? A week? Just two? I had been busy. And I had been trying not to think about the truth. They were wrong. I reached my hand up and ran my gloved fingers through my hair. The horns followed the lines the sacred oil had traced, still too small to be seen through my hair. Bigger and more sharply pointed than yesterday. The gloves were new, too. I hoped Father Gabriel, as sharp as he was, didn't notice them, but my fingernails were becoming claws. Not the sharp sickle claws of a cat or dog or any animal I knew. These were black like talons, and like the horns I knew they would grow.

I was told that I was too old for this to happen to me. They were wrong. I had been told it happens all at once, and they were wrong about that. No one had told me I could only become an animal, because they didn't need to. There were birds of prey with claws like this, but a row of little horns like sharp bone spikes? I was losing my body and soul.

My hope, my prayer, was in the one truth about Wild Children I had left. The transformation was a punishment for sin. I would give myself to virtue and hope it saved me.

The first step to that salvation was Father Gabriel's quiet crusade. I circled around, back to the crematorium behind the church. Normally it was a way of purifying bodies that could not or should not be buried, but it was suitable to cleanse anything with fire. The guards and novices who had helped me with the collection brought out the carts. There were a lot of books. I had felt that was important. Better to destroy a book on astronomy that suggested the scriptural Heavens were incorrect than to let pass a book of lies that would trick a man out of his faith. Anything that might be heresy, and especially anything that might be alchemy, I'd collected for burning. They were only one lure away from virtue, but one easy to remove now that the civil government was so disrupted. When we came to search their libraries, people simply assumed we were on the highest business of the church, and with no Emperor who was higher?

I was a secretary, trained as a clerk. I liked books and regretted seeing these go. They weren't evil really, but they were dangerous, like a sharp knife to be kept out of reach of children. Father Gabriel would be livid if I'd used a metaphor in front of him suggesting that we were more able to make moral decisions than the men on the street, but I couldn't think of a better one. This was just a danger we were removing from their path.

Shovels dug into the piles. Books ripped, but it didn't matter because they all went into the fire and stray pages could be collected. I gave the nearest wheelbarrow a regretful look and was relieved to notice something unexpected.

Lying on top was a book, old and mud-stained and warped, that obviously did not belong. It wasn't a real book at all, and had no title and wasn't properly bound. Picking it up and flipping through it, I found it to be some kind of diary, and the words were educated but the hand was shaky. I really have always liked books, and whatever this was it didn't deserve to go in the fire. Probably I'd end up discarding it as trash, but that would be different.

I ran my fingers back through my hair without realizing it. Horns. Little sharp horns, in rows. I glanced at the furnace, then. Would I fail and have to be cast in there? Would I do it myself?

Worry would do nothing at all. As the last few books were heaped into the oven, the ones around the edge already burning as it was sealed, I took the little book back to my room. As an ordained priest, at least, I had one of my own now. I needed to clear my head and focus on something pure, so I went over the list of libraries that had been searched and compared it to records from the central library itself. Anyone who borrowed books regularly probably had a collection themselves. It had led us to several collections in need of scouring.

It was pointless. I had done this too many times before, and the truth was I didn't like destroying books. It was the right thing to do and it wasn't like we were burning the owners, but it just felt like a grim task. So I flipped open the badly mauled diary and tried to figure out if it was worth keeping.

It was certainly odd. The first few entries were dated, but the days didn't always go forward. Then there was one from the month before. After that the writer seemed to give up and just listed the day of the week, but they either wrote down entries rarely or lost track of weekdays, too. Mostly it seemed to be discussions of housework and books read. I settled on one of the longer entries to get a feel for the oddity.

THURSDAY – I had ice cream today! I've always wanted to try it. I can't even remember when I first read about it. I do remember when I was learning to cook for Mister Thornback and I found a recipe. I lost the book before I could show it to him, though. Well, I didn't lose it, Mrs. Shekel took it from me, because she thinks I can't learn to cook. Thought, I guess. I wonder what happened to her? But without the recipe, I couldn't tell Mister Thornback what I wanted. When Vick was first studying with us, I wrote to him that I'd always wanted to try ice cream, but I thought he forgot.

He didn't forget! Today he came over with ice. In the middle of summer! Big chunks of it, and some vanilla, he brought everything, and he told Mister Thornback he thought I'd enjoy making ice cream, and I got so excited I tried to TELL them I wanted to before I remembered and nodded. A lot.

The ice cream was wonderful. It's so rich, and vanilla is wonderful too. I can see why people are willing to pay so much for it. But best of all was that Mister Thornback and I made it together, and he told me all about the process and why we had to use salt and the grinding and mixing, and that it's a recipe thought to have been invented in Xian on the other side of the world more than two thousand years ago. And he let me do the stirring. It's taken a long time for him to realize I can do things like that with hooves, because without a human voice, I can't tell him to trust me. I've had to show him.

All this time, Vick's just been waiting for a chance to do this for me, I guess. And he let me do it with my owner, and we hardly knew he was there. I didn't even know he could be so nice. I'm going to go to bed now, and hope I have the same day all over again in my dreams. Okay, that sounds stupid, doesn't it? Goodnight!

I was reading the diary of a Wild Girl. One of the donkeys of the city. She could write, and write well, with hooves, and that was the smallest of the things that didn't make sense. I sat there until it got very dark, looking at the book without really reading it, and feeling the claws under my gloves, and I wondered – what kind of child could sin so badly she turned into a donkey but write something like that?

I guess eventually I went to bed. I had to get up early for the confessional.

Which meant that the next morning I was sitting in a tiny booth listening to a muffled litany of soft prayers and praying, myself, that I could suddenly become wise and understanding and virtuous. Instead I kept drifting off into trying to remember what I'd dreamed about last night that had been so horrible but hadn't stayed with me.

That was just nerves, of course. They went away when I heard a door close gently and heard those ritual words, "Forgive me, Father, for I have sinned."

A man's voice. I had to be wise for a grown man twice my age. But I had an example to follow, and perhaps he could follow mine.

First, he was more nervous than I was. I heard guilt and fear in his voice, and I could hear it more easily because I could not see his face. "However terrible you think your sin may be, my son, the Lord has seen worse and forgiven it. Tell me what you have done, and I will help you seek absolution."

It sounded very stiff to me, but it seemed to work. The man on the other side of the screen trusted me. He had faith. "I committed the sin of theft, Father," he told me, barely audible. "The guards were gone and there were men fighting down the street and someone threw a brick and broke the window of a shop. No one was looking, and I took a gold candlestick. Every day food costs more. I was worried we would not be able to eat soon."

"Yes. That is how temptation works, and how good men are dragged down," I told him solemnly. "You had your reasons. You may have had more reasons, all of them good. But you are responsible before God for your own decisions. Did you do the right thing?"

He struggled for a moment, but he knew the answer. That was why he was here. "No," he finally told me. The fear and shame were back.

Shame had its place, but fear did not. "And now you want me to tell your punishment, but punishment will not make you a good person. Do you still have the candlestick?"

This wasn't what he was expecting. "Yes," he told me carefully.

"Is the shop still there?"

He saw where this was going, of course. "Yes, but the owner is gone. He died or ran away. If I put the candlestick back, someone else will steal it."

"And if that happens will you be the thief, or will he?" I continued as calmly and gently as I could. This was what Father Gabriel had told me. Absolution does not come through punishment. It comes from not sinning again.

The man on the other side did not answer, but there was only one way for these thoughts to go. "You are responsible for your own soul, my son," I guided him as carefully as I could. "Do you want to be a thief, or do you want to do the right thing?"

Again he was quiet, and so was I. Until, after a little while, he told me, "Thank you, Father." And I heard the door move, and he was gone.

Looting. He had been in the crowd yesterday and heard Father Gabriel's speech, and realized that he had done wrong. And now I had helped with the other half of the lesson. Nothing would erase his sin, but he was back on the path of virtue.

Eventually I heard the other door close again. "Forgive me, Father, for I have sinned," came a woman's voice.

She was not as afraid, so I waited for her to speak. I was starting to realize why I had not been trained for this. All that was important was opening these people's eyes to what was right.

"I committed the sin of wrath, Father," she eventually told me, nervous now due to my silence. "I have committed this sin before. I lost my temper. I spoke blasphemes. I scolded my servant... harshly. He's so lazy. All he has to do is pull a cart, but we always stop, over and over."

Oh. "You own a Wild Boy." It wasn't really a question, but she hadn't wanted to admit it.

"Yes," she answered guiltily. "I know it's still a sin, but he makes me so angry."

"He will always make you angry, my child." Once again I felt the irony of using those words to someone who, while young, was surely older than me. "They are creatures of temptation. You've heard that before."

"Yes."

"You are responsible for your own virtue, daughter, always. While you are with him your eyes will always be clouded. Can you overcome that challenge?"

And she was quiet for a moment. I had made her think, too. "I can try, Father." Her words came too slow and too heavy. She was worried that she couldn't.

"You must either overcome that temptation or remove it, daughter. You know that." I paused so that she could have a chance to recognize that she did, then pressed on. "For now it is enough that you see clearly the problem you must overcome."

"Yes, Father," she answered meekly. I said nothing. I let her think. "Thank you," she added eventually, and she did sound grateful, and I heard the sound of the door. She was gone.

Which left me with my thoughts. Father Gabriel had been right. I did not know if I had helped these two become better people, but it was a better path than meaningless chastisement. If only it would work for me.

I didn't even hear the next person enter the confessional. Suddenly there was a voice, a young girl's voice, calm and modest. "Forgive me, Father, for I have sinned."

Children were supposed to confess just like adults, but they rarely did. Her voice hadn't betrayed anything, but she must have something on her mind. "Then I will try to help you, child," I answered. "Tell me of your sins."

I heard a sigh. "My sins are too many to list," she answered. There was a kind of wistful sadness in her voice.

That wasn't the kind of response I expected from a young girl, and I wondered if she simply had a young voice, and what kind of woman sat across the screen from me. Still, I had to help her. "But you came to me for a reason, daughter," I tried, seeking the way past that defensive calm. "Some sin must bother you more than the others."

"Yes," she told me, still sadly. "But it's not my sin, Father, it's yours." For a moment I was trying to figure out what kind of trick this could be, when she added, "I know what you're becoming."

It was very, very hard to sound calm. "You're not making sense, child."

Another sigh, and then she asked me, "Are the horns bigger than yesterday, Father?"

It wasn't a trick. She knew. Before I could stop myself my gloved hand slid through my hair. They were. They were bigger than yesterday. Bigger than when I'd combed my hair that morn- no. No, they couldn't be growing that fast. But that didn't matter. She knew.

So there was no point in lying. "I think so."

"Have you looked at your back yet?" It was a gentle tone. She was handling me as I had handled the sinners before her.

I was grateful, because that question made me afraid. I was not someone who could easily reach his own back, but I tried and felt over my shoulder bones something hard and ridged, one on each side. I was sure they hadn't been there yesterday. Or was I?

"You're still changing, Father. What kind of sin are you still committing?" she asked again. She was guiding me. I was suspicious, but it was the question I should have been asking myself.

"I don't know. I sin like every other man."

"You believe that donkeys earn their transformation." Her voice was serene. She was making sure I didn't know what answer she was looking for.

"Yes," I had to tell her. And then I thought about that journal back in my room. Did I? They had to. I had seen what they did to men and women, hadn't I? Heard the evidence of it just a little while ago.

"But you're not becoming a donkey. You're becoming something worse. What kind of person are you to have earned this?"

"How do you know that I'm changing?" I demanded. But she was silent. Too silent. Like I would have been if someone had tried to change the subject during a confession. "I don't know. I thought I knew, but I must have been wrong." It was the only thing I could say that wasn't a lie.

"I think there's still hope, Father. You're still changing. There may be a long way to go yet. Do you want to save yourself?"

This question shook me even worse. I had claws on my fingers, horns on my head, and scales on my back, and this was just the beginning. We both knew that. Wherever this would end, it would be bad beyond anything I could imagine. "Yes." My voice was raw.

"I want to save you, too," she told me, calm and gentle like she was the one taking confession. "If you will do everything you can, so will I."

I sat there for a minute wrestling with my feelings. Everything she said was right, but I had no faith in this mysterious voice. Who was I talking to? Suddenly I leapt up and rushed out of the booth to yank open the door used by supplicants.

No one was there. I wasn't going to be given any easy answers. I certainly wasn't going to be able to help in the confessional any more today, so I headed back to my room and tried to think.

I couldn't. Eventually I opened up the journal again, hoping to find some clue as to why whoever wrote it deserved her fate. I read about her measuring shadows to learn about angles, and putting up wallpaper, and making soup for her owner when he was sick. I read her confessing to saying angry things she knew no one could understand about another donkey's owner. Apparently she did it all of once.

I would laugh and embrace a child who thought that was a terrible sin. There were no answers here, either.

Now that I was ordained and the library clean-up was finished, I wasn't quite sure what my duties would be, although I was sure I would still be attached to Father Gabriel as his secretary somehow. In the morning I received a note. One of a priest's most sacred duties is delivering the Last Rites and attending upon the dying. Few people die so predictably, but if we could ensure that they were in a state of grace at the moment of their passing, that was the greatest blessing we could provide. A man named Lusef Viaremus had been taken ill, struck down in some way but not immediately died. It was certain he would not last much longer though, and I needed to learn to attend to the dying.

It was a grim task but an undeniably virtuous one. If I was barreling down some road to corruption and self-immolation, I was happy to have a chance to do something I knew was good, some clear direction to follow.

I considered a hat, but my hair still hid my horns. That was a relief, but it wouldn't last. Soon I wouldn't be able to hide how I was falling. One of my sins surely was that I felt more afraid of what I was turning into than the idea that I was corrupted that deeply.

I had a task of simple virtue to focus on today. Painful to the heart perhaps, but morally clear. I was grateful.

So, in the mid-morning, I found myself entering the garden of a house just inside the walls. It was a pleasant building but not spectacular, with a small and simple garden. The fact that there was a garden at all, this deep in the city, and that one person owned this house told me it was a much wealthier home than it looked. This was a grim occasion, so I made sure I looked very somber and respectable and, above all, calm as I rapped on the door with the knocker.

My knock was answered by a woman of moderate age, and like the house her clothing was good but not showy. It made me warm to her immediately. These were good people who did not flaunt their blessings, I felt. But the lessons of my teacher came back to me. I should not hold up anyone over anyone else, only be mindful of how I could help them. Right now I should focus on the task at hand.

She did not seem to have been crying, but her grief-stricken countenance made my next step clear. "Mrs. Viaremus?" I asked.

She nodded and told me shyly, "Thank you for coming, Father." The ecclesiastical clothes I was wearing were dark for this purpose, but people saw the church, not my age.

I tried to put her at ease. "Just Elijah, Mrs. Viaremus. I have not yet earned a title like that, but I have advanced more than enough to help you and your husband as he seeks Heaven." I tried to have faith in that.

"He's in the bedroom," she told me as she led me through the house. "It was very sudden, Father." I would let the title drop, since it seemed to comfort her. That one sentence said everything. She was trying to hold herself together.

I needed to be calm for her. "We never get to choose the hour, daughter. Remember that I am here to help you as well as him. For now, let me perform the rites and make sure he is prepared. You do not have to attend, but I think it would be good for you to see and know that even after he dies, God will be taking care of him." Yes. The living were just as important, and I had to sound confident that I knew what was best for her.

The bedroom was the shock I had known it would be. It was a pleasant but not extravagant room, like the house and its owners, and clean and orderly. The man in the bed, though, was horrible to look at. There were no wounds, no obvious signs of sickness, and he seemed still and asleep. He had a pallor, though, and his face was drawn, and he was too still. Anyone would know, looking at him, that he was slipping away as we watched. That he might already be gone. Almost as disturbing, a Wild Boy sat on a little stool, watching the bed silently. He was one of the uglier donkeys, with fur on much of what could be seen and a face that jutted forward too much with too flat of a nose, neither a human nor an animal shape. His expression, what of it I could read, was as bleak as the wife's.

I did not think he should be here, but I also didn't think he could do any harm, and I wanted this to be as peaceful a process as possible. I confirmed that the man in the bed was still breathing, set out the sacraments for the ritual, and went through it immediately. I felt good about this at least, because I knew that the reminder of Heaven and the soft droning and simple melodies of the prayers were soothing, and would comfort the widow even as they requested forgiveness for whatever sins Mr. Viaremus was carrying. He couldn't confess. I was becoming very certain he would never wake up.

I was right. When the last prayer was finished, and I snuffed the incense and laid it in my case, I checked the body – and it was, now, a body.

"I was just in time. He has passed, but you can be at ease at least that he has passed into Heaven." I will never be able to describe how it felt to give her that news, but I clung to the hope that it was the easiest way for her to hear it.

She began to cry, but softly, and I hoped the shock had been eased a little. It was my duty now to focus her on the future, not the past. Keeping my voice soft, I told her, "You should have some time to grieve, but when I get back to the cathedral I will tell my brothers to come and prepare him for burial. This is going to be a difficult time for you, and we want to make it easier as best we can. Was his will made out properly?"

"...yes," she told me distantly, dragging herself back to practical affairs. "He was able to write it yesterday."

"Then that is one thing less to be worried about," I murmured approvingly. "You are very vulnerable right now, but I want you to remember that you are young and you have a life ahead of you. I would also like you to remember that you can come to the church day or night for advice or comfort or companionship. It will be hard to deal with the loneliness for a while, and you may feel a loss of purpose. We will ease you through that if you let us."

"Thank you, Father." She still sounded distant, was not really listening, but she would remember when she started to think again.

"I would like to make one request now and give you one piece of guidance," I broached gently. "This is a vulnerable time, and I see you have a donkey in the house."

I dragged her again out of her brooding. She was going to have far too much time for it, but at least I could help her right now. "Jack? Yes. He's been very helpful. He was very close to Lusef."

Jack. Almost a human name. And the Wild Boy was just sitting there, staring at nothing, looking much like the widow. They had let themselves get dangerously attached.

"This is not a good time for you to be alone with a Wild Child, daughter," I continued as delicately as possible. "I have seen what they can do to a person's soul. You will feel very lonely for a while, and that can make you cling to what will hurt you most. Please let me take him away."

She looked at me with confusion, trying to think but failing because of her grief.

"You don't need him to take care of you, daughter. He can't help you, and right now he's a danger to you. The church will take care of him, and we know he was expensive. He will certainly pay for the burial. Have faith in us, Mrs. Viaremus. Let us help you."

She was shaking, so I helped her into a chair, and while she cried into her hands she nodded and told me, "Alright."

I wanted to stay and comfort her, but if I did she would change her mind. "Come with me, Jack," I told the Wild Boy, and took his hand. I worried for a moment at that, but when I felt the glove between my hand and his I realized that the claws, growing so large and sharp I didn't think gloves would hide them much longer, made my hands at least as corrupt as his. Possibly more. And his expression held nothing but grief, like the widow's. He hadn't spoken a word, and didn't speak as I led him outside and started on the path back to the church. I would treat him with all the gentleness I could. Whatever he was, cruelty was a sin.

Which is why it was an almost chilling coincidence when a voice asked me, "Are you sure that was the right thing to do?"

I knew that voice. It was that soft, little-girl's voice. And it came from a little girl. Well, she was younger than me, anyway. She really wasn't a child anymore. Beyond that it was hard to tell, because her mourning clothes were rich but somber, everything black, from respectable shoes just visible below her skirts to a broad hat and a veil that obscured her face. She had appeared without warning like a ghost, and that was how she walked, almost floating from step to step.

"Yes," I answered. At least, I had been, but just her asking the question shook me. "I did it only to protect her."

"She's lost one family member, and you just took away the other. She has no one left now," the girl pointed out. In all the black I'd missed something. Hanging from one hand was a doll, some sort of stuffed black animal toy with red button eyes. It made her look a little younger and a little more ethereal, and she didn't need either.

"I couldn't leave her to live only with a creature of sin." Suddenly it didn't seem like enough. "I've seen the sins that the owners of Wild Children fall into."

"Are they worse than the sins that men and women fall into without one?" She hadn't even had to stop and think. I felt like a blind person being led by the hand, when it should have been the other way around.

Besides, nothing she said had been wrong so far. "I only have to look at him to know he's a creature of sin, not a human." I was falling back, but I was falling back to the most undeniable truths.

And they didn't trouble her for a moment. "You've looked at him. Have you listened to him? Have you listened to any Wild Child? Do they act like creatures of sin? Do they talk like demons, or like people?"

The only Wild Child I had listened to was the one in the diary. A little girl who wanted nothing but to be with the man who owned her. No, it was worse than that. She wasn't so simple. Like any human, she wanted a lot of things, but none of them seemed to be very bad.

I didn't know what to say, but I had to try. "Who are you? You seem to want nothing but to make me doubt. Men smarter and wiser than me have decided these things, and I have faith in the goodness of the church. Why are you trying to turn me from what I know?"

"I think the most important reason is that something very bad is happening to you." She paused for a moment to let that sink in. It wasn't something I could deny. "I want to save you. I want to save this boy, too."

She kept saying things I didn't expect or understand. "Save him from what?"

"You tell me. What will the church do with him when you bring him back?"

I hadn't thought about that. At all. "Sell him, I suppose. I'll turn him over to one of the bursar's clerks. Maybe they'll find him a home out on a farm."

"Where he'll corrupt someone else? That's what they believe he does. Do you think they'll allow that? They might as well have left him where he was."

I started to realize where she was going with this. "They wouldn't imprison him or execute him just because of what he is." I could hear the tightness in my voice.

"No, probably not," she agreed, still calm – and still sad. "Those are things you do to humans. You think he's an object of temptation. What do you do with those?"

The furnace. With the books of blaspheme. "They wouldn't do that. We wouldn't do that." Now my voice really was shaking.

"When you tell me that, do you have faith?"

I couldn't answer. And she knew what that answer meant. I had stopped walking, and I wasn't sure when. She walked around me to the Donkey Boy, lifted her veil, and took his face in her tiny hands so that he could look into her eyes. I could see hints of white hair. Her face was pretty in a way that didn't look real. But she could touch him, so she wasn't a ghost. And that silly doll still dangled from one hand down over the boy's shoulder.

"What's your name?" she asked him.

"Jack," he told her. It was the first thing I'd heard him say, and the hoarseness of his voice told me everything. If he spoke again, it would be a sob.

"I can't take you back to your Mistress, Jack," she told him with the same quiet and gentle voice she used for me, "But I can take you somewhere that you'll be treated well, and your work will be appreciated, and you'll be loved. Will you come with me?"

He nodded. I couldn't argue with her. She had to be wrong about the furnace, but if she wasn't... I couldn't finish that thought.

She pulled her veil back down, and as she took Jack's hand I let go of the other one. And as she looked up to me, again, her face held the same sad kindness she gave him. "What's your name?" she asked.

"Elijah," I answered dumbly.

"I can't save you as easily, but I will save you, Elijah. I'll see you again soon." And she and Jack walked off into the crowd. In a few moments I couldn't even see them anymore.

I had to return to the church. I needed Father Gabriel's wisdom. I knew now that wisdom was something I didn't have.

We knelt side by side, praying before the icons. It was our place now to lead others to prayer, but Father Gabriel felt that we needed to reaffirm our personal attachment to the Lord at every opportunity. I was honored that he let me join him sometimes, and it gave me a chance to seek private counsel now.

"Father, I need your wisdom. I am not certain if I did the right thing," I told him during a moment of quiet.

"You need more faith in yourself, Elijah. All men have goodness inside them, but you have an innocence that withstands every test. When you see the right thing to do, you follow that path faithfully and without hesitation. That is why I want you by my side."

"Knowing the right thing to do is not as easy for me as it is for you." I knew his faith was not completely justified, because I couldn't bring myself to tell him about the horns, the claws, the plates on my back. But I did not need to keep the doubt and worry I felt from my voice, either. "Today I attended a deathbed. I wish I had been better at comforting the widow, but I did my best and I am not ashamed of that. They had a Wild Boy, though, and I convinced her, while she was stricken with grief and could not think for herself, to trust me and let the church buy him from her. I worry now that it was the wrong thing to do."

For a moment Father Gabriel was silent. He had been my teacher for nearly a year, and there was both a thrill and a sense of anxiety easing inside me when I heard the warm tone that followed next. "Elijah, I am proud of you. Dismiss your fears. They are the path of temptation, making the bad seem good. You not only stuck to the principles of virtue you knew were right, you acted on them. You took initiative and seized a chance to remove a terrible lure to sin from a woman who was weak."

"That is part of why I am troubled, Father." There was so much that suddenly seemed wrong about this, and I needed answers. "She could not make her own decision. I made it for her. And I think she loved the Wild Boy, and he loved her. If she had been able to decide she would never have let him go."

"That is not a sin, my son." His voice, if anything, sounded more approving, and I confess I could feel tears forming in my eyes. "You have learned already what it means to be a shepherd among the flock. People are good, but they are also flawed. If we take temptation away from them they can only become better people. If you did not take the donkey away and she turned to it and it obsessed her, she would have been pouring love on an empty vessel that could not be filled. Soon there would be nothing left of her. When that happens, good people break. They become filled with rage, or fear. They deny God entirely. They hurt, in the cruelest fashion possible, even the thing they profess to love. You saw how to save her. If you had not done so and she was destroyed by her decision, could you have lived with yourself?"

"No, Father," I admitted. When the ghostly little girl had spoken, everything was in doubt. When Father Gabriel spoke, everything was clear. Almost everything.

"Do they really destroy a man so, or a woman?" I asked him gently. I was confessing to a doubt that was almost heresy. I was afraid, but I trusted him.

"It is a truth I have seen absolutely in my life. You are young yet, so I understand that you haven't. They are creatures steeped in sin so deeply that they could not remain human even in appearance. The only question is how far someone who is close to them falls. But you need to see this for yourself, and when you see it you will do the right thing. Not once, but always, because that is the kind of person you are. Which is why I have a task that I can trust only you to perform. You may not see the truth of it until it is finished. Will you have faith in me and let me open your eyes?"

"Absolutely," I told him, and I meant it.

Which is why I sat in a confessional booth, in a church I had never visited before. It was unusual, but I was entitled and the priest considered that I was doing him a favor, and he returned it by letting me practice this difficult and holy responsibility. The time was chosen carefully, and when I heard a door close on the other side and a grown woman's voice speak, I knew this was what I had come for.

"Forgive me, Father, for I have sinned." The ritual words, passed down from before the line of Peter was severed.

"I am here to help you free yourself of those sins, daughter," I told her, trying to keep the nervousness and doubt out of my voice. "Tell me what troubles you."

"Jealousy, Father. It is consuming me. I can barely keep a hold on my anger, sometimes. I think terrible things, about her and my husband. I know it is wrong." Yes, there was passion in her voice. She was struggling even to admit it was a sin.

But it was, and it was etched straight through to her heart, from the sound of it. "This is not something new, I take it. You have made this confession before."

"Yes." I heard more guilt in her voice. She was mastering her sin, for the moment. "I never seem to escape it."

"And it is getting worse, not better," I added. This part I hadn't been told. Father Gabriel had left me to see what was happening to this woman on my own.

"Yes." More guilt. "Sometimes I strike her. Even when I don't I feel a terrible rage when I least expect it, towards both of them. And I know that's another sin."

"It is. There is no sin that can't be forgiven, but only if you can free yourself of it first. If things go on like this, that will never happen. I would like to help you find a way out. Can you tell me more?"

The woman on the other side of the screen was breathing hard. Confessions were meant to be anonymous, but I knew her name was Lady Margay, because I had been waiting for her at the time and place she always came to confess. And I knew something of what she was about to tell me. "My husband has a Wild Girl, Father," she explained, with venom as well as guilt in her voice. "One of the expensive ones. She is prettier than I am, and she always will be, and she never disagrees with him except to beg with a whine that scrapes my nerves raw. She's lazy and stupid, but she's always there with him even when I'm not, and he spoils her and… loves her more than he does me."

I was silent for a moment. I didn't just want her to know I was taking this seriously. I had to take this all in. "The church fathers have taught us that a creature like that cannot return love," I told her carefully. "So let me ask you. Is she making him a better person, or a worse person?"

"Worse." I could hear how hard she was breathing, but also the thoughtfulness in her voice as she was led down new paths. "She just begs, she never gives anything to anyone. And every day he loves me less, and the children, and is less concerned with our position or our estates. All he cares about is her."

"Then you're telling me that she is corrupting both of you, and as long as she is there it will continue, and neither of you can break free." This was what I had been sent here for. I had been left to see the truth on my own, but my task had been spelled out.

"He'll never give her up. She can do no wrong in his eyes, which is ridiculous. She's mean-spirited and selfish and she says bad things about me when I'm not around, I know it."

She was getting a little hysterical, so I kept my voice as soothing as possible as I told her, "Calm yourself, daughter. If she has that tight a hold on him it will take something extreme, something unthinkable to break him free. And if she dies, he will never learn his lesson. He will only fall into some new sin, missing the old one. You have to make him see the truth."

"How, Father?" I didn't like what was in her voice, but if she was this deep in jealousy and wrath she would not recover until the temptation was removed.

"You will have to decide that for yourself. But you know you must do something or you will both be destroyed, don't you?"

There was a quiet moment. "Yes, Father," she told me, and I could hear the sincerity in her voice as she added, "Thank you," before she stepped out.

I came back to myself hunched over Father Gabriel's body, or what was left of it. His blood dripped from my fangs and my mouth was full of the flavor of it, hot and with an exquisite tang like the most delicious of spices. I could taste what kind of person he'd been. It hardly mattered. The thread of destiny had been severed. He'd needed to die to save everyone else.

Just like the guards in the hall had to die, because they were in my way. And when Ohm from the novice ward came running in shouting something in a language I'd forgotten how to make sense of, it just took a flick of my tail and blood was spraying everywhere. He had been part of the problem. Weren't they all? And anyway, it was fun.

I used an armored hand to shove a window out of its socket and sniffed the air outside. The blood of many, many people. The streets were thick with sin, and I had a very simple solu-

I had never been so grateful to be woken up from a dream before, although it meant I remembered it and I didn't want that either. Someone was rapping urgently at my door. I wasn't used to having this kind of privacy. It took a moment for me to realize I had to pull a shirt on and open it.

It was Ohm, and it was more than a little weird seeing him, but the images were blessedly fading. Anyway, he looked terrified.

"There's a mob outside! They heard that Lord Margay's donkey was taken in for poisoning him, and I think they're going to storm the jail! At least... I don't know. But there's going to be a riot right here!"

I could hear the distant, muffled sounds of yelling, which told me how loud it must really have been. "Does Father Gabriel know? If anyone can do something, he can."

"He's gone out there already. I saw what he did last time, but they're angry this time. They'll stone him or tear him apart."

I reached out and took hold of Ohm's shoulder. I was quieting the panic of someone three years my elder. "Have faith. I do. I need to go with him. Make sure everyone else knows, but try not to scare them."

And by trying not to scare them, he would reduce his own fear. He nodded and went to knock on the next door while I returned to my room and dressed quickly.

Going out the front gate would be an invitation to trouble, and I wouldn't be able to get through the crowds, but a cathedral and its outbuildings have a lot of exits. I slipped out a back door, noticing how bright the city was. A brightness that let me see the little figure in black sitting on a bench. Waiting for me.

It was jarring, but I was already off balance and this didn't make it any worse. For that reason I felt no qualms walking right up to her. She looked harmless, if out of place, although in what I guessed was reflected torchlight the button eyes of her doll gleamed unpleasantly.

"How did you know I'd be here?" I asked her accusingly, trying to take control of the conversation before she turned everything on its head again. "Where do you keep coming from?"

She looked up at me, although I couldn't see her eyes in this light thanks to the veil hiding them. "You say that like it was hard to figure out. I knew you couldn't sleep through a riot, and I need your help."

"My place is with Father Gabriel. He'll calm the crowd. He knows how to make people see the truth." I was being stubborn, but I knew I would have to be.

"Does your Master need you, or do you just want to be by his side?" she returned, quiet and penetrating as always.

"He's not-" I started. She had baited me. "You can call him that if you want. It's as true as any other title. And he doesn't need me, but if he does, what could you want from me that's more important?"

She was stroking the doll like it was a real cat, in some kind of nervous gesture that was the only sign I'd seen that she wasn't completely unflappable. There was emotion in her voice too as she told me, "I need your help to save someone's life."

That only threw me off a little, but I was able to follow that thought through to the end, which helped me recover. Reason told me where this was leading. "Lord Margay's Wild Girl. You want me to let her go." She was going to say something that would throw me in doubt again. I had to stay strong. "She's a murderer and a monster. I'm not going to help you set something like that free."

She just looked at me. I couldn't see her eyes, but I didn't need to. Her silence gave me time to think. I wasn't being asked to save a murderer. Whatever had happened, it had been something Lady Margay had done because I had pushed her into it. But I had pushed her because Father Gabriel had pushed me, for the right reasons. Whether she was a killer or not, she was still a monster.

Except she didn't have horns or claws. She didn't have the taste of blood from a dream lingering on her tongue. I was the monster.

I wasn't going to make it worse by committing this crime, and I kept my stare hard so that the ghost girl would know it. Which was why, after a moment, she told me, "You're determined. You've closed your mind, and nothing I can say will change it."

I kept glaring, then realized that even letting her talk was too dangerous. I started to turn and set off to join Father Gabriel. The yelling had stopped. He had already begun to talk to them.

I was brought short by the strange sound of a little girl's voice that was tired and resigned like an old woman's. "I am at least as stubborn as you are, Elijah. I am going to save Mane, and so are you. Your claws are still growing, but I can make sure everyone knows what you are sooner rather than later."

That brought me up short and froze me with panic – and hatred. The kind of hatred that made me think of those claws, how sharp they were, and how easy it would be to remove this obstacle to my virtue. I forced myself to think of that as just an echo of my dream. I would, absolutely, do the right thing. Killing this girl wasn't it, no matter how dangerous or weird or misguided she was.

'She had no fear of me. My continued silence earned me only a stern and mildly impatient lecture. "You have a choice, Elijah. You can help me rescue a girl from being killed for a crime you and I both know she isn't guilty of, or you can be absolutely honest and face your Master when he finds out that you're a Wild Boy yourself – or something worse."

Father Gabriel's faith in me wasn't justified, I knew. I was too afraid and I wasn't sure, I wasn't totally sure what was right enough to overcome that fear. All I could manage was an excuse. "I can't do anything anyway. I'm no one important. I can't set a prisoner free, and Father Gabriel is there at the jail right now, keeping the mob from breaking in."

"Which must be why they're keeping her in the garden shed, not the jail." Her tone remained flat and hard. "As for what you can do, you'll figure something out."

I had no choice. I even had to strangle my seething anger when we approached the shed, well behind the cathedral, far away from any crowds. At least, when *I* approached the shed. The mystery girl was nowhere to be seen, probably because there were a number of lamps lit and a guard standing by the locked door of the shed. The shed was a sturdy little brick building, and no one was getting out of it, especially not a child.

"What's your business?" the guard challenged me. I'd seen him around, but didn't know his name. "No one is allowed into the shed tonight. You'll have to come back tomorrow, or the day after maybe."

It just popped into my head. "I know." My anger actually helped. I certainly sounded grim. "That's why I'm here. Father Gabriel wants the donkey disposed of tonight, not tomorrow. You know what's going on out front. We may not be able to wait."

He wasn't expecting that, but he had absolutely no reason to distrust me either. "Disposed of how?" he asked cautiously.

"You don't want to know. You had nothing to do with it at all. You know what things are like right now. Father Gabriel would rather you get to honestly say you weren't there. You were relieved of duty and have no way of knowing what happened afterward."

He took a deep breath, and then another. He did know what it was like. The Archbishop was dead, and so was the Emperor. Politics. Lots of politics, even in the church. He gave me the sign of benediction as a salute, and I returned it and I took his keys and he walked off, turned a corner around a greenhouse, and then we couldn't see each other anymore. Which was how we both wanted it.

I was committed now. What I would do tomorrow, I had no idea. Someone would find out. I unlocked the padlock and heaved the door open, which had always been rusty.

I only realized the young girl with the mourning veil was there when she walked past me into the shed. It had been cleared out of tools. All it contained was a young woman in a heavy yoke that held her wrists and neck, fastened by a chain to a bolt in the wall from which some gardening implement used to hang.

Not a young woman, a girl. Just a little younger than me. And not a girl, a Wild Girl, although the only signs of it were long, fuzzy donkey ears and a tail with a black brush tip. She was naked, and might have been beautiful like Lady Margay had described. I couldn't tell. Every inch of her that wasn't bruised had bright red wheals that I was afraid were burns. She slumped against a wall, and the look of helpless, resigned dread in her eyes when she watched me open the door was going to haunt me.

The girl in black was no longer calm at all. She yanked the keys out of my hand and rushed forward, so impatient she had to struggle to get the lock of the yoke open as she gasped, "Mane! Are you going to be okay? How bad is it?"

"Hind?" the Wild Girl husked, sounding incredulous. As the yoke came off she reached stiffly up and pulled the hat off the girl in black's head. Hair, which glowed white in the lamp-light, came spilling out down to her hips, and out of it stuck the ears of a donkey. She'd been a Wild Girl herself all the time.

I didn't care. I was staring at Lord Margay's girl, Mane. I couldn't believe she could stand, much less embrace the girl in the black dress who I supposed was named Hind. "Is this real? Are you alive? Why would you rescue me? You hate me!" She was babbling and she flinched every time she moved, but she still held on to the other donkey.

"You can answer those questions yourself," Hind told her. Her voice was controlled again, calm, soothing, and she held the beaten donkey girl like she would break. She might. I couldn't stop staring. "How badly are you hurt?" Hind pressed. It was an answer I was suddenly desperate for myself.

The hopelessness in Mane's eyes gave way to tears. She was taller, obviously older, and her black hair was almost as long as Hind's white hair. The whole scene seemed increasingly like a dream, except that Mane's hoarse, pained voice made it all too real again. "They think I poisoned Rikter!" she babbled hysterically. "Why would I do that? You and I were the best treated girls in the city! Even Clip and Charcoal were jealous. Rikter was so- is he alive? Hind, is he alive?"

"He is. Whoever poisoned him wasn't very good at it," Hind answered, stroking the girl's hair.

"Her Ladyship gave me the bottle. It was supposed to be a special brandy. She's kind of a shrew, but she loves him. It couldn't have been her, either! Who-" She cut herself off. "He'll never take me back. Even if I convince him I didn't do it," she whispered. No, rasped.

Hind kept stroking the donkey girl's hair, whispering, "You'll be taken care of, Mane, but we have to get out of here and-" Even this girl who looked and acted like a ghost hesitated before continuing. "Are you going to live long enough for me to get to a doctor?" Looking at Mane, it was a question you had to ask.

But Mane was getting a little less hysterical, and was able to answer, "Yes. Everything… hurts, so I'm not sure if any bones are broken, but they didn't want to risk killing me because I hadn't answered their questions yet. They wanted Rikter's secrets. I didn't tell them anything." Her voice husked vehemently about it, and despite everything she looked proud. And the expression on Hind's face was exactly the same. But then Mane's expression twisted up in pain for a moment. "You'll have to hold me up. Or can your friend carry me?"

And Hind gave me a look. Without the hat and the veil I could see dark blue eyes, but I didn't understand her expression. "No, but you know I can manage," Hind assured her… friend, I supposed. "And Elijah is in enough danger already. You and I are just going to disappear, and he will go back to his life."

Mane nodded. Whatever energy seeing us had given her, she was hanging off of Hind like a rag doll now. Which left Hind still looking at me. "I lied to you, Elijah," she told me softly, still petting the other girl's hair. "I would never have given up your secret, but you had to see this. And after this the furnace, or the stake, or the blade. Did you do the right thing, helping me? Do you regret it?"

I closed my eyes. I didn't want to look at Mane, or the marks on her, or the way she kept twitching when some new pain hit her. Then I made myself open my eyes again because Hind was right. I had to see this, because it was my fault. I had taken the complaints of a woman consumed by jealousy at face value, and even if they were true this Wild – this girl, Mane, hadn't deserved having her life destroyed and her body tortured.

"Saving her was the right thing to do," I told Hind helplessly.

She looked at me for another moment. Somehow she managed to pick up her fallen hat with her foot and flip it up into the air and catch it. I watched her set it back, tucking her ears under her hair and her hair under the hat, and when the veil was pulled down she was just a young girl grieving a relative again.

"You need to be away from here right now," she told me finally. "You'll see me again soon. Neither of us has much time."

She was right. I couldn't think of a single thing she hadn't been right about. Some small part of me wanted to go to bed, to hope that in the morning what I knew would be right and what I'd seen would be wrong, but there wasn't much hope. All I could do was drag myself back to my room and go back to bed, and pray I didn't have another nightmare.

TODAY – When I think about things like this I usually try not to write them down, but yesterday we went to the library again. I got in easy. Sometimes people just don't notice me, and this was one of those times. While we were there I found a copy of The Republic. Mister Thornback has a copy, of course, but it's in Latin and I can't read Latin well enough to make sense of it. I really needed a vernacular copy. But then I read this one, and it still didn't make any sense! I feel like I must be missing something, because he just seems like a windbag who likes to talk about things he doesn't know anything about.

But you know, maybe he's got a point. Maybe, if we don't have any answers, it's not useless to at least try and think about something and make the best guess you can. It bothers me sometimes that I can never remember the date, and I'm pretty sure a lot of the other donkeys have the same problem. Maybe it's because we don't change much, so it always feels like the same day. Vick has grown a lot since I met him, not just physically but as a person. And Mister Thornback laughs a lot more than he used to. But I'm still exactly the same.

But we do change sometimes. I was a lot of trouble at first. So maybe I don't know what I'm talking about after all. Anyway, he's calling.

There was nothing in the journal that was useful, nothing that applied to anything. But I had woken up shaken and uncomfortable and somehow reading it made me feel better, even though it was only what any bright, well-meaning little girl might write in her diary. I hadn't done the safe thing last night, but at least I felt like I had done the right thing.

That was all that gave me the strength to show up at Father Gabriel's office for work. I had no special duties today, and he always had books and journals of his own to be copied and letters to be taken or read and sorted. If you went by rank and title he was nobody at all, but it seemed like everybody wanted his advice. Really, sometimes I thought he just wanted me to be there. In quiet moments he would tell me moral parables, or discuss the city.

I was inscribing his initials on a wax seal when the moment I knew was coming arrived. "I have a question, Elijah," he remarked, looking up from a list of how tithes were divided. "Last night you destroyed the donkey we took in, or so I'm told. If anyone else had used my name for anything, I'd worry. From you, I'm wondering what your reason was."

Again I was a coward. I was going to put the moment of revelation off as long as possible. "Yes, Father. I apologize, but the matter weighed on me heavily. I felt that I would not have a clear conscience until it was over."

It was a weak excuse, but kind of true. It made him smile, though. "Yes, I remember those days," he told me warmly. "You see what needs to be done, but your heart wants so badly to do what is right that it worries about things that feel wrong that you know are right. And you felt you needed to take personal responsibility as well, didn't you?"

"Yes." And there was something else. "Father, someone had been interrogating the donkey about her former owner. That doesn't seem like something you would do."

Father Gabriel sighed in exasperation, although it was mild, like most of the things he did. "Politics. I'm sure that was Bishop Murus's doing. Everyone wants to be the Archbishop, it seems like. It is causing men who should never have joined the priesthood to betray themselves."

There was a knock, and it was my job to let visitors in. It was Ohm again. He was a runner a lot. "Sealed letter for you, Father." He set it on the desk and hurried out nervously.

A moment later, after it had been opened, Father Gabriel continued dryly. "How timely. Bishop Isaac wants me to know that he is withdrawing his nomination and putting me forward instead. He feels that his chances of being chosen were too low, but that I am a candidate that a general consensus could accept, and he's ensuring the new Archbishop will be a man whose faith he agrees with."

"You don't seem surprised."It was big news. I could hardly imagine bigger.

"I'm not. I will probably be chosen. I have little interest in the title, although I can't deny it would be useful. I will be chosen because I understand that this isn't about politics."

Suddenly he was standing, heading over to look out the window, perhaps to try and look over the wall at the city itself. "This is a moral reformation, Elijah. First and last, that is what this is about. The next Archbishop may be in a position to choose the next Emperor, and reverse the balance of power that has held for more than two centuries, but passing laws to outlaw sin is a half-measure that doesn't hold. When the people open their eyes and follow the path of virtue, the government and the church itself will have to follow. In the end, all that matters is that the Empire turns away from sin. I seem to be the only man who has realized this so far, and that is the only source of my power."

"That is why you arranged for me to take Lady Margay's confession," I pressed gently. I didn't need it confirmed, I needed it explained.

"It was the right thing to do," Father Gabriel replied firmly. "We excised a cancer from her household, we turned a powerful man and his family from sin, we destroyed one of the beasts previous Archbishops allowed to infest this city, and in so doing we opened the people's eyes to the dangers all around them. You feel it was distasteful to manipulate the woman and so do I, but that is what a shepherd does. All that matters is that it was, unquestionably, the right thing to do."

Which meant that I wasn't allowed to question it. I shouldn't question it. I had heard all of the answers before and knew them by heart. They didn't seem to mean anything when I compared them to my memory of Mane, every inch of her red or purple, which wasn't as bad as the look in her eyes when I opened the door. None of those answers explained the diary of a little girl who talked about her hooves like any other girl talked about her hair. I knew two things, and they couldn't both be true.

"You are quiet, Elijah." Despite Father Gabriel's mild tone, cold fear washed through me for a moment. "You, too, are going through an awakening. You have always done what is right, and now you're being asked to look at a bigger picture. One day you may have to lead as I have led, because there are few men so dedicated to doing good. That is why I have another task for you."

I couldn't do to another person what I'd done to Mane. I couldn't. But instead of spitting that back in his face, I merely admitted, "It weighs on me, Father. What would you have me do?"

"It is a weight you will learn to bear. This task may be easier on your heart, although it will require much more from your head. You know that donkeys aren't the only kind of Wild Children?"

I nodded. "The church fathers argue about the nature of the doves sometimes."

"Yes. And if you had grown up in the country like I did, you'd hear stories about wolves as well. Sin comes in ever more nightmarish forms. It is true that there is a nest of pigeons in the city. I would like to know where it is." His back remained turned to me. I couldn't see his face, but he sounded calm despite the harsh description.

"I have no idea how to find that out," I confessed.

"Neither do I, but if I had time, I could find a way. I have faith that you can, too."

Which is why, a little bit later, I was walking the streets of the capital, taking turns randomly and just letting my feet guide me. They didn't know what they were doing, but neither did the rest of me. I wasn't sure what would happen if I succeeded in this task, and I wasn't sure what would happen to me if I refused.

I ended up in the park. I wasn't quite sure how, or why. I had just been wandering. It wasn't a place I normally went, although I had heard it was very popular and parents liked to take their children there to play. With mobs and riots almost every day I hadn't expected anyone to be here at all, but a couple of children were building things in a big pit of sand while a woman I supposed was their mother or nanny watched. There was a Wild Girl too, but they stayed well away from her. She rocked back and forth on what was mainly a rope hanging from a tree.

I had too many questions, the ones I had been ordered to ask and the ones I was forbidden to ask. Instead, as I walked up to her I found myself saying, "That must be hard with hooves."

Suddenly the girl was clinging to the rope tightly, in no control as she swung around in odd directions, but it seemed to be stopping itself. "I'm sorry, Father. Should I go?" she asked timidly.

265

She was afraid because I was dressed like a priest. I felt a pang about that, but I tried to smile and put her at ease again. "I don't mind. I just don't see a lot of Wild Children getting a chance to play, so I was curious. It's charming," I found myself saying.

"My Mistress is buying makeup. Mister Artax is-" She didn't want to speak ill of someone in front of a priest. Like pretty much everyone I met. "Well, he just pitches a fit if I come in. Some of the craftsmen are like that, and my Mistress will eat day old bread before she'll put second-best rouge on her cheeks." The girl grinned. Her teeth, I had to admit, were very flat, but didn't have the gaps a donkey's teeth did.

"You seem to like her." I was honestly curious, even enjoying the conversation, and she seemed to sense that and it relaxed her. I realized that this might be the first conversation I'd ever had with a Wild Child, unless you counted mysterious girls in black dresses with white hair.

She hesitated a moment, but then the girl nodded. "I've had a few owners. My Mistress is a little strict about respect and being obeyed, but if I'm good to her, she's good to me. She said that if I couldn't wait on her in the store, I might as well be out here having fun."

"You seem a little old for a toy like this," I noted, trying to keep it light, "And I can't believe you can stay on it with hooves."

She actually giggled, although she tried to restrain it. "You're never too old for a swing, Father." She was starting to sound impish, and was having trouble staying formal and respectful. "And the hooves aren't so bad. I figured I'd be losing my balance all the time when I got them, but I don't. And I figured I'd never stub my toe again, but instead rocks keep getting stuck in them."

And since I was asking questions, "Do you know many other Wild Children? I've heard there are doves in the city, too."

"I know a bunch of other donkeys." She started twisting and rocking to get the swing moving again. "We don't get to spend a lot of time together, but you know, most of the folks who can afford a Wild Girl like me are just rich enough to know each other, right? So when our owners get together, sometimes we can get together and talk too, or play Catch-As-Catch-Can or something."

"And the doves? You think they're just a story?" I wondered if I was betraying my principles or just curious myself. The whole idea made me look up at the sky.

"Oh, they're real," she told me immediately. "They never talk to me, though. They mostly visit the donkeys with the really bad owners. Like, the

266

really, really bad owners. The kids who need to be talked out of killing themselves. Um… I think that girl is waiting for you, Father."

I hardly had to look, but I did anyway. Hind was there. Hat, veil, dress, shoes, and doll, all in perfect black. She looked human, just grim. "We should go, Elijah. You don't want to get Brand in trouble, and her owner may worry if she finds her Wild Girl talking to a priest."

That name… The girl on the swing saw my look, and her own face twisted up in distaste. Then her smile came back, just as fast. "It was a long time ago, Father. I hardly remember it. Now it's just like a birthmark." Hind was pulling gently on my hand, and Brand added, "It was a pleasure to meet you," before I turned away.

Walking next to Hind made it impossible to forget that I had a task, and how my last task had turned out. When we were out of earshot I asked her bleakly, "You're going to talk me out of doing this, aren't you?"

"No, I'm not."

I couldn't make out her tone at all. "Why not?" I had so many doubts and arguments against this myself, but I was sure she knew all of them.

"Because the church will find out anyway. It's not really that hard." Her tone was serene, but sad. She sounded entirely too much like Father Gabriel, but that was the only way they were alike. "You're on the edge, Elijah. I can't save you if you're found out first because you betrayed your Master. I can't let you get innocent children killed, either. But here there's nothing you can do anyway, and I would rather you be the one who finds out. It's the best of a number of bad options."

"That doesn't make me feel better," I told her, because it didn't.

"Good." Hind's voice held just a hint of a haunted tone. Compared to her normally noncommittal calm, it made her sound emphatic. "When you learn to make hard choices without feeling bad about them, we'll both have lost."

I didn't know what to say to that, but I was full of questions. "You're a Wild Girl, too." It wasn't really a question. It was every question all at once.

She shook her head. "You don't want to talk to me, Elijah. You want to talk to them. You can't trust me, yet. You just want to."

I didn't know what to say to that either, so I let her shadow me, a step back but at my side as I wandered the streets and looked for Wild Children to talk to. I spoke to a couple and they were like Brand, more or less. A little suspicious, only available until their owner called them, and they had seen doves in the air but never met one. The next child I talked to was a little human boy waiting in a cart while his mother bought a hat. He'd never seen a dove, but he complained about having to do chores the same way the donkey I'd spoken to last groused to his friend about how many dishes there were to wash.

I was getting somewhere I supposed, but I didn't know where. I wasn't learning where the doves lived. So I walked for a while not looking for any donkeys to talk to, just thinking, and for awhile I forgot that Hind was there at all.

Then I heard yelling, a woman's voice, screams of fury going on and on. I couldn't make out the words, but I followed the sound off a main street to a side street. When the yelling stopped, I still followed my memory of it. When people are that angry, a priest should find out. It was cleaner work than my other duties.

I turned a final corner. It wasn't quite an alley, but it was definitely a back street. In front of some kind of tavern sat a little one-person carriage much too rich for the street itself, and on its knees harnessed to the carriage was a donkey, an actual donkey. Except that crouching over the animal was a tiny figure in white — white feathers, white shirt, white wings. There was a movement in the church that said that Wild Children were part angel, not part demon. I'd always considered it a strange, fringe belief, but looking at this apparition in white I understood how someone could think that way. The white bird flew away as I stepped onto the street, and I felt guilty as I marked the direction.

Helplessly fascinated, I walked over to where it had been standing, but my fascination became a lot more grim as I got close. The donkey was crying. Not crying like an animal, in neighing shouts of pain or unhappiness. These were the sniffles and light sobs of a human child trying to get himself under control.

This was another story I had heard but never seen. Every Wild Child I'd seen was different, more or less an animal than the others. The only thing human about this one was its voice and its cloudy green eyes. Otherwise it just looked like a real donkey, if a young one, hitched up to a cart. A cart that despite its size I couldn't help thinking was too big for this little animal.

This little boy, I supposed. I tried to think of him that way as I knelt down myself and put my hand on his hairy neck. "Are you alright, son?"

He wasn't guarded like the others. I guess he was ready to accept sympathy from anyone. "I guess. I guess." He sniffled. "Egg always seems to be watching me. Mistress Faubelle just... she yells."

'Yelling' hardly described what I had heard from blocks away, the fury and harshness of it. I wasn't sure if this was right, but I petted his mane slowly. "Did she hit you?"

"No," he told me softly. He really looked just like an animal, but the tears and the voice were so human. And the voice was full of guilt. "I know a lot of boys and girls who get treated worse. But I'm not strong enough and I can never make her happy, ever, whether I try or not. If her parents are around she just says bad things, but if they're not, she yells."

I remembered what Hind had said about Brand. I didn't want to leave this child, but I didn't want to get him in more trouble, either. "Where is she now?"

"She's inside getting a drink. She got thirsty."

There was a weight in his voice that a priest was meant to listen for. He wasn't telling me everything, and what he didn't want to say is that she'd yelled until she lost her voice.

"I'll be okay, Sir. I've caught my breath. Mistress Faubelle won't be as angry when she comes out, and Egg is watching out for me and she says she's proud of me because I'm still trying."

"Do the doves talk to you often?" I asked him. I didn't want to lead the conversation here, but I was going to.

"Egg, mostly. Mourn brings me sweets sometimes, and Hatch makes me laugh, and Coo can make it all make sense for a little while. It's almost always Egg, though. I can try my hardest if it makes her happy."

I couldn't press too hard to make him feel better. There was nothing I could do. "I would very much like to meet her. I know you can't arrange that, so don't worry. Do you know where she lives, so I can go find her?"

"Kind of." He'd stopped crying, although the flatness of his voice sounded physically tired and emotionally drained. It was a little better than sounding defeated. "I take Mistress Faubelle all over the city. She's usually flying from the center of town, or heads back there. Actually... you know, that big church? Not the cathedral. The other one."

The second biggest church in the city was the one in the enclave of the Monks of St. Francis. Among other things, the abbot who led the order was one of the most vocal opponents of the doctrine that Wild Children were evil. As a monk he could never have become Archbishop, and I regretted it for a moment. I supposed that in this Father Gabriel was right. What mattered was what the congregation itself believed.

I was interrupted by a young woman's voice becoming rapidly more shrill as she demanded, "Mange, are you bothering a priest? Are you still lying down? Do you know how late we are already? I don't know why I even put up with you. I should have sold you to-"

I couldn't let it go on. "Daughter!" I interrupted sharply. I was praying she didn't notice how ridiculously young I was. But once you were a priest, you were a priest, not a person. She stopped long enough for me to tell her in a quiet but firm reminder, "Wrath is a sin. It is a very hard sin to give up, but it is a terrible sin that eats you from the inside."

"Yes, Father." She was staggered, but she'd stopped yelling. Mange – and I couldn't imagine naming anyone or anything that – had scrambled up onto all four legs the moment he saw her. There wasn't anything else I could do. There was also a bottle in her hand, not nearly full enough, and I gave it a pointed look. But making her feel guilty might hurt as much as it helped. I walked away and left them both behind. At least I could try to not make her embarrassment the boy's fault.

Hind hadn't said anything at all. Maybe the other two hadn't known she was there. When we turned the corner I felt her hand on my wrist, though, giving me a brief squeeze and then letting go. Yes, she probably knew what I felt like right now.

There was only one thing to do. I headed over to the enclave. The monastic orders and the church hierarchy were separate, and I supposed Father Gabriel's authority would not hold much weight there. Anyway, he might not have said it, but I was surely supposed to do this quietly. Wild Children didn't count. I had never spoken to one before Hind. Probably no other priest in the city had, either.

Instead I waited across the street. This close to the center of the city, the enclave's wall pressed right up close to its buildings and wasn't all that high. I was able to look over the wall and admire the church. It might not have been the cathedral, but its sweepingly pointed roof, its gables and its tower and its flying buttresses were all beautiful enough to be worth a look. One of the monks was sweeping the sidewalk in front. The monastic orders tended to view physical labor as valuable for spiritual discipline, so that made sense. But he saw the way I was staring and took a break to wander across the street talk to me. "Lovely, isn't it? Every morning I see the sun rise over it, and I want to be a better person just to thank the Lord for that gift."

That was the kind of sentiment that had drawn me to the priesthood in the first place, so I couldn't help returning his grin. "It is. Our cathedral's bigger, but a simpler beauty like this makes me feel the virtue of devotion. It is the monastic ideal in stone, and I think I'm feeling the sin of jealousy."

He chuckled a little, and as he turned to go I saw something in the sky, a figure in white too big to be a bird, landing on the roof and climbing in through a window. I reached out and touched the monk's shoulder, and as he paused I asked, "There's a lot of gables on your roof. Do you really have attics that big?"

He laughed. "I have no idea. They've been locked for as long as I've been here. Not only is the key lost, I think the lock is jammed, and the abbot's just told everyone not to worry about it. We don't really need the storage space."

This time I let him go. Hind was standing a building farther down, the picture of a very young woman contemplating God in the form of a church as she grieved for a lost relative. Somehow, I thought she had heard every word we'd said. I walked over to her, and she looked up at me, and said simply, "Do what you have to do."

I walked back to the cathedral alone. I told Father Gabriel that the doves lived in the attic of the monk's church and I'm sure he praised me for it, but I wasn't listening. I could not have been more relieved when his next order was just to go get some rest because I was obviously exhausted.

The next day, nothing happened. I copied a manuscript, I ran letters, and I sat and wrote down the words of other men of the church trying not to say anything dangerous as they discussed the choosing of an Archbishop with Father Gabriel, who didn't seem to care. There were no special orders at all.

It was the same the following morning. Father Gabriel seemed annoyed that men kept coming to him about the election, and I was writing out a letter as he spoke, instructing Patriarch Calius to ignore both threats and favors and simply vote with his faith. I had tried to relax, to think that things were calming down, but my claws were making it difficult to hold a pen. Nothing was over, and I was almost waiting for the timid knock at the door to the office.

I opened it and a sub deacon looked in. Father Gabriel was never harsh, and this young man's expression of fear was another sign. "Have you heard the news, Father?"

My nerves were raw. I had to bite back anger of my own at such a vague question. But Gabriel was as always calm, in control, and sympathetic. "I haven't heard any news that would make you so nervous, son. What has happened? Something that I must try and fix, it sounds like."

"There was... a killing, Father," the messenger explained. "In the town. A merchant by the name of Loave. He and his family, all cut apart by their Wild Boy before it turned the knife on itself. He had children, Father. One of them was quite young."

"There is nothing I can do to bring back the dead," Father Gabriel responded. "I cannot make a crime like that not have happened. Please leave us, my son. I must think about if there is anything I can do in the aftermath."

The room was quiet when the sub deacon left. Father Gabriel stared out the window, letter forgotten. I wrestled with myself, until I lost and blurted out the most offensive question I could imagine. "Did you arrange this?"

He wasn't angry. "I didn't have to," he told me peacefully. "I only had to wait. I am glad you understand the power of this event. These deaths will tear away the last veil between the city and the truth. Our congregation will understand how bad things have become, what they have allowed to fester here. And when they recognize one temptation, they will open their eyes to the others. First they will be afraid, of course, but fear will give their reformation urgency."

"It's just that I've never heard of something like this happening, Father." I couldn't stop myself. I needed to know how bad this was. "For it to happen now seems so convenient." Describing murders that way made me nauseous, but I just couldn't believe this crime was real.

"If you were my age, you would have expected it." Father Gabriel's words were calm and dispassionate, the tone of a wise and solemn man. It just turned my stomach more. But he stood very still, watching the street, and seemed at ease. "Donkeys take their own lives. They don't usually take others with them, but creatures like that also know that the rules are breaking down and there is no one to stop them. Oh, someone might have arranged it, because the church and the court are full of greedy men with devious little plans right now. I didn't need to plan. When you see a cup filled right to the top you don't have to tip it over, just wait for it to spill."

"What will happen now?" Whatever he was going to say, I hoped he would be wrong.

He only had to point out the window for me to know that he wasn't. "That will happen." Over the wall, just barely, I could see people drifting steadily into the plaza. Soon they would be a mob.

"They'll be scared and angry," I told Father Gabriel, feeling scared and angry myself. But whatever he thought about Wild Children, no one else would be able to stop what was about to happen out there.

"Yes. If we let them get worked up, it will be too late. We will talk to them now."

Which is why a few minutes later I was standing at the back of the execution stand again, and Father Gabriel was sitting at the edge, facing the plaza. His legs hung over the edge of the platform and he watched the crowd as they watched him, but he hadn't said anything yet. Still, the crowd wasn't shouting, and every minute more people showed up to watch as word spread.

I knew it was deliberate, but he stood up slowly, giving them something to watch. The crowd was absolutely still by the time he began to speak. "A crime has been committed. You have heard about it, like I have, and like me you are angry. Like me you worry about what is happening to our city. And now you are waiting to hear what I am going to do about it."

"There is nothing I can do about it at all," he continued, his voice grave, and it was good that he knew how to make his voice carry because there were ugly murmurs to talk over. "I am just a man and a priest, of no particular rank. I have no special power. All I have done is tell you the truth and let you do what is right. You have heard that I am being considered for Archbishop, but politics is wild speculation and games that drag on forever. If I could somehow make everything right if I were chosen, how much time would it take? How much worse can we afford to let things get?"

He gave them a moment of quiet, but wasn't calming them down this time. While he was silent there was a noise, a steady rustle of a thousand people about to speak. His voice cut through that again and his head shook slowly, weighted with the gravity of the moment. "I can't ask you go to home again and live in peace. You wouldn't listen, because you know, now, that peace won't happen by itself. You know now that the problem isn't scared nobles or a dead Emperor or a leaderless church. The problem is that we have let evil in, given it our blessing and pretended it is something harmless. Fear and sin are feeding on each other in this city, in the whole of the Empire, and now you can see how it is dragging us down. Only you have the strength to act, so you tell me. What are you afraid of? What is the sin you cannot drag yourself away from?"

Shocked silence dragged on for a moment. Then random voices, brief shouts, but before they got longer Father Gabriel raised his hands in sympathy. "Wild Children are only one of the sins that are dragging us down, my children, but until now they were the sin you refused to face. They seemed harmless. Too many of you saw them as almost human, and even in the church there were those who would debate their nature. Now you can see what they are, but you are still not sure. It seems too much to accept that we could be destroyed from the inside by something that hides behind an innocent face, but that is exactly how temptation works. You know you need to do something, but you are not sure, not entirely sure, what is right. Are you?"

Father Gabriel stood ramrod straight and still. His face was like a rock and his voice was stern, but matter-of-fact. The crowd was frozen. "If you want to see the truth for yourselves, I will show you where to look. You know where the monastery of St. Francis is. In their church, in the attic, they are hiding the doves from you, the prettiest face sin ever wore. I cannot tell the monks what to do. I will not even set a foot over their threshold without permission. But they have to listen to you. I make only one request. Let me send good men who work for the church. Go with them, but let them act in your name, seize these creatures and bring them back so that you can see the difference between innocence and sin for yourselves."

Now there was shouting, a lot of shouting, and all of it affirmative. They were almost cheers. And Father Gabriel gave me a look, and I knew instantly what he wanted me to do. I wondered for a moment if I could refuse, and when the crowd went wild for blood if Father Gabriel would be their first target, but I was haunted by a dream, a dream of taking a life I thought needed to be taken. And after we were torn apart, who would be next?

So I found myself leading a half dozen or so guards, trailed behind by a wall of flesh and noise, a thick crowd of angry people who I knew would become violent at the slightest sign of weakness. Hind couldn't save me, couldn't lead me by the hand to solve this. She was out there somewhere watching, but if she tried to interfere the balance would tip into chaos.

I couldn't let that happen, but there I was, standing at the gates of the monastic enclave telling their white-faced abbot, "I apologize, brother, but our congregation wants to see what is hiding in your attic. Please let us through." I didn't have to make any threats, because he knew what would happen if he refused. His church would be stormed by a mob rather than a few soldiers.

The monks stepped back to let us by, faces tight and disbelieving, and I looked up at the sharply pointed roof of this beautiful church. I thought about the children who must be inside, perhaps starting to wonder what was going on, and I yelled much louder than necessary, "The attic will be locked, and there is no key! Find some kind of battering ram. To get in we'll have to break at least one door down!"

The crowd roared, a bottle and a brick flying up to clatter off the roof, doing my work even better than I had hoped. There was no way the doves would miss that noise and nothing to stop them from simply flying away. I didn't know what would happen then, but an empty attic was the only hope I had as the church guards took a few crowbars and rather than beat it open levered a trapdoor at the top of a stairway off its hinges.

The doves had heard my words. Inside was a chaos of scattered books and spilled cups to mark a hasty exit. But also, standing waiting in front of the trapdoor, were a young boy and girl with white feathers and white wings. They just stood there holding each other's hand, watching us as my guards lunged for them. I closed my eyes, because I didn't want to watch and I couldn't make this any better.

Father Gabriel had, at least, pacified the mob. As I marched up the steps onto the execution platform leading guards holding the pair of doves we had caught in chains, there were no shouts. I stood well back, a little bit grateful that I was no longer even pretending to be in charge, but the truth is I felt numb. I had stopped wondering what I could do or what was right at all.

The girl was held up by guards at the edge of the platform next to Gabriel. She had been gagged. They both had, when we got back to the plaza. I hadn't ordered it or the shackles on their wrists and ankles. It had just been done. There was no point. They hadn't said anything or tried to get away. They had just waited for us to take them.

It was a shock to me when Father Gabriel began speaking to the crowd again. "I have led you to these creatures, and it is time for you to decide for yourselves. The donkeys who lurk in the streets tell you they are doves. The monk who shielded them thinks they are angels."

In the first violent action I had ever seen from him, he reached out and grabbed the shirt the girl was wearing. The cloth was clean and white but ragged and worn to begin with, and had been heavily cut and retied to accommodate her wings. He yanked at it viciously until the shirt tore, stripping her bare, and then grabbed her chin and held it up to demand of the crowd, "Is this an angel?"

I knew what they saw. The guards had not been gentle and a huge, livid, puffy bruise had spoiled a face almost as ethereal as Hind's. But her body was worse. Naked, haphazard patches of feathers white enough to make her skin look pink mottled her body. She looked weird and ugly, not like the shining white child I'd seen comforting a crying donkey.

The angry noises in the crowd confirmed it. "What do you see?" demanded Father Gabriel again. "I see a dirty pigeon. I see the features of an animal cast upon what was supposedly once a human girl. I would call that the mark of the demonic, but that would be giving them too much credit. These are beasts of flesh and blood." His hand moved, grabbing one of the long, white pinion feathers of the girl's wings, and he pulled sharply. It resisted, then came free. When it did the girl made a shrill, sharp noise only half-muffled by her gag, and suddenly there was blood staining her feathers red, dappling the wooden platform.

Father Gabriel threw the feather into the crowd and the blood matting it made it fall rather than float, although the people crowded away rather than touch it. "Open your eyes and look at what is in front of you. This is nothing holy. This is an animal, but worse than an animal because it can smile at you and lure you into sin. The monk who hid them said they were gentle, pious, and harmless." He grabbed another pinion and pulled it out faster, more savagely than before. The girl's self-control failed her. She screamed into the gag and behind her the boy suddenly came alive, thrashing in the grip of the guards that held him, beating his wings against them and yelling furiously as he glared at Father Gabriel.

"Would those have been words of prayer or of blaspheme, do you think?" Gabriel asked the crowd. They were very, very quiet. "I don't have to tell you what's in front of you anymore. You know, now, what the donkeys are like. You have seen the true nature of even the prettiest seeming Wild Children. Are you going to live in fear of what they will do next?"

Now the crowd was shouting, and it was only because Father Gabriel's voice cut over them that there wasn't a riot then and there. "I am just a priest. Just a man, with little rank. I do not claim to make decisions for the church, or the court, or for you. I can only ask. I ask you now to have faith in me for a little while. You have made your wishes known. We will not have these monsters in our city anymore, and I will ask the leaders of the church in your name to gather them up. Every Wild Child will be collected, and no more allowed in. Once we have them we will pass the judgment on them that they deserve, and there will be no fires or mobs in the process. Will you give me your faith?"

They yelled, cheered. He made the sign of benediction and turned to leave, to take the stairs down to the jail below. As he passed me he paused. He had seen my expression, and his was serious as he laid his hand on my shoulder. "The truth of Wild Children is ugly, Elijah. I am sorry you had to see it this way, but our work has now truly begun. Today the first temptation will be purged from this city. For now I ask you to rest. You have performed beyond my hopes, better than men three times your age famed for their holiness. It was the right thing to do."

He led the guards and the shackled Dove Children they carried down the stairs, and he left me behind. A bloody handprint was soaking into my robes where he had touched me.

I couldn't sleep. I couldn't even lie in bed for long. I couldn't read, and I flipped through the beaten old journal aimlessly without taking in even a word. I could wash, but not enough. I could smell the blood on me.

The church was in no better shape. There was a lot of activity, people hurrying back and forth. Often there were loud arguments. Nobody knew what was going to happen next.

What was going to happen next? For me? Father Gabriel would send for me, of course. Tonight, or tomorrow, he would need me. Whatever it was, big or small, I didn't want to be a part of it anymore. It only took a moment's thought to know what my next job would be, anyway. The collection was going on right now. Someone would have to take an inventory, count and mark off children as they were fed to the ovens. It was a job anyone could do, that didn't make things better or worse, but it wasn't going to be me that did it.

The only thing I took with me was the journal. A book wasn't alive, but I still wasn't going to let it be burned just because a Wild Girl wrote in it. I walked out, left my rooms, left the church. Whatever horrible thing happened next, I wasn't going to take part in it.

I had to find Hind so we could do something, whatever that might be. I decided that as I stepped out of a side door from the clerical quarters, and I could not have been more relieved to see a petite figure in black, a darker shadow in an already dark night, standing in the garden. She ran her thumb over the strands of a willow tree, and for once I was the one appearing magically behind her pleading, "I need your help, Hind."

Not that she showed any sign of surprise. She just turned around and looked up at me, although her face was only a pale mask behind the dark veil. "And I need yours." Her tone was a little warmer and less calm than usual. "You must have passed my message in the hall. It's better this way. You're doing this because you want to."

"But doing what? Father Gabriel was right. He doesn't have to do anything at all. It will all be done for him. By now they'll have seized most of the Wild Children in the city."

"All of them," Hind corrected me, then corrected herself, "Barring a few of us who are particularly well hidden. I understand he's planning public executions to begin in the morning, which gives us tonight. That's all the time we'll need."

"You have a plan," I realized incredulously. I didn't want to hope.

"I've had a plan for months now. Only the details change. Having a priest with me will make things much easier."

I broke in. "I'll do anything, Hind. I can't live with myself already." I meant it. I couldn't wait while she tried to be gentle about what I was throwing away. "I'll go with you right now if you'll just tell me what to do."

I thought she smiled behind the veil. "First, can you find a hat or something? The more priestly you look, the better."

I carried a skullcap with me as a matter of course. I rarely thought about it. It was just something I did as a priest. More importantly, I didn't want to go back inside to get anything more formal. "Will this do?" I asked, drawing it from a pocket and laying it over my head.

Now I thought she was grinning, but it was too dark and her voice was as even as always as she told me, "It's an improvement."

She really did have a plan. There were nearly a hundred donkeys in the city, much more than I'd imagined, too many to just throw in jail cells. Since they were merchandise they'd just been thrown into a warehouse down by the river Ister instead. They didn't have to be heavily guarded either, because they were just donkeys.

Which apparently meant that I could walk down a street near the docks and give two guards standing in front of a freight door a letter. They read it by the dim light of the lamp over the door, glanced at each other, handed me their keys, and just walked away into the night. When Hind stepped out of the dark I asked her in amazement, "What was in that letter? Where did you get it?"

"I've been in correspondence with Bishop Murus for some time now," she told me, as I wrestled with an old and tired lock until we could step inside. "He's getting quite desperate right now, enough to adjust a few guard postings if he thinks it will embarrass Father Gabriel. I knew something like this was coming as soon as the Archbishop died. So did a lot of other people."

And then she stepped back behind me, disappearing as she did so well. It took me a moment to figure out why. It looked like there were a couple of side offices, a few stalls for horses, some support beams, but mainly the building was nothing but a huge empty room. Empty, that is except for a bewildering variety of boys and girls. All of them looked younger than me, and I almost felt like no two had the same combination of animal traits. I could see two that just looked like donkeys from the door, and I had no idea which one was Mange or if neither of them was. What had made Hind disappear was the guard. He wasn't an official soldier of the church, although he wore a badge. He was just a man holding a heavy stick, walking up and down the clear spaces, watching the donkeys.

As soon as I saw him, he saw me, and I kept my expression as casual as possible as we approached each other. This had not been in the plan, but I had a good idea of what to do. "I see they left you to watch the animals," I told him. He would want an explanation, so I wouldn't give him time to get suspicious. "I was asked to come replace you for the night. You'll be on the pay sheet for the full shift, but Father Gabriel wants this handled a little more personally."

He was suspicious already, but the instructions came from a priest and he wasn't going to argue. "No point in either of us being here anyway." He grumbled as he handed over the stick. "Donkeys never put up a fight. I've had to tap them a couple of times to keep quiet, but that's all."

I smiled as convincingly as I could and blessed him, and he walked out into the night. I dropped the stick immediately, but he'd been right. The children weren't even tied up. They just sat there, or lay there. Some of them watched me and some of them didn't, and a lot of them had red, puffy eyes.

Hind stepped past me again. Only one lamp hung from the middle of the roof, but she stepped right into its light and took off her hat. As she threw it aside, white hair fell out down to her waist. Her hair was paler than her skin, a white I'd never seen even bleach give a human's hair. It marked her, but not as dramatically as the long, furry grey ears.

"My name is Hind," she announced to the crowd of donkeys. The ones who hadn't been watching us were looking up now, and when she asked,

"How many of you know who I am?" quite a few raised their hands. A couple of them raised hooves.

"We're getting out of here," she told them, firm and commanding. "Your owners would rather you run away with me than see you killed tomorrow. If anyone's locked up, Elijah has the keys. If anyone can't walk, help them. Where are the doves? Is anyone else hidden?"

I couldn't see the doves. I was just starting to worry they weren't here when a girl I recognized, Brand, pointed towards one corner of the badly lit warehouse. "They're in one of the stalls. The guards had to keep them chained up." She wasn't talking to Hind. It was me she was staring at.

My heart was still tight until I got to that corner and could peer into the old horse stall. The doves, boy and girl, sat there. No one had given the girl clothes, but they had at least tied a rough bandage tight around the gap in her wing feathers. The bandage was an ugly red, and most of her wing was black from drying blood. They'd been chained so heavily it seemed ridiculous too, but they were both alive and didn't seem to have been hurt any more. There were several locks and I had to find the key to each, and I only started to relax again when the last key turned, the collars fell away, and I pulled the gags out of their mouths. The boy's hand had already taken the girl's.

"Can you walk?" I asked them anxiously, helping them both to their feet. They seemed stunned, and clumsy, but they got their balance back after a few steps.

We'd gone just far enough to get them out into the room when the girl's hand squeezed around the boy's and she stopped short and announced, "No. You can go. We want you to go. But we have to stay here and face the church."

"You did," Hind told them approvingly. When the two didn't move, she spread her hands to either side of her and added, "Anyway, I think they want you to come with us."

Donkeys were shuffling past her. Green eyes let me know that it was Mange who bumped his nose up against the girl's hip, but the doves were surrounded by boys and girls asking quiet, worried questions that all ran together. The girl's name was Egg apparently, and the boy was Mourn, and they didn't so much agree to go with us as not fight as they were pulled along towards the back door.

Hind waited for me next to it, and the donkeys piled together behind her. It was nothing like the big front gate, just a little door in the corner of the building. For staff, perhaps. I unlocked it and opened it up, and the guard on the other side leveled a short poleaxe at me.

Hind had stepped out of sight beside the door. The look she shot me was wide-eyed and warning. She hadn't known this man would be here. As she slipped away past the gathered mass of children I realized I had only one card, but it had worked perfectly so far. In fact this was a real church guard, a lay brother, and he might even recognize me.

"What are you doing here?" I demanded shortly. "Father Gabriel wants the animals moved, and you don't want anyone to even think you know where they went, do you?"

The blade of his spear lay right against my chest. I'd always thought they were silly, ornamental. It looked and felt entirely too sharp. "Anyone can say they work for anybody," he told me. There was doubt in his voice, but it went both ways. "The only orders I've seen were for us to make sure no one came in or out until the shift change at dawn. Prove to me you work for him."

"You're not supposed to be here to need proof," I snapped back crisply, trying to sound impatient rather than scared, "But if you need it, I'm Father Gabriel's secretary. If you've seen him you've seen me, and you should know I'm carrying out his private instructions."

I had never met this man, but I was hoping he'd seen me. He did take a moment to study me closely, lifting up the lantern he'd kept next to him so that he could see in the dark alley behind the warehouse. I thought perhaps he knew who I was, until he suddenly barked, "What's with your hair?"

The question was so unexpected, I didn't even move as the blade of his spear lifted and knocked the skullcap off my head. "Stripes," he told me curtly. His face turned a lot harder now. His eyes fixed on me angrily, and the spear point dropped back to my chest and pressed against it. If I didn't back up, I'd be cut open by it. "I've never seen stripes before, but you're one of them, aren't you?"

There was one man and a hundred donkeys. If he was busy killing me they could trample him flat, or just run past. I was sure they wouldn't do it. I was very, very surprised when Hind stepped up behind the man, silent as a ghost, and pressed what I thought was a knife against his back.

He felt it, and he certainly knew what it was. We all stood still for a moment, the balance of the situation changed, until I told him, "This isn't an impasse. You can kill me and die yourself, or back away and we'll let you go when all the children are free. Decide quickly, because I already have." I meant it, and my voice was steady and my eyes stayed set on his.

He took a couple of deep breaths, but his mouth was still flat, his eyes glaring. "Mike!" He yelled suddenly. Around the corner came another guard, with another poleax and another lamp. This had just gotten more complicated.

"What in the name-" the new guard started to swear, but the first one cut him off.

"Look at his hair! He's trying to free the other animals. The one behind me can't kill me before you take care of it."

The new guard, Mike, nodded. There was a very tense moment which ended as Mike swung his lantern up and clubbed the first guard over the head with it.

I didn't know what to think, and I hesitated long enough for Mike to lay the tip of his spear against the other guard's back, pinning him like I'd been pinned a moment ago. My face must have asked the question for me. "I saw what Gabriel did to the dove today," he explained, his voice low and grim. He knew this was trouble, and like me he'd made his choice. He was only telling me why. "A man like that doesn't speak for God. Get them out of here."

Hind already had my arm. The Donkey Children filed out silently, following us as she led me down to the docks. She pushed the first girl up the plank onto a ship and in moments they were all filing up, a knot of them tugging the still-reluctant doves along.

"Stripes?" I asked Hind dumbly, reaching up to run my hand back through my hair. Was it thicker than before? The horns were still there, but they weren't sharp anymore. In fact, I could barely feel them.

Which meant I should take off my gloves. The claws certainly weren't gone, but they were duller, flatter. I didn't know what to think of them.

Hind's face was very solemn. "No one ever gets their humanity back, Elijah. I'm sorry. Whatever you're becoming now, I don't think it's a monster."

"When you said you'd save me, you meant you'd save what's good in me," I realized. It didn't hurt as much as I thought, giving up the hope this change wouldn't go through to the end somehow. "I didn't understand then, but now I do. Thank you."

"Actually, Elijah, that was only kind of what I meant." Her voice held a hint of playfulness I wasn't familiar with. A few Donkey Children still lingered on the dock watching us, and she gave them a nod. "Help him on board before he starts to argue, would you?"

Hands grabbed me, pulling and pushing. A broad nose prodded against my back, and I looked over my shoulder into Mange's green eyes. Like Egg, I couldn't argue with that, and I let myself be pushed onto deck of the riverboat, then almost forced to sit down in a pile of rope.

Almost instantly Hind was there, seated a lot more daintily on an unlabeled crate. At the same time I heard the gangplank scrape across the wood and felt the boat lurch gently. We were moving, and as the dock started to drift away behind us Hind smiled. She leaned back on one hand, and instead of calm and controlled and knowing she just looked relaxed. "We made it. There are no Wild Children left in the city, and it'll be a long time before they let any more in. Nobody will have to wear a collar they don't want."

She pulled that cat doll out of a pocket in her heavily ruffled skirt, and tucked it under her arm as she unfastened the buttons on her dress's high collar. Underneath it there really was another collar, a metal one, although I'd never seen a collar so thin and elaborately inlaid.

Other things were more urgent. She was getting more relaxed by the second, and I was getting more tense. "We haven't done anything. There'll be an Archbishop Gabriel within a week. There won't be anywhere a hundred Wild Children can hide."

She was still smiling, but there was something faintly sad in the line of her brow. "I'm sure he'll get the title. The Empire will probably get an Emperor sympathetic to his views, too. And outside of the capital no one will care. A hundred miles away there are towns where they think Wild Children are ghosts, or fairies, or myths that don't exist at all. He can rule his own little world. We'll just find a new one."

I had more questions. Even as they formed on my lips I realized she'd asked herself all of them, and answered them. I threw up one, at least. "Where did you get a boat?"

"Rich people who love their pets enough to not want to see them killed," she answered easily, and then added, "You can ask me everything you want later. I just want to enjoy this moment."

She didn't get to. Mange came stumbling up, and even with a donkey's face he looked guilty as he bumped his nose up against Hind's knee. "Excuse me, Miss Hind, but Mourn is worried about Egg's wing. He doesn't think the bandages are good enough. What should we do?"

As she slid to her feet, I looked again at the collar she wore around her neck. It had a clasp but wasn't even locked, and I asked, "Can they really live without an owner?"

The smile she gave me was the widest yet. "They don't have to. I'll be their Master and they will be mine, and you know, maybe someday we won't need one."

I had hardly started thinking about that when her fingers trailed through my hair on her way past and she added, "But if I were you I'd be figuring out what animals have black and white stripes in their hair, and what kind of person turns into one."

DENOUEMENT

DAY ONE – My name is Violet Amaranth Fromme. I don't know if I'll ever want that name again, and I wouldn't know Violet if I met her on the street. I don't want to forget her, though. Bray, if you ever get this back your name was Jenny McThresh. Left and Right, your name was Mikhael. I don't think Bray ever got to ask. I'm going to bed now. Tomorrow I have to pretend I'm an adult, but Jinx doesn't need me to be something I'm not. He's just going to tease me again because he thinks this stupid bump on my forehead means I'm growing a horn. I mean, a donkey with a horn?

Richard Roberts

THANK YOU FOR READING.

Curiosity Quills Press
http://curiosityquills.com

Please visit http://curiosityquills.com/reader-survey/ to share your reading experience with the author of this book!

Richard Roberts has fit into only one category in his entire life: 'writer.' But as a writer he'd throw himself out of his own books for being a cliche. He's had the classic wandering employment history – degree in entomology, worked in health care, been an administrator and labored for years in the front lines of fast food. He's had the appropriate really weird jobs, like breeding tarantulas and translating English to English for Japanese television. He wears all black, all the time, is manic-depressive, and has a creepy laugh.

As for what he writes, Richard loves children and the gothic aesthetic. Most everything he writes will involve one or the other, and occasionally both. His fantasy is heavily influenced by folk tales, fairy tales, and mythology, and he likes to make the old new again. In particular, he loves to pull his readers into strange characters with strange lives, and his heroes are rarely heroic.

Sweet Dreams are Made of Teeth, by Richard Roberts

Have you ever had the nightmare of being chased by a beast? Then you've met Fang. He'll be the first to admit that he's a very simple nightmare. All he knows is hunting your dreams and dragging them into the Dark.

He's not ready to be dragged into his best friend's schemes to make dreams so terrifying they break people. He's not ready to love, or to be loved, or to meet someone who makes him happy.

He's not ready to grow up. When he does, one thing will stay the same: he'll stay an artist, and he'll paint your dreams with fear until they're beautiful.

Quite Contrary, by Richard Roberts

The secret of having an adventure is getting lost. Well, Mary is lost. She is lost in the story of Little Red Riding Hood, and that is a cruel story. She's put on the red hood and met the Wolf. When she gives in to her Wolf's temptations, she will die. That's how the story goes, after all.

Unfortunately for the story – and the Wolf – this Little Red Riding Hood is Mary Stuart, and she is the most stubborn and contrary twelve year old the world has ever known. Forget the Wolf's temptations, forget the advice of the talking rat trying to save her, she will kick her way through every myth and fairy tale ever told until she finds a way to get out of this alive.

CPSIA information can be obtained at www.ICGtesting.com
Printed in the USA
BVOW11s0207200715

409511BV00002B/72/P